THE UNFORGIVEN DEAD

FULTON ROSS

Published by Inkshares, Inc., Oakland, California
www.inkshares.com

Edited by: Adam Gomolin
Cover design by: Tim Barber
Interior pages: David Scott, *The Fall of the Damned. Copy after the Painting by Sir Peter Paul Rubens.* National Galleries of Scotland. David Laing Bequest to the Royal Scottish Academy on loan 1974.
Interior Design by: Kevin G. Summers

ISBN: 9781950301096
e-ISBN: 9781950301102
LCCN: 2022938638

First edition

Printed in the United States of America

ACT I

"There is no trace in Highland folk-lore
of the idea of benevolent gods."

—"A Highland Goddess,"
Donald A. Mackenzie, 1912

CHAPTER 1

THE voice whispered to Angus as he lay in that otherworld between wakefulness and sleep. A woman's, the accent honeyed American with a hint of Scottish bleeding through. He smelt her warm breath on his neck, faintly rancid, like meat on the turn.

You could have saved me.

His hands bunched into fists, gripping a wad of bedclothes. He squeezed his eyes shut and heard the thundering of distant hooves. The hammering grew louder. Closer. The harsh caw of a crow cut above the din.

Then silence.

Cold sweat beaded on his forehead, crawled like fingernails down his back. He could taste salt on his sandpaper tongue. Behind the soft membrane of his eyelids, his vision flickered.

He saw a flock of birds circling an island with a distinctive, snoutlike peak, but before he could get a handle on the image, he heard the frightened whinny of a horse. He was transported to a grove, where a woman knelt in a halo of light. Behind her stood a figure in a deer-skull mask. The figure looped a thin ligature around the woman's neck. Angus tried to shout, but words stuck like rocks in his throat.

The thing jammed a knee in the woman's back and yanked—

Angus sat bolt upright. Beside him, Ashleigh groaned in her sleep, flame-red hair fanned out on the pillow. She pulled the duvet back over a milky-white shoulder. He tore his eyes away from his wife, and forced himself to look.

Three shadowy figures stood at the foot of the bed.

The Burned Man.

The Strangled Woman.

The Drowned Boy.

An unholy trinity whose eyes begged for answers.

He heard his father's voice, a dim whisper.

These things you see, they're all in your head, son. All in your head.

The boy's mouth opened, but no sound came out. He choked, heaved. His eyes bulged.

You could have saved me!

The woman's voice rang around the room, but his wife did not stir.

Angus sprang from the bed, bare feet slapping on the warped oak floorboards. He swayed, like a fisherman on a rolling sea, and threw out a hand to steady himself. His fingers found the bedroom wall, but the textured wallpaper—a flowery motif Ash had chosen from Moy's in Silvaig—felt alive, like the flank of some great beast. He could smell the feral stink of it, feel the blood course beneath its soft pelt. He whipped his hand away as if burned, and lurched towards the bedroom door, grabbing yesterday's clothes as he went.

What felt like a second later, he was pounding down the rocky path past the Lost Village. Flecks of phlegm flew from his lips. His breath plumed into the cold air. Ahead of him, sheep scattered, bleating in fright as they bounded for the safety of tumbledown black houses. The ruins of the old crofting community littered the glen like piles of broken teeth, gaping and eerie in the wan dawn, the hillside scarred from claw-mark furrows of long-abandoned lazy beds. Heart thrashing, he hurdled a stile and was swallowed by the bracken, hawthorn, and gorse that carpeted the lower slopes. Thorns raked his hands and face as he ploughed blindly forward, heading downwards, ever downwards, guided by shadows.

He burst from the gorse and powered across the raised beach towards the sand dunes. Marram grass bit at his ankles, and the memories he had buried came flooding back—thrashing in the cobalt-blue sea, the boy's dead weight in his arms.

With one final push, he reached the top of the dunes. There he paused, gasping for breath, as the kneeling woman had at the end.

The sun now crested the callused shoulder of Sgurr an Teintein. A dark crust of seaweed curved around the bay, marking the high-tide level. Past it, silver sand stretched out to the sea, Eilean Coille rising from the waves like a kelpie, the Small Isles of Eigg, Rum, Muck, and Canna cowering in the background. Everything was exactly as he had seen it: Eigg with its distinctive peak, even the rocks covered in blooms of *crotal ruadh,* the red lichen that Gills claimed was congealed blood left after nocturnal battles between the fairies.

You could have saved me. . . .

A sound made him look up. From the west, a flock of black birds surged across the sky: starlings, hundreds of them. The din as they passed overhead was awful, like the wails of tormented souls.

He returned his attention to the beach. Something lay on the sand, halfway between the scab of seaweed and the waves. A small mound, with a greenish tint, like a dead seal coated in algae.

A breeze whipped in off the sea, carrying with it a scent of decay.

No, not a seal—

The object moved.

Angus flinched. The movement had been little more than a twitch, as if anything more were too great an effort. Hope and disbelief rooted him to the spot. Then he leapt, arms flailing in midair, before he landed, fell, and tumbled down the dunes. He hauled himself upright, spat sand, and ran. His feet crunched across the shingle until he reached a plateau of soft marbled sand, pockmarked with lugworm castings. Footprints meandered hither and thither, left by the seabirds his father had taught him to identify—herring gulls, oystercatchers, and curlews. None were human.

The cloying reek hung in the air like a smirr of rain. He ran, head down, into the teeth of the wind, until he could go no farther.

A marionette on a string, he raised his eyes from the beach.

It was no seal.

She lay in the foetal position on a smooth blanket of sand, her back to him. He leaned over her body and a ragged sob escaped his cracked lips.

He fell to his knees beside her broken body as if seeking absolution. But there was no forgiveness in her lifeless stare.

He screwed his eyes shut and clenched his fists, digging his fingernails into his palms until the pain thumped inside his head. Only when the skin was close to breaking did he stop. He opened his eyes and forced himself to look at the girl. Her eyes had been emerald green and had sparkled like dewdrops when she'd talked about art and horses. No more. Her irises were empty grey voids that somehow reminded him of the ruined houses in the glen. Her purple lips were slightly parted, as if she were mumbling something in a dream.

Only, nobody slept with their wrists bound like that.

She wore a green velvet cloak over a diaphanous silver gown. The front of the gown was spattered with gore as if she were a gutted fish. A thin ligature caked in dried blood arced around her throat, cutting deep into her alabaster skin. A fold of her cloak flapped in the wind, like the wing of a dying raven, which accounted for the movement he'd seen from the dunes. Her damp hair had lost its golden lustre and was matted in blood on one side. There were no footprints in the sand around her body, but if the sea had spat her out, wouldn't her clothes be sodden? He placed a tentative hand on the girl's arm. Her cloak was damp but not waterlogged. If she hadn't washed up on the tide, how had she gotten here?

His hand shook as he placed two fingers on her neck, not to check for a pulse—it was obvious she was dead—but to feel her temperature. Her skin was cold. She had been dead for hours. His hope had been in vain.

He sat back on his haunches and screwed his eyes shut. He clenched his fists, again digging the nails into his palms.

Too late, always too late!

He felt the shadows crowd around him again—man, woman, and child—their dead eyes boring into him.

He could have saved them all.

CHAPTER 2

THE sea was an enemy. Tide on the turn. He should have carried her beyond the high-tide mark, but training had told him that would be a mistake. The dictate warning against contaminating a crime scene had been drummed into him as a cadet at police college in Tulliallan, all those years ago.

His legs felt heavy, as if the marrow had been scooped out and replaced with lead. He followed the same path as on his descent, but it now seemed impossibly steep, the bracken denser, brittle heather like rabbit snares waiting to trap his feet. Sweat stung his eyes. He swiped a sleeve across his face. The skeletons of black houses leered at him. Laughter rose from their ruined maws, a cacophony that climbed in pitch until it was almost unbearable.

Angus needed to think, but his mind went back to those green eyes. The eyes of a girl on the cusp of womanhood. So much life unlived. All that potential snuffed out.

You could have saved me!

Within the hour, the waves would creep up the beach to claim the girl's body. Perhaps he should let the sea take her. Return to his cottage, to his pills and his tidy life, climb into bed beside his wife, and pretend it had all been a dream. That it was all in his head, like his father had told him. But even as the thought formed, his hand fell on the wrought-iron gate of the Old Manse. He froze, momentarily confused. When had he decided to come here? On the flight from the beach? When he had first seen the girl's body? No, his path had been set long before that.

He hauled open the gate and ran towards the sanctuary of the ivy-coated house, boots slapping on the herringbone-pattern slabs of the path he'd helped Gills lay five summers ago: hard toil in the sweltering sun, cold beers on the bench under the apple tree afterwards, warm breeze keeping the midges away.

He slumped against the door, gasping for breath, and pressed his forehead into the cold wood. He saw the girl then, brushing the chestnut-coloured mare in the stables at Dunbirlinn. He drove his forehead against the door.

"All . . ."

Thump!

"In . . ."

Thump!

"Your . . ."

Thump!

"Head!"

There was a high-pitched ringing in his head, like a scream. Manic barking joined the symphony—Bran and Sceolan, Gills's excitable border collies. He staggered backwards and saw a light flick on in the upstairs dormer window. He swayed, his vision slowly returning to normal. The pain felt good. He heard feet stomping down the stairs inside the house. A second later the door creaked open and there was Gills, a sight in fur-lined moccasin slippers and a tartan dressing gown, white hair standing on end.

Angus choked back tears.

A dawning realisation crept across the crags of Gills's face. His keen blue eyes, so often lit with humour, misted over. Gills sighed, a breathy, drawn-out sound, like wind soughing through the boughs of the yew tree in the cemetery where his mother lay buried. He placed a bony hand on Angus's shoulder.

"Ah, my dear boy."

He let Gills pull him into an embrace. The old man's body felt thinner than he remembered, no longer the great oak that had enveloped him and held him tight when he awoke from his nightmares.

"I'm sorry." A sob escaped his lips.

"Mollaichte!"

He was cursed.

CHAPTER 3

CLOUDS had amassed out to the west in the time he'd been away, chased landward by a strengthening wind. The tranquil sea of earlier was now a surging mass of spume-topped waves crashing onto the shore. The girl's body looked insignificant set against the sweeping panorama of sky and earth and sea, a dark speck at the mercy of Mother Nature.

He glanced at Gills, who was doubled over, hands on his thighs. Although a member of the local rambling club and spry for his age, his friend was struggling on the scramble down the hillside. What did he expect? His self-imposed exile from Gills meant that it had been many years since they'd hiked together.

"Take it easy, *a'bhalach*," he said, using the Gaelic term of endearment.

Eventually Gills straightened up. "Ready."

Angus hesitated, reluctant to revisit the body.

He saw the girl smile up at him from her Merc after he had pulled her over on that midge-infested evening three months ago.

"I need you to film the crime scene," he said, swatting away the memory.

Gills fumbled for his mobile phone. He jabbed the screen with a shaking finger.

"Take a general sweep of the beach, then follow me," Angus said. "But watch your step: the kelp's slippery."

Gills gave him a withering look, raised the phone, and swung it slowly through one hundred and eighty degrees.

Angus set off down the shingle, then picked his way over drifts of seaweed before reaching the sinewy rivulets that crisscrossed the beach. The wind was an invisible foe now, trying to force him into retreat. Waves crashed onto the shore, a rhythmic refrain: *Go back, go back, go back. . . .*

By the time he reached the girl, the sea almost had her in its grasp.

"Quick," he told Gills. "Film the body and the surrounding sand, then I'll lift her and carry her beyond the high-tide mark. Okay?"

Gills, though, was frozen to the spot, staring at the body. His breaths came in short, sharp bursts, like a man who had jumped into a pool without realizing the water was freezing. Angus clutched his arm. "Gills!"

The old man's eyes snapped to him. This time there was no withering look. Gills could only nod and film in silence, the grim diorama played out to the sound of breakers and the plaintive cry of an oystercatcher.

"Right, time to move her."

"No footprints," Gills wheezed.

Only Angus's own boot marks from earlier were visible.

"Probably the wind," Gills said. "It could have blown sand into the footprints."

"Aye, probably," Angus said, unconvinced.

They stood in silence for a long second, heads bowed. "I'll tell them I found her while out walking the dogs," Gills said.

The wind howled across the sound. "You'll have to go get them—otherwise, it'll look suspicious."

"I'll say I left the dogs back home after contacting you."

"Why didn't you call 999?"

"Panicked. Figured you'd know what to do."

A detached part of his brain told him there was no CCTV between the Old Manse and the beach or his home. The story would hold. Angus nodded, his eyes on the coarse rope cinched around the girl's wrists. A compact bowline knot, tied by hands that knew what they were doing.

Summoning up his strength, he squatted and worked his fingers under the girl's body. She smelt of dew and there was a lingering hint of perfume, a slightly saccharine note that conjured up an image of her stabling her horse at Dunbirlinn.

In one fluid motion, he lifted the girl. Her head lolled back, the wound around her neck parting like lips.

He heard Gills stifle a cry. "Poor lassie," he murmured, lowering the phone.

Angus could only nod, although "poor" was a word rarely mentioned in the same breath as this girl. She was sixteen but looked unbearably young.

He turned his back on the wind, cradling her body the same way as he had the Drowned Boy. Ethan Boyce had been even lighter.

Angus had barely taken three stuttering paces when something fell from under the girl's cloak. He half-turned, in time to see Gills crouch and reach for the object.

"Wait! Don't touch—"

His warning came too late.

"Sorry," Gills said with a wince.

Angus closed his eyes and muttered a curse under his breath. "What is it anyway?"

Gills stood and dusted sand off the object. A startled look rippled across the old man's face. He glanced at Angus and then back at the object.

"Gills, what the hell is it?"

The old man stepped closer, his arm outstretched, the object lying on his palm. Angus frowned. He looked down at the object and felt a shudder run up his spine. It was a macabre doll, about six inches in height, with golden hair and bulging, beady glass eyes. It was crudely carved, but even so, the doll had an uncanny lifelike quality.

"A *corp creadha*," Gills breathed. "It's a Highland voodoo doll."

CHAPTER 4

A thin mist closed around Ashleigh as she reached the summit of Glenruig Hill. Her thighs and lungs burned from the climb, but she knew she was far off her personal best. No surprise, really. She'd slackened off since winning the Games back in August. The key was to peak at the right time, and she'd managed that. Winter had now arrived, though. A few races would still be held in the coming months, but she wouldn't compete. Instead, she'd train, then emerge stronger and fitter in the spring. Everything was cyclical, wasn't it? A time to kill and a time to heal.

Ash wiped a sleeve across her sweat-streaked brow. Where had that thought come from? Sounded like something that bigoted old goat Reverend MacVannin would come out with. She shivered, and not just because of the icy wind that scoured the summit. The minister gave her the heebie-jeebies. That MacVannin now thought they were allies in the fight against Chichester's wolf reserve needled her. His support she could do without.

She put the minister and his roving eye out of her mind and jogged across the summit, the notes of a new clarsach melody running through her head. As always, she'd been mentally composing music on her run. The stone cairn appeared from the mist. Every time she reached the summit, she made a point of adding another rock to the cairn. She had no idea where the tradition had come from, but generations of hillwalkers had been adding stones. The cairn now stood almost as tall as she was. Ash slid a flat rock into one of the crannies. Her fingers caressed the ribs of stone. She felt a fizzle of connection in her fingertips, as if a gossamer-thin thread connected her to those distant others who had laid stones here in the past.

Her descent was cautious, in contrast to the race day months earlier when she'd flown down the scree, feet hardly touching the ground. It had been drier then, of course, one of those rare cloudless days in the Highlands when the colours were so vibrant, they seemed otherworldly. Such a shame her victory had been overshadowed by the presence of the laird, strutting around in a kilt like a cock pheasant. He had been asked to present the prizes, but she'd refused to shake his hand. She'd taken some flak for that gesture afterwards, but most folk were supportive.

Soon, Ash emerged from the mist and the village spread out below, like a child's model creation. She picked out the village hall, Lachlan Campbell's bookshop, the Glenruig Inn, and the small cluster of houses around it, her and Angus's own cottage farther along the coast. They all looked so small, dwarfed by the surrounding mountains, tracts of pine forest, ochre moorland, and the leaden expanse of sea to the west. A road snaked along the lochside like a black tongue. On it she saw a blue flashing light blinking furiously. Ash felt a tremor of apprehension. Angus had not been in bed when she'd risen that morning. She had presumed he had gone for a swim, but it now looked more likely he'd been called out to some emergency.

Instead of heading home, she took the alternative route alongside the burn that led past Granny Beag's cottage. Perhaps the old woman would know what was going on.

There was no response when she knocked on the door of Granny Beag's sturdy, well-kept house. She was about to go inside—Granny Beag never locked her door—when she heard a sound of splintering wood coming from the rear. Rolling the tension out of her shoulders, she walked around the side of the cottage and found Granny Beag splitting logs.

"Och, Granny! I said I'd chop those for you."

Granny Beag glanced towards her. Her face was a scored and wrinkled, like the bark of the clootie tree. Two sharp grey eyes glinted from the whorls of flesh. Her thin lips puckered into a scowl. "Pah!"

"You shouldn't be hefting that big axe at your age."

Granny Beag drew the axe back and split the log in one fell swoop. "See. No bother."

Ash couldn't help but smile. The woman was as immutable as the land.

"Don't stand there grinning like a gowk," Granny Beag scolded. "Fill up that log basket and carry it inside for me."

Ash bit back a retort and lifted the log basket. Granny Beag had a knack for making her feel like the same frightened, destructive child she'd been when they'd met in Kintail House. She gave the old woman a tart smile as she slipped past her into the house. She dropped the log basket by the hearth and threw a couple of blocks onto the smouldering fire.

"Not so many, Ashleigh! It's like a sauna in here as it is."

She stepped across the room and took Ash by the hands. Her skin felt like dry leaves. She rubbed the pads of Ash's fingers, as if testing the quality of a fine dress.

"Soft," she declared. "You're not practicing enough."

Ash extracted herself from the old woman's grip.

"I've a lot going on, Granny."

"Aye, so I've heard. Up at the castle every day waving your placards."

Ash frowned. "I thought you'd approve."

"I do, but a bunch of middle-class villagers stamping their feet won't change a damn thing. You need to be on the inside to affect change. You should run as an independent at the next local elections. The folk like you."

Ash rolled her eyes. "We're not going over this again. I was just wondering if you know what's going on in the village? Saw a police car wheeching past when I was out for my run."

"No idea. I haven't been out for my messages yet. But whatever it is, I'm sure Moira will have the inside track, nosey old besom that she is."

Granny Beag smiled, and for Ash it was like the sun appearing from behind a cloud.

"Now, *a luaidh*, you'll take a cup of tea?"

Ash found Moira Anderson at the back of her shop, gossiping furtively with the so-called beautician Geraldine MacAuley. The local store was little more than a trumped-up Portakabin shoehorned into a tight scrap of ground overlooking Glenruig Bay. Moira stocked an odd assortment of goods: fishing tackle, midge spray, the obligatory tartan tat for the tourists, garden ornaments, hardware, and—for reasons Ash could never fathom—a whole cabinet full of sun cream.

Despite Moira angling for secrecy with Gerry, Ash could hear every word of their whispered conversation.

". . . it's a real shame, Moira. And her only gone fifteen." Gerry's smirk belied her expression of sympathy. Her makeup looked as if it had been applied with a trowel. Hardly a great advertisement for her business, although Ash had heard she did a line in knockoff clothes, which she sold from a stall at the Sunday market in Silvaig.

"Aye, poor Ethna, and after the husband was done by the police for flashing the nuns. God alone knows what will become of the child. She's only a child herself, the daughter. A flighty one by all accounts. They say she's been with half the lads who work on the fish farms. . . ."

Moira glanced at Ash, a gleeful set to her thin lips. "How's form the day, Ashleigh? Have you heard the news? They're saying there's been a suspicious death." Moira rolled the word "suspicious" around her mouth like a fine malt.

"We all know whit that means," Gerry added. "Someone's been done in. Murdered."

CHAPTER 5

BLACK wraithlike shapes drifted through the dunes, a ragged line of uniformed police officers like a funeral procession. Angus sat a couple of feet from Gills on a large barnacle-studded rock in the lee of the wind. An awkward silence had descended, the partial estrangement of the past five years wedged between them. Farther along the beach, the small white tent erected by forensics to protect the girl's body from the elements bucked and jerked, a tethered animal.

Angus gazed at the point where the sea kissed the horizon and thought of Tír na nÓg, the mythological Celtic otherworld that Gills had taught him about. It was said to be an island paradise, a realm of everlasting youth, beauty, joy, and abundance. If he were to wade into the sea now and keep on swimming, would he reach it?

Gills gave his shoulder a brief squeeze. "Are you all right, old bean?"

"Aye," Angus mumbled.

Out of the corner of his eye, he sensed movement at the tent. He turned and saw the pathologist emerge. Dr. Orla Kelly tugged down the hood of her white Tyvek suit, unleashing her corkscrew blond curls. She stood for a second, staring out to sea, then turned and beckoned him over.

He crunched across the shingle towards her.

"Christ! I need a stiff gin after that," she said in a thick Irish accent.

"Bad?"

"You know yourself, Angus. The young ones are the worst."

Aye.

Orla wrapped her arms around herself.

"Come on, I'll show you."

He hesitated for a beat too long and Orla noticed his reluctance. "You don't have to—"

"No, it's okay."

She gave him a sympathetic smile, then disappeared back inside the tent. He steeled himself, then pulled back the flap and entered.

The girl lay exactly where he had left her, on her back on the shingle, the green cloak like a mound of moss growing over her body. Her wrists were still bound, but plastic bags had been secured over her hands to preserve evidence. For a brief second, he saw her pulling a comb through her horse's mane. Bessie, the mare had been called.

"She was found farther down the beach?" Orla asked.

"Aye. Underwater now. There were no signs of blood on the sand, though. Deposition site, most likely, although there were no footprints in the sand."

Orla frowned. "I'll leave that conundrum to you lot. Who's SIO?"

"No idea. Local CID should be here soon, then whatever major investigation team is free."

"They'll all be after this one, if the victim's who you say she is," Orla mused. "That geebag McQueen, Stirling, Bennet . . . something this high-profile, we might even get Crowley."

He nodded, although the last name was the only one he recognised. He couldn't wait until the MIT arrived. Yes, he'd still be involved in the case, but as a constable, it would be a minor role. Pointless house-to-house inquiries. Manning a police cordon like a spare part. It suited him fine.

"I've a daughter around her age," Orla said in an almost-whisper. "She's a stroppy wee cow at times, but—" Orla let the sentence hang in the air.

They stood in silence for a moment, then a switch seemed to flip and the pathologist was all detached professionalism.

"Deceased has suffered several blows to the back of the head, but cause of death appears to be strangulation by garrotte."

The ligature was still intact, a few inches spiralling from her slit throat. Something about the garrotte bothered him. Subconsciously, he'd noticed this earlier, but only now did he realize what it was—the ligature had an unusual fibrous texture and was an almost translucent light brown colour. "I haven't encountered many garrottes," he said, "but I'd expect them to be made of wire, nylon, or cord. That's none of those."

Angus realized he was rubbing his own neck. He let his hand fall to his side.

Orla dropped to her haunches and inspected the garrotte with a gloved hand. "You're right. I'm not sure what material this is. I'll extract it when I get her back to the mortuary, and run some tests."

She stood, hands on hips. "No obvious defensive wounds. Signs of trauma to the back of the skull, around this area"—she pointed to a section of the girl's head where her fair hair was matted with blood—"suggest she was struck from behind with a bladed object. The blows would likely have incapacitated the victim rather than killed her, but I can't say with any degree of certainty until the postmortem examination."

"Time of death?"

Orla stood, folded her arms. "She's been dead for between twelve and fourteen hours."

He glanced at his watch. It was just after noon, meaning she had been killed between midnight on Friday and two a.m. on Saturday morning.

Too late. Always too late. He could taste the acrid words in his mouth.

Suddenly the hair on the nape of his neck stood on end. Over Orla's shoulder, he saw a shadow pass outside the tent, an elongated stick figure that made no sound on the shingle.

He felt Orla grip his arm. "You okay, pal?"

He refocused on the pathologist.

"Aye, fine."

Orla eyed him for a long second, then returned her attention to the body. "That's some getup she's wearing. Mind you, it was Halloween last night."

He had been wondering about the cloak. It looked like something a Hobbit would wear, but he hadn't made the connection to Halloween.

He imagined her dancing, spinning around in her silver dress, light bursting from her like a supernova. A few short hours later she would be dead. A cold husk to be prodded, photographed, and processed.

You could have saved me!

Her voice rippled around the enclosure.

"Thanks, Orla," he muttered, then swept from the tent. Outside, he sucked in a mouthful of salty air.

"Constable MacNeil!" The familiar high-pitched accent of Inspector Stout carried to him on the wind. Angus closed his eyes, muttered a curse under his breath.

He turned and watched his boss waddle, stiff-legged, towards him. The marram grass on top of the dunes bristled in the wind, like a cat's hackles rising.

Stout stopped a few feet away, spat, then snatched the tweed fisherman's bonnet from his head and swiped a sleeve across his sweaty brow. He replaced his trademark hat and eyeballed Angus.

"Do you not answer your phone, Constable? I've called you about a hundred times."

"Left it at home. Doubt there's reception here anyway, sir."

"For God's sake! I've ruined my good brogues coming all the way down here. All because *you* forgot your bloody phone." He sniffed, contemplating his muddy shoes. "Weren't cheap, these boys. Real Italian leather, so they are."

"Err, sorry, I think."

The short rotund man glared up at him. "And where's your uniform, Constable? You look like you just fell out of bed."

"It's my day off, sir."

Stout sniffed again. "Not anymore. The uniforms tell me the victim is Chichester's girl? That right?"

"Aye, sir."

"For God's sake, MacNeil! This is going to cause mayhem!"

He knew why Stout was irked. The murder would generate a huge amount of media interest and extra work, which in turn would keep Stout away from fly-fishing.

"Who found the body?"

Angus jerked a thumb over his shoulder towards Gills. "A local walking his dogs. He's a friend, lectures at the uni in Silvaig. . . ."

"Okay, okay, MacNeil. I don't need his life story."

Stout fumbled in his pocket and pulled out a squashed packet of Pall Malls. He took out a bent cigarette and turned his back on the prevailing wind to light it.

"Bad news," he said, after taking a deep draw. "The MIT has been delayed. Accident on the A82. Road's closed. Motorcyclist played chicken with the Sheil bus to Glasgow and lost. They'll be scraping him off the tarmac for a good few hours yet, which means *we* have to tell the laird his daughter is dead before he hears about it on Nevis Radio."

CHAPTER 6

ANGUS watched the old graveyard flash past out the passenger-side window of Stout's Lexus. The big yew tree, under which his mother lay buried, stretched its boughs over the crumbling Celtic crosses and lichen-encrusted headstones like a grieving animal protecting its dead. A sudden glint of gold snagged his attention. On the front step of a decaying mausoleum, the girl sat brushing her long flaxen hair. Angus dug his fingers into his thigh and willed away the hallucination. He felt the rounded edges of the bottle of pills in his trouser pocket. Stout had insisted he return home to change before they met the laird. Ash wasn't home, so he'd scampered to the bedroom for his bottle of Seroquel, which he kept hidden at the back of his sock drawer.

All in your head, son. Take the pills.

"You say something?"

He turned to Stout. Had he?

"No."

He imagined the little yellow pills dissolving in his stomach as Stout swung the Lexus past the small group of protesters outside the gates of Dunbirlinn Castle. His wife, for once, was not amongst the handful of placard-wielding locals. Amber wolf eyes glared down on the protesters from a billboard advertising Wild West Highlands Nature Reserve. The animals seemed to sneer at the pitiful demonstration. James Chichester's pet project—the American billionaire's obsession if the press was to be believed—was due to open next month, despite the opposition.

"Folly," Stout snorted as he drove past the billboard. "What's going to happen when a wolf mauls some poor child, eh?"

Angus gave a noncommittal grunt. He rather liked the idea of wolves roaming the mountainside, but kept his own counsel in case Ashleigh found out. None of it mattered today, anyhow.

Up ahead, the ramparts of Dunbirlinn loomed through the mist like something from a Gothic horror, the only colour the red slash of a MacRuari flag with its wolf-head crest flying from the battlements. The car glided past a stable block and a row of squat stone houses that were staff quarters, before reaching the ancient stone bridge that led to the gatehouse. Angus glanced warily out of the passenger window. A hundred feet below, the sea was a broiling, living creature, thrashing against the rocks. Wind threw shrapnel bursts of rain against the cliffs. Herring gulls, gannets, and fulmars sat hunched on ledges, heads tucked tight against their bodies.

Stout nosed the Lexus through the gatehouse. Angus glanced up at the iron teeth of the portcullis, like the jaws of a beast ready to snap shut. A few yards farther, a row of murder holes was punched in the vaulted ceiling. He imagined boiling oil pouring through the shafts onto the clansmen who had besieged the castle in the sixteenth century. MacLoughlins they were, if he correctly recalled what Gills had told him. Their howls of agony must have been amplified in this narrow space. To the soldiers at the rear, it must have seemed as if their kin were being devoured by the castle itself.

Once through to the inner courtyard, Stout parked between a gleaming burgundy Aston Martin and a mustard-coloured Range Rover, which looked as if it had never seen a dirt track in its life. A Porsche Cayenne and a sporty Mercedes he recognised completed the set of luxury cars on show.

Stout popped a mint into his mouth, eyes scaling the turrets. "Remind me of her name again?"

He forced her name from his throat. "Faye."

"And you knew the girl?"

"Wouldn't say I knew her, sir. Met her when I was investigating that fire a couple weeks back."

"What fire?"

"Shed up at the visitor centre. Nothing of value in it apart from the GPS trackers for the wolves. We think that might be why the shed was targeted."

"Did you question the protesters?"

"Aye."

Stout grinned. "That must have been awkward, with your missus being rabble-rouser in chief."

He shrugged. "They're mostly wee old women. Can't see them creeping about in the dead of night with a jerrican full of petrol."

"Hmmph! So, what was she like, Miss Chichester?"

Angus gave a faint smile. He hadn't told Stout, but he'd met the girl weeks before the fire. Pulled her over for speeding. He saw the window of the Merc slide down, Faye's 110-watt smile.

"Do you know why I stopped you, Miss?"

"To compliment me on my excellent driving?"

"Eh, no. Your brake light's gubbed and you're not wearing a seat belt."

Stout crunched the mint. "MacNeil, what was she like?"

Charming, funny, down-to-earth. She'd also been under the legal driving age for Scotland, but he couldn't bring himself to issue a fine. Instead he had driven her home and explained the situation to her father, who had been grateful to avoid any more press coverage.

"Err, she seemed like a typical teenager, sir."

"Your typical teenybopper doesn't live in a castle."

He recalled Gills's words from earlier.

Poor girl.

The irony of the statement lingered in his head as he eyed the luxury cars. But for all the wealth on display, the simplistic brutality of the castle left him cold. It was a place of fear and death.

"This place is supposed to be haunted. A ghost known as the Druid."

Stout squinted at him. "And that's relevant why?"

He shrugged.

"Right, once we're inside, let me do the talking. And don't mention ghosts."

He reached across Angus, opened the glove compartment, and took out a garish salmon-pink tie. "Have to look our best for the landed gentry." He slipped the tie over his head and tightened the Windsor knot.

"How do I look?" he asked, turning to Angus.

Like you dressed in the dark.

"Very smart, sir."

Stout nodded, as if this were only to be expected. "Right, let's go."

Eddies of wind laced with the promise of snow swirled around the courtyard. Where once archers would have observed them from the walls of the keep, now they were watched by a host of CCTV cameras. He glanced in the Merc's window. A pair of miniature pink boxing gloves with the letters *F* and *C* hung from the rearview mirror. He imagined Faye driving along the Road to the Isles, windows open, radio on, singing at the top of her lungs as windswept lochs and rugged mountains flashed by.

Angus dug his nails into his palms as he and Stout mounted the castle steps. A great wooden door swung open and an elderly woman appeared from the shadows of the portico. Her deeply furrowed face had a greyish tinge, as if hewn from the same coarse stone as the castle itself. She wore a tweed two-piece and observed them with cold blue eyes, hands clasped behind her back, lips stretched into a thin line. Her slate-coloured hair was pulled back from her lined forehead and collected in a tight bun. A wolf-headed broach glinted from her lapel, like a fleck of quartz in a block of granite.

"Police," Stout said, brandishing his ID. "We're here to speak to Mr. and Mrs. Chichester?"

The woman did not even glance at Stout's ID. "I know who you are."

Angus inclined his head and asked how she was doing. *"Ciamar a tha thu,* Mrs. MacCrimmon?" Her eyes softened. *"Chan eil gu dona,* Angus."

Stout, who wasn't a native speaker, scowled.

"Can we come in?" Angus asked.

Mrs MacCrimmon gave a brisk nod, spun on her heel, and led the way into the castle, her back ramrod straight.

Angus shoved the wooden door shut behind them. Inside, the cavernous entrance hallway was wood panelled and gloomy, decorated with stag heads, tapestries of hunting scenes, and a large portrait of a wild-eyed clan chief named Dòmhnall MacRuari, also known as *an Droaidh.* The Druid.

Two suits of armour stood guard at the foot of a crimson-carpeted staircase, which rose to a landing then split in opposite directions leading upwards. Both guards brandished Lochaber axes, vicious-looking weapons with a large curved blade attached to a six-foot-long shaft.

Mrs MacCrimmon turned and glared at them. Slithers of light gleamed from the housekeeper's eyes. She stood in front of a wall-mounted stag's head, which, in the dim light, gave the impression she had sprouted antlers.

"So, have you caught them yet?" she asked Angus. Although Stout was the senior officer, Mrs. MacCrimmon ignored him. *Probably because he doesn't speak Gaelic,* Angus thought.

"We've not come about the fire," he said, disconcerted by the eerie optical illusion. The antlers reminded him of the figure from his vision. "We're here to deliver some bad news to the laird and his wife."

A flicker of emotion flitted across the old woman's face, the wrinkles on her forehead and the crow's feet around her eyes creasing like crepe paper. "Why? What's happened?"

Stout cleared his throat. "We're here to speak to Mr. and Mrs. Chichester. In private."

Mrs MacCrimmon gave Stout a stare as cold and furious as the Corryvreckan whirlpool, but relented, leaving only a bare concern.

"Follow me."

Heels rapping out her disapproval, the housekeeper led them down a long corridor hung with gilt-framed paintings of famous battles: kilted Jacobites being massacred by bayonet-wielding Redcoats on Culloden Moor; William Wallace swinging his broadsword at the neck of a foe on Stirling Bridge. The paintings disconcerted Angus, but it wasn't just that—the air itself seemed charged with threat, as if Dunbirlinn's bloody past had been scorched into the walls.

Presently, Mrs. MacCrimmon led them into a vast room that must at one time have been a banquet hall. Now, though, it was a museum to the Highland's martial past. A row of cannons sat behind a red rope barrier, their barrels trained on glass cabinets that housed swords, maces, and crossbows. A whole wall was devoted to muskets, another to shields, pikes, and axes, whilst further cases held military medals. He'd read in the *West Highland Mail* that Chichester planned to open parts of the castle to the public once his nature reserve was established. Tourists, their imaginations fired by Hollywood movies romanticizing Scotland's gory past, would love this room, but Angus saw the nicks and scratches on bare steel. Screams of pain seethed beneath the still, cold air. This was a room of death.

Breathe, Angus. Breathe.

"Wait here," Mrs. MacCrimmon barked.

Once she had gone, Stout blew air through his cheeks. "Bloody harridan," he muttered. "Who the hell does she think she is?"

"That's the housekeeper," Angus told him. "Mary MacCrimmon. Her son's the famous piper—"

"I don't care," Stout spat. "And don't speak Gaelic. It's unprofessional."

Stout harrumphed over to inspect a display of medieval torture devices. Angus walked in the opposite direction. His stomach churned when he contemplated the conversation to come. Language crumbled when breaking the news of a child's death. Words fell like rocks and there was little anyone could do to soften the blow.

He paused beside a large display that featured stuffed animals in a re-created Highland landscape. A hind and her calf nibbled at mountain grass, a wildcat bared its teeth from the heather, a pine marten clung to the trunk of a Caledonian pine, a red fox padded by with a grouse in its jaws, all watched over by a golden eagle from its eyrie high up on the fiberglass cliff face. The scene, however, was dominated by a large stuffed wolf with a luxurious silver pelt and bright amber eyes that gleamed with an otherworldly glow.

A placard claimed the wolf was the last of its species in Scotland. The creature had been pursued by a legendary stalker named—appropriately enough—Roderick Hunter, who had cornered the wolf and slain it in a cave above Loch Morar in 1753.

Angus felt a stab of pity for the wolf. Harried to the ends of the earth and butchered in a cave.

Death and more death . . .

He shook his head and moved on to the next display, which contained a hunting horn decorated with intricate spirals and symbols in gold and silver. He flinched at the sound of a door opening at the far end of the hall. His pulse quickened as Mrs. MacCrimmon reappeared, then stepped aside to let the laird pass. James P. Chichester ambled towards him with the leisurely, confident stride of a man who knew his worth. He wore a dark three-piece suit that Angus reckoned had cost more than his monthly salary. The American's face was furrowed and wrinkled, but rather than seeming old, he reminded Angus of a seasoned explorer or round-the-world yachtsman. His tan was a deep mahogany, the type earned on a Caribbean island. His smile when he saw Angus was easy and charming.

"Constable MacNeil, good to see you again," he said, extending his hand. His eyes were warm, but his grip was like iron, his hand rough like a workingman's. The nails, although manicured, had dirt under them. His hair was shot through with silver but thick, like the pelt of the wolf in the display. He fixed Angus with smiling eyes the colour of verdigris. "Thanks again for that solid you did me with Faye," he whispered.

The laird was blissfully unaware. He glanced at the hunting horn Angus was examining. He opened the glass case, lifted the instrument from its stand, and held it up to the light. "The Fairy Horn of the MacRuaris—stunning, isn't it? Pre-Celtic. One of a kind. Impossibly old. Legend has it that sounding the instrument in battle will lead to a MacRuari victory. Although it can only be used three times, and has already been blown twice." Chichester raised the horn to his lips. "What do you think, Constable—should I? One good blare to scare off all these protestors who hate my wolves? Do you believe in the Good Folk?"

The Good Folk, Angus knew, was another term for the fairies from Scottish folklore. The epithet was used so as not to rouse their anger.

"Err, no—I don't think so."

Chichester sighed, like a teacher given the wrong answer by a star pupil. "That's the problem with the world," he said, replacing the horn carefully on its stand. "Nobody believes in anything nowadays."

He didn't argue the toss. Stout was heading his way, scowling. "Mr Chichester," Angus said, "this is my—"

The inspector cut him off. "I'm Inspector Stout. My colleague and I need to talk to you."

Chichester was a good foot taller than Stout and observed the inspector with a look of mild amusement.

"Of course. Please follow me, gentlemen. I'll have Mrs. MacCrimmon fetch us some coffee."

The housekeeper, who had been standing like a statue a few feet away, took the hint.

Angus's heart thumped in his chest as he followed the two men into what turned out to be a library.

"Take a seat," Chichester said, gesturing to a three-seater Chesterfield of weathered brown leather in front of a roaring log fire. Angus did as instructed, resisting the urge to tug at his shirt collar. The room was stifling from the heat of the fire. Weak daylight filtered in through a large arched window that overlooked a tiny interior courtyard. Books lined almost every wall, reaching all the way to the intricate cornicing on the ceiling. A wooden ladder set on wheels and attached to a railing allowed access to the tomes on the top shelves. A framed family tree was displayed prominently, Dòmhnall MacRuari's name at the top. He could just make out Faye's name at the bottom, a snapped twig.

The heady scent of woodsmoke, leather, and musty old books made Angus's head spin. The aroma took him back to the study of the Old Manse, where Gills, feet up on the leather surface of his writing desk, was riffing on the topic of the day. He blinked away the memory and watched Chichester lower himself into a wingback chair at right angles to the Chesterfield.

"Now, gentlemen," he said, crossing an elegant trouser leg over the other, "I take it you're here to update me on the progress of your investigation into the fire. You have made progress, yes?"

Stout frowned. "I'm afraid you've got the wrong end of the stick, Mr. Chichester. We're not here about the fire. We're here about your daughter."

"Faye? Why? What's she done? Wait—she didn't take the Benz out again?"

Angus glanced at Stout. Chichester might be wealthy, and perhaps he was the eccentric recluse the media cast, but he didn't deserve to receive the news with Stout's tactless delivery.

"There really is no easy way to say this. . . ." Angus faltered. Sweat prickled his brow. "Early this morning, the body of a young woman was discovered on a beach near here. The deceased was your daughter, Faye. We believe she was murdered."

Chichester looked at him uncomprehendingly.

"But . . . but that's not possible."

Angus kept his voice level. "I'm truly sorry, sir, but there's no doubt."

"You're wrong. Faye's upstairs. In her room. She's—"

Chichester sprang from his chair. "She's in her room!"

A second later the laird was gone. Angus heard his futile footsteps recede into the distance.

"That went well," Stout muttered. "I told you to let me do the talking."

The inspector stood and strolled around the room, lifting ornaments and pursing his lips, as if weighing up how much they'd cost. He plucked the stopper from a crystal whisky decanter and sniffed.

"Hmmph! That's no' Famous Grouse. Probably costs about a hundred quid a dram."

Angus watched Stout with barely concealed anger as the older man reached for a glass. Only the sound of approaching footsteps prevented him from pouring a measure. Angus stood as Chichester reentered the library. The laird had been away barely a minute but seemed to have aged a decade. His shoulders were hunched, and his face had taken on a sallow hue, the skin around his cheekbones and jawline flaccid, like melting wax. His eyes were desolate pools. Chichester trudged across to his chair and sagged into it.

After an awkward few seconds, when no one appeared to know what to say, Angus cleared his throat.

"I'm very sorry, sir." Not the first time he'd used those words. Not the first time he'd thought how insufficient they were.

Chichester's shoulders began to shake, but he held his sobs in check. "Who would . . ."

"It's really too early to say, sir."

Angus dug his nails into his palms, the abused skin aching, pain the only way to silence the biting, accusatory voice in his head.

You could have saved me. . . .

"Can we get someone . . . your wife maybe?"

Chichester looked up at Angus, as if seeing him for the first time. He swiped a hand across his face. "My wife? Yes, my wife. Of course, she must be told." He tried to stand, but his legs seemed to buckle. Angus caught him before he could fall.

"You're okay, Laird. Just take it easy."

He eased Chichester back down onto the armchair. No sooner had he done so than the library door swung open and Eleanor Chichester breezed in like an exotic cat. She could have been anywhere from forty to sixty years old, with sleek platinum-blond hair, pouty lips, and thin arched eyebrows that gave her a look of permanent surprise. She wore tight jeans and a white wrap blouse that left little to the imagination.

"Mrs MacCrimmon said we had guests," she exclaimed in a high-pitched drawl. "Ah fantastic, the fire's lit. It's so very cold in this country." She noticed Angus hovering over her husband and the smile vanished. She put a hand to her cheek. "Oh my God, what's happened?" Her eyes darted from Stout—who was staring at her, agog—to Angus, before settling on her husband. "Oh, James! What's the matter?"

The appearance of his wife seemed to rally Chichester. He locked eyes with Angus. "Thank you, Constable."

He levered himself upright using the armrests of the chair and planted his feet wide apart, like a sailor braced for a high swell. "Perhaps, gentleman, you could give us some privacy."

"Of course, sir," Angus said. "We'll be outside if you need us."

He walked to the door and held it open for Stout, who barrelled past him without a glance. "Well handled, *Constable*," he hissed.

Angus bit back a snarky response and followed his boss from the room. Outside, they met Mrs. MacCrimmon. The housekeeper held a silver tray laden with a coffee carafe and fancy china crockery.

"What's going on?" she demanded.

Angus could just about hear Chichester's voice through the door, deep and level.

Mrs MacCrimmon flinched when the sudden, inevitable wail came from the library.

Angus stepped forward and took the tray from her shaking hands.

CHAPTER 7

GILLEASBUIG MacMurdo threw down his pen and let out an exasperated sigh. Words were not flowing today. His writing pad contained more scorings-out and doodles than actual sentences. His paper on the Devil as represented in Highland folktales was not going to write itself, but he simply could not concentrate. To make matters worse, he had agreed to give a one-off lecture on Highland mythology to a group of German exchange students who were visiting Silvaig University this afternoon. He *could* cancel, but he admired the research of their leader, Professor Tanya Berman, and didn't want to disappoint her. Besides, they'd travelled a long way and were taking the ferry to Skye later, so the lecture couldn't be rearranged.

His mind kept returning to the beach and the dead girl. The sight had affected him more than he cared to admit. But that wasn't all. Perhaps he was imagining things, but when he'd seen the girl, he'd sensed a fundamental shift, like the first frigid autumnal winds blowing away the dying embers of summer. He shivered—cold, even sitting in the warmth of the study. This killing had meaning. The violence had a pattern, but the object on which that pattern was etched lay buried in the peat bog of his brain. He needed to dig deeper. And he needed to find out more about that damned clay corpse.

He worried about Angus, too. He'd been running from this for so long. He'd swallowed Uisdean's words—that it was all in his head—and the doctor's pills. But now he would blame himself for the death, like he did the others. It wasn't the lad's fault. Gills had told him that on numerous occasions, but Angus seemed to welcome the burden. Which was damaging. There was plenty of guilt to go around. Gills knew this better than anyone.

If there was one small chink of light in this morning's dark events, it was the chance to rebuild bridges with Angus. He could take encouragement from the fact that, when in crisis, Angus had come to his door. Surely that showed their relationship was not damaged beyond repair?

He sat back in his chair, hesitated, then pulled out the drawer. He dug under piles of envelopes and paperwork and felt the glossy surface of the photograph. Gently, he teased it out and placed it flat on the desk. The smiling eyes of a pretty woman gazed at him. She sat on a barnacle-studded rock, overlooking the sea, dark hair whipping around her face. Gills closed his eyes. Even after all these years he could hear her laughter that day, could smell the warm sea breeze and her perfume. He had not looked at the photograph for months, and felt the same stab of emotion: love, remorse, and—yes—guilt. Ach, always the guilt.

He turned over the photograph. The words "Caitlin '82 Roshven" written in his own hand. Below them, he'd neatly copied a short Gaelic poem by Sorley MacLean. His eyes welled up as he whispered the verse into the dusty silence:

> *"I spoke of the beauty of your face*
> *yesterday and today, not often but always;*
> *and I will speak of the beauty of your spirit*
> *and death will not say it is idle talk."*

A fat tear rolled down his cheek. Just in time, he jerked the photograph away and the glistening drop landed on his thigh. Annoyed with himself, he swiped his sleeve across his eyes, slipped the photograph back under the papers and envelopes, and closed the desk drawer.

He would not malinger. The Devil could wait while he walked the dogs.

Bran and Sceolan scurried along the shoreline, sniffing and peeing, pink tongues lolling happily from their mouths. Bran splashed into the shallows and retrieved a piece of driftwood. He returned to land with his prize clamped between his teeth and dropped the stick at Gills's feet, his chestnut eyes filled with hope.

"Oh, to be a dog." Gills sighed, lifting the stick and throwing it back into the waves. Bran set off after the stick, yipping excitedly. Sceolan watched Gills with his mismatched eyes, one a cobalt blue, the other milky white. "Your brother's an idiot," he told the dog.

Sceolan cocked his head to the side, as if in agreement. He'd never had any interest in playing fetch.

A biting wind cut across the bay, bringing with it a flurry of sleet. Snow wouldn't be far behind, judging from the leaden clouds draped over the Small Isles. He turned from the sea and headed towards the village. Grant Abbot, a wiry, bearded fisherman in his early thirties, was mending nets on the jetty.

"How's the wee one getting on, Grant?"

The man grinned. "Ach, they dinnae do much at this age. Sleep. Eat. Shit. Repeat."

"My idea of heaven," Gills joked. "And Nualla?"

A faint shadow flitted across the fisherman's weather-beaten face. "Aye, she's grand, Gills. Tired, like . . ."

Gills clapped Grant on the shoulder and left the fisherman to his nets. He set off towards the bookshop, the dogs at his heels. Some hillwalkers sat on a wooden bench outside the Glenruig Inn, studying a map, their rucksacks propped against the drystane dyke that encircled the pub's beer garden. Gills was still in need of that dram, but forced himself to keep walking. The metal sign above the door of Campbell & Boules bookshop flapped in the wind, emitting a banshee wail. The cobwebbed window display hadn't been rearranged since last summer, judging from the year-old bestsellers. A dog-eared poster Sellotaped to the window offered "expert genealogy services." "Come inside, and meet your ancestors!"

How disappointed customers must feel, he thought, when they ventured inside and found nothing but a curmudgeonly cheroot-smoking bookseller.

Gills turned to the dogs.

"Stay," he commanded. Sceolan lay down to wait, but Bran tried to follow him into the shop, stick still clamped in his jaws. "No, stay, you silly mutt!"

A bell jangled an off-key note as he slipped inside, leaving Bran pawing at the door. He glanced around the dusty interior. There were books everywhere. Not just on the maze of shelves, but crammed in teetering piles on the floor, making it impossible for customers to pass without performing an impromptu waltz. Not that the bookshop ever had more than two customers at once.

A ginger cat sprang from the top of a shelf and padded over to meet him, wrapping itself around his legs. "Afternoon, Issy," he said, bending to stroke her. "And where's the master of the house?" The cat looked up at him with sharp green eyes and meowed.

"This way, you say? Why, thank you, Issy."

He found Lachlan Campbell sitting in his customary leather chair behind the counter, a gas fire humming away close by. As if the fire weren't risky enough, Lachy had a cheroot balanced precariously between his fingers, ash flaking from the glowing tip as he sat engrossed in a book. Gills thought it one of life's miracles that the bookshop had not yet burned to the ground.

"It's yourself, Gilleasbuig," Lachlan said, without looking up from the book in his lap. Smoke hung around the old bookseller like a shroud.

"How are you keeping, Lachy?" In truth, the bookseller was not looking well. His skin had a jaundiced tinge and hung loosely from an emaciated face. As always, he wore a suit, waistcoat, and tie, but the clothes were crumpled, as if Lachy had slept in them. Which, Gills reflected, he probably had.

Lachy shut the book and took a draw of his cheroot. The off-white collar of his shirt was speckled with blood from where he'd nicked himself shaving. "I'm muddling by, Gills," he said, blowing smoke into the stale atmosphere. "I suppose you've heard about this murder?"

Gills nodded gravely. Nevis Radio had led its hourly news bulletin with a report on the "suspicious death." Faye had not been named, but soon the world would know. Nothing stayed secret for long in this era. He recalled how small she had looked cradled in Angus's arms. Billionaire's daughter or not, she'd been just a child. Who could do such a thing to a wee lassie?

"You okay there, Gills?"

Lachy's question snapped him back to the present. "Aye. Listen, old bean, those books I sold you a while back, have you still got them?"

"Uh-huh. Nev says they're too esoteric for the passing trade."

Gills snorted. "Too esoteric? For here?"

Lachy sucked on his cheroot. "Aye, well, this isn't exactly Waterstones, is it?"

Gills wafted smoke away from his face. "You can say that again. Anyway, I'd like to buy them back."

"It's your money to waste, I suppose. Why did you sell them in the first place?"

Gills hesitated. "I thought we were done with them."

"We?"

"That's the royal 'we.'"

Lachy scrutinized him for a second. The whites of his eyes were tinged the same nicotine yellow as his fingernails.

"Hmmph! You'll find them over by the parish records." He dismissed Gills with a flick of his hand and returned his attention to his book.

Gills cleared his throat. "Err, could I trouble you for a box?"

Lachy, grumbling, got to his feet in a plume of cheroot smoke. "Bet you don't get this kind of service in Waterstones."

"You don't get lung cancer, either," Gills coughed.

Lachy shuffled out from behind the counter and disappeared through a velvet curtain into what Gills presumed was another room, although it could easily have been another dimension. He turned and walked over to the shelves Lachy had indicated. Smiling, he ran his fingers along the titles, something comforting in the familiar texture of the spines. He plucked out a tattered volume from the *Proceedings of the Mythopoeic Society*, which, he recalled, contained an article on supernaturalism and water in Highland folklore.

Gills was reminded how mysterious nature must have appeared to the ancient tribes of the Highlands. All nature, in fact, must have seemed supernatural to them. Seas, lochs, springs, and rivers were the abodes of divinities, even divinities themselves. They were populated not just by gods and goddesses but by a plethora of monsters, both benign and terrifying: sea trows and mermen, selkies and kelpies, sprites and serpents.

From the Hebrides, Gills recalled tales of the Seonaidh, a sea sprite that drowned sailors and made a death necklace with their teeth. Until relatively recently, the islanders of Lewis observed a custom on Samhain of wading into the sea and propitiating the Seonaidh with cups of ale.

Then there was the Highland *each-uisge*, or water horse. A shape-shifter, it would come ashore as a beautiful horse, but if any man should mount it, the *each-uisge* would gallop towards the nearest body of water and plunge into the deepest part. After the rider had drowned, the *each-uisge* would tear him apart and devour his entire body, except for the liver, which would float to the surface.

It occurred to Gills that the girl's body had been left intentionally on that liminal place below the high-tide mark, known in Gaelic as the *Cladach Dubh*, or black shore. That area of the beach was laden with supernatural associations, a watery frontier where the known and unknown worlds collided. It was a threshold between life and death, a metaphysical realm where the supernatural impacted on the physical world. The shoreline was where humans encountered fairies and selkies, the seal folk who came ashore to shed their skin and dance naked under the moonlight.

Gills's reverie was broken by Lachy returning with a cardboard box. "Much obliged."

Lachy grunted in response.

"One more thing. Something I need to pick your brain, old bean."

Lachy sighed theatrically. "Whit now?"

"Your specialist subject, of course—witchcraft."

A mischievous smile spread across the old bookseller's face. "I told you last time, Gills, there's no spell to fix that little problem of yours. But fear not, you can get pills for everything these days. I should know—I'm on most of them."

"Very drole." Gills took out his mobile phone and showed Lachy a photograph of the clay corpse he had snapped that morning. The effigy was female, that much was obvious from the greyish-blond strands of hair attached to the head and the curvaceous figure. Her face was pinched, the cheekbones, forehead, and nose pronounced. The lips were disproportionately large, as if collagen-injected, like one of those glamor models the tabloids always plastered on their front pages. The eyes were tiny shards of glass that glinted out from hollow eye sockets. Despite this, the doll was clearly dead—its throat had been slashed, just like Faye's.

Lachy studied the doll, his eyes narrowed. "Haven't seen one of those in a while. How did *you* come by it?"

Gills slipped the phone back into his pocket, as if afraid the effigy might leap from the screen. There was something deeply unsettling about the doll. "Afraid I'm not at liberty to discuss that, old bean."

"Has it anything to do with this murder?"

Gills saw the gash on Faye's neck yawning open, the thin garrotte still intact. The poor lassie had been executed. No, not executed—sacrificed.

"No! No! I'm writing a paper on black witchcraft. I don't suppose you know anyone who still makes these . . . err . . . totems."

"Sorry, we're strictly white witchcraft."

"You've never dabbled in the darker side?"

"Of course, when I was young and foolish. But now that you mention it, there was one woman. She tried to join our coven last year, but Nev and I turned her down. Her interests were . . . somewhat extreme for us."

"She sounds delightful."

"Aye, she's quite something."

"Can you tell me where to find her?"

Lachy hesitated. "Aye," he said, drawing out the word. "You'll find her in Rhu. But be careful, Gills. You're an irritating old reprobate, but I wouldn't like to see you cursed."

CHAPTER 8

ANGUS nervously eyed the two suits of armour at the foot of the staircase and started to climb. Stout was in the staff kitchen, stuffing his face with scones and drinking tea. Angus had broken the news of Faye's death to Mrs. MacCrimmon in Gaelic. She had grasped the back of a chair and let out a small exclamation of despair. Her eyes had welled up, but she did not shed any tears. She wasn't the sort of woman to cry, which was why her reaction had affected him more deeply than Lady Chichester's shriek.

Once he'd been sure the housekeeper was going to be all right, he had slipped away, telling Stout he was going to check on the ETA of the family liaison officer. Instead here he was, mounting the stairs, footsteps muffled by a crimson carpet that reminded him of the legend of the bloody cataract. The gory waterfall was said to have sprung out of the hillside behind Dunbirlinn in the immediate aftermath of a calamitous battle.

He had no good reason to go snooping around, but his legs seemed to be acting of their own volition. Bronze busts of esteemed gentlemen watched his passing as he circumnavigated the first floor, opening doors with his sleeve over his hand to avoid leaving fingerprints. Most of the north-facing rooms were guest bedrooms, but none appeared occupied. All were decorated in Highland chic—sheepskin rugs, tweed cushions, paintings of stags, the obligatory tartan. They reminded him of rooms in upmarket hotels, not that he got to visit many of those on his constable's salary.

It took him a few minutes of searching to find Faye's bedroom. She might not have been a typical teenager, but her bedroom showed all the hallmarks. It looked like a hand grenade had gone off in a suitcase. Shirts hung limp from the back of a chair, a pink bra dangled from the wardrobe door handle, and discarded underwear lay, forlorn and twisted, on the thick carpet.

He stepped farther into the room and let the door swing shut behind him. It was then the scent hit him, the same sickly sweet fragrance he'd smelt earlier when he lifted her body. He closed his eyes and for a second fooled himself into believing she was here—lying on the four-poster bed that dominated the room, or sitting at the dressing table near the window, brushing her golden hair in the mirror.

He could keep up the pretence no longer. His eyes snapped open. A scruffy teddy smiled at him from the bed. The stuffed toy was clearly old—an eye was missing and rough stitching across its belly showed where it had been mended over the years. He felt something cold twist inside his stomach. He imagined Faye as a child, dropping off to sleep, the teddy held in the crook of her arm. He'd had a similar comfort toy as a child—a stuffed seal pup that his mother had bought him in the gift shop of the Sea Life Centre in Oban. After she'd died, he couldn't sleep without Sammy beside him. But one morning he woke to find the seal gone. Gills had tried to cheer him up by telling him a folktale about selkies. Sammy, he said, had probably returned to the sea, to his own kind. Angus, though, knew what had happened: Dad had decided he was too old for cuddly toys and thrown Sammy in the bin.

His eyes darted around the walls of the bedroom. There were no posters of pop stars here. Framed paintings and prints hung everywhere. There was a distinct style to the paintings: thick vivid colours applied in manic slashes, built up layer upon layer until the subjects—horses, hares, various birds—appeared almost three-dimensional. Looking closer at a sinister raven, he noticed the initials *F* and *C* scrawled in red in the bottom left-hand corner of the canvas. He was no art critic, but it was clear Faye had possessed talent. Potential that would be forever unfulfilled.

Because you did nothing.

No! No! It was all in your head! There was nothing to do!

He turned and his eye fell on a pile of notepads strewn under her bed.

Diaries.

He fell to his knees, reached under the bed, and pulled out one of the notepads, again using his sleeve to avoid leaving prints. He took a pen from his pocket and flicked to the first page, but rather than a diary entry, there was a symbol etched in pencil. The image—three interconnected circles—snagged something at the back of his memory. A band logo, perhaps? As a teenager he'd gone through a heavy metal phase and often sat with *Kerrang!* magazine, copying logos for Metallica, Sepultura, Anthrax, and Megadeth onto his school jotters.

Using the pen, he flipped over to the next leaf and discovered the same symbol. With growing unease, he flicked through the rest of the notepads.

They all contained the same drawing—sometimes in pencil, sometimes crayon, sometimes a reddish brown that looked like dry blood, but always this same symbol.

His hand shook as he took out his phone and snapped some photographs. There was something mesmerizing, almost spiritual, about the symbol, like the intricate designs on the ancient Pictish standing stones Gills had shown him as a child.

A sudden draught swept through the room, as if someone had opened a window. The pages of Faye's sketch pads ruffled, then flipped and began to whirr forward. He scrambled away, the hair on the nape of his neck standing on end.

He felt the dead girl's eyes on his back, but didn't dare turn around. He heard the hiss of wind through trees, and a monotonous murmur, like an off-key waulking song that rose and fell in time to his own heartbeat. Faye's paintings were suddenly alive: the raven hopped from foot to foot and let out a loud caw; an otter's silken body slid silently into a brooding pool; a white horse pawed the ground and shook its mane, bulging eyes rolling back in its head like those of the Drowned Boy. Angus screwed his eyes shut, but the girl was waiting for him in the darkness, an inky black slither of blood running down her neck. Behind her, that presence he had felt earlier at the beach now had shape and form. It towered over the kneeling girl, a cloaked, elongated figure with gleaming white orbs for eyes. Large antlers protruded from its head. He tried to back away, but what had been a thick rug in Faye's room was now ivy and bindweed crawling over his hands and feet, pinning him to the ground. He jerked and thrashed, straining every sinew as he attempted to rip his limbs free, but it was no good. He felt her warm breath on his cheek then, her whispered words ripe and rancid.

You could have saved me. . . .

His eyes snapped open and Faye was there, in the room, sitting at the dressing table, brushing her hair. She looked just as he remembered, only her pallor was deathly pale. He noticed clumps of hair spiral to the floor as she brushed. The ghostly Faye glanced at him in the mirror. Her lips were purple bruises.

"Oh, howdy, Constable MacNeil. Sorry about the mess."

His mouth contorted, struggling to form words.

"You're . . . you're not real. . . ."

Her eye roll was a masterclass in teenage contempt. "Well, duh . . ."

He backed away from her, upsetting the pile of sketch pads.

"You're not real!"

He spun round and lurched towards the door. Faye's words chased him from the bedroom.

"I'll be seeing you, Constable."

Back in the kitchen, he found Stout sitting at a long table, polishing off a scone and jam.

He scanned the room. It was dominated by a fireplace of blackened stone big enough to spit-roast a pig in. It was unlit, and the wind whistled from its dark maw in an eerie banshee wail. Sleet splattered onto a row of small arched windows fifteen feet from floor level, but the thick castle walls dulled the sound of the elements. The kitchen, thankfully, was bereft of his ghosts.

"These are delicious," Stout said, spraying crumbs across the table. He pushed the plate towards Angus. "You should try one."

"I'm good, thanks. Where's Mrs. MacCrimmon?"

On cue, the housekeeper appeared in the doorway. She glanced at Stout, lips puckered in distaste, then turned to Angus. "Lady Chichester has gone for a lie-down. The laird is attending to her but will speak to you shortly."

"Can we ask you a few questions, Mrs. MacCrimmon?" he asked.

The housekeeper sighed. "If you must."

He pulled out a chair for her. She sat and placed her hands in her lap.

"Excellent scones," Stout remarked. "Did you make them yourself?"

Mrs MacCrimmon shook her head.

"That's a shame. Mrs. Stout would have liked the recipe." He pushed away the plate. "Do you live here, in the castle?"

"No. I have a cottage near the stables."

"You live alone?"

"My husband passed five years ago."

"I'm sorry to hear that," Stout said mildly. "How long have you worked here?"

"Since I was thirteen. I've seen two lairds come and go—Mr Chichester is the third."

"And is he a good boss?"

"Aye."

"What about Faye?"

Mrs MacCrimmon twisted a silver ring round her bony finger. "Och, she was never any trouble. Her room was always a tip, but she was a good girl. Quiet. Lost her mother a few years back." *Lost.*

Angus clenched his teeth. He hated that euphemism.

"There's a story attached to this castle," Mrs. MacCrimmon continued. "Legend has it that the adulterous wife of Chieftain Dòmhnall MacRuari was bricked up alive in a secret room. Some nights I fancy I've heard her, clawing at the walls of her prison. In a way, Faye was a prisoner here too. She had the run of the place, but she was lonely. The laird never paid her much attention. Too busy. Sometimes she'd help me out in the kitchen, peeling potatoes and carrots like a scullery maid. She seemed content, though, humming away to herself as she worked."

The old woman's eyes misted over. "And baking—she loved baking, too—cookies, fairy cakes, Victoria sponge, that kind of thing. It was Faye who made those scones you like so much, Inspector."

"Doubt I'll be getting that recipe, then."

"Please excuse him, Mrs. MacCrimmon," Angus said in Gaelic, adding: "'Ceann mor air duine glic ach mar as trice air amadan.'" His father had often used this derogatory phrase: "A big head on a wise man, but more often on a fool."

"Speak English!" Stout scolded.

"Sorry, sir. Force of habit. I was asking Mrs. MacCrimmon when she last saw Faye."

A half-smile tugged at the corners of the old woman's mouth.

"At dinner last night. Around half past seven. She left the table rather abruptly after the starter."

"Why was that?"

She hesitated. "She and Lady Chichester exchanged words."

"They argued? What about?"

"Och, I don't want to be telling tales."

"This is important, Mary. We need to know everything, even if it doesn't seem relevant."

Mrs MacCrimmon nodded to herself. "Faye and Lady Chichester were not on the best of terms. Eleanor wanted to send her to some fancy finishing school in Switzerland, but Faye had her heart set on art college."

"Was that what they rowed about last night?"

"Lady Chichester told Faye she'd chartered a jet to take her to Zurich before term started. Faye . . . did not take it well."

"Did you see Faye after that?"

"No . . ."

"You don't seem too sure," Stout prodded.

"When I was getting ready for bed, I heard the sound of horses' hooves outside my window. This would have been about ten o'clock. I glanced out but didn't see anyone."

"It would be pitch black at that time anyway."

"Actually, Inspector," Mrs. MacCrimmon replied tartly, "there was a full moon last night, so I could see just fine."

"Faye rode, didn't she?" Angus asked.

"Aye, every day, she took Bessie out for a hack. Beautiful chestnut mare." She sniffed. "Faye adored that horse. Spent hours grooming her, pleating her mane and tail. Even mucked out the stable."

"Isn't there staff for that?"

"Och, there's staff, all right, but Faye didn't act the pampered heiress, Angus. If she could do something herself, she would."

The old woman worried at the silver ring. "A few months ago, when it was warmer, I found her sleeping beside Bessie in the stables. She looked so peaceful. I couldn't bring myself to wake her."

He blinked away the image of the golden-haired girl sleeping in the hay beside her horse.

"Can you take us to the stables?" he asked. "I'd like to check if Bessie is still there."

Mrs MacCrimmon swiped a hand across her eyes. "Of course."

He rose, but Stout showed no sign of moving.

"You two go on ahead," he said as slivers of sleet hit the windows. "I've some important phone calls to make."

Angus and Mrs. MacCrimmon lapsed easily back into Gaelic on the walk to the stables. The sleet blew in horizontally off the sea, but the housekeeper had found them both yellow oilskin jackets before they ventured outside. The sleet hammering off their waterproofs pitched him back to an isolated lay-by, to the sound of rain pounding his mother's Renault Scenic, and a cold knot of dread in his stomach. He throttled the memory before it could become fully formed.

Once past the gatehouse and across the bridge, the wind eased and they were able to talk without shouting.

"You don't seem to have a very high opinion of Lady Chichester," Angus said.

Away from the castle, and Stout's bad manners, Mrs. MacCrimmon was less guarded.

"She's a pain in the proverbial. Treats us staff like dirt, but only when the laird's not around. If he's there, she pretends we're best of friends. She does . . . *did* the same with Faye."

"She certainly sounded distraught when Chichester broke the news."

"Pah! Distraught! It's not just Her Ladyship's *glagan-mhòr* that are fake, Angus. She's rotten to the core, that one."

They walked along a gravel road that led past manicured lawns to the stable block, an impressive three-winged granite building complete with clock tower.

"That's my house over there," Mrs. MacCrimmon said, pointing to a neat one-story building with crow-stepped gables and a jaunty purple door. "I'm used to the sound of folk on horseback riding past. And I'll swear on the Good Book I heard someone last night."

"What about the staff? Where do they stay?"

"Staff quarters are behind the stables, but only Ewan lives there now." She glanced up at him through the sleet. "Have you spoken to Ewan since—"

He shook his head. "I've tried, but you know what he's like."

"Aye, stubborn as a mule."

"Were he and Faye close? I wouldn't have thought they'd have much in common."

"You'd be surprised. There're only four years between them, and it's not like there are many young ones around here. Sometimes Ewan took her out on the boat, and during that fine spell we had in July they were swimming up the river almost every day."

The wrinkles on Mrs. MacCrimmon's face looked taut, like tiny threads about to snap. "Poor Ewan, he'll be devastated. He's not been the same since his father died."

Angus recalled John Hunter lying on the heather, his lips blue, Ewan pounding his chest as rain fell like skeins of yarn from the grubby clouds.

"Would you say Ewan and Faye were an item, Mrs. MacCrimmon?"

"Ewan had a soft spot for her; a blind man could see that. But Faye . . . she is—was—still a wee girl at heart. But she was at that age where girls start to understand the power their looks give them over men. Och, I don't know . . . Maybe she led Ewan on a wee bit."

"Did Faye have any other friends?"

"Well," Mrs. MacCrimmon said uncertainly, "she did hack out to the commune most days."

"Teine Eigin?" he asked, surprised. "Again, wouldn't have thought she'd have much in common with that lot, either. Pagans, aren't they?"

"I believe so. Doesn't make them bad people, Angus. Once upon a time, we were all pagans."

"No, of course not," he spluttered. "I didn't mean that."

The old woman gave him a look, then turned and stomped across the courtyard, which was dominated by an ornate fountain—all prancing horses, dancing nymphs, and leering satyrs.

A sudden image of Faye flashed into his head. He saw her trotting towards him from across the courtyard on her chestnut mare. Bessie was beautiful but temperamental. She'd spooked when he'd tried to stroke her nose, shied away from him. What was the phrase she'd used to calm the horse down?

Two as one.

That was it. Said she'd learnt the phrase from her old riding instructor, who himself had been a member of a secret horseman society.

Two as one.

"Angus, are you coming?"

He almost flinched at the sound of Mrs. MacCrimmon's voice.

"Aye, sorry."

He jogged after the housekeeper and followed her through a stone archway flanked by Grecian columns and topiary trees. If he didn't know better, he would have thought he was entering a grand hotel. He almost expected to see a bellboy in livery waiting in the lobby to take his suitcase.

There was no mistaking the tang of horse dung, however. It hung in the air, reminding him of policing football matches with the mounted unit when he was a beat cop in Inverness.

Rows of stalls were arranged down both sides of a central aisle, forks, buckets, net bags of hay, and boxes of feed stacked neatly at regular intervals. A pigeon flitted across the vaulted ceiling and settled on a thick timber joist, cooing. Only one of the stall doors stood ajar.

Mrs MacCrimmon hurried down the aisle, stopping outside the unoccupied stall. He didn't need to ask if this was where Faye's horse had been kept—a gold-plated plaque screwed to the wood panelling next to the door was inscribed with the name Bessie.

"Gone," Mrs. MacCrimmon whispered. "She's riding with the wild host now."

He frowned at the cryptic comment. "Perhaps she'll come back," he said. "Horses have a knack of finding their way home."

The old woman turned to him, her eyes hard as flint. "I wasn't talking about the horse."

CHAPTER 9

DUNBIRLINN was a maze of staircases, cloisters, narrow passageways, and dead ends. Like a palimpsest in stone, the castle had been modified over the centuries, many parts destroyed then overlaid with new constructions according to the whims, and defensive requirements, of its occupants. It had evolved into a disjointed, brutal behemoth, an eerie hybrid creature full of rattles and wails as the wind ransacked hidden nooks and crannies.

As Angus climbed to the room at the top of the tower to meet the laird, he fancied he could hear scratching behind the walls. Mice probably, or rats, although he couldn't help recalling Mrs. MacCrimmon's story of Dòmhnall MacRuari's adulterous wife, entombed alive.

He glanced over his shoulder at Stout, who was wheezing his way up the narrow spiral staircase. Slashes of light filtered in through arrow loops.

"Christ! Please tell me we're nearly at the top."

"One flight to go, sir."

Stout took off his cap and mopped his brow. "I need to lay off the fry-ups," he gasped, shooing the constable on ahead.

Angus climbed the final flight of stairs, tapped on a solid oak door, and entered. James Chichester stood like a bronze statue at the window, hands clasped behind his back, staring out at the rugged coastline.

Heart thudding, Angus stepped into the room at the top of the tower. His eyes were immediately drawn upwards to a stunning fresco that covered every inch of the vaulted ceiling. It depicted a great cosmic battle: angels, demons, men, and beasts locked in combat in a fantastical landscape. Strange mutant creatures—like something from a Hieronymus Bosch painting—stalked the scene, devouring the dead and living alike; naked people plummeted, lemming-like, from a cliff into a sea of flames; wolves tore a woman limb from limb; naked bodies writhed on the ground in an apparent orgy; ravens soared across the sky with severed limbs in their beaks.

Angus was aware of Stout wheezing into the room, but he could not take his eyes off the fresco. In his head, he heard his father's voice, denouncing the painting as zealous nonsense, the work of a deranged mind.

One as deranged as mine, Dad?

But in the other ear was Gills, inviting him to look deeper, to peek beyond the curtain of science and scepticism to another realm, an otherworld that coexisted beside their own. He'd closed his mind to that world, turned his back on Gills, but it had found him anyway.

The voices argued in his head as he took in new details of the fresco. In the middle of the carnage, a fair-haired boy sat against the trunk of a hulking oak tree, reading a red book. Above the raging battle, presiding over it, was a woman with two faces: one, a beautiful maiden with blue eyes and rosy cheeks; the other, a one-eyed crone with blackened skin and straggly grey hair. She hovered in the air, set against roiling masses of angry clouds and barbs of lightning. The colours—vermilion, turquoise, ultramarine, gold, and silver—made the ceiling seem alive.

"Impressive, isn't it?"

He tugged his eyes away from the fresco and found Chichester watching him.

"Aye."

"It's allegorical, of course. Probably completed in the 1300s. The artist is a mystery, however."

The laird let out a long sigh. "I'd often find Faye up here, lying on her back, staring up at the ceiling. What was she thinking? I wonder."

"Who knows the mind of a teenage girl, eh?" Stout joked.

Chichester ignored him.

"I met Faye a couple of weeks ago, when I was investigating the fire," Angus said. "She told me she wanted to go to art college."

"Eleanor thought it was a passing phase," Chichester mumbled, as if to himself. "It's strange: for a former actress, my wife doesn't have much time for artists. I think, perhaps, she had a bad experience with one in the past."

"What about you, sir? Did you have an opinion on the subject?"

Chichester raked his fingers through his silver-flecked hair. "I didn't give it much thought. My mind's been on other things."

"Oh, aye—like what?" barked Stout.

Chichester eyeballed Stout like a predator assessing a rival. Apparently satisfied, he turned from Stout and addressed Angus. "My every minute has been taken up with plans for the nature reserve. There's so much to do before the wolves are finally released into the wild."

Stout let out a snort, but Angus did not want to be sidetracked by an argument. "When did you last see Faye?"

Chichester pinched the bridge of his nose, screwed his eyes shut, probably replaying the argument of the previous evening in his head. Angus understood. He'd done the same when his own mother had died. He'd scoured through their last conversation together, strained and distilled the words, torn them apart looking for a meaning they didn't possess.

Chichester swallowed, his Adam's apple bobbing. "At dinner, last night. It was not the most . . . cordial of occasions."

"She rowed with Lady Chichester?" He met Chichester's questioning stare. "Mrs MacCrimmon mentioned she heard raised voices."

A spark of anger fizzled in Chichester's eyes then went out.

"I see," he said at length. "Yes, it's true they did have a disagreement. Over that goddamn art college. Stupid argument, really. In hindsight, I should have supported Faye, but like I said, I've been too wrapped up in my own affairs."

"How did Faye and your wife get along generally?"

"What are you getting at, Constable?"

Angus shrugged but held his stare.

"Elle loved that girl like she was her own. If you'd seen the state my wife's in, you wouldn't ask such a question."

Angus nodded, feeling chastened. His intention was not to rile Chichester.

Stout, though, had no such qualms. "Did Faye have any enemies, Mr. Chichester?"

The American swatted away the question. "No."

"What about yourself? I'll bet you've rubbed a few folk up the wrong way in the course of your business?"

Chichester was silent for a long second. "No one who would do this." His eyes snapped towards Stout. "How did she die?"

"I'll ask the questions if you don't mind," Stout blustered.

Angus cringed as Stout grilled the laird on his whereabouts the previous evening. He had worked for a little after dinner then watched a movie with his wife in their private cinema before turning in around twelve. Angus felt suddenly exhausted. It was their job to ask these questions, but Stout seemed to take a cruel delight in badgering Chichester.

Angus suspected the laird had dealt with worse irritants than Stout in his time. The inspector's probing soon petered out and Chichester took the initiative. "Perhaps you can tell me *exactly* what steps you are taking to catch my daughter's killer?"

"That's above my pay grade," Stout sniffed.

"Mr Chichester," Angus cut in, "the CCTV cameras at the front of the castle, I presume they're not just for show?"

"Of course not."

"Is there any other way in or out of the castle apart from the front entrance?"

"Not unless you can climb one hundred feet of sheer cliff. Or fly," Chichester said with a bolt of pride amidst the storm of melancholy. "Dunbirlinn has been besieged numerous times over the last eight hundred years, but its walls have never been breached. Today, anyone entering or leaving the castle would be picked up on the CCTV."

"That makes things easier," Angus said. "The MIT will want to see the footage from last night."

"MIT?"

"Major investigation team. They're on their way from Glasgow, but a serious accident has blocked the road."

"So who are they, the Scotch G-men or something?"

"Aye, if you like. They investigate all murders and serious crimes in Scotland. Since MITs were established in 2013, they've solved every murder they've investigated."

Chichester walked over to the arched window and stared out. "Very impressive. Why aren't you on one of these MITs?"

Angus looked up at the fresco. He saw violence, mutilation, death. Mankind would always kill. It was in its nature. And he would be there to pick over the aftermath like a raven on a battlefield.

Always too late.

"I'm happy enough being a constable," he lied.

He stepped across the room to stand with Chichester at the window. His legs felt suddenly weak, head in a vertigo spin. From the window he had a bird's-eye view over the blasted coastline and inky expanse of sea. Great banks of charcoal clouds smothered the Isle of Skye and the mountain ranges to the north. A grey ribbon of road meandered along the coast, following a route used for centuries. New forestry plantations checkered the hillside, but otherwise the landscape was relatively unchanged, the same wilderness those first tribes wandered into millennia ago and laid down roots.

"How did my daughter die?" Chichester asked again, his voice little more than a whisper.

"Strangulation," Angus said, keeping his voice low so Stout couldn't hear.

Chichester again pinched the bridge of his nose. "Was she—"

"She was fully dressed, sir," he said. "That's all I can tell you until after the autopsy."

The American nodded several times, then ran his hands over his face, the movement somehow jerky and unnatural. Angus had seen it before: shock and grief made puppets of men.

"Thank you, Constable," Chichester said. "I appreciate your candour."

Stout cleared his throat loudly. "Anyway, I think that will be all for the time being, sir. Family liaison officers have been assigned, and will be with you in due course—"

"Where is she now?" Chichester asked, cutting across Stout. "Can I see her?"

"Faye has been taken to the mortuary in Silvaig," Angus replied. "I can arrange for a formal identification to take place, if that's what you want?"

Chichester gave a brisk nod. "Please, do."

"Right, we'll skedaddle," Stout said. He turned, pulled open the door, and shuffled out. Angus placed a hand lightly on Chichester's shoulder. "I'm truly sorry, sir," he said. "She seemed like an exceptional girl." He wanted to add something, some words of comfort, but when he opened his mouth to speak again, nothing else came out.

Sadly, he turned away, leaving Chichester alone in the room at the top of the tower, save for the company of his gods and monsters.

CHAPTER 10

THE smell of blood and damp clung to his clothes. Ewan Hunter had the heater on full blast to clear the Pathfinder's windscreen of condensation, but the recirculated air only made the stink worse. A saccharine pop song warbled from the radio, some silly American teenybopper caterwauling about getting dumped. He poked the stereo and caught the end of a news report on Nevis Radio. The DJ's thick West Highland accent immediately put him at ease.

"With less than two months before the opening of the controversial nature reserve, a local minister has again hit out at the venture. Established by eccentric American billionaire James Chichester on his Kilcreggan estate, the reserve has split the community over plans to reintroduce wolves to the land. And now Reverend John MacVannin of Glenruig Free Kirk has accused the laird of running roughshod over crofters' rights. Earlier, the minister spoke exclusively to Nevis Radio."

Ewan gripped the steering wheel tighter as the minister's voice filled the cab.

"This nature reserve is an act of vandalism that threatens the livelihoods of the local crofting community. Mr. Chichester would have us believe these wolves will bring ecological and economic benefits, but locals, in particular crofters like myself, will see none of these.

"Not only does this harebrained scheme go against crofters' wishes, but by bringing wolves back, Chichester is playing God. What can you expect from an arrogant foreigner who has already brought shame on himself by allowing a pagan commune to flourish on his estate?

"He tells us that wolves will keep down red deer numbers, and that we will be compensated for loss of livestock. Well, he better get his checkbook out, because our sheep will be easy pickings—"

Ewan jabbed the radio, silencing the minister. "Not if I have anything to do with it."

He drove the Pathfinder into the courtyard of Dunbirlinn Castle and skidded to a halt. He sat for a long second, a lump in his throat. Steam rose from his tweed breeks, and although his father's Barbour jacket had kept his top half dry, he was eager to get home and change out of his gory clothes.

If the weather had been fine, he might have stayed away from Dunbirlinn for a few days. Might, in fact, never have returned. The laird had warned him that his days as a stalker were numbered. Barely turned twenty and already being put out to pasture. The wolves, apparently, would keep red deer numbers down far more efficiently than he could. He ground his teeth. What wolf could take down a hind from a kilometre in flat light and a blowing gale? He'd learnt to stalk at his father's knee, just as his father had learnt at *his* father's knee, all the way back to the famed Roderick Hunter, who had killed the last wolf in Scotland. At least his father's passing meant he had been spared the indignity of being told he and his bloodline were obsolete.

Ewan had inspected the stuffed animal on display in the laird's ridiculous museum. He'd hoped to find the wounds his ancestor had inflicted with his sword, but there were no signs. Probably wasn't even the same wolf. You could never tell what was fact and what was fiction these days. Everyone lied. Politicians, celebrities, journalists, certain police officers. He'd thought Faye was different.

Involuntarily, he raised a bloodstained hand to his cheek, felt again the sting from her slap. The way she'd looked at him hurt even more. Disgusted. Repelled. As if he were an ogre in a fairy tale.

That was another good reason to stay away—he could live off the land. The idea appealed to him. All he'd need was his gun and his fishing rod.

Forget wolves, *he* was the apex predator.

Hundreds of years ago it had been different: the Highlands, his father told him, had been infested with rabid hordes of wolves. They stole newborn children from their beds, attacked travellers, and, when food was scarce, scavenged graveyards for freshly buried corpses. Some forests had become all but impassable because of the beasts, and it had taken men with the courage and skills of his ancestor to quell the menace. That same hunter's blood coursed through his veins. It was hardwired into his very being. This rugged, starkly beautiful landscape was in his bones, its natural rhythms as familiar to him as his own heartbeat.

So yes, he *could* live as a wolf in the wild, but why should he? He was no base animal. One thing was certain—he couldn't go crying back to his mother. He'd thoroughly burnt his bridges with her after beating seven shades of shit out of her new boyfriend.

And now he had a criminal record, thanks to holier-than-thou Angus "Dubh" MacNeil.

Ewan yanked open the door and hopped out. Wind whistled around the battlements. For a second he imagined corpses hanging from the castle walls. His dad had had a passion for history, and had told him all about Dunbirlinn's bloody past—Dòmhnall MacRuari and his thirst for sacrificing prisoners to the old gods and hanging them from the ramparts, the sieges where the occupants of the castle were forced to eat rats, then each other.

Dad had been a great one for stories and books. Ewan was not academically inclined but loved reading, and the old boy had taught him the lore of the hunter.

He walked to the rear of the Pathfinder and jerked open the door. The deer stared at him with huge doe eyes. She was a beautiful animal, with a sleek fawn coat. He almost felt sorry for shooting her.

"Grow up," he muttered.

He grabbed her by the hind legs and hauled her out of the jeep. He'd gralloched her out on the hill, slit her from anus to throat, and pulled out her innards. This meant he left a clarty snail trail of blood on the cobblestones as he dragged her towards the storeroom. Mrs. MacCrimmon wouldn't be happy, but so what?

He kicked open a stout wooden door and hauled the carcass inside. The storeroom was dim, its warped wooden shelves crammed with enough cans and tins to survive the apocalypse.

He reached for a vicious hook that hung from a pulley rig attached to a wooden joist. The iron was freezing, so cold that it burned. He rammed the hook into the deer's hindquarters the way his father had taught him, ignoring the squelchy sound. Using a chain, he pulled the deer into the air, head down, until she was a couple of feet off the floor. Some stalkers liked to hang deer by the head, but not him. The method seemed disrespectful, as if the deer were a murderer being hung on a gibbet.

He secured the chain, placed a bucket under the carcass to catch the blood, then stood back. A muscle in his jaw twitched. He watched the hind spin on the hook and suddenly he was at the ceilidh in the Great Hall again, spinning Faye on his arm as the band belted out an Orcadian Strip the Willow, her golden hair flying out behind her as he propelled her down the line of dancers.

He shook away the memory and ran a hand down the deer's hindquarters. Her fur felt so soft. Tears stung behind his eyelids. How many deer had he shot in his lifetime? A hundred? A thousand? Killing was his way of life; it was what he was born to do.

"I'm the apex predator!"

He drew back his fist and slammed it into the deer's side, then unleashed a flurry of blows, spittle flying from between his lips. At length he stopped, breathing heavily. He closed his eyes and saw Faye dancing at the ceilidh. She smiled at him, but then the image distorted and the girl he'd loved was gone, replaced by a deer carcass, spinning around and around on a hook in the darkness.

CHAPTER 11

STOUT wet his finger and rubbed at a jam stain on his tie, tutting loudly. "Goddamn it," he muttered. "This is the last thing I need."

Angus couldn't be sure whether Stout meant a stain on his tie or a murder on his patch. The latter, he hoped.

Stout gave up on the tie and turned to him. "Some silly wee DI from major investigations has just been on the blower. She reckons the station in Silvaig is too far away from the locus, so she's established an incident room in the Glenruig village hall. Some numpties from CID are there helping her get set up. I want you to join them. No doubt you'll be given some thankless task—house-to-house inquiries probably—but remember you've still got your own workload, MacNeil."

"It's supposed to be my day off, sir."

"Boo-bloody-hoo! I was meant to be fishing the Monarch beat today. It's hotching with salmon apparently." Stout sniffed. "My advice—answer this DI's questions as succinctly as possible, then leave this case to the big boys. You've got smaller fish to fry."

Angus watched Stout's Lexus recede into the distance. For a moment he imagined that his anguish and ghosts were receding into the distance with it. The sleet had cried itself out, but the temperature had dropped too. Snow wasn't far away. He turned and walked towards the village hall, but rather than go inside, he took out his mobile and placed a call. Gills picked up on the second ring.

"How are you? I meant to call sooner, but . . . you know how it is."

"Och, I'm fine. Tough as old boots, me. More to the point, how are you?"

Angus leaned against the village hall, watched his breath plume into the air. On the phone, Gills's voice sounded older than he remembered.

"Dog-tired."

Angus closed his eyes, heard the rattle of the pills echo in his ear. The guilt ate at his throat like imagined bile.

You could have saved her.

"Listen, Gills, I was just phoning to say thanks for earlier. Those detectives should be coming to speak with you soon."

"Don't worry, old bean, I'll stick to the story. Look, Angus, I have to go—I'm in Silvaig, about to give a lecture to a group of German exchange students."

"On a Saturday?"

"I'm in demand," Gills joked.

Angus nodded to himself. "Okay, well, I won't keep you."

He stuffed his phone back into his pocket, turned, and entered the village hall. He'd passed this way on countless occasions but always for a concert or ceilidh. As he walked through the lobby, it felt odd not to hear a band warming up or the sound of raucous laughter. Instead of the usual villagers milling around, joking and drinking from plastic glasses and cans, two constables loitered, one tapping at his mobile phone whilst the other crammed a sandwich into his mouth.

He strode past them and pushed open the double doors to the auditorium, which was about the size of two badminton courts, with a small stage at the front. Wooden beams ran up the walls to meet at a vaulted ceiling, giving the impression of being in an upturned boat. No, not a boat, he thought. A coffin.

He remembered the press of warm bodies in the darkness. The smell of sweat and lager. The wolf whistles as a woman with a tumult of auburn hair took the stage. The hair on the nape of his neck standing on end as Ashleigh began to sing . . .

He blinked away the happy memory and grabbed a harassed-looking policewoman heading for the exit. "Who's in charge?"

She gestured over her shoulder to a petite woman with long raven-black hair who was busy sticking crime scene photos to the murder board. Unlike the rest of the officers, she was dressed casually in jeans, ankle boots, and a thick sweater.

"Shortie over there."

He dredged up a smile. "Thanks."

"You're welcome. Here to help."

Angus ignored the sarcasm and walked over to the woman. He stopped a few feet away, waiting for her to turn around. When she didn't, he cleared his throat. "Eh, ma'am. I—"

The woman spun around, her smile melting like snow off a dyke. Her eyes widened, gold flecks dancing in the almond brown of her irises. She quickly recovered her composure.

"Angus MacNeil. Fancy meeting you here."

He tried to speak, but his throat felt like a drain clogged with dead leaves. He forgot how strong her Glaswegian accent was, how much he loved the lilting cadence. He worked saliva into his mouth and swallowed. "Hello, Nadia."

She folded her arms across her chest and gave him a penetrative stare.

"So this is where you've been hiding, Angus?"

His name on her lips sent a quiver through him. "Err . . . aye."

"How long's it been? Eight, nine years?"

He shrugged, remembering that awful car journey home from Tulliallan in his father's old Volvo, when the pain was raw and he could hardly see the road for tears.

He didn't need this right now. Today had already been full of ghosts from his past.

"Aye, something like that."

"Long time."

"Aye."

"You look like shite, by the way."

A smile tugged at his lips. "Thanks."

"No, seriously. Do folk age quicker up here in the Highlands or something?"

"It's nice to see you, too, Nadia."

Nadia gave him a faint smile, then turned her back on him and resumed studying the crime scene photographs, hands on hips. He recalled his own hands on those hips, the chamomile and lavender scent of her hair.

"So, why are you here, Angus?"

"This is my patch. I was first officer on the scene. It was Gills who found her—"

She turned around. "There's a name I haven't heard in a while. Is it *that* Gills?"

"Aye."

Out of the corner of his eye, he saw the sarky WPC from earlier approach. She thrust a mobile phone towards Nadia. "DI Sharif, you're ringing."

Nadia took the phone with a nod of thanks. "Wait here a sec," she told him.

He almost flinched as she brushed past him, that lightest of touches catapulting him back to Tulliallan, to the tiny creaking bed, the taste of peach schnapps, and the sound of Cowboy Junkies drifting from her old Sony stereo. He blinked away the memory and stepped towards the murder board. Faye's laughing green eyes beamed from the photograph pinned to the centre of the board. Suddenly he felt a presence. His body went rigid.

Why was this happening again, after all these years? He'd been punished enough already, hadn't he?

A waft of familiar perfume caught in his throat. Slowly, he twisted his head to the left. The background churn of the incident room faded. Faye stood next to him, staring at her own photograph. She wore the same green cloak as when he'd found her on the beach, but the colour had faded. She appeared so real but less substantial somehow, a washed-out image of the vibrant young woman in the photograph.

All in your head, son.

"Who was that?" she asked.

Angus opened and closed his mouth like a fish, but no words came out.

"She's very pretty," Faye said.

She dragged her eyes away from her own image and gave him a tepid smile. "You oughta watch yourself there, Constable MacNeil."

Angus shook his head in disbelief. He closed his eyes for a brief second, and when he opened them again, she was gone. *See, all in your head, son.* He glanced around the room in panic and saw Nadia walking back towards him.

"My boss is still stuck on Loch Lomond-side. C'mon," said Nadia. "You can take me to see Gills. It'll be nice to put a face to a name. At last."

"Constable MacNeil! Constable MacNeil!"

They had barely set foot outside the hall when Alice Seaton's phlegmy rasp lassoed him from across the car park. The reporter stood outside a police cordon, cigarette glowing from between her bony fingers. She was only in her late-thirties but looked twice that age. Her face was pale and thin. From this distance, she looked to Angus more like a wraith than Faye had moments earlier.

"Do you know her?" Nadia asked.

"Aye, chief reporter for the local rag."

He gave Alice a baleful look and shook his head.

Nadia took a set of car keys from her pocket and bleeped open a black Audi.

"Come on, Angus, give me a break!" Alice yelled. "There are rumours it's Chichester's daughter. Is that true?"

He hauled open the door of the Audi. "No comment!"

He folded himself into the passenger seat beside Nadia. She crunched the Audi into gear and drove out of the car park. Angus gave the reporter a blank look on the way past. Alice snarled something he couldn't hear, but he didn't need to be a lip-reader to comprehend the insult.

"She seems friendly," Nadia commented.

He gave her a sidelong glance. "You made DI already."

"Yeah, but I had to sleep my way to promotion."

"So that's where I've been going wrong."

The laugh died on her lips. "Do you live around here?"

He jabbed a thumb over his shoulder. "Back there. The cottage up on the hill."

"A wee bit remote."

An awkward silence hung between them as they drove towards Silvaig, where Gills was lecturing the class of exchange students.

Suddenly Nadia broke the silence. "You're married."

It was a statement, not a question, but he nodded anyway.

"Kids?"

"No. You?"

She gave a humourless laugh. "Nah, I've not even been married off yet."

He heard the barb in her tone. "Nadia, it was never about that—"

"It was a long time ago, Angus. Water under the bridge and all that."

She leaned forward and fiddled with the heating dial. He caught a whiff of her perfume, delicate and fresh, familiar even after all these years. She used to wear his old shinty hoodie so often that it had become infused with her scent. After it had all fallen apart and he'd returned home, he'd found the hoodie scrunched up at the bottom of his rucksack. For weeks he'd kept it under his pillow, breathing her in as he fell asleep and cursing his cowardice.

"Anyway," Nadia said. "Tell me about the victim. I've read about Chichester and this wolf reserve but know nothing about his daughter."

"Aye, she was a good one. Only sixteen. She grew up in New York but otherwise lived with her father and stepmother at Dunbirlinn Castle."

"No siblings?"

He shook his head. "There's been some bother up at the estate recently. Vandalism and the like. Not everybody's happy about the nature reserve. I spoke to Faye just last week when I was there investigating an arson attack."

"What was she like?"

It was the second time that day he'd been asked that question.

"Not the spoiled heiress you might think. She was down-to-earth, friendly. A fine painter, too. Wanted to go to art college . . ."

"Any boyfriend?"

"I don't think so."

"Bit strange for a sixteen-year-old girl, no?"

He shrugged.

"Who was the last person to see her alive?"

"Her parents saw her at dinnertime yesterday. She was supposed to be going out last night to a party at Teine Eigin—"

"Teine what?"

"Eigin. It's a pagan commune out in the wilds of the estate. Faye was a frequent visitor, apparently. Last night was Samhain."

"That's Gaelic Halloween, right?"

"Aye, it's where Halloween has its origins—an ancient Celtic festival marking the start of winter." He suddenly recalled the Quran that had sat on Nadia's shelf in her room at Tulliallan, next to Blackstone's *Police Manual*. The books had been equally well thumbed. "Samhain's pagan Muharram if you like."

"Except we don't dress up as witches and devils."

"What do you do?"

"Fast. Pray. At least I used to."

He couldn't miss that sadness in her tone. "Used to?" he asked gently.

She had her eyes fixed on the road. "My dad died a couple of years ago. Massive stroke. He was the one who brought me to the mosque."

"I remember."

"Aye, well, I can't bring myself to go back without him."

"I'm sorry. That must have been"—he fumbled for the right words—"fucking awful."

The ghost of a smile flitted across her face. "Aye, that about sums it up. Anyway, do we know if Faye actually made it to this commune?"

"No, although the housekeeper says she heard someone passing her house on horseback around ten. I checked earlier, and Faye's horse is gone."

Nadia puffed out her cheeks. "A dead heiress, some pagans, and a missing horse."

"You can add witchcraft to the list."

She frowned a question at him.

"Faye was found holding a small effigy. Gills recognised it as a *corp creadha*, or clay corpse. It's basically a Highland voodoo doll."

Nadia made a clicking sound with her tongue, a quirk he remembered she had when she was deep in thought. She caught his look and gave a faint smile. "Sorry. Old habits . . ."

He shook away the apology.

"Is this your first murder victim?" she asked.

He hesitated, images of all those he could not save flashing through his mind—Ethan Boyce's limp body lying in the shallows, his Spider-Man T-shirt plastered to his thin frame; Lewis Duncan's charred corpse seared into his wheelchair; Barbara Klein sprawled in the dew-soaked grass—smudged pink lipstick, hoop earrings, dead eyes staring at him.

"Aye," he lied, "first one."

Nadia wound the Audi through the campus of Silvaig University and parked in front of the main building, in a bay reserved for the vice-chancellor. She glanced at Angus and shrugged. "What? We're on important police business."

"I didn't say anything," he replied, climbing from the car. The university towered over him, a huge Gothic pile with elongated arched windows, gargoyles, and flying buttresses.

"This way," he said, leading Nadia towards a side entrance that opened onto the cloisters and the west quadrangle. An ancient oak grew in the middle of the quadrangle—a tree of knowledge in Celtic mythology according to Gills. Fitting for a university, then.

"This place reminds me of Glasgow Uni," Nadia said wistfully.

"Do you ever wish you'd finished medical school?" he asked.

She gave a bitter laugh. "Every day. But you know why I couldn't."

"Aye, I know," he replied.

Their eyes met briefly, and he felt that old, instinctive sense of understanding flow between them. He glanced away, embarrassed. "The lecture hall's over there," he said, pointing to a small arched doorway in the corner of the quadrangle.

They walked towards the door, climbed a flight of dusty steps, and slipped into the lecture theatre. The tiered seating was almost empty, a group of thirty or so exchange students occupying the first few rows. Gills leaned casually against a lectern, a large screen behind his head. He wore a loose-fitting tweed suit, and his white hair stuck up at all angles. Angus lowered himself into a seat in the back row, Nadia next to him. Gills's voice carried to the back of the lecture hall, his strong Highland brogue rich with humour.

"When Saint Columba landed on Iona's sandy shores in AD 563, he stepped into a pagan world controlled by fearsome monsters and wrathful deities," Gills intoned. "The druids—a learned caste of priests, teachers, and judges—held sway. Their rigorous training lasted twenty years, and covered everything from natural philosophy and astrology, to ancient verse and divination. They were the conduits to the gods, of which there were many.

"In this world, magic was real and to be *mollaichte*—cursed—was greatly feared. Shape-shifting was unquestioned. Seals were the souls of people drowned at sea. Crows were messengers from the otherworld. Deer and hares were fairy women in disguise. Lochs were populated by human-eating water horses, and the sea by giant serpents. The shore, in particular, was a dangerous, liminal place, where the known and unknown worlds collided. It was the haunt of the nuckelavee, a skinless half-man, half-horse creature with black blood squirming through its veins. Lonely waterfalls were plagued by glaistigs and brownies. Mountains were the abodes of giants. Rocks contained the souls of our ancestors. Trees were sacred. Caves were entrances to the underworld."

Gills began pacing in front of the students, smiling amiably. "I'm sure much of this resonates with German mythology, and the tales of the Brothers Grimm. Take, for example, changelings: Highland folklore is full of stories about babies, and sometimes adults, being inhabited by entities from the Gaelic otherworld, usually elves and fairies. Some academics have argued that this changeling motif developed amongst rural societies as a way to discuss mental illness. Even today people considered mad are said to be away with the fairies. Stripped of its supernatural associations, a changeling becomes a euphemism for a mentally handicapped person. However, in the Victorian era, there developed a strand of academic thought that posited that fairy possession was real in the truest sense: that certain entities *could* inhabit the minds of people and compel them to act in certain ways. In many different cultures, these entities would be equated with demons and aligned with the devil, which owes much to the burgeoning influence of Christianity.

"However, before the first missionaries arrived, these fairies and elves would have been nature deities worshipped by the native tribes. An echo of this remains in the name of the river that flows through Glasgow—the Clyde—named after the goddess Clota. Trees, lochs, mountains, as well as rivers, would all be associated with specific deities. Highland fairies are a folk memory of these old gods, denuded of their power by Christianity, stripped of their associations, until we are left with nothing but the slightly absurd creatures we know today."

Gills ambled across to a laptop and tapped a key. The screen behind him sprang to life, revealing costumed figures dancing around a bonfire. The word "Samhain" was written above the flames. "Who can tell me what this word refers to?"

A goth girl in the front row raised her hand. "Samhain is the pagan festival that spawned Halloween," she said in German-accented English.

"You're quite right, my dear, although to be pedantic, it's pronounced *sow-een*, or *sow-in*. The festival ushers in the dark half of the year, when the veil between our world and the otherworld is at its thinnest. On this date, the dead are free to roam between the physical and spiritual realms, as are a whole gamut of supernatural beings. Perhaps most fearsome was a fairy host known as the Sluagh, or the Unforgiven Dead. They were said to come from the west, often appearing as a flock of starlings."

Gills tapped a key, and the picture changed to that of a hideous old crone with blue-tinged skin, rust-red teeth, and one eye. She carried a staff and rode on the back of a wolf.

"Wolves played a prominent role in the Celts' belief system," Gills said. "In the Highlands, they were associated with one figure in particular—this fearsome crone behind me. She is known as the Cailleach, a name derived from Old Irish and meaning 'the veiled one,' although to modern Gaelic speakers it translates simply as 'old woman' or 'hag.' She is the oldest goddess we have, perhaps worshipped by the first settlers who wandered to the frozen north after the retreat of the polar ice caps. She is also an expression of the crone archetype found throughout world cultures, such as the Slavic witch Baba Yaga, who is crone guardian to the otherworld, or the cave-dwelling Black Annis from English folklore who eats children, or the Inuit Mistress of Life and Death, Sedna, or the Egyptian funerary goddess, Nephthys.

"The crone guardian is one of countless mythologies common across ancient religions—a universality that should make us modern humans wonder whether our ancient, primitive—savage, even!—ancestors knew things we have forgotten. Alas, I digress. . . ."

Memories flitted through Angus's head like the starlings in Gills's lecture, dark shapes he refused to give colour to. He would not go back there.

"Like your Germanic god Woden, the Cailleach goes by many names—Beira, Queen of Winter, the Thunder Hag, and the Bone Mother, to name but a few. She is a complex deity, a creator goddess who fashioned the mountains and glens of Scotland, and a protector of deer. But she is also wrathful—a bringer of storms, destruction, and death. Samhain, ladies and gents, is the Celtic new year. It celebrates the arrival of the Cailleach to rule over the winter months. Sacrifices would have been made in her honour, fires lit, and rituals enacted."

Gills glanced at his watch.

"That's just about it for today. But I'll leave you with this—if any of you were out last night and saw something strange in the sky, it was not necessarily the result of too much *uisge beatha* in the pub. You just might have seen the Cailleach riding across the night sky on the back of a wolf, as our ancestors believed."

Angus heard disembodied laughter, before a murmur of conversation began as the students lifted satchels and checked mobile phones. Angus and Nadia stood, waiting as the students filed past them, jostling each other and chatting in a mixture of German and English.

Gills slung a familiar worn leather satchel over his shoulder and climbed the steps towards them.

"Gills," Angus said, "this is DI Sharif—she's with the MIT. She'd like to ask you some questions."

Nadia thrust out her hand. "Nice to meet you, Dr. MacMurdo."

Angus feared Gills would kiss her hand, like a knight in a fairy tale, but instead he gave a warm shake. "A pleasure, my dear. But please, call me Gills." He rubbed his hands together, blue eyes twinkling. "Now, do you mind if we chat back at my house, DI Sharif? I need to let the dogs out and, frankly, after the day I've had, I'm in sore need of a dram."

Ragged clouds scudded across the sky above the Old Manse, blotting out the sun. It was the middle of the day but felt like twilight. Angus stared at the ivy-coated house. Had it only been this morning he'd been here, rapping his head against the front door? It had been a mistake. Running to the beach. Returning to the Old Manse and Gills. He wanted none of it.

Bran and Sceolan struck up a chorus of barking as Gills wiggled his key into the door. Angus gave Nadia a sidelong glance. He recalled the sickle-shaped scar on her forearm, the result of being mauled by her aunt's Japanese Akita when she was twelve.

"It's okay, they're friendly," he whispered.

She glanced at him, eyes smiling. "I'm a dog's best friend now. A fortnight on duty with the K9 unit helped me conquer my fear. But it's sweet of you to remember."

The door swung open and the dogs wriggled past Gills, determined to sniff the newcomers. Bran bolted into the garden and found a stick, which he dropped at Nadia's feet, then looked up at her expectantly with his guileless chestnut eyes.

"Ignore him," Gills said. "Throw it once and he'll never leave you alone. Please, come in."

"Sorry, boy," Nadia said, giving the dog a conciliatory scratch behind the ears before following Gills into the house.

Angus crossed the threshold with a faint sense of trepidation. His eyes lingered on the door to the study, which was open a few inches. Books were scattered on Gills's writing desk. For a brief second, their eyes met and Gills pulled the door closed.

"Now," Gills said, again rubbing his palms together, "will you join me for a dram?"

Angus would have sold his soul for a large glass of Talisker, but shook his head. "Better not."

"DI Sharif?"

"I'm more of a gin girl."

"In that case, I think I have a bottle somewhere."

Nadia laughed. "No, thanks. Bit early for me."

"Come away through, then," Gills said, leading them into the snug room. He opened the door of the woodburner, which was set with balled-up newspaper and kindling. He sparked a match and set light to the paper before walking over to a drinks cabinet and pouring himself a glass of Talisker. "Please, sit," he said, gesturing to a familiar leather couch. Angus flopped down. His body seemed to fold into the contours of the couch like a warming hug. He closed his eyes for a second and allowed himself a brief respite from the turmoil in his head.

Gills lowered himself into his armchair and raised his glass in a toast. "*Slàinte,*" he said, then took a draught of the amber liquid. He let out a satisfied "ahhh" then placed the dram down on a coaster, next to a book Angus recognised—a well-thumbed edition of folklorist John Gregorson Campbell's *The Gaelic Otherworld.*

"Can you take me through what happened this morning, Dr. MacMurdo?" Nadia asked.

Gills clasped his hands. "Well, now, let me see. I must have left the house around eight o'clock to walk the dogs. We took the usual route through the woods, then past what's known locally as the Lost Village, towards the shore. There are sheep on the hillside there, so I had to get the dogs on the lead. I usually let them off again when we reach the beach, but they were acting strangely, barking like mad."

"What time did you reach the beach?"

Gills's eyes flicked to Angus for a moment, then back to Nadia.

"It's a good half-hour walk from here, so eight thirty, give or take."

"And what did you see when you got there?"

"Something was lying out on the sand. At first I thought it was a dead seal. You do, occasionally, get carcasses washed ashore there. But there was just . . . something about it that set me on edge. So I tied the dogs up and went to investigate."

"And when you realized it wasn't a seal, what did you do?"

"I had my mobile phone, but there's never any reception down there, so I ran as fast as I could—which, granted, isn't very fast—back to the village and summoned Angus."

Nadia made the clicking noise with her tongue, then seemed to catch herself doing it and stopped. "Why not go back to your own home and call 999?"

Gills threw out his palms. "Shock, maybe. Reckon I panicked. Thought Angus would know what to do."

Nadia nodded, apparently satisfied with the explanation. Angus, though, suddenly realized he had no idea what was going on behind her eyes. He'd never seen her in detective mode.

"Angus came back with me to the beach," Gills continued. "The tide was coming in, so we carried her . . . err . . . body farther up the shore."

Gills reached for his whisky glass and took a gulp. Angus noticed a slight tremor in his friend's hand. He wondered if Nadia noticed it too.

"Sorry, Dr. MacMurdo," she said. "Do you mind if I use your bathroom?"

Gills looked relieved to answer a simple question. "Not at all, my dear. It's the room directly across the hallway."

Angus watched Nadia leave the snug room, still finding it hard to believe she was here, with him in the Old Manse.

"She's young for a DI," Gills said. "Must be a brainbox."

"Nadia's always been very driven."

Gills squinted at him.

"We were cadets together at Tulliallan," Angus explained.

"Wait! That's not *the* Nadia, is it?" The old man shook his head, a wide smile transforming his face. "Good God! Of all the gin joints in all the world, eh?"

Angus glanced at Gills but instead locked eyes with Faye. The girl sat on a high-backed chair in a shadowy corner of the room. She wore paint-splattered overalls and Converse high-tops. Her hair was pulled back in a tight ponytail, which accentuated her sharp jawline. Her purple lips stretched into a wan smile. Of course she was here. This, of all places, was a house of ghosts.

"Better watch yourself there, old bean," he heard Gills say.

Faye cocked an eyebrow, as if she'd somehow put her words from earlier in Gills's mouth. Angus dug his fingernails into his thighs.

Faye held up her hands like a bank teller in a stickup. Etched into her palms was the same triple-spiral symbol he'd seen in her sketch pads.

He heard the door crack open and he jerked his head away from the apparition. Nadia reentered the room and lowered herself back down onto the couch.

"Sorry about that," she said. "Now, where were we? Ah yes. I was going to ask you about this doll Faye was holding. What was it you called it, Angus?"

His eyes flicked to where Faye had sat, but the chair was empty.

"A *corp creadha*," he croaked.

"I'm something of an expert in Highland folklore and witchcraft, DI Sharif," Gills said. "I recognised what it was straightaway."

"And it's used in much the same way as a voodoo doll?"

"Yes and no. In one story, a famous cattle thief from Ardnamurchan finds witches sticking pins in an effigy of his enemy, MacLean of Duart. He scatters the witches and rides with the doll to the chief's residence, finding him at death's door. He withdraws the pins and MacLean is cured. "More commonly, the *corp creadha* was placed in a stream, and as it disintegrated, the target of the spell would wither away. If the effigy was not found in time, they would die."

"Do you think people still believe in these spells?" Nadia asked.

"Undoubtedly," Gills replied. "Human nature is not so different today than it was thousands of years ago. We're not rational creatures, DI Sharif. And anyhow, belief in magic is not necessarily irrational."

"How so?" Nadia asked.

"We merely have to accept as true that not all events can be explained through scientific principles."

Angus noticed a slight tightening in Nadia's jaw. Did she still pray, he wondered?

"I get what you're saying, Dr. MacMurdo. There was an imam my father knew when I was young who believed having your photo taken was *haram*, forbidden."

"Because it diminished the soul?" Gills asked.

"Partly, but also because the image could be manipulated by others for nefarious means."

"Exactly, my dear." Gills beamed. "It's the same principle with a *corp creadha* or voodoo doll. Injuring a likeness of someone can maim, or even kill, for real."

He tapped a finger on *The Gaelic Otherworld*. "This book was compiled in the 1850s by a minister from Tiree. He recorded a whole gamut of Highland superstitions, including a belief in the efficacy of clay corpses." Gills's smile faded. "But so much of this folklore has been lost, known only to sad old academics like me. Gaelic culture has been under attack for centuries, DI

Sharif. Our heritage has been either appropriated or derided, depending on which way the political or religious wind of the day blew. History has cast us in the role of noble savage or barbarian. To others, we're no better than the beasts in the field—indolent kilt-wearing drunkards prone to inexplicable bouts of violence and depression. These attitudes have become ingrained, even amongst ourselves. Gaels have been made to feel ashamed of their native tongue, embarrassed by their *quaint* traditions—their music, customs, and folktales. . . ."

Angus loudly cleared his throat. "You're not in the lecture hall now, Gills."

The old man gave Nadia a sheepish smile. "Apologies, my dear. I shall now dismount from my high horse."

Nadia's smile was warm. "Don't mention it. I like a man with passion. You and my father would have gotten on like a house on fire. Sufis love nothing more than a cultural debate. And, believe me, we know exactly what it's like to have our beliefs torn to shreds."

She stood and held out her hand. "It's been nice meeting you, Dr. MacMurdo."

Gills stood and took Nadia's outstretched hand. "The pleasure is all mine, my dear. I've heard a lot about you. It would have been nice to meet under different circumstances."

"Yes, it would have."

Gills let go of her hand. Nadia fished in her pocket and handed him her card.

"My phone number and email are on there. If you can think of anything else that might be relevant to the case, anything at all, don't hesitate."

Over Nadia's shoulder, Angus gave Gills a warning look. The last thing he needed was him poking his nose in.

Gills's reply, however, was drowned out by the sound of Nadia's phone ringing.

"Sorry," she said, taking the device from her pocket. She glanced at the screen. "I've got to take this."

She stepped out into the hallway, and Angus heard a brief mumbled conversation. A moment later she was back, a trace of a smile on her lips.

"That was my boss. He'll be touching down any minute."

Angus frowned. Glenruig didn't have an airport the last time he checked. "Touching down?"

"Aye." Nadia grinned. "Touching down."

CHAPTER 12

ANGUS watched the helicopter swoop down over the village like a giant bluebottle. Agnes and Muriel—a couple of grumpy Highland cows—looked up from munching grass, glowered, then cantered towards the overhanging branches of a horse chestnut to watch the chopper land in their field. No sooner had the helicopter touched down than the door was flung open. A lean man of around sixty climbed from the aircraft and loped at a crouch across the field, his three-quarter-length coat billowing. Angus recognised him from the news reports on television last year—DCI Ruthven Crowley.

Nadia opened the gate for her boss, a smile playing about her lips. "A helicopter, Ruthven? Really?"

Crowley grinned wolfishly, little sharp incisors appearing behind thin, cracked lips. He was a big unit, six two or three at least, with a face that looked like a Peter Howson portrait—exaggerated musculature, knotted brow, hollow cheeks, and kinked nose. Not someone you'd want to meet down a dark alley, as Gills might say. More like a washed-up boxer than a cop. Angus couldn't help it—he glanced at Crowley's right hand and saw the stumps where fingers used to be, before he'd been taken hostage by the Priest.

"You know me, I like to make an entrance, DI Sharif." Crowley emphasized the "DI" and Angus saw Nadia smile. Clearly, her promotion had been a recent development.

"Congratulations. No one deserves it more than you." He gave Nadia a peck on the cheek.

"Thank you, sir," she replied, flushing. She glanced over his shoulder towards the chopper. "The chief's going to do his nut over that. We haven't even got a budget for biscuits, never mind helicopters."

"Good God! We're not paying for it," Crowley exclaimed. "When Chichester heard we were stuck, he phoned up and offered us the use of his chopper."

Crowley's voice was a throaty smoker's rasp, his native Edinburgh accent chiselled down by years spent in the States, like a Scottish actor who had spent too long in Hollywood. He shot Angus a suspicious glance over Nadia's shoulder. "Who's this fine specimen?"

"Sorry, sir," Nadia said. "This is Constable MacNeil. I know him from way back when. This is his patch."

Crowley stepped forward and offered Angus his mutilated hand. He shook it without hesitation and met Crowley's level gaze. His eyes were like a grey dawn.

"Ah yes, MacNeil. Mr. Chichester has requested your presence on the MIT. He's the paranoid type, but it seems he trusts you. He wants you as a point of contact." The DCI gave Angus a fake grin. "And what Chichester wants, Chichester gets." He clapped Angus on the shoulder and marched past him. "Happy days, there's a pub," Crowley muttered, clocking the Glenruig Inn.

Nadia cocked an eyebrow. "Don't worry, you'll get used to him."

She made to walk past Angus, then gave him a solid jab to the arm. "Welcome to the team." She smiled. "And don't look so worried. We'll be gentle with you."

He'd tried to hide himself away, but that once-imagined future had smoked him out.

Crowley smelt of Old Spice. A pungent waft of the aftershave smacked Angus in the face as he followed the detective through the double doors and into the incident room. For a brief moment he was a child again, watching his dad shaving in front of the mirror in the small bathroom, naked from the waist up. He saw the powerful shoulders, the solidity of him as he slathered foam on his face with a shaving brush, the deftness of touch as he scraped it away using the frightening razor with the mother-of-pearl handle. He'd wink at Angus in the mirror, then slap the aftershave on his cheeks.

"Fuck me! Is this it?"

Crowley stood with his hands on his hips, surveying the incident room as if it were a battlefield. He marched over to the murder board and squinted at the photographs Nadia had pinned there.

"Pretty. What we looking at, Nads? Sex crime?"

"Won't know until the PM. Angus was the first officer on the scene. Maybe he can tell you more."

Crowley swivelled his head and glared expectantly at him.

"She was fully clothed, sir. No sign of sexual assault."

"Hmmph. What were her last known movements?"

"We believe she attended a party last night at a pagan commune. For Samhain, that's the—"

"I know what Samhain is, Constable," Crowley cut in. "Have you spoken to them yet, these pagans?"

Angus shook his head. "The commune's pretty remote. No vehicular access."

A thin smile spread across Crowley's craggy face. "Right. Nads, you and Angus get yourselves up to this place. I'll arrange for a dog team to attend. I want this commune torn apart."

"How are we getting there?" Nadia asked. "I haven't brought my hiking boots."

Crowley's smile widened. "No worries—take the chopper."

Angus felt his stomach lurch as the helicopter banked over the gunmetal-grey sea and thrummed deeper into the Rough Bounds, as the mountainous area around Arisaig and Moidart was known. If there was anything in his stomach, he might have been sick. He swallowed the rising bile and stared out the window. He saw stick figures down below, the reporter Alice Seaton having been joined by other members of the press, drawn to Glenruig like carrion crows to a dead sheep. He saw the slate roof of the Old Manse, with the well-tended green rectangle of lawn that Gills was so proud of. From above, the house looked insignificant. Yet it had loomed so large in his life. He'd missed the place. Missed the dodgy plumbing, the creaky floorboards, and the warmth of the Aga. Missed the slobbery licks from Bran and Sceolan, the contented click of the grandfather clock, and Gills swishing around in his tartan robe and moccasin slippers.

A lump formed in his throat as the helicopter buzzed inland, over regimented swathes of pine forest, a patchwork of fields flecked with sheep, isolated crofts, and drab brown moorland. Thick clouds blanketed the islands to the west, but the chopper ranged north and was soon swallowed by mountain clefts. Great walls of stone towered around them, the rock callused and wrinkled like the face of an old crone, the streams gushing down the mountainside her wisps of hair.

As the helicopter swung low over the shoulder of the hillside, he spotted a large herd of red deer. Startled by the sound of the chopper, the deer were on the move, a brown mass that surged across the heather like a great beast. Perhaps, if James Chichester had his way, it would soon be wolves, not a helicopter, that spurred the herd on.

Nadia turned to him. "Tell me, Angus," she said, fighting to be heard over the chopper's rotors, "why are you still a constable?"

He gave a one-shouldered shrug.

"You used to be so ambitious. This case is the type of thing we always talked about. Something big. Something that makes a difference. So why do I get the impression you'd rather be anywhere else? Is it because of me?"

Angus clamped a hand on his thigh to stop it vibrating. "No, no—it's not you. I mean, it's a surprise to see you, of course, but no, it's not that. . . ."

"So, what's the problem?"

"Folk change, Nadia. Priorities . . . wither away."

She searched out his eyes. "Jeez, Angus. You always were a little distant, but since when did you become such a gloomy bawbag?"

The insult made him smile, as he knew she'd intended it to.

"Anyway," she said, the mood lightened, "I forgot to ask, what does Teine Eigin mean? Gaelic, right?"

"Aye, it means 'need fire' and refers to a ritual performed at Beltane. In the old days, villagers would douse their hearth and relight it from a communal bonfire known as *Teine Eigin*, symbolically binding themselves to the community."

"Right, and how long has the commune been here?"

"Not long. Couple of years. I remember it caused a bit of a stooshie at the time. We have a small but vocal Free Kirk in the village. The minister wasn't too happy that pagans were moving in next door."

Nadia returned her gaze to the window. "This is hardly next door. We're in the middle of nowhere."

"Said like a proper city girl."

From above, Teine Eigin looked like something out of Lord of the Rings—twenty or so dwellings huddled around the shores of Loch Dubh, surrounded by arable plots and linked by a network of paths. A crannog stretched on stilts out onto the loch with various small boats or coracles moored alongside. The whole community was encircled by what looked like a boundary wall, as if the inhabitants feared imminent attack from marauding clansmen.

Not that the pagans were a warlike lot. He'd occasionally spot them about the village, stocking up on provisions at Moira Anderson's shop, or selling crafts at Highland Games and agricultural shows.

His stomach again lurched as the helicopter dropped. He saw people in the fields down tools, and others emerge from doorways, as the chopper descended onto a flat patch of moorland on the outskirts of the village. The *thwump* of the chopper's rotor slowed, spluttered, then fell silent.

"Tourists would pay good money for that trip," Nadia said, unbuckling her seat belt and hauling open the chopper door. She hopped down and Angus followed, glad to feel the soft moss and heather under his feet.

A knot of people stood at the edge of the commune, staring blank-faced at the chopper as if it were an alien spacecraft.

"They don't look too welcoming," he said.

"You'll just have to use that famous Angus MacNeil charm on them, then."

He answered her sarcasm with a cool glance. She brushed past him and picked her way through the hummocky heather and mountain grass. He followed, careful to avoid the peaty pools of water. The last thing he needed was to fall in a bog.

As they neared the villagers, he clocked a huge man with a bald head and bushy ginger beard. He stood a good foot taller than the others and looked like a giant out of one of Gills's Highland folktales. However, it was an athletic woman with braided hair who stepped forward to greet them. She was in her mid-thirties, with the tanned, leathery skin of someone accustomed to outdoor work. Although it was freezing, she wore a vest top, her bare arms covered in swirling Celtic tattoos that reminded him of the symbol Faye had sketched in her art pads.

The woman eyed them with suspicion as Nadia took out her police ID.

"I'm DI Sharif, and this is Constable MacNeil," she said, brandishing the ID. "Are you in charge here?"

The woman gave a curt nod.

"And you are . . . ?"

"Chris . . . Chris Kelbie," came her reluctant reply. Her accent was odd—local, Angus thought, but with a foreign inflection. Scandinavian, perhaps?

"Is there somewhere we can talk, Miss Kelbie?" Nadia asked. "It's important."

"Must be, for you to come all the way up here in a helicopter."

Kelbie turned abruptly on the heel of her mud-caked boot. Her braids whipped out behind her head. "This way."

The rest of the villagers parted for Kelbie, who led them into the commune. Angus felt as if he were stepping back in time. A dirt path meandered through the village, past ramshackle dwellings thrown together using stone, wood, and corrugated iron. Some had thatched roofs, others turf. Many were painted in bright colours, the walls covered in arcane symbols or depictions of deities and animals. Swags of rowan and juniper hung over doorways, whilst garlands of pine cones and twigs twisted into stars and crude figures looped from under thatch roofs. Smoke puttered from the chimneys and the smell of peat hung in the air, undercut with something acrid, like charred timber. Somewhere, he heard the manic bray of a donkey.

He glanced over his shoulder and found the residents following a couple of meters behind. He couldn't help thinking of *The Wicker Man*, and Ed Woodward screaming as the flames engulfed his tomb in the final act of the movie. He tried to ignore the cold bead of sweat trickling down his spine.

It struck him that he was already lost. From above, the commune appeared small, but down here, amongst the higgledy-piggledy houses, it felt enclosed. He was glad when they emerged from the maze of houses into an open area near the loch, dominated by a stone circle. There were perhaps twelve standing stones in total, rough granite slabs, each seven or eight feet tall, forming a circle about twenty meters in diameter. There was something eerie about the stones, as if they were a council of elders formed to pass judgment on some unfortunate soul.

In the centre, he noted a large burnt patch where a bonfire had recently stood. Probably lit during the Samhain celebration that Faye had attended.

His eyes darted around the stone circle. He sensed the girl's presence in the prickling of the hair on his forearms, but she was nowhere to be seen. That sense of being watched lingered as he followed Kelbie and Nadia onto the wooden walkway that led to the crannog on the loch. At last, the snow that had been threatening all day began to fall, light flakes that landed on his cheeks and forehead like cold kisses of the dead. Beneath his feet, the dark water of the loch lapped against the wooden stilts on which the crannog stood. At the end of the walkway was a timber-built roundhouse with a conical thatched roof. A stag's skull leered down at him from above the entrance. Its eyes were dark pits, and a row of yellow teeth were set in a malevolent grin.

Angus's legs felt suddenly weak, as if he'd reached the end of a hard shinty match. He hauled himself along the walkway, and stumbled after Nadia through a small doorway. It took his eyes a second to adjust to the gloom. The space was divided up with wattle-and-daub walls, but the room he was in was surprisingly spacious, kitted out with mismatched furniture, a long rustic table, and macabre wood carvings. One wall was dominated by a bookcase, crammed with titles, some of which he recognised from Gills's library—*The Fairy-Faith in Celtic Countries, The Mabinogion, Carmina Gadelica, The Secret Commonwealth*. His fingers twitched, as if recalling the texture of the books' spines.

"Do you know why we're here, Miss Kelbie?" Nadia asked.

Kelbie gestured for them to sit. "No, but I imagine we're being blamed for something."

Angus slid out his notebook and lowered himself down next to Nadia on a tattered sofa.

"Oh? Why do you say that?"

Kelbie sat opposite them on a chaise that looked as if it had been rescued from a skip. "Past experience." She sighed.

Angus waited for Kelbie to elaborate, but she folded her arms and clamped her lips shut.

"So, you haven't heard the news?" Nadia asked.

"We're kind of remote up here. No Wi-Fi, no mobile connection. No TV. Look, what's happened?"

Nadia's eyes, he noticed, never left Kelbie's face. "We're investigating a murder."

For the first time, he saw a flicker of apprehension in Kelbie's gaze.

"What, like a cold case or something?"

"No, recent. Last night, in fact."

The tightness in Kelbie's bearing seemed to loosen.

"Well, no one here can have anything to do with that. It was Samhain last night. The biggest night of our year. We were all here."

"Yes, I know. We believe the victim attended the festivities. Her body was found on a beach this morning."

Kelbie picked at the blistered welt of the chaise, a dawning realization in her eyes. "The only nonresident here last night was Faye."

Nadia gave the briefest of nods. For a long second, Kelbie sat in stunned silence. Her braids hung over her face like rough cords. Was this woman really capable of such brutality? Physically, yes—her arms were knotted with muscle, like a boxer's. There was anger in Kelbie too, that much had been evident in the hostile reception he and Nadia had received. But you needed more than anger to kill a girl like that. You needed fury, or a belief in the righteousness of the act.

"What time did she arrive?" Nadia asked gently.

Kelbie flicked the braids away from her face. Her eyes were glassy. "Must have been around half ten. Made quite an entrance on her horse."

"How long did she stay?"

"I'm . . . not sure. I had quite a bit to drink. We all did. She was definitely here at midnight, though."

"How can you be sure?"

"We had a countdown, like you do at Hogmanay. I remember her dancing around the fire. . . . Wait—"

Kelbie sprang to her feet and walked to the bookcase. She hauled open a drawer, but rather than a book she slid out a thin tablet. "Rhiannon took some video footage on my iPad around that time. We have a Facebook page. Every so often someone takes a run into Silvaig to update content at an internet café."

She crouched next to them and tapped play on the iPad. Her strong-boned features were bathed in light from the screen. Her eyes, Angus noticed, were now dry. The sound of guitar and fiddle blared from the device, accompanied by the tribal rap of a bodhrán drum and whoops from costumed figures dancing in front of a large bonfire. The flames spat twenty feet into the sky, casting an eerie glow on the crannog and loch in the background as the revellers weaved in and out of the standing stones. Sparks floated above their heads like fireflies. Three musicians sat to the right of the fire on a large log, the bodhrán player's arm a blur as he beat out the rhythm. Angus recognised him as the giant from earlier. His face and bald head were painted with blue woad, a stark contrast to his orange beard. Round his neck dangled a gold torc that shimmered in the firelight. Beside him, the fiddle player's elbow jerked like a butcher sawing bone as she cut out the tune. Her face was painted metallic silver and crisscrossed with lines of black symbols and runes. Blond plaits of hair curled down her shoulders from under a headdress of leaves and branches. Completing the sinister triumvirate was a guitarist, his face half-covered by a demon mask with ram's horns. The black pupils behind the mask looked dilated. His skin was painted red and his lips were twisted into a rictus grin.

"That's Howie, Hazel, and Glen," Kelbie said.

The camera then swung around the scene, before resting on the revellers who pranced and spun around the flames.

"That's me," Kelbie said, pointing to a figure wearing a headdress of gold leaves. Her face was painted green. Shimmering gold lipstick and eye shadow highlighted the whiteness of her eyes. Her arms and midriff were bare, with strips of leather covering her breasts and hips, as if she were enwrapped in tree roots. A swirling mass of tattoos seemed to writhe around her body. As she spun past the camera, Angus thought he saw that same triple-spiral symbol Faye had drawn in her sketch pads etched onto the small of Kelbie's back. He looked up and found the woman watching him with cold, feral eyes. Almost immediately her expression softened.

He returned his eyes to the iPad, his heart beating quicker now, almost in time to the bodhrán.

Kelbie twirled away, powerful and terrifying, and soon Faye came into the shot. She was equally distinctive in her long green cloak. She danced gracefully around the fire, outstretched arms making sinuous loops and spirals in the air.

"We'll need to know the names of all these people," Nadia said. "And we'll need to speak to them."

Kelbie nodded, but her brow was knitted.

"What's up?" Nadia asked.

"It's probably nothing—"

Kelbie's eyes were still on the dancers.

"This guy here," she said, "appears to be dressed as Donn Fírinne, the Dark One—a god of death. But I don't know who's behind the mask."

Angus squinted at the screen, a chill creeping across his shoulder blades. The figure Kelbie indicated wore a long black cloak and a deer-skull mask like the creature from his vision. It lurched around the bonfire behind Faye, its movements jerky, discordant, somehow inhuman.

"We spend a lot of time on our costumes for Samhain, Detective," Kelbie said. "They mean something to us. No one was wearing this costume. And they couldn't have been here earlier in the night, or I'd have noticed."

"But I thought you said Faye was the only nonresident to attend?"

Kelbie tugged her eyes away from the screen. "Aye, she was . . . although we did have an unwanted visitor earlier in the evening."

He stared at Kelbie, willing her to talk, his pen poised over a page of his notebook.

"That Free Kirk minister who hates us," she said.

"Reverend MacVannin. He was here?" Angus asked, unable to keep the surprise from his voice.

"Aye. He started raving at us. All the usual stuff—how we were heathens who were going to burn in Hell for all eternity."

"What did you do?"

"I calmly asked him to leave."

"And he did?"

Kelbie offered a ghost of a smile. "Howie is six three and built like a brick shithouse. It helps when you have him standing by your side."

Nadia gave a slight chuckle. "Tell me, was Faye here when this altercation occurred?"

Kelbie sank down onto the chaise, the iPad held loosely in her hand. "Aye. Aye, she was. MacVannin grabbed her at one point. Told her there was still time to save her soul."

Angus gave Nadia a sidelong glance. "What did she do?"

Kelbie's eyes were hard as quartz.

"She laughed in his face."

CHAPTER 13

GILLS swung his 1967 baby-blue Ford Anglia down the Rhu peninsula. Loch nan Ceall flashed by in the driver's-side window—a palette of blues, greys, and scuzzy whites, darkened by the snow clouds edging closer to landfall. His mind, though, was not on the scenery. He was thinking about DI Sharif. She seemed nice. Sharp too. And those eyes! He could see why Angus had fallen for her. He remembered him coming home from Tulliallan one weekend, unusually cheerful because he'd met a girl. Angus had had girlfriends before then, of course. Whenever there was a ceilidh at the village hall, he was always in high demand amongst the young woman as a partner for a Gay Gordons or Strip the Willow. But this girl had been different; Gills had read it in his smile. And in his eyes, which were so much like his mother's, it hurt. His face had lit up when he talked about Nadia and that had made Gills happy. There had been too much darkness in Angus's life.

He remembered, too, the black mood that had engulfed Angus when college was over. The lad had never spoken about that, but Gills had guessed its cause. Only a romance snuffed out could bring such despair. His biggest fear was that he was to blame—that Angus had decided what they were doing was too important to jeopardize, even for someone he loved. He'd been unable to drag Angus out of that dark place, but Ashleigh had succeeded where he'd failed. She had saved him.

Some nights Gills lay awake in bed as that guilt stalked his consciousness like a starving wolf. It hung at the fringe of his memories, a shadow tainting fond recollections. He would whisper Caitlin's name into the still air on those hunted, insomniac nights, his mind's eye conjuring up her face. Burnished copper irises. Dimpled cheeks. Smattering of freckles across the bridge of her nose and forehead. Full lips always on the verge of breaking into a smile. But then the idealized vision would blow away like dust. The sweet wild strawberries they'd feasted on that summer at Roshven turned putrid in his mouth. The sea stirred, the sensual calmness broken by something writhing, unseen, just below the surface. Flies and insects descended upon the picnic rug on which they'd sat. They crawled across the food and drowned in the elderflower wine she had made from swags of flowers plucked from the tree behind the Old Manse. Still he whispered her name until the image dissolved and he was left, lying in his bed, an old man with tears in his eyes and a foul aftertaste in his mouth.

Gills forced the memories from his head and focussed on the narrow, winding road ahead. Lachy's directions had been rather vague. "Drive until the road runs out of tarmac," was all he'd said, but Gills had been driving for ages, deeper and deeper into the wilderness. He was beginning to lose hope when he rounded a bend and the road ended abruptly. He pulled up in a lay-by and killed the engine. He could see no house, but the view across the Arisaig skerries was stunning. Hundreds of tiny islands and rocks poked out of the sea, like shattered glass scattered by a giant. The sky hung low and threatening, bearing down on the larger isles of Eigg and Rum in the distance.

He climbed from the car and picked his way down a faint path to the shore as the first flecks of snow began to fall. Only then did he spot the house, lurking amidst a copse of ash and alder. The property looked derelict. Moss and grass sprouted from sagging guttering, loose slates slid from the roof, paint flaked from the walls like blistered skin. A small burn behind the property coughed peaty water onto the shore. There was no garden as such, and nature had taken its course, thickets of bramble, gorse, and ivy crawling over the house.

Gills swallowed his apprehension and rapped on the Witch from Rhu's warped front door. After a few seconds he heard movement from inside. There was no spyhole at the entrance, but he had the sensation of being watched for a moment before the door creaked open. A small woman stared up at him with the same mismatched eyes as his dog, Sceolan, one blue, the other a milky grey. Matted hair framed her preternaturally white face, which was marred by a livid scar on the right side of her forehead. The scar, he thought, still radiated the violence with which the wound had been inflicted. She wore an odd ensemble of clothes—woolly socks, tight leggings, a long silk cardigan over numerous layers of clothing, all chosen, apparently, for their different materials—chiffon, cotton, leather, Lycra.

"Who are you?" the woman spat.

Gills cleared his throat. "Sorry to bother you. My name is Dr. Gilleasbuig MacMurdo. I got your name from Lachlan Campbell—"

Her lips curled in distaste as she looked Gills up and down. "What dae ye want?"

"I was hoping you could help me with a research project. I lecture at the university."

"Research? On what?"

"I have a particular interest in . . . err . . . clay corpses."

He tried for his most amiable smile as the woman glared at him.

"Well," she said eventually, "you've come to the right place."

She stood aside and ushered him into the house. The door led straight into a kitchen-cum-sitting room. Sods of peat crackled and spat in a blackened hearth. White candles were positioned around the room, stuck into the tops of wine and Smirnoff bottles, the wax overflowing to create abstract sculptures. The air was heavy with the earthy reek of peat and lavender, although there was a meaty note, emanating from a large pot boiling on the stove.

The witch shooed him towards a rocking chair near the fire. "Sit."

He did as he was told, ignoring the bead of sweat that ran down between his shoulder blades.

"So, Dr. MacMurdo, you want to know about *corp creadha*?" She sank onto a wingback armchair of ripped green leather. "They're footery things to make." She grinned, showing little white teeth. "Or so I've heard."

"I . . . came across an example of one recently. Do you mind if I show you a picture of it?"

She shrugged her acceptance. Gills's hand trembled slightly as he slid his phone from his pocket. The device slipped from his clumsy fingers and clattered onto the floor. The woman leaned casually forward and plucked up the phone, a slight smirk on her lips.

"Don't worry, Dr. MacMurdo. You're quite safe here with me."

He didn't feel particularly safe. Only now, as the witch thrust the phone towards him, did it occur to Gills that he could be sitting with Faye's killer. Almost as soon as the thought formed, he dismissed it. What possible motive would she have?

No, you're letting your imagination run riot, old bean.

The thought, however, lingered like a smudge as he took his phone. His hand still shook as he scrolled to the photograph he'd taken of the *corp creadha*. The woman leaned towards him, and he couldn't help looking at her scar.

"A parting gift from my fella," she said. "Before he fucked off to America. As if the width of the Atlantic could save him."

Gills couldn't help imagining the gruesome fate that awaited this woman's partner in America. He pictured him withering in some hospice, neither medicine nor anodyne offering relief.

The witch took the phone from him and stared at the photograph for all of a second before handing the device back.

"Amateurish," she declared.

"It is?"

"Clumsy detailing. Poor proportions."

"Any idea who could have made it?"

"A child could have made it."

Gills stuffed the phone back into his pocket. "I see—"

"Or a killer." She cocked her head to the side and fixed him with a penetrating gaze. "Do you want to tell me why you're really here, Dr. MacMurdo?"

Gills felt a flush creep up his neck. "What? I . . . err . . . don't know what you mean."

"You're a terrible liar."

Gills chuckled humourlessly. Caitlin used to say the same when he phoned her from the Doublet to say he and Uisdean had been held up at work, when actually they were in the pub.

"One of my many failings, no doubt."

She shifted her gaze to the fire. "After the girl's sacrifice, I knew someone would come," she murmured.

For a second Gills was too stunned to speak. His mouth opened and closed like a fish.

"You have the gift?" he croaked.

"I have many gifts—*dà-shealladh* is not one of them. It's a curse, as I'm sure you know."

He saw the anguish on Angus's face when he'd opened his door yesterday, heard his cry that he was *mollaichte*.

She turned away from the fire and locked eyes with Gills. "You'll have heard of *slinneanachd*, Dr. MacMurdo?"

"Err, yes," he replied, frowning. "The ancient Highland practice of divination using the shoulder blade of a sheep. Although, I believe the art has died out."

The witch gave a snort of laughter. "Not quite."

She rose from the armchair and swished across the room towards the stove. Gills craned his neck to watch as she took a set of wooden tongs and drew a large triangular-shaped bone from the pot. She placed the bone on a chopping board in the centre of the kitchen table. Despite his wariness of this woman, Gills was intrigued. He'd read historical accounts of speel bone reading. Practitioners had, at one time, been treated with a wary reverence by the community. Many believed the skill was a remnant of druidic teaching, passed down through the generations, even after Christianity had supplanted the old religion of the Highlands.

His thigh muscles protested as he stood, reminding him he'd already covered a fair bit of ground today. More than a man of his age could easily bear, more than he was used to. He hobbled towards the kitchen table and watched the woman at work. Her mouth was a thin slash across her face as she scraped remnants of flesh from the bone with a wooden knife.

"No iron must be used, of course," she said. "If you scrape the bone, the reading will be skewed."

"Where did you learn the art?"

"Reading the bone is a skill like any other, passed down through the family. There's no magic to it." She glanced at him, her eyes cold as steel. "Do you really want to know, Dr. MacMurdo?"

"Yes!" he exclaimed. "Of course. We need to stop this man before he kills again."

She shook her head and returned to her task. "That's not how it works. The girl's dead. The past has ceased to exist. Besides, what makes you think it was a man?"

"I just presumed. . . ."

"Well, don't!" she snapped, then added more quietly: "Don't presume anything, Dr. MacMurdo. You don't know what you don't know."

She was quite right—didn't the greatest revelations strip bare the inconceivable?

He watched in awed silence as she tucked a strand of matted hair behind her ear and took the bone in both of her hands. She turned slightly, some forty-five degrees perhaps, and Gills recalled how the bone had to be held lengthways facing due south. She closed her eyes, then, and her knotted arthritic fingers traced the length of the bone, as if she were reading Braille. All the while her lips were moving, but Gills could not make out what she was saying. He bent closer, so close, he could smell her sour breath as she whispered in the strange tongue. After listening intently for a few seconds, he was able to pick up what he thought was the odd Gaelic word. But if it was Gaelic, it was a dialect he'd never encountered.

Suddenly the woman's eyes snapped open. Gills flinched and took a step backwards.

"Sorry," he muttered, "I was . . . err . . . trying to identify the language you were speaking just now. Was it Gaelic?"

The witch brushed past him, ignoring the question. She walked to the sink and washed her hands for what felt to Gills like a long time. Eventually she turned the tap off. Her hands fell limp to her sides. Beads of water dripped from her fingertips onto the floorboards, but she made no effort to dry her hands, nor did she turn around.

Gills stared at her back, his unease growing with every passing second.

He walked over to her and stared at her face. Her eyes were blank and held that same faraway look Uisdean's did in the care home.

"What did you see?" he asked gently.

She appeared not to have heard him. A sense of frustration, tinged with desperation, rippled through Gills's body.

"Did you see who's behind this? Did you see who killed her?"

He was about to place his hand on her shoulder, snap her out of whatever trance she was in, when her head whipped round to face him. He saw fear and hopelessness in her eyes.

"This is just the start," she rasped.

CHAPTER 14

THE snow was beginning to lie, a faint coating, like a gauze bandage wrapped around a wound. The tips of Angus's fingers were numb and the statements he'd scribbled in his notebook were almost illegible. So far, none of the residents of the pagan commune had aroused any great suspicion. They all appeared genuinely shocked by Faye's murder, but, of course, appearances could be deceiving. He thought of that unguarded look he'd caught Kelbie giving him.

"Who dresses up like that, and comes all the way up here, unless he has a sinister agenda?" Nadia asked.

The Dark One—whoever was beneath the visage of Donn Fírinne—remained a mystery. Angus stuffed his hands into his pockets and glared towards the commune. They stood in the middle of the stone circle, the snow swirling around them. He shrugged.

"Well, that's helpful," Nadia joked.

"Why do you think it's a 'he'?"

"Usually is, but point taken. It could be a woman."

That hadn't exactly been what he meant.

She spun on the spot, glaring at the granite slabs surrounding them. "Bit creepy, isn't it? What do you make of . . . all this? Paganism, I mean."

"No different from Sufism or any other religion."

The sentence was out before he could take it back. Nadia stepped towards him, her eyes burning. "Don't you dare disrespect my faith, Angus."

"I'm sorry," he spluttered. "I didn't—"

The corners of her lips twitched upwards. Her cheeks dimpled. "Gotcha!" She grinned.

Relief flooded through him. "That's not funny, Nadia."

"Aye, it is. Should have seen your face. Pure shat yerself."

He shook his head, now more annoyed than relieved.

She playfully punched his arm. "I'm only messing. Anyway, I'm hardly a model Muslim." The smile slipped from her face.

"Don't be too hard on yourself," he said. "You lost your dad and your wali."

"You remembered," she said, in an almost-whisper.

She'd told him her father was her wali, her spiritual guide—a strict man, but his faith was mystical and open-minded. Sufism, Angus recalled, urged the purification of the soul. It had seemed a gentler religion, certainly compared to the Christian fundamentalism espoused by the likes of Reverend MacVannin. Gentler, too, than Kelbie's paganism, with its strange rituals, votive offerings, and wrathful deities.

"Do you still believe, Nadia?" he asked.

She cocked her head to the side and stared at him through the snow. "I don't know. Since Dad died, I've reread all the Sufi poets he tried to get me interested in—Rumi, Hafiz, Kabir Das. But I haven't prayed, Angus. Not even once."

He held her open gaze for a long second, until the sound of barking shattered the moment.

"That'll be the dog unit," she muttered, turning away. "C'mon."

Castor the scent dog was going bonkers. His handler, PC Ronnie Blake, gave Angus and Nadia a tight smile as the white-and-tan springer spaniel yanked at his leash. "We like them a bit daft," Blake said in a strong Leeds accent. "More energy the better. Those types make the best scent dogs. The only problem is, they demand almost constant attention."

Angus gave Castor a good scratch under the chin. The dog looked up at him with big brown eyes, tail thumping against the ground. The dog was a bit of a star. He'd been used in numerous high-profile murder inquiries, his ability to pinpoint microscopic specks of blood meaning he was in high demand across the UK. He'd even had a trip to the US recently, where the FBI was keen to learn his tricks of the trade. His name had some Greek or Roman mythological significance that Angus couldn't quite recall.

"I read somewhere that Castor is paid more than the chief constable. Is that true?"

Blake gave a throaty laugh. "Bloody right it's true. And he earns every penny, unlike that bloated bastard. If your vic was killed here, Cass'll find where."

Angus smiled, but he wondered if the superstar mutt would have been employed had the victim been a binman's daughter, rather than an heiress. Budgets, so often the gripe of Inspector Stout and his ilk, had been blown on this case.

"Right, Cass," Blake said, "time to earn your corn, boy. Find Bob! Find Bob!"

Castor bolted away in a flurry of legs and wagging tail, pink tongue flapping ecstatically from his mouth.

Blake followed at a half-jog, the hand holding Castor's long leash outstretched.

"Who's Bob?" Angus asked.

"That's a command I came up with. Sounds better than 'find the dead guy' or 'find the puddle of blood.'"

They scurried after the dog, who ferreted around the huts and tents, nose to the ground, every so often letting out an excited yip.

"How do we know when he's found something?"

"He'll point at the spot."

"Really?"

"Aye, lad. Used to be a dog would lie down when they'd located the scent of blood or a body, but Cass is a different cookie."

A black sludge seemed to settle in his stomach as he followed Blake and the dog. Part of him wanted the dog to find something, but another part of him didn't want to contemplate the girl's end, up here in the middle of nowhere.

Because you could have saved her. Because without those pills, you would have seen in time.

No! He was too late! Always too late!

The flecks of snow had by now turned into sloppy, cold tears. The dog skirted the perimeter of a vegetable patch, his focus unwavering, then moved on to the open expanse where the Samhain bonfire had stood. He sniffed at the charred patches on the ground, then progressed onto the standing stones. In the thickening snow, the great slabs of rock looked even more like craggy old men. Ridges of granite became furrowed brows and thin lips; patches of lichen were transformed into beards and moustaches; scores on the face of the stone took on the appearance of wrinkled skin and battle scars.

Angus's heart thudded in his chest as Castor nosed in and out of the slabs. Every time Castor paused, he held his breath, but then the spaniel would yip and move on, tail wagging. The dog came lastly to a flatter stone that looked like an altar. It sat on its own, a few meters from the burnt patch where the bonfire had stood. Castor padded slowly around the stone. Perhaps Angus was imagining it, but the dog appeared to be giving the stone more attention than the others. At length, Cass sat back on his haunches and pointed a paw at the stone.

"Looks like he's got something!" Blake trotted across to Castor and scratched him under the muzzle. "Good boy! Who's a good boy!"

Blake turned his attention to the stone. Angus could see no trace of blood. "Maybe it's been washed down," Blake said. He glanced at Angus and Nadia. "But there's blood on this stone. I'd stake me house on it."

Cass growled, as if in agreement, but when Angus looked, the dog was staring into the mist, hackles raised.

"What's up, boy?" Blake said. Castor's snarl turned into a long, dolorous howl. Angus flinched at the racket, a banshee wail that set his teeth on edge. The dog jerked at his leash and his howl became an anguished cry. And suddenly Angus was back on the beach, fists pummelling the wet sand as the waves crashed around him and the gulls shrieked overhead. He felt his knuckles tear on fragments of shell, heard his own dry, rasping screams. All the while Ethan watched him with dull, lifeless eyes.

"Whoa, boy!" Blake chided, gripping the leash. "Cass! Heel!"

Angus blinked away the painful memory and squinted into the fog. He couldn't see what had spooked the dog but sensed a presence too, as if something were hidden in the roiling snow and mist.

"Cass, you silly mutt! What's got—"

Angus held up a hand to silence Blake. He took a couple of steps forward, listening intently. "Do you hear that?"

"Hear what?" Nadia asked.

"It sounds like, like—"

Suddenly the mist seemed to coalesce into the shape of a horse. Angus stood, rooted to the spot, as the beast galloped towards him at full tilt, nostrils flaring, teeth bared in an anguished grimace. He sprang to one side and the horse shot past him, so close, he could smell its ammoniac scent. The animal turned in a tight circle and reared up on its hind legs. It let out a loud whinny that sounded like a human cry. Angus stumbled backwards, away from the flailing hooves. The horse's eyes were wide and terrified, teeth clamped around the silver bit in its mouth.

Angus raised his palms. "Whoa! Easy there, girl." The horse shook its mane, sending an arc of snow into the air. He reached out a hand, but the animal shied away and stamped a skittish hoof on the ground, snorting in distress. "It's okay, girl. Easy now." His heart was thudding in his chest, but somehow he managed to keep his voice calm. Suddenly he recalled the words Faye had spoken, the secret phrase taught to her by her old riding instructor.

He edged forward, hands still upraised. The horse lowered its head and continued to paw at the ground, as if preparing to charge. He looked the frightened creature in the eye.

"*Two as one,*" he whispered, so softly that Nadia and Blake could not hear him. "*Two as one.*"

The horse's ears seemed to twitch back. Angus took another half-step forward. His hand reached out towards the horse's nose, so close, he could feel the heat of her breath on his fingertips. "*Two as one,*" he said again. He inched forward and his fingers brushed against the horse's nose. She flinched, but he maintained contact, still muttering the phrase. He feathered his fingers across her cheek. "See, there's nothing to worry about," he murmured. The horse nuzzled into him, calm now, like the sea after a storm.

"Where the 'eck did she come from?" Blake asked.

Angus took hold of the horse's reins and stroked her warm muscular neck. Her flank was matted down one side with a reddish-brown substance. He ran a hand over the stain, then raised his fingers to his nose.

"What is it, Angus?" Nadia asked.

He dropped his hand to his side and rubbed his fingers on his trousers. The substance had an unmistakable scent, like copper pennies.

"Blood."

A leather saddle sat askew on the horse's back. Underneath, a black padded saddle cloth was plastered to the animal's body. A word was embroidered in gold thread near the edge of the cloth. At first he thought it was the manufacturer's logo, but looking closer he realized it was a name—Bessie. This *had* to be Faye's horse, but Bessie was a chestnut mare.

This horse was completely white.

CHAPTER 15

DARKNESS had fallen by the time Chichester's helicopter deposited them back in the field near the village hall. Agnes and Muriel, the Highland cows, were two dark shadows standing sentry under the horse chestnut. Angus felt their gleaming eyes follow him as he scuttled after Nadia towards the beacon of light that was the Glenruig Inn. Through the window he saw tables of folk drinking and eating. Flushed, smiling faces. Their happiness seemed an affront.

Despite the snow, the *West Highland Mail* reporter Alice Seaton had kept up her vigil outside the village hall. Angus spotted her sucking on a cigarette as he ducked under the police cordon, which was manned by a big bear of a constable named Archie Devine. "How's it going, Archie?" he asked.

"Living the dream, Gus. Living the fucking dream."

He saw Seaton flick away her cigarette and stride towards them.

"Constable MacNeil! I hear you've been up at the pagan commune? Is it one of them? Did they kill Faye?"

Angus was startled to hear Faye's name, but shouldn't have been. The local gossip network would be in overdrive.

"That type of speculation isn't helpful, Alice."

"Helpful? Angus, I've been stood out here all day freezing my tits off—is it her or not?"

"Sorry, Alice, can't help ye."

"Ach, come on! Give us something before the big boys from the nationals show up."

Angus shook his head. "Keep the press back, would you, Archie?"

The big man's expression never changed from surly boredom. "Aye," he muttered, then turned to the reporter. "Could you step back please, ma'am?"

"Don't 'ma'am' me, Archie Devine. I used to babysit you, for Christ's sake!"

"I'm asking you nicely to step back."

"No, you're not! You're being a prick! I'm well within my rights to be here. . . ."

Angus left them to argue it out and followed Nadia into the hall. A laminated sign with the words "Major Incident Room" printed on it had been Sellotaped to the door of the auditorium. Inside, DCI Crowley was perched casually on a desk in front of the murder board. A couple of local CID guys Angus recognised were still there, but six or seven new faces had arrived, presumably detectives from the major investigation team.

Crowley glanced up and gave Nadia a lupine grin.

"Here she is," he boomed, "our latest DI."

All eyes swivelled towards them, quickly followed by an ironic cheer. Nadia pulled a mock curtsy and accepted a couple of handshakes and kisses on the cheek. Angus hung back, feeling like a spare part, as Nadia traded banter with a few of the detectives.

Crowley slipped off the desk and gestured for him to come forward. He slapped his mutilated hand down on Angus's shoulder and paraded him in front of the team, as if he were a new pupil joining the class.

"And this fine specimen of manhood is Constable MacNeil. He'll be on board for this one. You can all introduce yourselves later. But no touching, and I mean you, DC Lockhart."

A few good-natured cheers were directed towards a woman in her late thirties. She wore round-rimmed spectacles and a chunky cardigan, looking more like a librarian than a detective.

"Tossers," she replied primly, cheeks reddening.

Crowley, grinning, gestured for Nadia and Angus to take a seat in front of the murder board.

"Right, now that the gang's back together, here's where we're at. The deceased, as you all know, is Faye Chichester. She was only sixteen. Her father is the billionaire media-mogul-turned-environmentalist James Chichester. As well as being obscenely rich, he's famous, which means this case is going to generate significant press interest, both here and in the States. Already there are rumours flying about on social media, so we're going to release the victim's name tonight. After the late editions have gone to press, just to piss them off."

He turned to the murder board and wrote three words in cap letters. He then turned, raised his maimed hand, and counted off the words with his remaining fingers.

"Lust, lucre, and loathing." He paused for effect, then continued: "I've worked more homicides than Boaby has had haggis suppers."

A rotund man with the ruddy complexion of a farmer barked a laugh. "And believe me, that's a lot," he said.

"I'm no' boasting, it's just a fact," Crowley said. "And in every one of those cases, the motive was lust, lucre, or loathing. Occasionally more than one or even all three came into play, but one was usually the killer's driving force."

He took his pen and underlined one of the words.

"Let's start with lust. We need to find out if Faye had a boyfriend or lover. Statistically, when young women are murdered, it's about sex. Digital forensics are going through her devices as we speak, so we need to talk to her friends and acquaintances. A girl like Faye catches the eye—find out whose."

Angus thought about what Mrs. MacCrimmon had said about Ewan. He'd known the lad his whole life. He would never do something like this.

"Do we know if she was raped, sir?" the mousey woman asked.

"No indication of sexual assault, Vee," Nadia replied, "but we won't know until after the autopsy."

"Which is when?" Crowley asked.

"Nine tomorrow. We won't know cause of death till then either, but judging by the video of the crime scene made by Constable MacNeil, strangulation looks a safe bet."

"Fair enough. I want you and Angus to attend the PM, aye?"

Please no.

"Thanks a bunch," Nadia replied.

"Perks of being a DI." Crowley grinned. "Right, let's move on to lucre. Chichester's worth more than the GDP of a small country, so who benefits financially from Faye's death?"

"Easy," a young man in a tailored suit sitting to Angus's left said. "The stepmum, Eleanor."

Crowley scribbled her name under "Lucre," his pen squeaking on the whiteboard.

"Tell me about her, Ryan."

DC Ryan Fleet glanced at his notebook. A Cartier watch glinted from his wrist.

"Former actress," he said. "Starred in a load of straight-to-DVD horrors in the nineties and early noughties. She's apparently fifty-four, although she's been under the knife more times than a butcher's table. Married James Chichester eight years ago."

"Prenup?"

"Er, I don't know, sir."

"Check that, Rylo. With Faye out of the picture, likely Eleanor stands to inherit a fortune once Chichester pops his clogs. Bearing in mind he's the wrong side of seventy. What about Faye's birth mother?"

"Died two years ago," Fleet said. "Overdose. Likely intentional."

Crowley tapped his pen on the whiteboard. Side-on, his nose was hooked like a bird of prey's. His missing fingers transformed his hand into a talon. The digits had been severed by a serial killer who'd terrorized Glasgow the previous summer. The Priest had forced his victims to confess their sins before deciding whether or not to kill them. He'd used garden secateurs on Crowley, and had been in the process of chopping off his thumb when he was shot by police marksmen. Perhaps, Angus thought, this was why Crowley's eyes held a haunted look.

"Loathing," Crowley rasped. "Who hates this girl enough to brutally murder her?"

His question was met with blank looks. DC Lockhart gave a polite cough. "No one gets as rich as Chichester without making enemies. What if this is not about Faye at all? What if this is a message to Chichester?"

"Thanks, Vee. You've just volunteered to look into all Chichester's business dealings."

Crowley gave her an icy smile then moved on. "Right, we know from DI Sharif's sterling work today that Faye was last seen at a pagan commune. We've all viewed the video footage of her taken by one of the residents. Forensic searches will continue at first light, but the dogs have already detected traces of blood on both an altar stone and her horse, is that right, Nadia?"

"Aye . . . well, we're not sure it actually is her horse, sir."

Crowley's brow furrowed.

"Bessie had a brown coat," Nadia explained. "The one we encountered up at the commune was white."

"Then clearly it's a different horse," Crowley said. "Boaby, get a list of local horse owners, equestrian centres, trekking businesses—see if any of them are missing a white horse."

"Aye, aye, Captain," the big man replied.

"Anyway, you were saying, Nadia?"

"So, we took samples of the blood. They're being couriered to the lab in Inverness, but we won't get the results back until tomorrow. Myself and Constable MacNeil have taken initial statements from all the residents, but we'll need full background checks."

"Absolutely."

"Maybe she was sacrificed to the old gods?" someone joked.

Crowley ignored the comment.

DC Fleet raised a tentative hand.

"Put that down, Rylo," Crowley snapped. "You're not in flipping nursery."

"Sorry, sir. I just wanted to add that the residents of the commune have access to a . . . err . . . communal camper van."

Angus knew the vehicle Ryan was talking about. He'd seen it around the area, usually stocking up on provisions at Moira Anderson's shop.

"There's no road up to the commune, so where's it kept?" Crowley asked.

"They have an agreement with the Forestry Commission, who allows them to store it in a garage near the path to Teine Eigin."

"Okay, good work, Rylo. Get a warrant and ask forensics to strip this camper van to its axles. If Faye was killed nearby, they might have used it to transport her body."

"Yes, sir."

He turned back to Nadia. "Any luck in tracing the mystery figure from the footage?"

"No, sir. But we've learnt a local minister gate-crashed the party last night."

She turned to Angus and gestured for him to take up the story. He cleared his throat, nervous, painfully aware of all the sets of eyes on him, watching, assessing.

"Er, aye," he stuttered. "His name's Reverend John MacVannin. He's a bit of a firebrand. Vocal critic of Chichester's nature reserve. Being Free Kirk, he's not taken kindly to a pagan commune being set up within spitting distance either. Samhain is the most important night in the pagan calendar. Seems MacVannin went there to try to disrupt proceedings. He had a run-in with Faye, too. Tried to get her to leave, but she laughed at him."

"Interesting," Crowley said, writing MacVannin's name under "Loathing." "Do you think he's capable of it?"

It took Angus a beat to realize the question had been directed at him.

"Most of us are," he replied, "given the right circumstances."

Crowley fixed him with a cool glare. "You believe that, Constable?"

Angus felt sweat prickle at his hairline. Everyone was staring at him. "Aye," he said. "I do."

Crowley's face broke into a wide grin. "Me too. We all have it in us. But look, Angus, you know this place and its people better than we do: When you saw that girl lying dead on the beach this morning, who was the first person who sprang to mind?"

He thought of Donn, the Dark One—and whoever was beneath his mask of death.

"No one," he muttered. "I didn't think of anyone."

"What about any local sex offenders?"

Angus shook his head.

"Psychos? Ex-cons?"

"No, sir."

Crowley sucked air between his teeth. "Pity. I suppose it could be an outsider. It's not tourist season, but you still get a fair few visitors, I'd guess?"

"Aye," he said. "Hillwalkers mainly."

"So a stranger wouldn't exactly stand out?"

"No."

Crowley turned to the murder board, his clawlike hand cupping his chin. He examined the photographs for a few seconds, staring at them dispassionately. "Nah, this seems personal to me. This lassie was strangled and dumped on a beach like a piece of garbage. Someone must have really hated her. Let's find out who."

CHAPTER 16

ANGUS'S wife slept on the sofa like the stone effigy of the Crusader who rested in St. Columba's chapel on Skye. Gills had taken him to Skeabost to see the tomb one summer when he was thirteen or fourteen. He recalled the cold wind whistling around the ruins, the aura of the place. The Crusader's tomb was laid in the sixteenth century, but the chapel was older, much older, Gills had explained. Somehow he'd felt this, sensed a history of worship going back centuries, millennia even, before Colmcille and his monks had set foot on the tiny isle in the middle of the River Snizort. He'd felt the past reach up from the ground like ivy, encircling his ankles. He couldn't wait to leave.

He crouched next to Ashleigh. Rather than a sword like the Crusader, she loosely cradled an iPad across her chest. Small flames lapped at a log in the woodburner and cast a soft glow on her face and thick russet hair. Gently, he removed the iPad from her grasp. The screen awoke at the last website she'd been looking at—a medical forum on IVF. They'd already been through two harrowing, unsuccessful rounds of treatment. They would find out this coming Friday if the latest procedure—and last they would be allowed on the NHS—had worked. He sat back on his haunches, sad and shamefaced. It would be a failure, he knew. But at least it would save a future child from carrying this burden.

He switched the iPad off and worked his fingers under Ash's sleeping body, so warm and alive. He carried her to the bedroom and laid her down on the blankets, just as he had laid Faye down on the shingle. He drew the duvet over her body and kissed her softly on the forehead. She mumbled in her sleep, a ghost of a smile on her lips. He thought, then, of the moment he had first seen her, on stage at the ceilidh in the village hall. Ash was the music she played: enthralling, knowing, tender, beautiful, anguished. It hadn't been her music that had washed over him, he had thought so many times—it had been her.

She saved you. When you were broken and nothing.

Ash would be a great mother. She was strong-willed and didn't suffer fools, but she had a tenderness, too, that reminded him of his own mother. He understood her need for a family, even if he feared it.

You knew that, even then.

"I'm sorry," he whispered, choking back tears.

He stood and tiptoed from the room. He'd barely poured a hefty glass of Talisker when his mobile phone rang. He checked the caller ID and saw Sandy Robertson's name flash up. The owner of the Glenruig Inn was a friend, but he wouldn't phone at this hour unless it was important.

"Sandy," he said, raising the phone to his ear, "what can I do for you, *a'bhalach*?"

In the background he could hear music, laughter, and drunken chatter, a typical Saturday night down at the pub.

"Sorry to phone so late, Gus. It's Ewan again."

Angus closed his eyes and muttered a silent curse.

"Give me five minutes."

He hung up and stared longingly at the glass of whisky. Then he grabbed the keys for the police Land Rover and went out into the snow.

An impromptu ceilidh was in full swing when Angus flung open the doors of the Glenruig Inn. Iain MacFarlane sat in the corner like a giant oak tree, his fiddle sprouting from the crook of his neck like a bough. The instrument was tuned to perfection, and no matter how drunk the big man got, he could carry a tune. At the Games in August, Angus had seen him knocked to the ground by a couple of overzealous dancers, but Iain hadn't missed a beat.

Next to Iain was a young accordion prodigy, whose name escaped him, and old Cally Swein, who was rarely seen without his uilleann bagpipes. With difficulty, Angus skirted around a knot of dancers, nodding to the odd familiar face, and almost collided with Grant Abbott coming out of the gents.

"How's form, Gus?" the fisherman slurred. "Will you take a dram with us—we're wetting the baby's head." He gestured over to a group of lads sitting at a table next to the musicians.

"Sorry, Grant, I'm here to take Ewan home. But congratulations. A girl, eh?"

"Aye, she's a wee smasher." He grinned, eyes glassy with pride.

Over Grant's shoulder, a big bearded man with wild dark locks and mut-
tonchop sideburns looked up from pouring a pint of IPA. Sandy Robertson
caught Angus's eye and gestured with a thrust of his chin towards the rear of
the pub.

Angus clapped Grant on the shoulder. "Have a good night, mate. I'll
hold ye to that drink."

Grant gave something approaching a thumbs-up and sashayed back to
his seat, fist pumping in the air in time to the music. A half-smile on his
face, Angus slalomed through groups of red-faced drinkers. He found Ewan
sprawled over a small table in the corner of the pub, surrounded by empty
whisky glasses, loose change, and crumpled Scampi Fries packets. The ghillie
sat with his head drooped, wide shoulders shaking as he mewled into his
dram. At first Angus thought he was crying, but then he recognised a few
words from a rowdy song they used to sing on the shinty bus after a victory. Ewan had been the star player back then, strong and fleet-footed with a
deadly strike—a shy boy who came alive on the shinty pitch. He could hardly
believe the drunken, slabbering mess in front of him was the same person.

He leaned across the table and placed an arm on Ewan's shoulder. "Time
to go home, a'bhalach."

Ewan glanced up at him with bleary, bloodshot eyes. It took him several
seconds to focus. "Wha-tha-fu-d'you-wan?"

He walked around the table and pulled Ewan to his feet. "Come on, time
to go, pal."

Ewan shoved him away. "Ge-the-fu-off-me!" he roared. The music was
loud, so only those nearest heard Ewan shout. Out of the corner of his eye,
Angus saw them nudge each other and turn, hoping for a fight.

"Easy," Angus said, raising his hands. "Let's not make a scene, eh?"

Ewan, though, looked past caring. He stumbled forwards, fists clenched,
eyes blazing. The ghillie snarled something incomprehensible and swung a
right hook. He leaned backwards and the fist whistled inches past Angus's
nose. Ewan pitched forward, his momentum sending him sprawling to the
floor. There he lay, groaning.

"Okay, show's over," Sandy said, emerging from behind the bar. The
drinkers returned their attention to their pints.

With the bar owner's help, he hauled Ewan upright and, like a fallen
comrade on the battlefield, dragged him out through the emergency exit.
"Sorry about this, Sandy," he grunted as they levered the ghillie into the back
of the Land Rover.

"That's the third time in as many months, Gus." Despite his size, Sandy's voice was soft. "I should bar him, but"—he shrugged—"I feel sorry for the lad."

"Aye, me too. I'll speak to him. When he sobers up."

The publican clapped him on the shoulder. "Good luck with that."

Five minutes later Angus brought the car to a halt outside Ewan's cottage. The ghillie had been garbling on the drive, something about the depth of Scotland's lochs. He left him there and opened the door to the house, wrinkling his nose at the smell from inside, like a post-match shinty changing room, only worse.

He returned to the car and half-carried, half-dragged Ewan into the cottage. The ghillie grumbled and cursed, giving him a rancid blast of alcohol-laden breath as he barged into the bedroom. He grunted with effort as he swung Ewan around and tipped him onto the unmade single bed. He tugged off his muddy boots and let them fall to the floor. Ewan curled up into the foetal position. His stomach clenched as he recalled Faye lying in the exact same pose on the beach. As if the killer had been returning her to the womb.

He bent down and yanked the duvet over Ewan's sleeping form. As he did so, his eye fell on a cluster of photographs pinned to the wall next to the bed. One featured a younger Ewan standing beside his father with a fly rod in his hand. On the grass in front of them lay a large silver salmon, a fine cock fish with a hooked jaw. John Hunter had his arm around his son's shoulders and was smiling proudly.

The rest of the photographs—about fifteen or twenty—were pictures of Faye Chichester. Some were posed, Faye grinning or making silly faces at the camera, but others had captured her in unguarded moments—reading by a river, staring out across the sea, reclining on a rowing boat with the sun on her face. He plucked one photograph from the wall. It showed Faye in the stables at Dunbirlinn, brushing Bessie's mane. A slash of sunlight cut across the shot, illuminating both girl and horse. The angle of the shot suggested Ewan must have taken it from a hiding place. Angus glanced down at the sleeping ghillie and remembered the young man he used to take for chips in Silvaig after shinty training.

"Ach, Ewan . . ." he whispered.

The fire in the snug room was still smouldering when he got back home, faint red embers glowing from the hearth like devil eyes. He threw on some kindling, then lifted the glass of Talisker he'd poured earlier. Small flames began to lick along the kindling, a dog tonguing a bone. Soon the wood was well alight and he was able to place on a couple of beech logs.

He stood, drinking his whisky as the fire spat and crackled, trying to avoid the inevitable. Finally he placed his glass down and walked into the hall. The shoebox was shoved to the back of the airing cupboard, concealed behind old clothes and miscellaneous junk—rarely played board games, an inflatable mattress, a box of plugs and cables that were probably broken or obsolete.

He pulled out the shoebox and carried it back through to the sitting room. He placed the box on a coffee table, fetched his whisky from the fireplace, and slumped onto the couch. There he sat, staring at the shoebox. He'd made running repairs to it over the years but noticed the Sellotape at the corners was coming loose, peeling away, a snake slewing its skin. He could have easily found a newer shoebox: every time Ash visited Inverness, she came back with a new pair of shoes. To do so, though, would have been a tacit acknowledgement that this—what he was about to do now—was going to continue, that he would never be able to move on.

He sat forward and reached for the lid of the box, paused.

Put it back. Better yet, throw the fucking box in the fire!

He glanced at the blooms of orange curling around the logs. He imagined the whoosh as the shoebox ignited.

He flipped the box open—quickly, like pulling an Elastoplast off a cut knee. The newsprint was yellowing. Decomposing. Like them. Familiar images and headlines swam in front of his eyes.

"Mum Slain."

"Boy Drowned."

"Fire Tragedy."

"Community in Mourning."

He jammed the lid back on the box, as if afraid whatever was in there might jump out and attack him. He reached for his glass of whisky and took a gulp. He wasn't ready for this, not yet. He took another gulp, draining the glass. The whisky made his head spin, but rather than cloud his senses, he was suddenly back there, standing in the puddle as rain hammered off the roof of his mum's old Renault Scenic. He could feel cold water seep through his school shoes; he could hear the animal panting as the car shook. Why were the windows steamed up? He flinched as a hand slapped onto the rear window.

Angus dug his fingernails into his palms, but the pain could not banish the images in his head. He was back there, his sodden school uniform clinging to his body, water seeping into his polished shoes. His teeth chittered as the hand squeaked down the window, clearing a patch in the condensation. Peering out from the car, as if trapped under a sheet of ice, he saw his mother's face.

ACT II

"Our pagan ancestors, as Highland folktales show, lived in a world controlled by great and fearsome monsters, who were ever seeking to work evil against mankind."

—"A Highland Goddess,"
Donald A. Mackenzie, 1912

CHAPTER 17

ANGUS was familiar with Silvaig General Hospital. Too familiar. He'd lost count of the number of times he'd loitered in the wards or paced up and down the insipid mint-coloured waiting room. He was less familiar with the mortuary around the back of A&E, but only just. Whilst the rest of Silvaig General had benefited from a multimillion-pound investment a decade ago, the mortuary hadn't changed. It remained the same squat Victorian building with crow-stepped gables, tucked out of sight around the back of the hospital like a dirty secret. The last time he had visited was about nine months ago. A climber had fallen almost a thousand feet from the Cuillin ridge on Skye. The aftermath was not a pretty sight.

He thought of the girl lying in the adjoining room and his stomach spasmed. By rights she should be out riding Bessie or painting or smoking weed like any normal teenage girl.

Nadia handed him a pair of scrubs. He garbled a thanks and bent over to tug them on, the rustle of the material like a cracked voice that only he could hear, the same phrase, repeating over and over. He saw himself as a boy, sitting against the wall of his bedroom, thin arms around his knees, pulling them to his chest. His eyes stung, and his throat was raw and gritty as he muttered to himself.

It's not fair! It's not fair! It's not fair! It's not—

He felt someone shaking his shoulder. He was jolted back to the present, and found Nadia frowning at him. "Are you okay?" she asked, concern in her voice. "You're looking a wee bit peely-wally."

He choked down the gravel in his throat. "Can't stand autopsies."

Nadia squeezed his shoulder, then let her hand drop. "Me neither. I think that's why Crowley sent me. Ruthven's an old-school face-your-fears kinda guy. He sees himself as my mentor."

"But you don't?"

She gave a one-shouldered shrug. "Crowley's a machine. The job's his life, but if he weren't catching killers, he'd probably be one himself." She zipped up her white scrubs. "I don't want to end up like him."

"You won't."

"The signs are there. . . ."

"What signs?" He frowned.

She shook her head and refused to meet his eyes. "The usual: pushing folk away, drinking too much, obsessing on certain unsolved cases—"

He understood that, knew, too, the case she alluded to—a little girl murdered and dumped in the River Clyde. The River Angel. Nadia had found her body.

"Has anyone . . ."

She shook her head.

"You'll keep going, though?"

"Aye. Always." She placed a hand on his shoulder for balance as she slipped on a protective bootie. Her touch took him back to Tulliallan, her hand on his shoulder as she put on her black high heels for a night out in Stirling. He saw her straighten up and ask him to zip up her dress. He remembered the smooth tanned skin of her back, the fruity scent of her shampoo as he feathered her neck with kisses. The memory was fleeting and stung like a nettle.

She frowned at him, then pulled out a small tub of Vicks. He scooped out a pea-sized amount of the claggy menthol ointment and rubbed it on his upper lip. She tied her dark hair back using a bobble, then pushed open the double doors that led to the postmortem suite.

Angus closed his eyes for a second. He tried to convince himself that the girl lying on the slab next door was not Faye. It was a body, nothing more. Flesh and bone. His mind, though, could not make that leap. He'd tried to numb his senses with the pills, but they hadn't worked.

Steeling himself, he followed Nadia into the PM suite, a sinister windowless room of grubby wall tiles and flaking paint reminiscent of a public lavatory. Victorian-era porcelain sinks jutted from the wall like broken teeth. The stained tiled floor sloped gently to a drain in the centre of the room.

Dr Orla Kelly looked up from a trolley of surgical instruments she was busy arranging. "Angus, not you again."

"Hi, Orla," he croaked.

She cocked an eyebrow in question.

"Sorry," he mumbled, "this is DI Nadia Sharif from the MIT. Nadia, this is Dr. Orla Kelly."

"Pleased to meet you, DI Sharif."

The two women briefly shook hands.

"Likewise, but call me Nadia."

Orla gestured for them to approach the gurney. Angus took a deep breath, then wished he hadn't—despite the Vicks, the room still stank of formaldehyde and raw meat. He fought a wave of nausea as Orla peeled away the sheet that lay over Faye's body. The girl's clothes had been sheared away. She lay naked on the slab, eyes closed, hair a golden halo around her head. Her skin shone like alabaster under the harsh glare of the mortuary striplight. Red welts around her wrists marked where the rope had been tied. The garrotte had also been removed, but it had left its mark in a livid slash around the throat.

As he stared at her pallid body, he sensed a presence beside him, and saw a flash of blond hair out of the corner of his eye. Faye was standing next to him. She stared at her body on the slab with dull, washed-out eyes. Her look of utter desolation stripped him bare. Her hand dangled loose by her side. He let his fingers brush against her cold skin. Slowly, she took his hand in her own frigid grip.

"Okay, initial observations," Orla said, going into professional mode. "The victim suffered three blows to the head. We have two fractures on the crown accompanied by adjoining scalp lacerations, each with swollen wound margins, which indicate the victim was alive at the time. The sharpness of the wound edges suggest a heavy weapon such as an axe was used. However, although severe, these blows would not have been fatal. Likely, the victim would have lapsed into unconsciousness."

He felt Faye's cold grip tighten. His throat constricted, as if she were squeezing his throat rather than his hand. He noticed now that she wore a cornflower-blue dress, as if she'd been out for a walk on a summer's day.

"There's a similar laceration to the base of the skull," Orla continued, "but the fracture looks to have been caused by a blunt weapon, perhaps the reverse, or flat, of the axe blade."

Angus's breathing was shallow. He clutched Faye's hand as Orla worked her way meticulously over every inch of the body, like an archaeologist on a dig at some Neolithic settlement, scraping away the dirt and soil to reveal an ancient skeleton. Her words were warbled, as if spoken underwater.

"Right leg has been fractured below the knee—

"Narrow laceration—

"Bruising to the upper arm—"

Orla lifted a pair of tweezers from her tray of instruments. She used them to pluck something from a silver dish.

"We managed to extract this earlier. It's a simple garrotte, about forty centimetres in length, knotted in three places. Petechial haemorrhaging tells us that this is likely what killed her. The killer must have wound it around her neck, jammed his knee into her back, and pulled. Pulled with such force, he cracked two ribs and almost severed her spinal cord along with the jugular. Wherever she died, she lost a lot of blood."

He saw a thin trickle of blood run down Faye's neck. The crimson thread coursed down her arm towards their interlocked hands. He tried to free himself from her grip, but it was as if they were glued together. He felt her tepid blood pool between their fingers before it dripped like tears onto the floor.

"I'm sorry," he croaked. He immediately attempted to cover his slip with a cough.

Nadia laid her hand on his wrist. "Are you okay, Angus?"

He thumped the side of his fist against his chest.

"Sorry, I'm fine."

"Do you want a glass of water?" Orla asked.

"Only if it has whisky in it," he muttered.

He noticed Nadia and Orla share a fleeting glance, before the pathologist continued: "The garrotte itself is unusual, as you suspected, Angus. I knew from my initial examination it wasn't rope or wire, so I ran some tests. Turns out it's made from animal sinew."

"Animal sinew?" Nadia exclaimed.

"Deer, maybe."

The pathologist dropped the tweezers into a metal bowl, then let out a long sigh, gathering her thoughts.

"Anything else you can tell us, Dr. Kelly?" Nadia asked.

"Her hair and the top half of her clothing were wet. Fresh water, not salt water. But there was no fluid in her lungs. I think she was held underwater after she was dead. It's overkill. Literally. Whoever did this . . . they beat her unconscious, strangled her so hard, they exsanguinated her, then drowned her once she was already dead. They killed her at least three times."

He felt Faye relax her grip on his hand, then let go completely. His fingers flailed for her hand, as if trying to hold on to her, but when he chanced a look to his left, the girl was gone.

CHAPTER 18

ASH coaxed the clarsach case into her Renault Clio. The instrument was too big for the boot, so she slid it into the rear seats and strapped it in with a seat belt, as if it were a child. In a way, the clarsach was her baby, which she guessed was a pretty sad thing to admit.

She slammed the door shut and climbed into the driver's seat. The car coughed and spluttered, the engine cold, but after a couple of tries it started. How many more winters would the Clio last? Would it even last this winter? She'd lost a couple of clients last week, and although Angus made a decent wage, money was tight, what with the fees for his father's care home. Fewer young ones wanted to learn the clarsach these days. Traditional music was fighting for survival. Gigs were still relatively popular, though. She'd heard the Cach Mòr Ceilidh Band was after a clarsach player for a European tour in the New Year, but the hours were tough and she'd be away from home for weeks.

You might be pregnant by then, anyway.

The thought slipped into her head unbidden, carrying with it the usual anxiety. She'd been trying—and failing—not to think about the IVF. Dr. Morrow had sounded hopeful, hadn't she? There was nothing defective in their gametes. The procedure *should* work. Although it *should* have worked on their previous attempts, too. And they should have been able to conceive without any damn procedure at all. Sometimes it felt as if the universe couldn't let her be happy.

Sheep nibbled at grassy stalks along the verge of the single-track road, and appeared reluctant to move out of the way to let her past. She recognised their obstinacy—this was their home after all. She edged around a gimlet-eyed ewe and her six-month-old lamb.

No, we'll muddle by, she thought, although it would help if Angus went for a promotion. He'd been a constable when they met eight years ago and had seemed ambitious. That was one of the things she'd liked about him, one of the reasons she'd reluctantly jettisoned her own dream of going to the Royal Conservatoire. She thought he'd at least be a sergeant by now. She couldn't say she hadn't been warned. She could still hear Granny Beag scolding her: "Men always let you down, Ashleigh. Go after what you want, but dinnae expect any help from them lot." Granny Beag didn't understand that was exactly what she was doing. Building a life in the Highlands with Angus, starting a family, that was what she wanted more than anything. Did that make her a bad feminist? No, it fucking didn't!

She shook the thought from her head and concentrated on the road. It was slippy from the recent snowfall. Speed and icy roads could lead to tragedy—she knew that better than most. When she reached the village, Ash found a new hazard.

"Jeezo!"

The area surrounding the hall, stretching back down the road past the Glenruig Inn, was swarming with press. Outside, broadcasting units emblazoned with logos for the BBC, STV, and Sky News were pulled up on the verge. Wires snaked from them like entrails as techs in combat trousers fiddled with equipment and people with clipboards flitted around like hummingbirds. She recognised a few reporters from the national news, their smart clothes setting them apart from the rest of the crew. Malcolm Gladstone, the BBC correspondent, was doing a piece to camera in front of Agnes and Muriel. The cows watched the reporter, chewing sullenly.

"I know how you feel," Ash told the cows as she trundled the Clio through the scrum.

Moira Anderson and the so-called beautician Geraldine MacAuley sat on deck chairs outside the shop, watching the goings-on with greedy eyes. Ash waved and faked them a smile as she drove past. Once out of the village, she flicked on the stereo, but rather than listen to the radio, she slid in a CD—Karine Polwart's *Faultlines*. The title of the album seemed appropriate somehow. Didn't fault lines run through everything? She recalled an old geography teacher, Mr. Law, explaining how the Highlands was separated from the rest of Scotland by something called the Highland Boundary Fault. He'd described a schism in the earth that tore across the country, from Arran in the west to Stonehaven in the east. As she grew older, Ash realized this rift wasn't only topographical. To the urbanites of the Lowlands, Highlanders were callow kilt-wearing haggis-munchers. The stereotype persisted. Even after devolution, the Highland voice was ignored, or became fodder for lazy comedy sketches. These attitudes were insidious—they enabled the continued exploitation of the Highlands. Ach, maybe Granny Beag was right. Perhaps she needed to do more than stand on the sidelines shouting.

The music kept her mind off this morning's visit, but as she neared Kintail House, the old black anxiety set in. Her stomach was churning by the time she reached the road entrance that led to the house, almost hidden now by encroaching rhododendrons. The Clio's suspension protested as she juddered along the potholed track. Great Caledonian pines loomed around her. She remembered walking in the woods as a girl and finding a red squirrel's drey. Every day she'd visited, until the squirrel became comfortable with her. She recalled the squirrel's intelligent eyes and tufted ears that reminded her of a mad professor. Perhaps the squirrel's offspring were still here, scurrying through the branches like streaks of fire. It was a comforting thought, and by the time the old hunting lodge came into view, she was smiling.

She pulled up in the small visitors car park, killed the engine, and sat for a moment contemplating the building where she'd spent the best part of her childhood. No, she thought, not the *best* part—the *worst* part. Her childhood had been split in two, pre–the Accident and post–the Accident. Her dim memories of those early years were Edenic: the bright flowers in their garden, a vast blue sky, and a house by the sea; her mother's laughter; her dad's kind, smiling eyes, the scratch of his beard on her cheek. Then all that colour had drained away and she was brought here. Back then, the house had seemed like a scary mansion out of a horror film, but now she could appreciate its charm. Aye, it was a wee bit neglected—the window frames needed painting, and some of the wooden fasciae were rotting—but it was a well-proportioned imposing building, with a great outlook over a sweeping lawn down to a small lochan.

She climbed out of the Clio. The lawn itself was well tended, but the grounds needed some TLC. The borders were overgrown and the hedges needed a trim. Weeds sprouted between cracks in the paved area that the warden, Mrs. Gillies, used to refer to as "the patio." She could still hear Keira mocking the warden's posh accent.

Ash's smile faltered. Mrs. Gillies was dead; she'd read her obituary in the *West Highland Mail* a few years back. She wondered what had become of Keira. She hadn't kept in touch with anyone from the orphanage after Granny Beag had adopted her. She'd wanted to bury that part of her life, yet here she was exhuming it.

The knot in her stomach tightened as she unclipped the clarsach from the back seat and carried it towards the big arched doorway. Inside, the lobby was dim and somewhat shabby, the tartan carpet threadbare. The same dull landscape paintings hung from the walls, although new potted plants wilted in a corner. The reception desk was scored and worn, smaller than she remembered.

Ash closed her eyes and took a deep breath, sucking in the lingering scent of boiled meat and vegetables, combined with a mustiness that she would always associate with this place. A thousand images from her childhood danced in her head, each one too flimsy to grasp. She opened her eyes and saw a woman emerge from the office behind reception. Maureen MacCluskie was in her sixties now, but she still had the mullet of an eighties footballer and the arms of a shot-putter. Big Mo, they used to call her.

"Well, well, the One-Girl Wrecking Ball has returned."

Ash gave a sheepish smile. "Hello, Mrs. MacCluskie."

"Och! You're not a resident anymore, pet. You can call me Mo."

She waddled out from behind the desk and took Ash by the shoulders. Mo's big thick-fingered hands felt warm and clammy, even through her coat.

"You're looking well, Ashleigh. A bit scrawny, but all in all not too bad."

"And you haven't aged a day," she replied, truthfully. Perhaps she was stuck in the same time warp as her hairstyle.

Big Mo grinned, displaying a mouth full of fillings. Ash wondered if she still kept a hoard of sweets behind reception.

"Come on, they're waiting for you in the glasshouse," Big Mo said.

She led the way through the lodge, whistling tunelessly through her teeth, an early warning sign that they'd been grateful for back in the day. Ash's eyes darted around, taking in the familiar furniture, gaudy paintings, the staircase to the dorms that creaked on the eighth step from the top, as anyone who sneaked out in the middle of the night knew.

"It's kind of you giving up your Sunday for this," Big Mo said.

"Ach! What else would I be doing?"

"I can think of a million things I'd rather be doing," Mo said. "How's Granny Beag keeping?"

"You know what she's like, thrawn as ever."

Big Mo gave a black-toothed smile. "I hear you're married?"

"Aye, five years now."

Mo stopped outside the door that led to the glasshouse. A laminated sign stuck to the door read "Music Therapy."

"Married to a man of the law, no less?" Mo smiled. "If someone had told me seventeen years ago you'd end up snagging a policeman, I'd never have believed them."

Ash contorted her features into a smile. She glanced through the window and saw six or seven youths, ranging in age from about thirteen to sixteen.

"Your students await. Good luck, pet."

Big Mo waddled away, whistling. Ash scowled at her back. "Snagged a policeman," she muttered to herself. "Fuck off!"

She took a second to compose herself, then turned and pushed open the door of the glasshouse. The heat hit her immediately. Two boys were wrestling playfully on the floor, surrounded by lofty plants and ferns. The others were seated on chairs in the centre of the glasshouse.

Ash was used to playing to large audiences, and had no fear of public speaking, but in front of this group of kids she had to force confidence into her voice.

"Okay, if you two could stop killing each other and take a seat, that would be great."

The boys disentangled themselves, the bigger one red-faced and grinning. He was a sleekit youth of about fourteen, with acne on his cheeks and a few wispy hairs on his chin. She turned and noticed a painfully thin girl with dyed purple hair and a nose ring scowling at the boys.

She settled herself onto a chair and smiled at the girl. "Okay, so, my name is Ash," she started. "Like you, I was a resident here. That was a long time ago, but the cooking hasn't improved much judging by the smell."

The girl with the nose ring smiled encouragement, but the rest of the children were sullen.

"So," Ash continued, "can any of you play an instrument?"

"Naw, but you can play with my instrument any day," the acne-faced boy said. He nudged his pal and they chortled like hyenas.

"Grow up, Shuggie!" the nose-ring girl snarled.

"Bite me, Lilly!" he leered, grabbing his crotch.

Shuggie reminded her of boys who'd pawed at her when she'd first arrived here, twelve and still in shock from the Accident that had killed her parents. She'd been confused, angry, vulnerable, and they'd taken advantage. But then she'd stabbed Joshua with a fork after he'd felt her up in the dinner hall. They didn't bother her after that. Now, seventeen years later, watching these spotty youths laugh at this lassie, her anger returned.

"That's enough!"

Her voice was like a whip and the boys fell instantly silent. She glared at the troublemaker. He folded his arms and stared back at her, an insolent scowl on his face.

"Shuggie, is it?" she said. "Bet you think you're the big man around here, aye?"

He gave a one-shouldered shrug, chin jutting out belligerently.

"I knew boys like you when I lived here. Bullies. Cowards." Shuggie's glare faltered under her intense stare. He looked away and Ash savoured the small victory. "It didn't work out well for them on the outside, Hugh," she continued, intentionally using the less colloquial form of his name. "Lilly's right, you need to grow up. Fast."

Her warning sucked the heat from the room. Everyone was suddenly very interested in the tiled floor. Everyone but Lilly, who smiled at Ash in awestruck admiration.

"Look," Ash said, softening her tone, "I know it's not easy living here. When I first arrived, they christened me the One-Girl Wrecking Ball because I liked to smash stuff up. Angry wee thing, I was. But then I met a wonderful lady." Her fingers tapped the neck of the clarsach. "She taught me to play this, and many other things besides. I wouldn't be here today without her. I'd be in Cornton Vale. Or dead."

Heads slowly lifted. She knew she had their attention now. She strummed a few notes on the clarsach.

"Music kept me sane in here," she said, almost to herself. "It stopped me destroying things. Stopped me destroying myself."

She smiled, her eyes scanning the youthful faces in front of her. *Poor kids who'd been dealt a shitty hand*, she reminded herself. Even Shuggie.

"Right, who wants a go first?"

CHAPTER 19

ANGUS sat in the mortuary car park, knuckles turning white as he squeezed the Land Rover's steering wheel. He glanced in the rearview mirror and saw Faye sitting in the back seat, which was normally reserved for criminals, watching him curiously. She pulled up the collar of her tweed riding jacket and shivered.

"Well, that was fucking horrible," she said. "When I came to Scotland at the start of the summer, I never thought I'd end up with a ringside seat at my own autopsy."

"I'm sorry," he muttered.

"Yeah, yeah, you're sorry. You wish you'd done more."

"What do you want me to do?"

"Well, find my killer, of course."

"That would be easier if you told me who that was."

Her laughter filled the cab, a fraction off-key.

"You know it doesn't work like that, Constable MacNeil. We're not even real."

"We?"

"I've met them, you know? The burned guy, the woman, the little boy." She gave him a thin smile. "They say your fingernails keep growing after death, so I got Barbara to paint mine." She wiggled her fingers at him in the mirror. "What d'ya think? Black seemed fitting."

He ground his teeth.

Faye's smile faltered. "They need answers too, Constable."

"Then tell me! Tell me who did this to you? Who was it? Who was dressed as the Dark One?"

"How can I, if I'm not real?"

He spun round, but Faye was gone.

"Christ's sake," he muttered, turning back to face the front. At the entrance to the mortuary Nadia was on her mobile, no doubt talking to Ruthven Crowley, filling him in on all the gruesome details. He wanted nothing more to do with the investigation, yet his brain churned over the details of the autopsy. Who would have access to deer sinew and the butchery skills to extract it? A stalker like Ewan, maybe? Although anyone with access to YouTube could learn how to do it. The more relevant question was why use sinew in the first place? And why put Faye's head underwater after she was already dead?

Suddenly the police radio crackled into life and he heard the rough-edged voice of Marion Muirhead, M&M, as she was affectionately known.

"Control tae all units. We've a report of dogs attacking sheep up at old Rankin's croft. Can anyone attend?"

Angus ignored the request, hoping a colleague would pick it up, which they duly did.

Although he'd found Faye's body on the seashore, her top half had been soaked in fresh water. He already suspected this was a deposition spot—the lack of footprints suggested as much—so she must have been killed near a loch, river, or burn. But where? If there was one thing the Highlands didn't lack, it was water.

He watched Nadia end her call and pick her way through slushy deposits of snow towards the Land Rover. She climbed in beside him, bringing a blast of cold air with her.

"Who were you talking to?"

He stared at her for a long beat. "No one."

"First sign of madness, talking to yourself. Or is it hairy palms, I can never remember. . . ."

"Eh? Nah, I mean, it was Control, looking for a unit to attend some sheep-related incident."

She cocked an eyebrow.

"I know," he said, firing up the engine, "cliché or what? Right, where to now?"

"Crowley wants us to speak to Eleanor Chichester. Ryan has already pulled the CCTV from Dunbirlinn Castle and gone through it. Faye left the castle just before ten, and nobody else went out after, so that effectively rules Lady Chichester out as a suspect, but we need to talk to her anyway."

"Mrs MacCrimmon told me yesterday that Eleanor and Faye hated each other. Maybe we shouldn't dismiss her entirely?"

"Fair point. There might be another way out of the castle, not covered by CCTV, a secret tunnel or something."

"Aye, or maybe you've read too much Agatha Christie."

Mrs MacCrimmon greeted them at Dunbirlinn, her expression as cold as that of the stag heads that sprouted from the wood-panelled walls. "Lady Chichester is waiting for you in the drawing room. Follow me please."

He felt the eyes of Dòmhnall MacRuari, the Druid, following him from his gilt-framed portrait. The chieftain's face was lined and cruel, his mouth a perpetual scowl. It was the eyes, though, that were really disconcerting. Even centuries after the portrait was painted, his dark orbs glinted with a strange, malignant power.

Angus fell into step behind Mrs. MacCrimmon. Her heels beat a staccato rhythm on the wooden floor as she led them down a draughty corridor.

"How's Ewan?" he asked the housekeeper in Gaelic.

Mrs MacCrimmon glanced at him over her shoulder. "Hungover, no doubt."

"And the laird?"

"With his wolves. Seems to spend all day up there with them."

They reached the end of the corridor and Mrs. MacCrimmon turned sharply to the left into a wide rectangular hallway with a mosaic floor. The tiles snaked around the hallway in knotted patterns, framing creatures at each of the four quadrants—a deer, a peacock, a wildcat, and an eagle. In the middle of the floor, bordered by an intricately decorated circle, was a snarling wolf surrounded by tongues of flame. Light flooded in through a large arched window at the end of the hallway, making the floor shimmer like a page from an illuminated gospel.

Mrs MacCrimmon raised her bony knuckles and rapped on a stout wooden door, the sound echoing around the cavernous space. Without waiting for a reply, she pushed open the door and stepped inside.

Eleanor Chichester was sprawled on a plush damask chaise longue, framed in the large bay window of Dunbirlinn's drawing room. She wore a loose plaid shirt, leggings, and faux fur slippers. She clutched a glass of what looked like bourbon, and her mascara had run, making her look like a sad clown. *Did she dress for a role?* he wondered, following Mrs. MacCrimmon into the room.

"Police to see you, Lady Chichester," the housekeeper said, tone tiptoeing around the insolent.

"Yes, Mary, I can see that," she said. "You can go now."

Mrs MacCrimmon spun on her heel and marched from the room, but not before giving Angus what he interpreted as a warning look.

Eleanor gave him a watery smile. "Constable MacNeil, nice to see you again."

"Aye, well, sorry it's not in better circumstances." He shuffled awkwardly, then remembered his manners. "Lady Chichester, this is DI Sharif from the major investigation team. We'd like to ask you some questions, if that's okay?"

"Sure. Please, take a seat," Eleanor said, gesturing to an antique sofa with carved wooden armrests and gold-leaf upholstery. He lowered himself gently onto the sofa, as if afraid he might damage it. The room was well appointed, with a high ceiling, thick cornicing, and a beautiful marble fireplace. Light from the window bounced off gilt-framed paintings, a baroque mirror, and a crystal chandelier, but was swallowed by the wood-panelled walls and doughty furniture. The room, which should have been airy and bright, instead felt dark and claustrophobic, as if the opulent furnishings were sucking up all the light.

Nadia crossed one leg over the other and clasped her knee. "I appreciate this is a difficult time for you, Lady Chichester. Constable MacNeil tells me you were—quite understandably—not up to speaking to us yesterday."

Eleanor eyed Nadia suspiciously, her high cheekbones lending her a somewhat haughty demeanour. "You don't expect this kind of thing to happen in the Highlands."

"No, you don't," Nadia agreed.

"Do you have any . . . leads?" She chewed the word, as if suddenly aware how bizarre it sounded.

"It's early days, but yes, we're following a number of lines of inquiry."

Ice clinked as Eleanor sipped her bourbon, hand shaking.

"In the days leading up to the incident, how did Faye seem to you?" Nadia asked. "Was she worried about something? Did you notice anything out of the ordinary?"

Eleanor swung her slippers onto the parquet floor and cradled the glass, elbows on knees, like a hermit crab in its shell. "Myself and Faye tended to stay out of each other's way."

"I see. And why was that?"

Eleanor gave Nadia an even stare. "Do you have children, DI Sharif?"

"No."

Her gaze flicked towards him. "What about you, Angus?"

He shook his head, noting her flawless transition to first-name terms. "Not yet."

"Not yet?" She cocked an eyebrow. When he didn't respond, she let out a humourless laugh. "Never wanted children myself. I know women are supposed to crave a family, but I've never developed that maternal instinct.

Perhaps it's in the genes: my own mother abandoned me when I was ten—ran off with an insurance salesman, of all things."

She took another sip of bourbon, then stared down into the glass, as if looking for answers. "I was a failing actress sliding towards obscurity when James rescued me. We met at one of those awful gala dinners rich people host to feel benevolent. I'd partaken liberally of the vodka punch—was making a bit of a fool of myself, truth be told. He held me up, took me outside, fed me coffee to sober me up. He was . . . kind." She glanced up sharply. "You don't get many rich, powerful men who are kind, in my experience."

She gave another tremulous smile. "Anyway, I was flattered. But looking back, I think he took pity on me. James likes broken things. And I was one of his pet projects, just like these damn wolves."

Angus gave Nadia a sidelong glance. "You were saying, about Faye?" Nadia prompted.

"Faye"—Eleanor shook her head sadly—"was . . . difficult. Sullen, uncommunicative, sarcastic. Oh, at first I went out of my way to ingratiate myself with her. I had this naive vision of us becoming close. She was going to be the daughter I never had."

She gave a bitter laugh. "I even tried to take an interest in her stupid horses, despite being allergic to the fuckers. But Faye didn't give me a chance. As far as she was concerned, I was a gold-digging whore and nothing I said or did would change her mind. In the end, we came to an agreement to be cordial around James."

"And he never realized?" Nadia asked.

Angus recalled how defensive Chichester had been when he suggested his wife and daughter were at loggerheads. Perhaps, on some level, the laird knew but didn't want to admit it. So Chichester had deceived himself into believing everything was okay when it wasn't. Just as he had.

"We all wear masks, don't you think, DI Sharif? Being able to hide our true feelings is the mark of a civilized society. What would happen if we told people exactly what we thought of them? Anarchy, that's what."

"How do we know you're not wearing a mask now?"

She fixed Nadia with a hard glare. "You don't."

Nadia faked a smile then reached into her pocket and took out her phone. She tapped the screen and brought up a picture of the clay corpse.

"Have you ever seen anything like this?" she asked, holding out the phone for Eleanor to see.

Her eyes barely looked at the picture before she shook her head. "Nope. Why do you ask?"

Nadia said nothing, sliding her phone back into her pocket.

Eleanor's eyes had suddenly become glassy. Angus recalled how distraught she'd been when Chichester had told her about Faye's death. He cleared his throat. "We're sorry, Lady Chichester. I realize this is difficult."

She sniffed, as if annoyed to reveal a crack in her mask. "James loved that girl more than anything. I fear the news will destroy him. He's not well, you know?"

"The laird is ill?"

"He has cancer."

"I'm sorry," he said. "I had no idea—"

"Well, you wouldn't; he hasn't told anyone."

He pictured the laird on their first meeting, effortlessly suave and brimming with vim and vigour. "He seems in robust health."

"Perhaps, but every day I wake up worried this will be our last together. You see, despite what my late stepdaughter believed, I don't care about his money. All this"—she raised her glass to the opulent surroundings—"means nothing to me. I'd trade it all in an instant if I knew James and I could live another twenty years together."

Eleanor's eyes welled up, but were they real or fake tears? he wondered.

"What's the laird's prognosis?"

"He was diagnosed with pancreatic cancer not long after we started dating. The doctors said it was well advanced—*distant* is the word they use, meaning it had spread to other organs. They told him there was no chance the disease would go into remission. He was given twelve to eighteen months, tops."

She shot him a watery gaze. "That was ten years ago."

Angus glanced at Nadia, baffled.

Eleanor's chin began to wobble. "You've no idea. It's awful—waking up each day and not knowing. At first James withdrew into himself, but as the days and weeks passed and he was still okay, he became his old self again. A better self, even. I've tried to make an appointment for him, but he simply refuses to see any more quacks, as he calls them. I think James believes if he goes back to the doctors, his health will fail. Like a self-fulfilling prophecy."

She shook her head and let out a sigh that rippled down her whole body. "I'm sorry," she said. "You're here to talk about Faye, I know. But, really, there's not much I can tell you. The girl simply wouldn't let me in."

"What about boyfriends?" Nadia asked. "I know you said you weren't close, but did you see her with anyone?"

Eleanor nodded slowly to herself, again cupping the glass. "There was an incident on Friday evening."

Angus narrowed his eyes. "Friday evening? Why didn't you mention this before?"

Eleanor's shoulders sagged. "To be honest, I'd forgotten all about it until now."

"That's okay," Nadia said. "What happened?"

"Well, after dinner, James dismissed Mrs. MacCrimmon for the evening, so I was forced to venture down to the wine cellar myself. I was passing close by the pantry when I heard raised voices. I glanced through the door and saw Faye arguing with that brute of a ghillie—"

"Ewan Hunter?" Angus blurted out.

"Hunter, yeah, that's the guy. So here's the thing, Angus. I saw him grab Faye and try to kiss her. I say 'try' because Faye dodged out of his way. Then she slapped him."

She smiled faintly, and when she next spoke there was a note of pride in her voice. "Caught him a beaut."

CHAPTER 20

NADIA thudded the side of her fist against the door of Ewan Hunter's cottage, a proper police officer's knock. Nothing stirred inside. She pushed open the letter box and brought her mouth to the gap.

"Ewan Hunter, it's the police! Open up!"

After the state Ewan had been in the previous night, Angus was surprised the ghillie was still breathing, let alone up and about.

"His jeep's gone," he said. "Come on, let's ask after him at the stables."

Nadia gave the door a last, frustrated rap, then turned away. They marched around the side of the building, then across the courtyard with its ornate fountain. Nadia, having already updated Crowley on what Eleanor had witnessed, took out her phone and placed another call.

"He's not home, Ruthven," she said, without preamble.

Angus could not hear the other side of the conversation, but he saw Nadia nodding along.

"Aye, will do. If anyone's seen him, I'll let you know."

She cut the call and glanced at him. "Tell me about Ewan Hunter, Angus."

"I've known him my whole life. Coached him shinty when he was a boy, then we played on the same team up until a couple of years ago. He's a nice lad at heart, but shy, socially awkward. He left school at sixteen, although he was clever enough, always had his head buried in a book. He was at college in Inverness for a while, some game management course, but he packed it in before graduating. Not that he really had much to learn. His dad was the ghillie at Kilcreggan for decades, and what John Hunter didn't know about wildlife management wasn't worth knowing. Ewan was following in his father's footsteps."

"You say he *was* following in his dad's footsteps—what happened?"

Angus let out a long sigh. "Eighteen months ago John Hunter took a heart attack while out deer stalking. Ewan was with him. He watched him die. After that he hit the bottle hard. Started winding people up, getting in fights. I arrested him a few months back. Caught him beating up his mum's new boyfriend outside a pub in Silvaig. Gave the guy a real pasting. He was lucky—got off with a fine and community service. It's fair to say we've not been on such good terms since then."

"So he has a temper."

"He was drunk." He glanced at her and shrugged. "I know, that's no excuse. To be honest, I was surprised he and Faye were friends."

"Why?"

"They just . . . come from very different worlds."

"So did we."

They walked in strained silence into the stable block. "Nadia, I don't think Ewan is capable of murder, I really don't."

"We're all capable given the right circumstances—isn't that what you said to Crowley last night?"

Had he really said that?

"Fair point," he muttered. "I suppose I don't want it to be him."

"Christ, Angus! We're a long way from that yet. We have a witness—one I don't trust, incidentally—who says she saw Faye slap Ewan. That's it. We need to speak to him. He could have a pure belter of an alibi."

A faint smile flitted across his face.

"Pure belter? Don't get all technical on me, Nadia."

She grinned at him as they marched past the first set of gleaming mahogany-panelled stalls. Nadia paused at one of the doors and glanced in at the white horse they had found yesterday at the commune. After being checked over by the vet, the decision had been taken to stable her at Dunbirlinn until her owners were found. Angus knew that was a futile task. This *was* Bessie. She'd responded when he'd said the phrase Faye had used to calm her down. Somehow her coat had turned white overnight.

The horse plodded over to the door and let Nadia stroke her neck.

"Who knew you had a way with horses?" Nadia said. "You said something to her, didn't you? What was it?"

"Ach, nothing," he croaked. "An old Comanche trick, that's all."

Footsteps at the far end of the stable saved him from further interrogation. They turned as a figure pushing a wheelbarrow appeared from the tack room. The person let out a startled cry.

In the dim light, it took Angus a second to recognise Nualla Abbot, his friend Grant's wife. She wore muddy Wellington boots and a man's waxproof jacket, her long hair tucked under a peaked cap. But even dressed in man's clothing she couldn't hide her beauty. Today, though, her eyes looked red-rimmed and tired.

"Hi, Nualla," he said. "Sorry to creep up on you."

Nualla tucked a stray lock of dark hair under her cap. "It's okay, Angus. I've been a nervous wreck recently."

"The baby keeping you up?"

"God, aye! It gets better, right?"

"I wouldn't know," he replied.

Nualla winced slightly, as if aware she'd put her foot in it: she and Ash were friends, so it seemed clear his wife had discussed their problems conceiving.

"This is my colleague, DI Sharif," he said. "We're looking for Ewan Hunter—have you seen him this morning?"

"Aye, saw him a couple of hours ago heading in the direction of the clootie tree. I think he sets snares in the woods down there."

"Cheers, Nualla, we'll go and check. He's probably sleeping off a hangover somewhere, though. Which reminds me—how's Grant's head this morning?"

Her smile didn't quite reach her eyes. "Sore, Angus. Actually, I'd better get back before Rosie needs another feed." She propped the wheelbarrow up against one of the stalls. "Tell your missus to pay us a visit, eh?"

"Aye, will do."

She flashed Nadia a tired smile, then turned and walked towards the rear exit.

"Angus," Nadia said. "What's a clootie tree?"

He gave her a sidelong glance. "Come on, I'll show you."

The gabbling stream sounded like old women arguing. A dipper flitted low across the torrent and perched on a moss-covered rock. The water gushed down towards the sea, swollen by melting snow. He remembered paddling in this stream when he was a child, a bandy net in his hand, his mother lounging on the bank wearing a wide-brimmed hat as he tried, unsuccessfully, to net small trout. That hat. Gathering dust in the attic now, along with the rest of her clothes. Would he ever go up there and get rid of her stuff?

He drew in a long breath, picking out the scents of loamy soil, rotten leaves, and something sickly sweet, as if a dead sheep were decomposing somewhere nearby. The snow had by now turned to mush and his feet made a horrible sucking sound as he trampled the husks of conkers, acorns, and beechnuts into the claggy mud. He thought of Faye's caved-in skull and felt his stomach twist.

The path along the bank of the stream narrowed, fringed on either side by bramble and blackthorn thickets, still but for the odd darting shadow of small birds. Soon, though, the path opened out into a large clearing, about fifty yards in circumference, covered in patches of snow.

The clootie tree stood on its own, as if the other trees were scared to go near it. An ancient, gnarled ash, it clawed from the earth like the hand of an old woman at the point where two smaller burns gushed down the hillside to join the larger stream. Strips of colourful rags hung limp from the tree's branches like flayed skin.

He felt a shiver course through his whole body as he approached the tree. Nadia reached up and traced her fingers across the rags. "What *is* this?"

Angus had a sudden visceral image of the branches twisting around her arm, then curling around her body and pulling her towards a knotted maw in its trunk. He resisted the urge to yank her away.

It's only a tree, you eejit!

He stepped up beside her. "It's known as a clootie tree. According to Gills, this has been a place of pilgrimage for centuries, millennia even. In pre-Christian times, votive offerings were made to local deities. These beliefs were then absorbed by Christianity, only instead of water sprites and goddesses, they honoured saints."

He looked up at the fleshy strips of cloth. "These rags are linked to an ancient healing ritual. You're supposed to dip one of these cloots in the sacred well and then tie it to the tree. As the rag disintegrates, your ailment fades."

"Have you ever tried it?"

He had. So many times.

He shook his head. "Paracetamol or antibiotics usually work for me."

"Sure, but no harm in giving it a go, eh?"

From her pocket she produced a handkerchief. She gave the material a swift yank and it came apart. She handed him a section then climbed down the bank and dipped the rag in a glassy pool. He hesitated, unsettled. The rags on the tree fluttered as if alive, and for an instant he thought he could hear faint whispering. He strained his ears, but although the words sounded vaguely Gaelic, he could not make them out.

"Angus."

He started at the sound of his name. Nadia was frowning at him, the wet rag held in her hand. "You okay?"

"Aye, fine." He slid down the bank, then dunked the rag in the burn, the water so cold that it felt as if he'd been bitten.

"Christ! That water's freezing."

Nadia grinned at him. "Don't be a baby. Come on. . . ."

He scrambled back up the bank and stood next to Nadia to tie his rag to a low-lying branch, just as he'd tied red ribbons to the Christmas tree with his mother when he was a child. He fancied he could smell pine resin and cinnamon from the cakes his mother used to bake, but the memory was fleeting, gone before he could catch it, like the trout darting away from his bandy net. He yanked the knot tight on his rag and stood back.

"So, Angus, what did you ask to be cured?"

"Old shinty injury," he lied. "You?"

"Broken heart." He met her gold-flecked eyes, not sure whether she was being serious or not. A sudden blast from her mobile phone broke the spell. She turned away from him and fished the device from her pocket.

"Hi, Ruthven."

She began to walk away, the phone pressed to her ear.

"Nope, no sign of him yet."

He took one last look up into the tree. The rags dangled like slithers of rotten meat from the branches. He felt that familiar tingle of apprehension, as if an army of ants were crawling across his shoulder blades.

Suddenly he heard the sound of horses' hooves and an obscene gargle. He closed his eyes, wincing in pain as a series of images flashed into his head. He saw a chain biting into pale white ankles. A bloodied body hoisted into the air. The obsidian eye of a crow.

Then nothing but flames.

CHAPTER 21

THE old barman in the Clan Ranald stared at Nadia with rheumy eyes. He fiddled with an ancient hearing aid that was roughly the size of a satellite dish. Angus imagined he could pick up the whispers of the dead with it, yet he was having trouble hearing Nadia a foot away.

"Whit's that ye were saying, hen?"

"Have. You. Seen. Ewan. Hunter?"

The barman nodded along, slack-jawed. "Eh?" he replied after a too-long wait.

"Come on, Jamesey," Angus said, "everyone knows you can hear perfectly fine."

The barman knitted his wrinkly brow. "Eh?"

"Maybe a wee visit this Saturday night to check the ID of your customers would clear the wax from your ears?"

Jamesey grinned, showing a row of yellowing teeth. "There's nae need fir that, Gus. I wiz only havin' a laugh."

"Aye, hilarious, Jamesey," he said, growing tired of this. "Have you seen Ewan or not?"

The barman scratched his dimpled chin, as if deep in thought. "Naw," he said at last. "Barred him a few weeks back. He was pissin' off ma regulars."

Angus glanced at Nadia, but she was already turning for the door of the dingy pub. He shook his head at Jamesey, whose grin only lengthened, then followed Nadia outside. She had her phone pressed to her ear.

"We've been in every pub, lounge bar, and shebeen between Silvaig and Glenruig. No one's seen him, Ruthven. Could be he's out in the hills, shooting poor defenceless deer, or beating up grouse, or whatever the hell it is ghillies do."

A smile crept across her face. "Aye, I know it's cold. They breed them hardy up here." She glanced at Angus and rolled her eyes. "Aye, he'll probably be home later. We asked the housekeeper to phone when he gets back."

Nadia was silent for a few seconds, nodding along. "No problem," she said. "We're on the way."

She cut the call and smiled up at him.

"So?" he asked, drawing out the word.

"Take me to church."

The Free Presbyterian Church was little more than a barn clinging to the edge of Reverend John MacVannin's croft. The walls were rough stone and seriously in need of repointing if the crumbling mortar was anything to go by; the door was warped oak pocked with metal studs; and the roof rusting corrugated iron the colour of an infected scab. A steep, rocky hillside loomed over the church, casting it in shadow. The minister's crofthouse sat, unloved, at the edge of the sheep field, surrounded by ramshackle sheds, the rusting bones of farm machinery, and the fank.

Angus thought of the rusty chain biting into the ankles of the body he'd seen in his vision. It had seemed so real. He'd heard the flames devouring the corpse, had smelt the acrid stench of charred flesh. Why was this happening again, after so long? Why weren't the pills working?

He stared balefully at the black-faced sheep gnawing the sparse grass. Tufts of their wool and scraps of black polythene clung to a barbed-wire fence surrounding the field. Six or seven cars belonging to MacVannin's parishioners were parked nearby.

"Is that the church?" Nadia asked, incredulous.

"Aye. Lacks a bit of grandeur."

"It's no Glasgow Central Mosque, that's for sure."

"Maybe it's nicer inside."

"Doubt it," she replied, reaching for the door handle. A blast of cold air smacked him on the face as he climbed out of the Land Rover and followed Nadia. A crow was perched on the arm of a rusted iron cross bolted above the door of the church. It hopped back and forth, observing him with eyes as black as tar. It opened its beak, but the caw, rather than coming from the bird, seemed to come from inside his head. A heartbeat later he heard the sound of pounding hooves. He whipped his head round, half-expecting to see a horse galloping towards him, but the only animals in sight were MacVannin's sheep, gnawing at the grass.

He turned back to the church, and his breath caught in his throat. He froze, staring wide-eyed up at the cross. The crow was gone. In its place hung a body, chained by its ankles to the cross. There was no wind, but the corpse swayed as if tugged by currents of air. Rivulets of blood coursed down the contours of the body and plummeted to the ground. Angus tasted vomit at the back of his throat. His stomach spasmed. He doubled over, but the feeling of nausea quickly passed. He glanced back up at the cross, but the corpse had gone. He closed his eyes and tried to still the beating of his heart.

You're losing it, pal. Get a fucking grip!

He swallowed. His saliva somehow tasted of smoke and blood. He ground his teeth and trudged after Nadia. She hadn't seen the episode. But how long would that luck last?

Reverend MacVannin's haranguing voice seeped out of the church, becoming louder when Nadia shoved open the door. Heads twisted in their direction as he and Nadia slipped inside, but MacVannin's tirade continued unabated, his black robes flapping as he strutted, like the crow outside.

"Demons seek out idolaters because their souls are fertile ground to sow the seeds of violence," MacVannin snarled, his eyes bulging. "Look no further than the horrific crime that has befallen our community. This is what happens when idolaters are allowed—nay, encouraged—to take root. I refer to the so-called pagan commune, that hotbed of sin and debauchery that grows unchecked in our midst."

MacVannin's head looked like a turnip lantern left to rot on the doorstep, the features sinking into one another. Everything about his body was disproportionate: thick blubbery lips, but tiny fluted ears; wide powerful shoulders, but a cinched waist. One leg looked shorter than the other, which made him walk with an odd, rolling bowlegged gait, as if he'd soiled himself. Whenever Angus saw him, out tending his sheep, or driving his ancient Massey Ferguson tractor, MacVannin reminded him of an ogre from one of Gills's fairy tales.

Angus slid into an unoccupied pew beside Nadia. Icy draughts surged through nooks and crannies in the roof and walls. His eyes darted upwards. No ceiling frescos here, only rusty corrugated iron stretched across a skeleton of worn timber joists and rafters. Loose skeins of cobweb billowed in the breeze like tormented wraiths.

The congregation, barely twenty people, sat cocooned in scarves, although hats were forbidden. He noticed Raymond the Waver sitting in the second row, nodding enthusiastically to everything MacVannin said. Raymond worked as a greenkeeper at Traigh golf course, but Angus frequently saw him standing at the crossroads in Arisaig, bicycle propped against a nearby tree, waving to passing cars. Folk made allowances for him.

Next to the Waver sat Elspeth Cummings, a cheerful, stylish woman of about sixty who owned a craft shop in Silvaig. He was surprised to see her here. She didn't seem the fire-and-brimstone type. Nor did the elderly gentleman sitting behind her. Jim Gavin was a retired maths teacher who made radio-controlled model boats, replicas of warships and frigates that he displayed in the bay at community events. Angus sometimes met Jim walking his two golden retrievers along the shore. A pleasant guy, he would always stop for a natter about the latest village gossip or the fortunes of the local shinty team. The subject of God never cropped up in their conversations. Who knew that behind Jim's friendly exterior lurked a belief in what Angus could only describe as a doomsday cult? Why were all these people here? he wondered.

He heard his father's voice in his head, bitter and sarcastic: *If God does exist, he's got a twisted sense of humour. Either that, or he's a bloody sociopath.*

"Judgement Day is upon us," MacVannin declared, voice rising. "The Devil and his imps are everywhere. They are relentless in their quest to bring about the downfall of mankind. They play on our base desires, with a set of temptations tailored to each and every one of us." His eyes darted from the Waver to Elspeth to Jim Gavin and the other worshippers. "Money. Sex. Power. Materialism. Homosexuality. Drugs. Pornography. These are the chips demons use to gain entry to our soul so that they might overpower us and possess us!"

As if on cue, a faint rumble followed the minister's declaration. Angus wondered if someone, his wife, perhaps, was hidden out back with a tape recorder full of sound effects that she pressed at the appropriate juncture of the sermon. There was something kitsch about MacVannin's performance, as if he'd taken lessons from an American TV evangelist.

The minister locked eyes with Angus, as if he could read his scepticism. "Beware of false prophets who come to you in sheep's clothing but inwardly are ravenous wolves," he growled.

The rumbling noise came again, louder this time. It was not a sound effect, and the storm was closer. A few of the worshippers glanced at one another, frowning. Angus sensed a subtle shift in the barn, a collective anxiety. Storms had not been forecast, and besides, it was far too cold for thunder, wasn't it?

"Even now they prowl amongst us looking for someone to devour!" MacVannin roared, oblivious to the rumbling. The Waver was now nodding so hard, he was almost bouncing. "But He will strike back; He will punish those who follow false Gods, those who unleash the wolves!"

A fine shower of dust landed on Angus's thighs. He glanced up at the ceiling. Was the corrugated iron roof shaking slightly?

"We must fight this evil, we all must—"

The rumble came once more, so loud this time that it stopped MacVannin mid-flow. Angus felt a tremor ripple up his legs. He sprang to his feet and scrambled from the pew. "Everyone out!" he bellowed. "Now! Get out!"

The nearest parishioners jumped up, as if his words had sent an electric shock through their bodies. He grabbed the nearest man by the arm and thrust him towards the door. Over his shoulder, he saw Nadia staring at him with wide, fearful eyes. "Rockfall!" he yelled.

Around him, people began scrambling over pews towards the exit as the first rock smashed into the roof of the church. The noise reverberated around the barn like an explosion. Elspeth Cummings screamed like a banshee. Her usual politeness forgotten, she clawed past an old couple, causing the woman to fall on the floor. More rocks rained down on the roof. A section of the corrugated iron collapsed, the sound of shearing metal like a human cry. The old woman was being trampled by those behind. Angus shouldered through the fleeing worshippers and yanked the old woman to her feet. He dragged her towards the door, adrenaline making her body seem as light as dust. Another rock smashed through the roof and landed on the exact spot the old woman had lain. He pushed the woman outside and turned. MacVannin was nowhere to be seen, but Raymond the Waver was still inside. He stood amongst the carnage, smiling as if this were all some game.

"Raymond!" he shouted. "Raymond! Get out!"

The Waver did not respond.

"Ach, bugger!" Angus growled. He glanced at Nadia. She was the only one looking back towards the church. Everyone else was running for safety. Their eyes met, briefly, then he turned and ducked back inside the church. Great holes had been punched in the ceiling by the falling rocks and part of the gable wall had collapsed. The timber spine of the building was still intact, but wooden ribs hung from the roof, splintered and broken. He vaulted over smashed pews and darted down the central aisle. The air was thick with dust. It swirled around him like ash, making him choke. He hacked and coughed, and the sound made him realize the rumbling had stopped. The rockfall might have ended, but an ominous creaking suggested the building was close to collapse, a boxer who'd taken too many punches.

"Raymond," he hissed, grabbing the man by the shoulder. The Waver's head jerked round. His neatly side-parted hair was covered in a layer of dust. He grinned, then gave a weird, hiccuppy laugh. "God isnae happy wi' us."

Angus dragged him towards the aisle. They both stopped and glanced up at the roof. The whole building seemed to quiver. "Quick!" he yelled, thrusting the Waver down the aisle. He heard a rumbling, then, louder this time, more ferocious. The volume intensified, until it sounded like massed ranks of cavalry charging an enemy position. His heart pounded in his chest as he followed Raymond's shambling figure towards the door. He was almost there when a thick timber joist swung from the ceiling and caught the Waver a glancing blow. He went down hard. Angus scrambled over to him. Blood poured from a cut on Raymond's head. Angus saw the Waver's leg was trapped under the joist. He crouched and took hold of the coarse timber, but when he tried to lift the joist, it wouldn't budge. Out of the corner of his eye, he saw another section of wall collapse. Only seconds remained before the structure would buckle and the roof would cave in. He desperately worked his fingers further under the joist, then pulled with all his might. Nothing happened. He gritted his teeth and let out an agonized cry, drawing on every last vestige of his strength. The joist moved: a centimetre, an inch, three inches . . . enough for Raymond to free his leg. The Waver, though, just lay there, grinning.

Spittle flew from Angus's lips as he yelled: "Move! Your! Fucking! Leg!"

Raymond finally got the message and pulled his leg free as Angus's strength gave out. He whipped his hands away and the joist cracked to the floor in a puff of dust. He grabbed the fallen man by his lapels, hauled him to his feet, and half-carried, half-dragged him from the crumbling building.

They ran across the muddy ground, entwined like children competing in a three-legged race on school sports day. Angus chanced a quick look over his shoulder. Huge boulders, scree, and mud surged down the hillside. Suddenly the sheer cliff behind the church collapsed, like a condemned high-rise destroyed by explosives. A giant fist of rock smashed down on top of the church, pulverizing it into the ground.

Raymond the Waver gave another hiccuppy laugh and repeated himself, an echo unaware of its origin. "God isnae happy wi' us."

CHAPTER 22

GILLS watched the nurse flit around Uisdean MacNeil, chirping inanities.

"That's it, good man yourself. Let's get this TV on for you. *Countdown* should be on soon. You like that one, don't you? Not the same since Carol Vorderman left, mind you . . ."

She gave Gills a conspiratorial smile over Uisdean's tartan-robed shoulder. He smiled back, but this nurse—Lesley—grated on him; she spoke to Uisdean as if he were a child. The Uisdean he knew would have detested Lesley's relentless cheeriness. He would have much preferred the surly boredom of the other nurse—Catriona—who treated all the residents with the same detached indifference.

The nurse struggled to manoeuvre Uisdean from his bed onto the stain-resistant chair in front of the television. Gills took his friend's arm, noting how thin he'd become.

"That's the good fellow," the nurse said, placing a hand on Uisdean's shoulder and pushing him down. At first Uisdean's limbs resisted, but then he slumped onto the chair.

"Thank you, Lesley," Gills said. "You're a saint."

"Och!" She swatted away the compliment and bustled from the room.

His smile dropped. He reached for the remote and turned off the TV as the credits for *Countdown* began.

He stared at Uisdean, but his brown eyes that had once shone like ripe chestnuts were dull and lifeless, stripped of their lustre. They seemed to stare, unseeing, at a painting of Ben Nevis across Loch Linnhe that hung on the wall to the left of the TV.

"Your mob lost again yesterday," Gills said. "Thumped five nil by Kilmallie at Pairc nan Laoch. Could do with a new goalkeeper by all accounts."

He nodded to himself. "I know, I know, you don't care about the shinty scores. You want to hear about Angus."

He rubbed his sandpaper jaw. He'd forgotten to shave this morning. Standards were slipping. "I'm worried about him, old bean. A girl was killed. He found her body. Blames himself, of course. I told him there was nothing he could have done, but you know what he's like."

He heard again Uisdean's dry laugh. *Aye, he's a stubborn wee bugger, like me.*

"True." Gills sighed. "Ach, I knew it would happen sooner or later. Those pills he's been taking couldn't work indefinitely. He's at a crossroads now, though. And I don't want to lose him again. You know me, I'm not given to melodrama, but I have a feeling this murder is the start of something. I sense it, a kind of stirring."

He held up a hand. "I know what you're going to say: that I'm talking a load of old bollocks. But not everything can be explained and categorized, Uisdean. Feelings, emotions— and, yes, senses—are as valid as rational thought."

He pictured Uisdean cocking an eyebrow the way he used to. *That's a bit rich coming from a historian. I thought you lot dealt in facts?*

"All history is fiction," he said. "At best, all historians can do is present a facsimile of events and try to impose some sort of order on the chaos. That's what I've tried to do with Angus, but in truth, it should have been you, Uisdean MacNeil. You're a good man, but you let the lad down. When he needed your help, you pushed him away. You told him he was crazy, that it was all in his head. You knew it wasn't. He thinks he's cursed, and maybe he is, but he's not crazy. He's never got over that. For years he's been in limbo: a believer who's too scared to believe."

He clamped his mouth shut, surprised by the shake in his voice. He laid a palm on Uisdean's forearm. Blue veins forked across the back of his friend's skeletal hands, the skin stretched tight over his bones. He'd been good with his hands, Uisdean. Dexterous. Could tie a mean salmon fly and when his Ford Anglia had needed a new carburettor, it was Uisdean who had fitted it, doing a better job than most mechanics. Now his hands lay on the armrests of the vomit-coloured chair, shrivelled and lifeless.

"I'm sorry, old bean," he croaked. "That wasn't fair. I'm just . . . frustrated. I hate watching Angus this way, but I can't seem to get through to him."

In his head, he heard Uisdean's dry chuckle. *You're a persistent bugger, Gilleasbuig. I'm sure you'll find a way.*

Gills smiled sadly. He stood and clapped Uisdean on the shoulder. "I'd better be off. Things to do, people to see."

Uisdean's eyes never wavered from the painting on the wall—the great bulk of Ben Nevis looming over a stormy seascape.

An ambulance sped past Gills, its flashing blue light shattering on the choppy waters of the loch. His heart beat a little faster as he watched the ambulance recede in his rearview mirror, hurtling towards the main road and Silvaig General. *Probably nothing,* he told himself—*an old codger with a dodgy ticker*—but as he drove closer to Glenruig, that sense of dread only mounted. He rounded a bend, and across the bay he saw more blue lights flickering like phantoms between the trees. He floored the accelerator and the Anglia's engine growled in protest, unused to such brutal treatment.

"Sorry, old dear," he told the car, swinging left and powering along the lochside. The lights, he knew, were coming from John MacVannin's croft, and less than a minute later he skidded to a halt in front of the driveway. For a long second all he could do was sit and stare at the scene. Part of the hillside behind the croft was completely gone, as if sliced off with an axe. Two fire engines, and a similar number of ambulances, choked the access road that led to the croft. Yellow-suited firefighters crawled over what at one time had been Glenruig Free Church, but was now a pile of rubble. Gills saw Angus's police Land Rover and his heart seemed to miss a beat. He leapt from the car and stumbled towards a giant, bearlike police officer stationed at the road's end.

"What happened?" he asked.

The Bear gave him a blank stare. "I'm not at liberty to say." He leaned towards Gills and tapped the side of his nose. "But if I had to guess, I'd say there's been a landslide."

Gills ignored the sarcasm. "Is anyone hurt?"

The officer jerked a thumb over his shoulder. "See they big vehicles with the flashing lights on top? They're not ice-cream vans."

"Look," Gills said, exasperated, "I'm friends with Angus—that's his Land Rover over there. I just want to know if he's all right."

"Gus is fine," the Bear replied. "Got out just in time. He'll probably get a medal or something."

Gills took a few steps back, relieved beyond measure. "Well, thanks for your help."

"Aye, my pleasure," the Bear said, deadpan.

Gills plodded back to the Anglia and stood for a long minute, watching the firefighters at work. Three crows circled the ruins. At the edge of the rubble he spotted Reverend MacVannin in his black vestments. The minister trudged towards his house, dragging a mangled cross. Gills frowned, unnerved. The sight of the crows, the minister, and the flattened church kindled something deep in his memory, but he couldn't recall what exactly: some Highland myth or omen or prophecy.

Yes, that was it—a prophecy.

Years ago he'd written a paper for the *Celtic Review* on the prophecies of Coinnneach Odhar, the Brahan Seer. During his research, he'd come across a lesser known figure who, like Angus, was a MacNeil from the island of Barra: Gormshùil Mhòr na Borgh, or Gormla of Borve.

As if on cue, Angus himself appeared from behind an ambulance, DI Sharif at his side. Gills watched him crouch beside a man he recognised as Raymond the Waver, who was being treated by a paramedic. Angus straightened up, and their eyes met across the barren sheep field. Gills noticed a slight frown crease his friend's forehead before he turned away.

Gills ducked back into his car and caught a glimpse of his reflection in the rearview mirror. His face was grey as a wraith. Christ, he needed a dram!

As he drove away from MacVannin's croft, he scoured his memory for all that he'd learnt on Gormla and her seeings. She'd reputedly lived on the island some five hundred years ago, although there was no agreement on whether she was a real historical figure or an amalgam of characters from disparate folktales, twisted and altered over centuries by storytellers to suit the tastes of their audience. Gormla was perhaps best known for prophesying Bonnie Prince Charlie's defeat at Culloden, but she was also a healer and repository of omens and superstitions, scraps of which had been recorded in an early Gaelic manuscript. It was these fragments that had snagged something in his memory. He would visit the bookshop. Old Lachy held a copy of the manuscript, he was sure of it.

The bookshop was locked, but Gills knew where to find Lachlan Campbell. With Bran and Sceolan at his heels, he walked past a row of press vehicles and picked his way down onto the shore. Sheep nibbled at the salty seagrass. They had no fear of him, but bolted when they spotted the dogs.

"Heel!" Gills commanded, more for the benefit of Bran than Sceolan. The latter thought chasing sheep was beneath him, but Bran delighted in the activity. The dog looked up at him with pleading almond eyes, his tongue lolling out. "Don't try the puppy-dog eyes with me," Gills said. "You're too old for that now."

He watched the sheep scramble up a bank and hurtle past a group of bored-looking reporters smoking outside Glenruig Inn. One of the reporters raised an imaginary shotgun and blasted the animals. Gills gave a slight chuckle. He didn't want Bran frightening sheep, but he'd no great love for the animals either. In the eighteenth and nineteenth centuries, thousands of folk had been forcefully evicted from their homes across the Highlands to make way for sheep by rapacious landlords. He couldn't look on a black-faced ewe without imagining all those poor families, thrown out of their crofts and packed off to the New World. What Chichester was doing with his wolf reserve was hardly any better—in that, he was with Ashleigh, although they agreed on little else. For some reason, he and Ash had never clicked. Perhaps she resented the close relationship he had with her husband. Used to have.

Perhaps it is you who resent her, Gilleasbuig. She picked up the pieces of Angus and put him back together. It was you who broke him.

Rubbish, Gills thought. Don't give up on the lad yet. If he won't accept his gift, you'll have to make him see.

With a renewed determination, he strode along the shore towards the old boathouse, where he found Lachy buffing the gunwale of a sixteen-foot wooden clinker named *Lenore*. The boat sat on a timber ramp that sloped gently down to warped doors, which opened onto the sea. The boathouse was dim inside, the only light coming from narrow windows like half-shut eyes high up on the walls. Sagging shelves ran down one wall, a workbench, paint tins, and tools taking up most of the opposite space. In one corner, a pyramid of cardboard boxes full of books, an overflow of stock from the shop, rose towards the vaulted roof.

"Ah, here you are, old bean," Gills said. "I tried the bookshop, but you were closed."

Lachy gave Gills a quick glance, then sniffed. "Man's got to have a break, Gilleasbuig. It's not Waterstones I'm running."

Gills laid an appreciative hand on the prow of the boat. "She's looking well. Mind you, she's not wet her belly in a long time. . . ."

Lachy threw down his shammy. "I presume you're not here for a nautical discussion?"

"Quite correct. I'm looking for an old Gaelic manuscript. It contains, amongst other curiosities, the prophecies of Gormshùil Mhòr na Borgh." He shrugged. "I forget what the manuscript is called. Old memory's not what it used to be."

"I know the one you mean." Lachy sighed. "The Carntyne Manuscript."

Gills snapped his fingers. "Of course! Collected by Lord Carntyne in the eighteenth century during a tour of the Highlands and islands. I seem to remember you have a copy?"

"Hardly going to have the original, am I, seeing as it's in the special collections at the National Library?"

"Aye, quite," Gills said. "Could I trouble you for a loan of it?"

"Told you before—I'm not a lending library."

"Naturally, I'll make it worth your while."

Lachy climbed from the boat, grumbling. "Too right you will."

Half an hour later, with an expensively obtained copy of the manuscript under his arm, Gills returned to the Old Manse, poured himself a glass of Talisker, and retired to his study. He placed the manuscript flat on his desk and turned to Gormla's prophecies. His eyes roved over the tight script on the brittle brown page. Little was known for certain about the prophetess. Like Caitlin, she was probably born on the island of Barra, into a crofting family. Many of her prophecies, however, related to the mainland and the MacRuari clan. Indeed, she had predicted that the MacRuari line was doomed to extinction. For this, she had been executed—battered on the head with an axe, her throat ripped, then hung upside down from a tree over a stream, her head underwater.

The manuscript contained a gruesome illustration of the macabre ritual killing—the Celtic threefold death. On the facing page, he read out loud the prophecy that had sealed Gormla's fate: "When the Royalty Stone falls on a church, the MacRuari line will end and the land will be overrun by ministers without grace and women without shame. Glad am I that I will not see that day, for it will be a time of slaughter. The wretched will make bargains with demons and, thus possessed, make blood sacrifices to slake the thirst of the old gods."

The prophecy took a similar format to many of the Brahan Seer's. In English, the verse sounded stilted, and somewhat hokey to his ear, but in the original Gaelic it resonated deep within him. Clearly, the prophecy had angered Dòmhnall MacRuari, the clan chief, hence Gormla's brutal execution.

"A case of shooting the messenger," Gills muttered to himself. He placed the manuscript aside and wiggled the mouse of his doughty old Apple MacIntosh. The computer woke up with a grumble. Gills typed Dòmhnall MacRuari's name into a Google Images search. A number of pictures of the so-called Druid existed, most of them Victorian-era illustrations that depicted MacRuari as a frightening giant, a monstrous blood-soaked cannibal wielding a sword.

He cupped his chin and contemplated the images. There was no doubt in his mind that the Royalty Stone referred to by Gormla was the *Clach Rìoghalachd* that had stood on the hill behind MacVannin's church. Why then did the prophecy read as if the destruction of the church and the end of the MacRuari line were contemporaneous? Could some of the Druid's kin have survived the massacre, which had occurred in the fifteen century? And what to make of the reference to the old gods, whom Dòmhnall himself was said to have followed?

Gills clicked on an image of Dòmhnall MacRuari and hit print. The machine behind him made a sound like gnashing teeth as it disgorged a sheet of A4. He set his whisky glass down and cleared a space on the wall adjacent to his desk. Due to the accumulated books and junk of several decades, this was not an easy task, but eventually he had created enough room for his purposes. He took a sip of his dram and savoured the burn as the whisky slid down his throat. Then he lifted a large picture of Faye Chichester, which he'd crimped from yesterday's *Herald*. Using drawing pins, he stuck the picture in the centre of the space he'd just created, his very own *bòrd-murt*, or murder board. Next to Faye he pinned up the image of Dòmhnall MacRuari.

He stood back, finger and thumb cupping his chin, and contemplated Faye's smiling face. "Right, my dear," he said, "let's see what we can do to sort out this mess."

CHAPTER 23

ANGUS sat on the rear step of an ambulance and watched firefighters pick over the remains of Reverend MacVannin's church, like ravens over a sheep's carcass. Only a small corner section of the building remained upright: the rest was rubble, reduced to ruins, as had so many Highland villages over the centuries.

A young paramedic dabbed at a cut on the side of his head with an antiseptic wipe. It stung, but he stayed motionless. Out of the corner of his eye, he saw Nadia trudging towards him.

"How's my little wounded soldier?"

"I've had worse cuts shaving," the paramedic answered.

Angus glanced up. The paramedic looked about twelve, fresh-faced and blue-eyed. "Have your balls even dropped, son?"

The paramedic grinned. He applied a couple of Steri-Strips over Angus's wound, pushing them down a little harder than necessary. "All done, granddad."

Angus laughed softly at the cheek of him.

"You up for speaking to MacVannin?" Nadia asked.

"Aye." He stood too quickly and his head spun. He swayed, waiting for the dizziness to subside.

Nadia placed a hand on his arm. "Maybe you should sit this one out, Angus. You could be concussed."

"I'm fine," he answered. She stared into his eyes for a long second, then gave a slight nod. They turned and walked through a graveyard of rusting ploughs and harrows towards MacVannin's crofthouse. Nadia paused on the doorstep and turned to him. "Oh, I forgot." She jabbed him hard on the arm.

"Ouch! What was that for?" he whined, taken by surprise.

"Don't ever do that to me again," she hissed. "What were you thinking, running back into that church?" She again raised her fist but rather than give him another dead arm, she rapped on the door. "I thought you were dead," she whispered, staring straight ahead.

Perhaps that's what he'd wanted. It wasn't courage that had made him run back into that church. He was no hero. Raymond the Waver had just been an excuse to get himself pulped by a boulder.

He clasped his hands behind his back to stop them from fidgeting and plastered on his blank face as the door swung open. Reverend MacVannin's wife, a shilpit woman with a blue rinse and downcast eyes, let them into the house. A grandfather clock tutted loudly in the hallway, impatiently ticking off the seconds until the End of Days. Faded floral wallpaper covered the hall. There were no pictures to break up the pattern, which gave Angus the claustrophobic sensation he was trapped in a rosebush.

"My husband's in here," the woman squeaked, refusing to make eye contact with either of them. She knocked on a door and waited until she heard MacVannin's harsh caw.

"Come in!"

She pushed open the door then stood aside to let Nadia and Angus through. Reverend MacVannin sat behind a writing desk as if nothing were amiss, despite the blood on his collar and dust on his shoulders.

"Can I get you anything?" his wife asked timidly. "Tea? Coffee?"

"We're fine," MacVannin rasped. "Close the door on your way out."

The woman shuffled away. If she was put out by her husband's tone, she didn't show it. Angus almost felt Nadia's hackles raise.

"Thank you for speaking to us, Reverend," she said. "I appreciate that the circumstances are unexpected."

The minister looked Nadia up and down, nostrils flaring. "A church is mair than bricks and mortar. If needs be, we'll worship in the open air, like the old Covenanter martyrs."

His fat lips twitched upwards, as if quite taken with this idea. But then he returned his glare to Nadia. "Your lot knows all about martyrdom, eh?"

Nadia met his insult with a breezy smile. "Do other faiths scare you? Paganism, for example."

"Nothing scares me, save the wrath of my God."

"Believe me, Reverend, our justice system can be wrathful too."

A muscle in MacVannin's jaw twitched. "Whit's that suppose tae mean?"

Angus cleared his throat, trying to defuse the situation. "We need to ask you about Faye Chichester, John."

MacVannin turned his turnip-shaped head towards him. "Angus, how's your faither keeping?"

"As well as can be expected."

"Aye, it's a terrible thing—"

"It is," Angus said, cutting him off. "Listen, John, we know you were up at the commune two nights ago. We've witnesses who say you were abusive and threatening."

"Pah! It's them that's the threat. Infecting minds with their nonsense."

"So you admit you were there?" Nadia asked.

MacVannin leaned back in his chair, ignoring Nadia's question, his gaze still on Angus.

"You've the look of your mother about ye. Just awful what happened to her. Awful . . ."

Angus struggled to retain his blank expression. Despite the sympathetic words, MacVannin's eyes were cold.

"Just answer the question," he said.

"Aye, I was there. So what?"

"So, Reverend," Nadia said, "you were one of the last people to see Faye. Alive. Witnesses say you and she had a confrontation?"

"If by that you mean I tried to save her from those heathens, then yes. Blasphemers and idolaters, the lot of them."

"She laughed at you—Faye?"

MacVannin's eyes burned into Nadia. "Aye, well, maybe if she'd heeded my warning, she'd still be here."

"You've no love for Chichester," Angus said, "so why try to *save* his daughter?"

"Children aren't responsible for the sins of their parents. She was only a lassie; her soul was not yet completely corrupted. It was my duty as a Christian to try to make her see the light."

"It's been almost two days since Faye's murder—why haven't you contacted police to tell us you saw her that night? That would have been the Christian thing to do," Nadia said.

MacVannin seethed silently.

"Answer the question," Angus growled. "Why didn't you tell us?"

"Faye was alive and well the last time I saw her," MacVannin spat.

"Which was what time?" Nadia asked.

"Must have been around half ten."

"What did you do after the row with Faye?"

"It wasn't a row. I offered her a way out. She refused. I was then threatened with violence, so I left."

"Who threatened you?"

MacVannin sniffed, his lip curling. "Ach, I don't know. One of the heathens."

"Pagans," Angus corrected.

"So you returned straight home?" Nadia pressed.

"Aye, I was back here by about half eleven. Ruth will vouch for me."

He stood with a slight groan, hobbled to the door, and hauled it open. "Ruth! Ruth! Come in here would ye, woman!"

MacVannin's wife reappeared, looking pale and terrified.

"Tell these good officers what time I returned home on Friday night."

"Err, it must have been about half past eleven." She glanced at her husband. "I remember because *Today in Parliament* had just started on Radio 4. I was about to turn it off. Can't stand these politicians . . ."

"Yes, thank you, dear, that will do," MacVannin said.

He glared at Nadia, as if daring her to contradict his wife. He jerked his head at Ruth and she shuffled out of the room.

"Now, if ye don't mind, I've the tups tae feed." He faked a smile. "Then a church tae rebuild."

He stood by the study door and ushered them out.

"Thanks for your time," Nadia said. "But don't be running off anywhere, Reverend. We may need to speak to you again. After we've corroborated your story."

The minister's face turned an angry shade of beetroot. "Before you corroborate anything, you ought to be looking into the cause of this rockfall."

Nadia turned to him and frowned. "What do you mean?"

"An act of God, it was not."

Angus stood chittering by the sheep field and watched the geotechnical inspectors at work. In their hard hats and yellow high-vis jackets, they looked like canaries flitting around the hillside, dabs of colour in an otherwise drab landscape.

Nadia squelched up behind him. "So, Reverend MacVannin, eh?"

"Charmer, isn't he?"

"Do you buy the wife's alibi?"

They locked eyes for a second. "Nah, me neither," she said. "They'd rehearsed it. The question is why."

It was Angus's turn to shrug. "MacVannin's around the same age as Gills and my father, but they never had a kind word to say about him. I think he only found God later in life."

"We can speak to Gills later. I'd like to know all about the good minister."

"What do you make of his claim that someone deliberately set off the rockfall?" Angus asked eventually. "How would you even do that?"

"Explosives," she said doubtfully. "Some kind of pneumatic device?"

He nodded towards the mountainside. "Can't see anyone trekking up there with a jackhammer, can you?"

"Nope." They watched one of the geotechnical inspectors slither down a steep path and march towards a white jeep emblazoned with the company's logo. "Let's ask the expert," Nadia said.

They trudged across the muddy ground and found the inspector rummaging in the boot. Rather than some high-tech instrument, she emerged with a tartan thermos flask. She turned, flask in hand, and scowled. "If you're reporters, you can piss right off."

"Police," Nadia said, flashing her ID.

"Ah right, sorry."

"It's okay, can't be too careful."

The woman introduced herself as Dr. Willow Sedgewick, a name Angus thought sounded like an aromatic candle.

"Bloody Baltic," Dr. Sedgwick moaned, pouring herself a sludgy black cup of coffee from the thermos.

"How are you getting on up there?" Nadia asked.

"Probably another couple of hours at the least before we can declare the hillside safe."

"Any sign the rockfall could have been triggered deliberately?"

Dr Sedgewick looked at Nadia as if she were mental. "Err, no. Probably freeze-thaw weathering."

"What's that?"

"Well, it was extremely cold last night," Dr. Sedgwick said. "When temperatures plummet, water held within cracks in the rock freezes. And when water freezes, it expands, putting pressure on the rock. Then, when it thaws, the water seeps farther into the cracks. When this process happens repeatedly, the rock weakens and eventually breaks apart." She shrugged. "The gradient plays a part too. And that hill's pretty damn steep, as my thighs have discovered this morning."

"So," Nadia said, "it was an act of God."

Dr Sedgwick smiled thinly. "An act of nature."

CHAPTER 24

CLODS of mud spat from the Land Rover's tyres as Angus gunned the engine. For a second he thought they were stuck, which would have been bloody typical, but then the Landy lurched forward and found some traction on the churned-up ground. Nadia gripped the door handle as they bounced down the rutted track away from MacVannin's croft. He glanced in the rearview mirror and saw a black figure standing on the doorstep of the house, watching them leave—the minister in his robes.

Angus slowed for the road entrance, which was blocked with a "Police Incident" sign. Constable Archie Devine lumbered over to the sign and lifted it with one big paw, as if it weighed no more than a sheet of paper. Nadia wound down the window.

"Thanks, Archie!" She beamed.

Angus couldn't be sure, but he thought Archie smiled.

"Nae bother, DI Sharif."

"It's Nadia."

Angus gave the big constable a brief wave of thanks and turned right onto the single-track road, heading back towards the village hall. "You could charm the bears from the woods," he muttered.

"Just being friendly. You should try it sometime."

"Ha! You sound like my wife." He made the comment without thinking. Nadia's smile faltered. An awkward silence descended, and he was almost glad when the police radio crackled into life.

"ZS calls NR 34A!"

He recognised Stout's nasal whine.

"Go ahead to 34, sir." He sighed.

"Domestic out at High Cross Farm."

"What! Again? That's the third time this month."

"Just go and sort it out, eh? Make sure our star-crossed lovers don't kill each other. And, MacNeil, make sure *you* don't kill anyone either this time."

Stout hung up. Angus felt Nadia's eyes boring into him as he drove. After a long silence he gave her a sidelong glance. "I was involved in an altercation last year. A local thug called Mark Watson died."

"What happened?"

"Watson and his ex-girlfriend got into a row on Silvaig pier. He pulled a knife on her. I was patrolling the Esplanade and saw the fight. When I tried to intervene, he stabbed me. I was lucky. He missed my liver by half a centimetre."

"Shit!"

"Anyway, I shoved him backwards. He tripped on a mooring rope and fell into the sea. Turned out he couldn't swim."

The byre at High Cross Farm was nothing but a ramshackle shed, apparently held up by cobwebs and prayers. Rough stone walls; corrugated iron roof spread over a spine of sagging timbers; a heady reek of cow dung and damp straw. A bare bulb oozed light onto a dun-coloured shorthorn heifer that occupied one of the stalls. An old-fashioned clothes pulley hung from a joist, a solitary sock hanging on it.

"So what's the problem, Corky?"

Charlie Corcoran, a wiry rosy-cheeked crofter in his sixties, gave a hacking cough, then spat on the straw. He pointed up at the clothes pulley.

"I didnae touch anything in case youse want to do forensic."

Angus stared at the pulley, notebook held loosely in his hand.

Forensics. Aye, right.

He was glad Nadia hadn't decided to come along for the ride. She was already wondering what had happened to his promising career.

"You're saying someone's stolen your clothes?"

"Not someone. That witch next door. Took everything, except for that sock. Shirts, jeans—even my pants. All of them! Had tae go commando. I'll be chaffed tae buggery tonight."

From outside the byre, Angus heard a shrill woman's voice. "I've done nothing of the sort, Corky. It's you that's been stealing from my washing line."

He turned to find Lorna Cameron standing in the doorway. She was a formidable sight in a floral dress, body warmer, and mud-caked Wellington boots. He couldn't imagine a romantic bone in her body, yet she and Corky had been involved in a tempestuous on-off relationship for years. Now was clearly an "off" period.

Corky pulled a sprig of rowans from his pocket and held it towards Lorna as if she were a vampire and the rowans a crucifix.

"Get back!"

Lorna stepped farther into the byre. "Put that away, you superstitious old fool."

"Only if you remove the hex from Annabel!"

"I haven't cursed your stupid cow!"

"You're a witch, like your mother before ye. She's cursed my cow, Angus. Cannae get a drop of milk from her. And now she's pinched my clothes."

"Did I hell!"

"Shut your mouth, you old hag!"

Angus folded his arms and let the argument wash over him. He'd seen this all before. Corky and Lorna would go at it hammer and tongs, but they always kissed and made up. It was a complete waste of his time. He should be out there trying to catch a murderer, not listening to this.

"Okay, let's all calm down." He sighed, stepping between the bickering old lovers. He turned to Corky. "I noticed your field is a wee bit overrun with weeds."

"Aye, exactly," Lorna blurted. "I've been on at him for weeks to get them dug out."

Corky glared at her. "Who asked you?"

"What I'm saying, Corky," Angus said, trying to regain control, "is that . . . err . . . Annabel might have ingested some bracken. Before we start banding around accusations of witchcraft, it might be an idea to have Cruickshank check her over. Could be she's sick."

"Aye, that's exactly—"

Angus gave Lorna a stern look, cutting her off. "And as for the missing clothes, it seems you've both been robbed. You might remember there was a spate of this type of crime a few months ago."

The "Knicker Snatcher" had become public enemy number one in Inspector Stout's judgement.

Lorna and Corky stared daggers at each other.

Angus tapped his pen against his notebook. "Can you tell me what's been stolen, Lorna?"

"A few dresses, my best blouse, and an awful leopard-print top."

"You said you liked that top!" Corky blurted out. "It wasnae cheap. Went all the way to Monsoon in Inverness to buy that."

"You've got no taste, Corky."

"Clearly, otherwise I wouldn't have let you in my bed."

Angus again stepped between them. "Look, I think it'd be best if you two stayed out of each other's way, eh?"

Lorna stuck her nose up in the air. "Fine by me."

"Aye, me too," Corky spat.

Lorna spun on her heel and stomped from the byre.

"Hag," Corky muttered, heart no longer in it.

Lorna did not even turn around. "Arsehole," she said.

After leaving Corky's croft, Angus decided to try Ewan's cottage one last time before heading back to the incident room. Over his shoulder, the battlements of Dunbirlinn Castle stood out against the bruised sky like a row of teeth as he raised his fist and rapped on the door. When no one answered, he gave the door a shove, but this time it was locked. He crept around the side of the cottage, peering through windows, but saw only mess and junk. The curtains in Ewan's bedroom were pulled shut.

His mind returned to the burning corpse from his visions. The roaring flames made it impossible to say whether the victim was male or female. Not that it mattered, because it was a hallucination, a nightmare conjured up by some errant wiring in his head.

He stumbled back round to the front of the cottage, a sense of dread dogging his heels. He was about to get back in the Land Rover when he heard the sound of footsteps on gravel. He spun around and found James Chichester standing six feet away, watching him with his keen blue-green eyes. The laird was dressed in a three-quarter-length waxed coat with caped shoulders, tweed cap, and stout leather boots. He held a walking stick with a silver handle in the shape of a wolf's head.

"Err . . . Mr. Chichester," he stammered. "I didn't see you there."

"My apologies," the American said. "I didn't mean to startle you."

"You're okay," Angus replied, then decided an explanation was in order. "Just looking for Ewan."

"My wife told me she saw Faye slap him. Is he on the run?"

"No . . . well, to be honest, we're not sure. No one's seen him today, but if he's out on the hill, that wouldn't be unusual."

"Do you think he did it? Do you think he killed my daughter?"

Angus hesitated. "My instinct tells me no."

The laird stared at him hard. "If that's your instinct, Constable, then I, for one, believe you. Man has become over-reliant on empirical evidence. In our voracious appetite to explain the universe and label everything in it, we've sacrificed a deeper, innate knowledge. We're now so far removed from our true selves that I fear there's no way back."

Angus shuffled awkwardly, not sure how to respond to that.

Chichester rapped his stick on the ground and barked a laugh. "I'm walking up to the wolf enclosure. Care to join me? You can fill me in on the case."

Angus shrugged. "Sure, why not?"

The gloom closed in around them as they walked, Chichester's stick tapping out a rhythm on a new path that skirted the stable block and led through woods towards the wolf enclosure.

"You're the one Mrs. MacCrimmon calls Angus Dubh?"

"That's right. Everybody knows everybody around here."

"'Dubh' means black in Gaelic, right?"

"Yes."

"Sounds a bit bleak, if you don't mind me saying."

"I suppose it does, but there's nothing sinister about it, really. You'll have noticed quite a lot of people around here share the same name. In school there was another boy in my class called Angus MacNeil. He had red hair, so he was Angus Ruadh, and I was Angus Dubh. Usually they would have differentiated us by stature, either Mòr or Beag—meaning big and small—but we were the same height."

"I like it," Chichester said. "What's the Gaelic for 'grey'?"

"Glas."

"Then from now on I'll be James Glas."

"Has a certain ring to it."

They walked on in silence for a few minutes, Angus quickening his pace to keep up with the laird, whose long stride seemed to eat up the ground. He found it difficult to believe Chichester had cancer, as his wife had insisted. Perhaps the disease had gone into remission, despite the doctors' prognosis. The American's back was ramrod straight, and although he held the walking stick, he never actually leant on it. His face still had the rugged glow of a yachtsman, and his intense eyes darted around, taking in everything, like a tiger on the prowl for prey.

"Tell me, Angus Dubh," Chichester said at last, "do you have children?"

The question took him by surprise and rekindled the embers of guilt that burned inside him. This man might still have a child if only Angus had acted sooner.

"No, sir. Not yet."

"Not yet?"

"My wife and I have been trying for years. We're in the middle of IVF treatment."

Chichester swung his walking stick at a stray nettle that leaned over the path, scything the stingy stem in half. The movement was rapid, a mere flick of the wrist, like a cobra's strike. "It's not always straightforward," Chichester murmured. "Faye was an only child. She always wanted a little sister. That was the one thing I couldn't give her."

Would that have made a difference? he wondered. Single children—like Faye, like him—were often alone. They made their own decisions and mistakes. They carried their problems around like a loaded mule.

Chichester glanced at him. "Have you and your colleagues identified any suspects?"

"She was at Teine Eigin on the night she died. We have video footage of the celebrations and there's one person on there we've not managed to identify."

"The killer?"

"We're keeping an open mind."

Chichester swiped at another weed. "So why hasn't this person's picture been released to the media? Surely someone must know who he is?"

"We're not even sure it is a 'he.'"

Chichester gave him a sidelong glance. "What else could it be?"

"What I mean is, we can't tell whether the figure is male or female because they're wearing a full-length cloak and mask."

Chichester pondered this as they neared the wolf enclosure. Angus heard rustling in the tangle of rhododendrons that now fringed the path. He peered into the undergrowth. Branches and boughs twisted up from the ground, dark and alive, like the symbol Faye had drawn in her sketch pads. He heard scurrying feet. A high-pitched yip. Then silence.

Chichester pointed with his stick. "This way."

He bounded up a flight of wooden steps to a viewing platform, a curved timber structure with information boards and binoculars on revolving metal posts positioned every twenty yards or so. Angus could smell the musky scent of the wolves on the breeze, like wet dog, but stronger and redolent of damp forests, of Nature herself. Away in the distance, he glimpsed movement at the edge of a small copse that grew in the enclosure. A second later a howl that made the hair on the back of his neck stand on end rang out across the landscape. The lone cry was taken up by others, and soon the chorus filled the twilight. It seemed to reverberate around the rocks and hills like a proclamation, a warning to all the other species in the vicinity, including man. It struck a chord deep within him, touching some lost nerve, a race memory perhaps of a time when humans shared the land with these predators.

Chichester watched him, eyes smiling. "Amazing sound, isn't it? Wolves haven't been heard here in three hundred years."

"Aye," he said. "It's . . . quite something." He knew it was a tame response, but he couldn't put into words the impression the howling made on him. It was like hearing an ancient language, one he'd spoken and dreamt in but had somehow lost.

Chichester took a hip flask from his inside pocket. "They know this place: instinctively, they can tell this was once wolf country. I'm so proud these animals are back where they belong, back in my native land."

He screwed off the lid and took a sip, then offered the flask to Angus. "Macallan 1926."

Angus accepted the hip flask. It felt heavy and was decorated with intricate Celtic motifs, which wound around the flask and framed hunting and battle scenes, like a miniature Bayeux Tapestry etched in silver. He lifted the flask to his lips and drank deeply. Vanilla, woodsmoke, and marzipan burned deliciously down his throat, and for a brief second he forgot about the shadows stalking his subconscious—about the girl with the garrotte around her throat, about Ewan and the Dark One. He longed to drink the hip flask dry, let the alcohol smog fill his mind the way the yellow pills used to. *No.* Reluctantly, he handed the flask back to Chichester.

"What did you mean when you said 'my native land'? I thought you were as American as apple pie."

Chichester's lips twitched upwards. "True, but I'm descended from the notorious Dòmhnall MacRuari."

Angus now recalled the family tree he'd seen in the library, not to mention the portrait of the scary clan chief that greeted visitors to Dunbirlinn.

"The Druid," he said.

"That's right." Chichester nodded. "A genealogist friend's been helping me research him. I think I've read everything there is about Dòmhnall, and he's not the monster many academics make out. He is . . . misunderstood."

Chichester shook his head, as if dislodging the thought. "Anyway, at one time the MacRuaris were lords of all this—" He swept his stick out, as if to encompass the landscape. Dying light clung to the rocky shoulder of the hillside, like a child hanging on to his mother. For a second it appeared as if the rock were on fire.

"Was that why you decided to buy the estate?"

Chichester pursed his lips. "Certainly, the symmetry appealed to me. But, no, it was something deeper, fated even, if you believe in that kind of thing."

He smiled at Angus's confused expression. "My life had no meaning until I came to these shores. Everything before then—my media empire, the mansions around the globe, the yachts, the parties, the women—none of it gave me anything but the most fleeting satisfaction. It's a cliché, but money really can't buy you happiness. Sure, you can have fun testing the theory, but that's all it is—fun. And there's only so much fun you can have before you crave something deeper, something that feeds the soul. Believe me, you can't buy that kind of purpose."

He felt Chichester's gaze slide over him, sharp eyes evaluating. "You have a purpose too, Angus Dubh."

He tensed. How many times over the years had Gills said these exact same words? Too often, perhaps, because he had crumpled under the weight of the responsibility. No, that wasn't fair on Gills—Angus had crumpled because he was weak and selfish.

Chichester handed the hip flask across to Angus, who raised it to his lips. The scent of the whisky drifted from the open cap, like the whisper of a lover, or a siren's call. He tipped the hip flask back, but allowed only a dribble to pass his lips. Something that tasted so good had to be dangerous.

"I discovered my purpose quite by chance," Chichester continued. "A decade back I had a health scare, which forced me to think about my mortality. Until then I'd never considered myself old, you know? Naively, I thought I'd go on forever, a mighty oak that just kept growing. But when one gets old, Angus, they no longer reach for the sky anymore; they look to the roots. And that's what I did."

Chichester's fingers caressed the silver wolf's head atop his cane. "I'd always been aware of my Scottish ancestry," he said, eyes fixed on the middle distance. "One of the enduring memories of my childhood is my grandpa standing in our front room on what he called Hogmanay. He'd be dressed in a kilt, his cheeks inflating like a balloon as he played *Auld Lang Syne* on the bagpipes."

The laird seemed lost in some bittersweet remembrance. In profile, his nose thrust up slightly, as if he were sniffing the air for predators. Shadows pooled in the hollows of his cheek and eye socket. Wrinkle lines around his mouth yanked his lips downwards. "He was originally from Canada, Grandpa," Chichester went on. "His ancestors were amongst a group of Scottish colonists who settled Prince Edward Island in the first decade of the 1800s. He spent his early years in the province of Manitoba, but his father was a cattle dealer and decided to move the family south to Texas just before the turn of the century. Grandpa went into the same business, but he was no simple cowboy. He was well-read—self-taught, all of it, but he could debate philosophy and religion as well as any sonofabitch from Yale. I remember him reading me bedtime stories—tales about giants and banshees from the old country, passed down to him from his own grandfather."

Chichester smiled at the memory, but then his face clouded over. "Grandpa passed when I was ten. My own father had no interest in our Scottish heritage, and I was too young to care either way. It was only later, after the health scare, that I felt compelled to delve deeper."

He half-turned towards Angus. His sinewy neck twisted, the skin puckering into deep creases. Specks of light shone from his eyes, like the stars coming alive above the viewing platform. In that moment he resembled his murdered daughter. It was something in the expression, an almost childlike earnestness.

She was part of him, that's why. His blood. Gone, because of you!

Angus felt the guilt etched across his face, but the laird did not seem to notice.

"I felt a burning desire to see the land of my kinsfolk then," he said, "so strong, it was almost as if something were calling me here. Of course, I'd been to the UK a hundred times before—I own a town house in Knightsbridge and a stud farm in Kent—but I'd never been north of Edinburgh. This place"—he threw out his arms—"blew me away. Like the wolves, I felt a sense of coming home. But you know what my first thought was?"

Angus shook his head and handed back the hip flask.

"I thought this would be an amazing location for a championship golf course." Chichester guffawed. "Can you imagine anything more pointless than golf? Yet I used to obsess over the damn sport—spent tens, hundreds probably, of thousands on coaching, hours on the range, all to shave a couple of points off my handicap."

"What changed your mind about the golf course?"

He traced his gnarled fingers around the hip flask, like a blind man reading braille. "I was out hiking, alone, when I was caught in a storm. The mist was so thick, I could hardly tell which way was up and which was down. The wind was fierce, and the sleet soon soaked through my clothes. I was close to death from exposure when I stumbled across a cave. I later discovered that this was the exact cave where my ancestor Dòmhnall MacRuari met a grisly end, but that's another story. Anyway, I lay down to wait for the weather to change. I remember shivering uncontrollably, my teeth chattering so hard, I thought they'd shatter. Then I fell into this trancelike state of hyper-awareness. I started hallucinating, seeing all kinds of strange things. It was . . . spiritual. I made a pact, right there and then, that if I made it out of that cave alive, I'd change my ways. I would use my influence and money to do good in the world, to protect the environment and ignite the rewilding movement. That's where my plan to reintroduce the wolves was born—there, in that cave."

He glanced at Angus. "The idea did not come quite as out of the blue as it sounds. I've always had an interest in wolves, and several years previously I had donated to a wolf reintroduction project in Yellowstone Park. That initiative had been a remarkable success, and my notion was to create a Scottish Yellowstone, right here."

Angus gave an awkward-sounding cough. "Full disclosure, sir. My wife, Ashleigh, is one of those placard-wavers outside Dunbirlinn. In fact, she's a founding member of the Glenruig Community Trust."

Chichester grinned, then surprised him by clapping him on the shoulder. "I know. Mrs. MacCrimmon told me. I did wonder whether you'd mention it."

"You're not—"

"Angry?" Chichester interjected. "Of course not. I've heard your wife speak at one of the meetings. She's articulate, passionate, and a talented musician, too, I hear. Not to mention beautiful. You must be very proud of her?" He thought of the trauma Ash had endured after her parents had died when she was so young. It took a warrior to emerge intact from that battle. And now, scathed though he knew she was, she spent her time fighting for the underdog, championing those without a voice. Ashleigh was a better, stronger soul than he was.

"Aye," he said. "I'm proud of her. She's the most selfless person I've ever met. Sometimes I think I've held her back."

"In what way?"

"Ach, I don't know. Before we met, she had plans to go to music college. She could have done anything, but she wanted to get married and raise a family here, in the Highlands. But that's not quite panned out."

Chichester nodded, as if to himself. "Nothing in life ever turns out exactly as planned."

He took a long drink from the hip flask, then wiped a sleeve across his mouth. "The irony is, your wife and I are fighting for the same thing."

He surveyed the barren panorama. "Tourists come to the Highlands, Angus Dubh, to bask in the wilderness, but this"—he swept his walking stick across the landscape again—"is not wilderness. This is make-believe, an artificial creation of man, first branded by the Victorians and flogged to death by successive governments ever since. No landscape can truly be called a wilderness when its top predator has been eradicated."

Angus saw a flash of ruthlessness in the American's eyes that sent a chill down his spine. It was a mere flicker, but in that moment he saw something wild and untamed. The incandescent light fizzled and seemed to ripple across Chichester's face before his expression returned to urbane neutrality.

"The wolf kept this ecosystem in balance for centuries. She drove the deer through the wooded glens, picked off the weakest with an efficiency no gamekeeper—not even your pal Ewan Hunter—could match. Red deer were forest dwellers back then, perhaps a third bigger than the deer that ravage the hillsides now. They would still be here, had the wolf not been hunted to extinction, like so many other species—moose, reindeer, wild goat, wild boar, lynx, bear.

"These deer were conditioned not to linger for fear of wolf attack. Constantly on the move, they had no time to graze on these lower slopes as they do nowadays, destroying the forests before they've even had a chance to take root."

His eyes narrowed to slits, like the arrow loops in Dunbirlinn Castle. "In ten years" time—if the reintroduction project is allowed to progress unhindered—the view from here will be quite different. Where there is barren moorland, there will be trees and grass. Insects will flourish, as will the birds that feed on them. Wolves have a symbiotic relationship with nature, Angus. Rather than decimating deer numbers, they will keep the herds fit and healthy. She is the missing link in the chain."

Angus shifted nervously from foot to foot. He didn't disagree with Chichester, but he was also beginning to see why some newspapers had branded him a crazed environmentalist.

"What about the crofters?" he asked. "Won't the wolves kill their sheep?"

"Perhaps." Chichester shrugged. "But they'll be compensated for their losses. I appreciate they fear for their livelihoods, of course I do, but it is their mindset that must change. For too long, land managers have put the interest of people first. And have failed spectacularly. The Highland Clearances of the eighteenth and nineteenth centuries not only destroyed the ecosystem with the introduction of large-scale sheep farming, it also broke communities. We've learnt very little since then. Sheep farmers, hillwalkers, hunters, billionaires like me, they must learn this land is not here to serve them. They have taken everything from nature and given nothing back. If a wolf takes a sheep, it is not the fault of the wolf. It is only doing what comes naturally. The fault, Angus, lies with the shepherd who has failed to protect his flock."

"I doubt that argument will float with the likes of John MacVannin."

A muscle in Chichester's jaw tensed. "An odious little man. Sheep farmers and preachers have been the wolves' biggest enemies—he is both. Christian propaganda poisoned minds against the wolf, created the conditions where the extermination of a species was seen as a noble pursuit, a crusade, even.

Christianity perverted our relationship with the natural world. Suddenly God gave us dominion over all the other creatures and if Christ was the Good Shepherd, then the wolf was an agent of the Devil."

Chichester's tone was level but flint-edged, as if he were challenging Angus to disagree.

"Human beings used to revere wolves," he continued. "She was the first mammal we ever domesticated, long before horses or cattle. All dogs are descended from that source, but here's the irony"—he turned to him, his furrowed handsome face incised with sorrow—"over the centuries through selective breeding, we've fashioned dogs for our specific needs—guard dogs, retrievers, scent hounds. Eventually we got around to breeding the wolf-hound, an animal designed to kill wolves." He shook his head sadly. "How did we ever reach this point? How did our relationship with wolves change from one of respect and admiration, to one in which we wanted to annihilate the species? By its own descendants, no less."

Angus had no answer. He tugged his gaze away from Chichester and watched the animals in the distance. The sunlight had dipped below the shoulder of the hillside, but slivers of pewter and gold still feathered the sky. Stars blinked between the clouds as shadows swallowed the moorland. From here, the wolves looked like grey ghosts—insubstantial, as if made of vapor.

"They're smaller than I imagined," Angus said at last.

Chichester grinned, showing little canine teeth. "Everything about the wolf is exaggerated, especially their size. The mature European wolf is around five and a half feet from nose to tail and weighs about eighty-five pounds on average. But when people are asked—and, boy, have I asked—they'll say wolves weigh around two hundred pounds."

Angus squinted into the distance. One of the wolves had split from the pack and loped towards the viewing platform. The creature was graceful, feet hardly seeming to touch the ground as it glided across the heather.

"Ah, here she comes, the alpha female," Chichester said. The skin around his eyes crinkled and a wide smile broke like a wave across his face. "She does this as a show of strength," he said, like a proud parent watching a child perform onstage. "A quiet reminder that this is her territory."

The wolf halted some ten yards from the platform. She raised her head and sniffed the air. Her coat was a striking blue-grey colour, apart from her neck, which was lighter, almost white. The amber eyes, which were now looking straight at him, were outlined in black, as if painted with kohl. They seemed transfused with an otherworldly light. He held the wolf's gaze, transfixed. There was wisdom in those eyes, but something feral, too, a cold ruthlessness, like the brief glimpse that had flickered across Chichester's face.

At last, the wolf released Angus from her glare and strutted imperiously back towards her pack. The other wolves crowded around her, yipping in sublimation like fawning courtiers. The alpha ignored their adulation and loped off into the forest.

Chichester took a pull from the hip flask then passed it to him again. They stood in silence, watching as the wolves melded back into the shadows of the trees, grey ghosts returning to their graves.

He tried to hand the hip flask back, but the laird shook his head.

"Keep it," he said. "A gift from James Glas to Angus Dubh. Raise a toast to me when this is all done."

CHAPTER 25

THE hip flask sat snug against his chest in the inside pocket of his coat as he walked back to the Land Rover. He could almost feel the heat of the whisky radiating out from it, a warm glow to stave off the freezing mist that had descended with the night. In the woods, the visibility was so poor, he could only see a few meters in front of him, but once clear of the trees he could easily make out the dark silhouette of Dunbirlinn Castle and catch his bearings.

Soon he reached the sweeping road that led past the stable block. Water spat from the ornate fountain outside the stables, making an obscene noise in the darkness, like a horse pissing. No lights were on in Mrs. MacCrimmon's cottage. Presumably she was still at work in the castle, waiting on Lady Chichester's every whim. He pictured Faye riding out on Bessie two nights ago, dressed in her long green cloak, her path lit by a full moon. What had she felt? Excitement at the Samhain celebrations to come? Anger after the row with her stepmother? Embarrassment over Ewan's clumsy attempt to kiss her? Certainly no inkling of what was to come, no sense of the horror that lay in wait for her.

But you did, Angus. You did. . . .

He dug his fingernails into his palms, then reached for the hip flask. The metal felt warm and heavy. *Drink up,* said a voice inside his head. He unscrewed the cap and raised the hip flask to his lips. But before he could take a sip, he heard the distant sound of engines growling in the darkness, heading his way. He replaced the cap and strode past the stable block. Once he rounded the corner, he saw three sets of dim headlights probing the mist. The convoy began to take shape, two police cars and a bigger vehicle, a fluorescent blue-and-yellow liveried Transit that he recognised as a crime scene investigation van.

The vehicles skidded to a halt next to his Land Rover, which was still parked outside Ewan Hunter's cottage. Doors were flung open and police officers jumped out like coiled springs. Heart thumping, he ran towards Ewan's cottage. He heard a familiar Glaswegian accent rapping out orders. Nadia turned at his approach, a frown wrinkling her brow. "Angus, what are you doing here?"

"Err, nothing," he stuttered. "I was heading back to the village hall, but thought I'd check if Ewan was home yet."

"And is he?"

"Eh . . . no." He glanced over her shoulder and saw Constable Archie Devine wrestle a Big Red Key from the boot of a police car. Archie gave the metal door ram an affectionate pat with his meaty paw.

"What the hell's going on, Nadia?"

"We got a warrant to search Ewan's cottage."

"But why? What's happened?"

"He's gone missing, Angus. Nobody's seen him since Mrs. MacCrimmon broke the news of Faye's murder to him yesterday."

"Aye, but he could be out on the hill?"

"True, but Crowley doesn't want to take the chance. He could be halfway to France by now."

"What about port authorities?"

"On alert."

"Any hits on ANPR?"

Nadia rolled her eyes. "No, but he could have changed the plates or taken a road with no cameras. Look, Angus, we have thought this through and the sheriff in Silvaig agreed to a search warrant. Faye was seen slapping Ewan on the night she died. He has previous for violence, an unprovoked attack that left his victim in hospital for a week. He must have known where Faye was going that night and he has no alibi worth a damn."

She glanced at Archie and gave him a brief nod. The big man almost smiled, then stalked towards the door with the Big Red Key.

"But he might be back," Angus protested. "Is this really necessary?"

"Motive, means, opportunity," Nadia said. "He had them all. If we're wrong, we're wrong, Angus. Worst-case scenario we might have to fork out for a new door."

She gave him a faint smile, then walked past him.

"Okay, Archie," she said. "Let it rip. Wait! Check it's locked first."

Another uniformed officer stepped forward, twisted the handle, then shook his head.

"As you were, Archie."

The big man drew the ram back deliberately, then thrust it forward with amazing speed. Angus saw nothing but a red blur before he heard the sound of splintering wood. The door flew backwards and crashed against the inside wall where it came to rest, askew on its hinges. Archie stood aside, satisfied with his handiwork. A couple of uniformed officers funnelled past. Angus heard them stomping around inside, calling Ewan's name. Twenty seconds later they reemerged, shaking their heads. "Naebody here," one of them said.

"Right, tell Forensics to stop hiding in their van and get in here," Nadia said. She turned to Angus and threw him a pair of blue nitrile gloves. "Shall we?"

He snapped on the gloves. "S'ppose so."

Nadia stepped past the shattered doorframe.

"What exactly are we looking for?" he asked, following her into the hallway.

"Evidence, Angus. He's a gamekeeper: Maybe we'll find an actual smoking gun?"

Angus stared at her, not remotely amused.

"Sorry," she said, "I make shit jokes when I'm nervous." She wrinkled her nose. "Bit pongy in here."

The uniformed officers had already turned the lights on. Nadia glanced through the door to the right into a living room that was barely big enough for the couch, coffee table, armchair, and TV. Pizza boxes, fish and chip wrappers, and crumpled Tennant's cans covered the coffee table, overflowing onto the rug below.

She backed out and gave Angus a tight smile, then glanced over his shoulder as the forensic team waddled in, rustling like dry leaves in their Tyvek suits.

"Hope you've not touched nothing, DI Sharif?" one of them barked.

Nadia raised her hands. "That's a double negative, Scobbie."

"What are you, the grammar police? Beat it!" He jerked a thumb over his shoulder.

"Okay, keep your hair on, Scobs," Nadia said.

They squeezed past the forensic team out into the night. Angus sucked in a lungful of clean, cold air. He watched the scene of crime officers unload some lights from the back of the van. They clicked the tripods into place and a few seconds later the front of Ewan's cottage was bathed in a sodium glow.

He blinked, dazzled by the brilliant white light. His eyelids fluttered, and in those fractions of a second when his eyes were closed a series of images flitted through his head like electrical pulses. Drops of ruby blood hit the surface of a pool, diffusing on impact before being carried away on the current.

Phosphorescent flames tore at a corpse that hung from the branch of a tree. He could smell lighter fluid and the sickly sweet stench of rendered fat and charred flesh. He saw skin blister and ignite in a purple flame. He saw Donn Fírinne—the Dark One—arms outstretched. Behind the ravenous sound of the blaze he could make out a low murmur, a raspy incantation in a language he could not understand.

He spun around, away from the blinding lamps. The afterglow from the burning body was seared into his retinas. He clenched his fists, willing the vision away. Slowly, the image faded. He stood for a second and waited for his heart rate to return to normal.

"Come on, let's sit in the car. It's freezing out here," Nadia said.

"Aye." He nodded. He waited for Nadia to turn towards the car, then dug the bottle of pills out of his coat pocket. He tipped two yellow tablets into his palm and swallowed them dry, working them down with his saliva. The pill bottle felt light. He gave it a shake and realized with dismay that it was empty. "Fuck," he muttered. *"Fuck, fuck, fuck . . ."*

Grinding his teeth, he followed Nadia towards the car and climbed in beside her. She already had the heater on full blast and was warming her hands. "You okay, Angus?"

"Aye, bit of a headache."

"Did you get your case sorted?"

He frowned at her, momentarily confused. "What? Oh, aye . . ."

He scrubbed his hands over his face, bone-weary. "Ewan will probably turn up. I don't think he's our man, Nadia. And even if they find forensic evidence that Faye was in his cottage, it proves nothing. They were friends. She probably visited loads of times."

"Aye, true. Could be a waste of time. About ninety percent of the stuff we do is. Still has to be done."

He sighed. "So what do we do now?"

"We wait."

As it happened, they didn't have to wait long. The car had barely heated up when a uniformed officer rapped on the window. Nadia wound it down. "Something you have to see, boss."

Nadia cocked an eyebrow at Angus. Despite the tiredness, he felt a surge of adrenaline. He was out of the car and marching alongside Nadia towards the cottage before he knew it. A white-suited SOCO waved them forward.

"What have you got, Scobs?"

"I'll show you," he said, leading them down the corridor to the last door on the right, which Angus knew was Ewan's bedroom. Inside, another SOCO was crouched on the floor like a big maggot amongst a drift of empty crisp packets, sweetie wrappers, and lager cans. He was lifting small scraps of shiny paper with tweezers and dropping them in clear evidence bags. Angus glanced on the wall by Ewan's bed and saw faint rectangles where the photographic collage of Faye had once been. His heart sank.

The SOCO held one of the shreds up for Nadia, a photograph of Faye, torn down the middle. "They're all of the victim," Scobbie said. "Must be about twenty or thirty. All torn to shreds."

Nadia's eyes flicked towards Angus. "Right, thanks."

Suddenly another voice boomed from somewhere else in the house.

"Boss! Boss! We've got something here!"

Scobbie swished past them, practically running from the room. Angus and Nadia were right behind him as he barrelled into the kitchen. The smell was worse in there, the main culprit an overflowing bin in the corner of the room. Dirty dishes were piled high in the sink, and the kitchen table was covered in snares, fishing equipment, bowls, cereal packets, and empty whisky bottles. The SOCO, however, was kneeling on the scabby linoleum beside a washing machine.

"What you got, Felix? Oh . . ."

Angus and Nadia peered over Scobbie's shoulder. His guts seemed to clench as he saw what the SOCO with the ridiculous name was holding in his gloved hands. He heard Nadia blow out a breath of air. She caught his eye and gave a tremulous smile.

"Smoking gun," she said.

CHAPTER 26

ANGUS trudged towards the front door of his cottage as if his boots were filled with lead. After the discovery at Ewan's place, there had been a frenzy of activity. The ghillie's name had been released to the press. Angus had sat with the rest of the MIT in the incident room to watch the *News at Ten*, which had led with the story. Ewan, the news anchor informed them, was armed and potentially dangerous. Immediately after the segment, the phones began to ring— callers from as far apart as Thurso and Galashiels calling to say they'd spotted Ewan Hunter out walking a dog or doing a grocery run or shopping for cable ties in B&Q. The photograph the media had been given by the PR department was a police mug shot, taken an hour or so after Angus had nicked him for assault. Ewan's hair was wild, his complexion pasty, and he glared at the camera with hatred in his eyes. He looked like any two-bit psycho spotted every night of the week outside pubs and clubs up and down Scotland. Which probably accounted for the volume of useless phone calls.

It was impossible to run down every lead, but ironically, there were no local tip-offs from folk who actually might know Ewan. By midnight, Crowley had ordered them to call it a day, although the DCI himself did not seem in the least tired. Nadia and the rest of the MIT detectives were billeted at the Glenruig Inn, which had a separate accommodation block, but Angus wouldn't have been surprised if Crowley had a sleeping bag in the village hall. Or perhaps he slept standing up, like Agnes and Muriel.

As Angus put his foot on the bottom step, he still could hardly believe what they'd found. How could Ewan be so stupid? Angus slid his key in the lock and was about to open the door when he heard the sound of footsteps. He turned and a familiar gangly shape emerged from the shadows.

"Are you ignoring me, old bean?" Gills asked.

"Bit busy, Gills. What with the murder and everything."

"It's the 'and everything' I want to talk to you about."

"I don't follow."

Gills stepped into the puddle of light around the doorstep. "They tell me you got out of the church just in time?"

"Aye." He sighed. "It was a bit close for comfort."

"You saved Raymond the Waver's life."

He shrugged.

"Did you . . . see anything?" Gills asked.

Angus shook his head, eyes downcast. "It's not what you think," he murmured. "I heard the rockfall, nothing more."

"But there is more," Gills insisted. "There's much more to all this."

Angus briefly closed his eyes. All those missed calls today—he'd known Gills was concocting some theory; that's why he'd ignored them.

"Listen, Angus, that rockfall, it fulfils a prophecy."

He stared at his friend, expression blank. "Really?"

"Aye. When I saw that flattened church this morning, I knew it meant something. It's late, and I won't bore you with every detail, but it concerns something foretold in the 1500s by a reputed seer, Gormshùil Mhòr na Borgh."

"Borgh, as in the village on Barra?"

"Aye. That's where she lived. And died. She was executed, but that's by the by. The point is, Gormshùil made any number of prophecies that have come to pass. She said, for instance, that one day windmills would rise from the North Sea, which must have seemed nonsense to folk back in the sixteenth century. But look at the number of offshore wind farms we now have in the Highlands."

"She was a green-energy visionary—so what?"

"One of her prophecies remained unfulfilled," Gills continued, undeterred by Angus's scepticism. "Until today."

The light flattened the deep wrinkles on Gills's face, but he still looked old, like a sage in a fantasy film. "There's a huge rock that sits on the mountain, above MacVannin's croft. It used to be known as *Clach Rìoghalachd*, the Royalty Stone. At one time it was part of a stone circle, probably where early tribes inaugurated their kings. Gormshùil said the day would come when the stone would slide down the mountain and crush a church. I was there today, Angus. I saw that stone lying amidst the rubble of MacVannin's church."

"Gills," he said, growing tired with this nonsense, "that may be so, but I don't see the relevance—"

"I'm getting to that," Gills said, cutting him off. "The second part of Gormshùil's prophecy says that when the *Clach Rìoghalachd* falls, the

MacRuari line will come to an end, and the wretched will be possessed by demons—"

The old man's hand shot out and grabbed Angus's bicep. "Listen to me, Angus," he hissed. "This is just the start. The prophecy warns there will be more sacrifices to the old gods. I spoke to the Witch from Rhu today, and what she said confirmed—"

"Who the hell's the Witch from Rhu?"

"She's a seer, Angus, like you. . . ."

Angus shook himself free of Gills's grasp. "I'm not a bloody seer!"

He took a deep breath, trying to control his temper. "I shouldn't be saying this, Gills, but Ewan Hunter did it. He was infatuated with Faye and killed her when she turned him down. That's all there is to it: no prophecy, no witches, just a horrible crime committed by someone who couldn't take rejection. Now, if you don't mind, it's been a long day, and I need a fucking dram."

He turned his back on Gills and fumbled with the front door key. He could feel Gills's eyes boring into his back, but when the old man next spoke, his tone was soft.

"How many more must die before you see?"

Angus hesitated, then pushed open the door and stepped inside.

"Close your eyes and see, *a'bhalach*," Gills pleaded. "Before it's too late, close your eyes and see."

Angus poured a hefty measure of Talisker into a cut crystal glass. He'd barely taken a slung when the snug room door opened and Ashleigh padded in, half-asleep, a dressing gown wrapped around her.

"You're home," she said, blinking away sleep. "I thought I heard voices?"

"Nope, just me talking to myself."

"First sign of madness." Ash yawned.

Nadia had said the same that morning. He took another pull of his dram, feeling somehow guilty.

"Christ, Angus! What happened to your face?"

Ash raised her hand and brushed the back of her fingers down his cheek.

"It's nothing, *a ghràidh*. I've had worse cuts shaving," he said, recalling the words of the cheeky young paramedic.

"But what happened?"

He put down his dram and took her hands. "Did you hear about MacVannin's church?"

"Aye, Moira said it was destroyed by a rockfall, that there was a service on at the time and folk were lucky to get out alive."

"For once that nosy old besom was right. I was there. A stray rock left me this souvenir, but I'm fine, honestly."

Ash wrapped her arms around him. "Bloody hell! You could have died," she said, choking up. She was so strong, so kind, it was easy to forget how much she'd lost. More than he had.

"I'm fine," he repeated, as if trying to convince himself.

She brushed her lips against his. "Come on, time for bed," she whispered.

Sleep, though, evaded him. Well after Ash had drifted off, he lay staring up at the ceiling, thinking about Nadia. Her taste. Her smell. Dancing drunk with her at the Fubar in Stirling. Skinny-dipping in the sea at St. Andrews. That first night together. Her sequined dress discarded on the floor like a mermaid's skin. Her tears. The hurt and betrayal in her parting stare. Eventually he gave up trying to sleep, and swung his legs out of bed. Being careful not to wake Ash, he crept from the bedroom and pulled the shoebox from its hiding place at the back of the cupboard. He carried it through to the snug and placed it on the coffee table. His glass of Talisker sat on the mantelpiece, where he'd left it before his mind had switched to other things. He retrieved the glass and took a swift drink before easing the lid off the shoebox.

Lewis Duncan grinned up at him from the dog-eared front page of the *West Highland Mail*. "Disabled Man Dies in Arson Attack," read the headline. He reached for his glass and drank. The whisky burned its way down his throat, making him cough. And for a second he was back in the house, black smoke filling his lungs as fire rippled across the ceiling.

"A wheelchair-bound man died when his home was engulfed in flames in an incident police are treating as arson.

"Lewis Duncan was pulled from the burning building by a passerby, but despite attempts to resuscitate him, the 21-year-old died at the scene.

"The fire was started around 2 a.m. yesterday morning at a property on the outskirts of Arisaig. Initial investigations suggest an accelerant was used. Police believe the blaze was started deliberately by the victim's mother and carer, Elizabeth Duncan (50)."

Angus knew the story off by heart. He read it anyway, then put the clipping to one side.

Barbara Klein gave him a coquettish smile. "Murder Probe after Woman Found Dead in Woods," read the headline. He recalled the way her body had lain twisted in the dew-soaked grass, a ligature around her neck, face bloated and purple. Her lacquered fingernails were painted red with black spots, like ladybirds.

"A murder hunt is underway after a 26-year-old woman was found dead at a local beauty spot.

"The victim has been identified as hairdresser Barbara Klein.

"Her body was discovered by police early yesterday morning after a tip-off from a member of the public.

"Police are keen to trace her partner, Joseph Carver (28), who they believe may have vital information."

He placed the cutting aside and dug down to the next layer, where the Drowned Boy was buried. Perhaps he hoped that by placing these clippings below the others he would prevent Ethan Boyce from invading his dreams.

He sniffed, that old unhinged sensation in his chest, as if everything that moored him to the earth was coming loose. "Boy Dies in Murder-Suicide Horror."

"A community is in mourning today after a father drowned his son in the sea before taking his own life.

"Eight-year-old Ethan Boyce was killed by his father, Jonathan, yesterday morning at Camusdarach Beach near Morar.

"The *West Highland Mail* understands the youngster—a P4 pupil at Morar Primary School—was drowned.

"An off-duty police officer intervened and managed to drag the boy from the sea, but Ethan was pronounced dead at the scene.

"It is understood Mr. Boyce—a well-known local artist better known as JoBo—fled the beach. He was hit by a train travelling on the West Highland Line some thirty minutes later. Police are treating his death as suicide."

Angus's eyes flitted to the picture of Ethan—big cheesy grin, school uniform, fair hair neat apart from a bit that stuck up at the side. It was that detail that always got him. He imagined Ethan's mother, Janet, trying to flatten her son's hair in the morning before the school photograph. He remembered his own mother doing the same, fussing around him with hair gel and tutting at his obstreperous locks.

Janet had moved away after the killing, back to Black Isle, where she'd grown up. The memories must have been too painful. He could understand that, but distance didn't necessarily make the trauma any easier. He ran his fingers over Ethan's picture. His eyes were blue and innocent, not the blank eyes of the dead boy who visited him in his dreams, the boy with crabs coming from his mouth. He'd supported Inverness Caledonian Thistle Football Club. He liked superhero comics and wanted to design and build boats when he grew up.

Angus closed his eyes and felt the marram grass biting his ankles as he sprinted along the dunes. He saw the deserted beach, curving like a scythe between two rocky outcrops, the sea a deep blue, the same colour as the boy's eyes. In the distance, he heard the sound of water thrashing. . . .

His eyes snapped open. He reached for his glass of Talisker, took a gulp, then dug down to the final layer. With clumsy fingers, he lifted out the dog-eared case file and placed it on the coffee table. A memory flashed in his head of Detective Inspector Hood, the gaunt, sad-eyed officer who had handed him a copy of the case file, giving in to years of badgering from Angus. "You'll no' find what you're looking for in there, son," Hood had said, tapping the side of his nose. "Maybe ye should be looking closer to home."

He took a sip of whisky and sloshed it around his mouth, swilling away Hood's insinuation. He flipped open the case file. His mother smiled at him from the brittle pages of newsprint clipped to the file. Tears nipped behind his eyelids. He wished he could reach through the newspaper, into the photograph, and drag her back from that otherworld where she lingered. He imagined the warmth of her hand in his, the sweet, comforting scent of her as she pulled him close. A tear slid down his cheek and plopped onto the headline: "Murder Hunt after Local Mum Slain."

Sobbing quietly, he lifted the newspaper articles and began to replace them, layer on layer, as if interring the memories. However, he did not put the lid back on the shoebox. Instead he stood and, on unsteady legs, walked through to the kitchen. He took a pair of scissors from the drawer and returned to the living room. He lifted a recent copy of the *West Highland Mail*, eyes scanning the headline: "Laird's Daughter Slain."

He lifted the scissors and began to cut.

ACT III

"In our folk-stories of giants who thrust great hands through roofs and snatch away new-born babes, we may have a softened although persistent race-memory of human sacrifices."

—"A Highland Goddess," Donald A. Mackenzie, 1912

CHAPTER 27

THE first thought Angus had when he woke the next morning was about the empty bottle of pills and whether he could get through the day without them. He fumbled for his mobile phone and clumsily typed in the message.

Ash's side of the bed was empty. She would be out for a morning run. Her dedication shamed him—it had been almost a week since he'd last swam. He stood, swaying slightly, then staggered to the bathroom. He hardly recognised the man staring back at him from the mirror above the sink. His eyes looked raw, pupils like two piss holes in the snow. He needed a haircut and a shave and a nose job to fix the kink caused by a blow from a shinty ball when he was eighteen. He turned on the cold-water tap and ducked his head under the jets, twisting his mouth up to swill away the whisky taste in his mouth.

He turned off the tap and placed his forehead against the cold porcelain of the sink. Pearls of cold water dribbled down his cheeks, beaded on his jaw, and dripped onto the bathroom floor. He straightened up and stared at his reflection in the mirror. Over his shoulder, a pair of green eyes stared back at him.

"Morning, Constable MacNeil," Faye said.

He let out a yelp and spun around, but no one was there. His head throbbed. "Jesus!" he hissed.

"Nope, just me."

The voice came from his right. He shot out a hand to steady himself against the towel rail. Faye sat on the toilet seat, filing her nails. She wore jodhpurs, a tweed riding jacket, and tan leather boots. Her hair was pulled into a tight ponytail.

She was using his wife's nail file. She paused mid-file and glanced up at him. Her eyes were like puddles coated in a film of ice.

"You need to get your shit together, Constable," she muttered. "Before some other poor bastard dies."

"It's . . . got nothing to do with me," he stammered.

"Keep telling yourself that."

She splayed her fingers, inspecting her handiwork.

"I can't believe Ewan killed you."

"Why not?"

"I just . . . can't."

Apparently satisfied with her nails, she glanced at him. "Then who?"

"The antlered figure—Donn Fírinne—who is he?"

"You tell me?"

He screwed his eyes shut.

She's not real!

"I don't know!" he yelled.

His eyes snapped open. Faye was gone. Ash's nail file was on the shelf where it always sat.

Even wearing his wetsuit, the cold drove the air from his lungs as if he'd been punched. He kicked hard, the way his swimming coach Mr. Latimer had drummed into him on countless early-morning sessions in the Silvaig pool. He glided for a few seconds underwater, enjoying the silence in his head. Thick strands of kelp billowed in the gentle swell, reaching up from the seabed like soft hands, entreating him to join them. He thought of Gills's tales of selkies, the seal folk who came ashore to shed their skin and dance in the moonlight. A mortal man might meet a selkie woman and fall in love with her. They would marry, and she would bear his children, but always that longing for the sea remained. The husband, sensing his wife's yearning, would hide her skin to prevent her returning to the sea. But eventually she would turn the house upside down and—finding her skin—abandon the family she loved and return to the ocean. "These stories show," Gills used to say, "that we cannot deny our nature. We have to accept who we are."

Angus kicked again, fighting to stay underwater, imagining he was a selkie. His chest tightened as the oxygen in his lungs depleted, though he clung on until he had no option but to break the surface.

The sound of the world crashed in. Arms thrashing the waves, he ploughed forward, Mr. Latimer bellowing in his ear: *Your elbow's dropping on entry! Don't over-rotate! For Christ's sake, kick!*

Angus gritted his teeth and did as he was told. The coach's voice faded. His arms were a blur, fingers puncturing the waves with each stroke. But he could not outswim the flashes in his head. They came fast, like bolts of electricity: Lewis Duncan's charred corpse. The smudged lipstick on Barbara Klein's lips. Ethan's accusing stare. His mother's terrified eyes. Faye's hair matted in blood.

Angus let out an anguished scream, sucked in a mouthful of frigid air, and dived. He swam down, deeper into the freezing water, as if respite hid in its darkest depths. A voice in his head told him to stay down here forever.

An hour later, dressed in his uniform, Angus walked along the Esplanade in Silvaig, buffeted by the wind. He watched a CalMac passenger ferry docking as fishing boats moored in a small harbour bucked on the swell. His eyes lingered for a second on the old rotten wooden pier, jutting into the sea like the decaying skeleton of a dinosaur. The scar on his side seemed to throb. Rust-red seaweed clung to the legs of the structure, as if the creature were wading through blood.

Shuddering slightly, Angus clattered down a set of steps and through the piss-smelling underpass that linked the Esplanade to High Street. He scuttled past shops selling outdoor clothing and tartan tat, the wind a firm hand on his back, shoving him forward. The pressure only eased when he turned down a small dank lane. The lane was known locally as Shaggers' Alley, because it was frequented by amorous couples after the nearby disco spilled out. Angus had lost count of the number of young ones he'd interrupted in the throes of a knee-trembler. He now tried to avoid the lane on a Saturday night.

Although narrow, the lane was home to a number of businesses, including Ossian Fine Arts, the Steamie laundrette, Belle's Beauty Salon, Brandon's iron-monger, and his destination—GWA, Glenda Wright Associates, Counselling & Psychotherapy. He paused in front of the discreet glossy black door. He'd been coming here every month since the incident, although he'd missed the last session. Glenda would understand if he cancelled today as well, wouldn't she? He could say he was working the murder case, which had the added benefit of being true. He hesitated, eyes on the selection of large kitchen knives that glinted from the window of the ironmonger opposite. Not the most comforting sight for Glenda's potentially suicidal clients to see as they exited.

"Ach, bugger it," he muttered, pushing open the black door.

The office was bright, Scandi-chic, and smelt of the expensive pomegranate-infused Jo Malone candles that Dr. Glenda Wright favoured. Angus sat fidgeting on a wooden-framed accent chair as Glenda poured them coffee from a fancy machine behind her tidy walnut desk. She was in her late forties and wore an elegant camel-coloured suit over a brilliant white blouse. When she turned, two small cups of coffee in her hands, her wide-set eyes behind trendy dark-framed glasses were not entirely friendly.

Dr Wright held his gaze for a long, awkward second then gave a small laugh. "Look, Angus, I know you don't want to be here. This is a box-ticking exercise. Your boss demanded it, so here you are. But to be honest with you, we've not even scratched the surface. Killing a man is no small thing."

"It was self-defence." He took a sip of coffee, lest his eyes betray the weakness of his reply.

"Quite. Your use of force was deemed proportionate, in the circumstances."

"It was."

Glenda cocked a neat eyebrow. "Hardly your fault Mr. Watson couldn't swim. Although it was you who put him in the sea."

"We grappled. He stabbed me. I shoved him. He tripped and fell off the pier." Angus threw out his hands, palms up. "That's it."

"I hear you're a strong swimmer, Angus. A Highland champion in your younger days. Yet you didn't even attempt to save Mr. Watson?"

"I had a bloody great knife stuck in my ribs."

Dr Wright held his gaze, then flashed a tight smile. "I appreciate this is a difficult time of year for you. The anniversary of the incident." She flicked through some notes in front of her, but it was clearly for show, the blow ready. "And also the anniversary of your mother's death, I notice."

She glanced up, both neat eyebrows raised in a question. He clamped his mouth shut.

"Do you want to talk about your mother?"

He gave a small shrug, as if it were of no consequence.

"Tell me what you felt when you saw Mr. Watson at the end of the pier, the knife at his ex-girlfriend's throat?"

When he didn't answer, Dr. Wright cocked her head to the side. "Fear? No, anger, I think. If cops carried guns in this country, you'd have blown him away, right?"

"No," he said.

"That would be understandable, Angus. It was, after all, the anniversary of your mother's murder. And here was a man with a knife holding a woman hostage. It would only be natural to conflate the two. Perhaps, subconsciously, you wanted to kill Mr. Watson. You wanted to satisfy that childhood revenge fantasy. And by saving Mrs. Watson, save your mother."

"My mother's dead."

"Avenge her death, then."

"It was self-defence," he said through gritted teeth. "The court said so."

A sudden flash of anger coursed through his body. Why was he having to justify this?

Dr Wright pinched her bottom lip. "But you feel bad about killing Mr. Watson, don't you? The guilt is eating you up inside."

Angus had to stop himself from laughing out loud. "Do you remember, five years ago, a father drowned his son in the sea at Camusdarach?" he said.

Dr Wright's brow furrowed. "Vaguely. An artist wasn't he, the father?"

"Jonathan Boyce, better known as JoBo," Angus replied. "His son was called Ethan. It won't be in your notes, but I was there that day. I saw what happened, but I was too late to save Ethan."

He recalled the boy's lifeless eyes staring up at him, and how he'd taken an involuntary step towards the sea. He'd felt the pull of the waves and it had taken all of his strength not to simply walk into them, let the ocean claim him. He rubbed his hands over his face, as if trying to scrub away the memory. Dr. Wright remained silent, but he could feel her steely gaze on him. At length, he looked up. "Not being able to save Ethan, that's what keeps me up at night. Mark Watson"—he shrugged—"he can burn in Hell for all I care."

CHAPTER 28

THREE magpies fought over roadkill beside the tiny graveyard where her parents were buried. The birds were the first thing Ash saw when she got out of the Clio. She watched them for a long second, tearing at the flesh of what had once been a rabbit. She picked up a rock and drew back her arm, intending to throw it at the magpies. Instead she dropped the stone to the muddy ground. What did it matter? The rabbit was already dead, and the magpies weren't what killed it.

She hefted her clarsach from the car and pushed open the grave-yard's rusty gate. Autumn hadn't always been a melancholy month for her. Squirreled away inside her she held a faint recollection of happy days collecting chestnuts with her parents, wrapped up in mittens and woolly hats. She remembered the fresh, crisp scent of frost, the eruption of colour on the trees behind their house—deep reds, burnished coppers, fiery oranges, and golden yellows. She remembered trips to the seaside—thick, hot tomato soup from a thermos, jam sandwiches that left her fingers sticky, the bright flash of a kite and her father's strong arms around her.

Now death and decay were all around her. She could smell it in the rotten leaves that wilted in drifts by the drystane dyke, see it in the naked branches of the rowan trees outside the small church, hear it in the faint caws of the magpies as they continued to feast.

Her mother and father were buried in the same plot overlooking the sea. They would have approved of their final resting place. Dad, in particular, had loved the sea. Ash had a dim memory of them sailing to the island of Lismore, of salty spray on her face and a school of porpoises playing in the boat's wake.

Ash stood for a second, staring at the headstone, which was beginning to show signs of weathering. The surface was pitted and crumbly in places, and the base had taken on the green hue of algae. One of the disadvantages of such a view was its exposure to the elements.

She lifted the clarsach from the case, and took a long, raking breath. Her fingers flickered across the strings, coaxing out a sad lament she'd composed especially. The piece had come to her as if sent on the wind as she walked by the shore.

She closed her eyes and let the memories of her parents wash over her. Every year her recollections seemed to fade a little more, which was partly why she came up here to play every so often. She couldn't explain it, but the music seemed to graft those treasured memories to the core of her, like a branch to a tree.

As she played by the graveside, she let her mind drift, untethered, like a feather on the wind. It was something Granny Beag had taught her—how to free her mind when she played, how to let all the anger and sorrow drift away on the music.

Memories floated around her, sometimes little more than sensations, like the texture of her dad's fingertips, or the smoothness of the skin in the crook of her mother's neck. She swayed slightly, her fingers dancing across the strings. A faint smile touched her lips.

But then, suddenly, she heard the crunch of approaching footsteps. Her eyes snapped open. She let out a small gasp and her hands fell from the strings. Standing a few meters away, watching her with his big bulbous eyes, was Reverend MacVannin.

"Apologies, Mrs. MacNeil, I didnae mean to frighten ye. I was passing when I heard the music."

Ash flushed, embarrassed, but also annoyed that the minister had thought it was okay to intrude on her private moment.

"It's okay," she said. "No harm done."

"You're a fine musician," he said. "Of course, all music is the devil's work, but I think even God might make allowances for something so beautiful."

"I'd hope so," Ash said. "Anyway, I'd better be going." She lifted the clarsach and began wrestling it into the case. Out of the corner of her eye, she saw MacVannin look her up and down, as he might one of his cattle. "We've been keeping an eye on ye, Mrs. MacNeil. Metaphorically speaking," he said.

"Who's we?"

"Myself and my congregation. We're impressed with the way you've stood up against our deluded laird. If there were more folk like you around, perhaps we wouldn't find ourselves in such dire straits."

Ash slung the case over her shoulder. "Aye, er . . . thanks."

MacVannin stood on the path, meaning she'd have to go around him to get out of the graveyard.

"You should come to church this Sunday, Ashleigh. . . . Do you mind if I call you Ashleigh?"

"But I thought your church had been destroyed?" she asked, sidestepping his question.

"The Orange Hall in Arisaig has kindly agreed to help us out while my church is rebuilt. You should come. You'll find like-minded people there, Ashleigh. Good people."

"I'll think about it," she said, taking a step towards him. The minister made no effort to get out of her way. Up close, he had a rank odour of sheep dip, sweat, and cow dung.

MacVannin's tongue shot out, wetting his thick lips. "Perhaps we can help each other out?"

Ash resisted the urge to knee him in the balls. "No offense, but I don't think so. I'm a Humanist, Reverend."

The minister smirked. "Then what are you doing here, in a Christian kirkyard?"

"My parents are buried here," she said simply.

He shook his head. "Pah! I'd have expected better of you, Ashleigh. In my experience, Humanists are the most naive folk you'll ever meet. They're little gods who use their faith—and Humanism is a faith—to justify doing whatever they like on the basis of reason alone. Essentially, you lot don't like being told what to do."

"By the likes of you—absolutely."

MacVannin's cheeks began to colour. "I'd have thought what has happened here in recent days, not to mention history, would shake your belief."

"What do you mean?"

"We were born into sin. Human nature is not driven by ethics. We are base creatures. Only the fear of our Lord prevents us from acting upon our dark desires."

"Speak for yourself," Ash replied. She could refute these arguments, but there was no point. His mind was closed.

"Seems I was mistaken about you," he snorted, eyes bulging. "Not everyone's soul is worth saving."

She gave him a sweet smile. "I'm sure that's not all you're mistaken about. Now, if you'll step out of my way—"

MacVannin glared at her for a long second but finally relented. He took a small step sideways. His nose seemed to twitch as she squirmed past him, as if sniffing her scent. "I pity you, Ashleigh," he hissed. "I pity you."

CHAPTER 29

ANGUS ran into Crowley outside Glenruig village hall. The DCI was smoking a menthol-scented cigarette and glaring at the press gathered along the roadside some fifty yards away. "Cutting it fine, MacNeil," he rasped, glancing at his watch.

Apart from the American-tinged accent, Crowley sounded just like Inspector Stout. Perhaps all senior officers were schooled in talking down to their underlings.

"Apologies, sir," he said, offering no explanation.

"How are you after yesterday's incident?" Crowley asked with a slight smirk. "No need for a hugging session with occupational health?"

Already covered on that score, he thought. "Nah, I'm fine."

"Good man!" Crowley said, slapping him on the shoulder with his mutilated hand. "And how are you finding it, being a cog in the MIT machine? Must be a change from collaring sheep worriers and speeders?"

"Aye, it's certainly . . . different."

Crowley sucked at the cigarette, eyes narrowing. "And DI Sharif? You pair rubbing along okay?" he asked, blowing smoke into the chill air.

"Aye, grand."

"Good. Nadia's a fine officer. One of the best." He scrutinized Angus with his sharp eyes. "You know something, I've never been married, Angus, never felt the need for a family. The polis has always been my pack. And Nadia's like a daughter to me."

A frown crept across Angus's brow. He didn't like the direction this conversation was going. "Okay," he said uncertainly.

"Just watch yourself, aye?" Crowley said. "She doesn't need distractions."

"Distractions? Sorry, sir, I've no idea what you're talking about."

Crowley stubbed his cigarette out on the wall and flicked the butt into an overgrown hawthorn bush. All traces of American inflection fell away as he said: "Aye, ye do."

Crowley brushed past Angus and disappeared inside the village hall. Angus waited a few moments, mulling over what the DCI had said, before following him inside. As far as he could tell, all the MIT were already in the incident room, their numbers buoyed by local CID and a squad of uniforms. Most were looking busy, or pretending to be, phones pressed to their ears or fingers bashing their laptops. The queue for the coffee machine evaporated at the sight of Crowley. Nadia was over at the murder board, sticking new photographs onto the wall next to the large map of the local area. Red string, like a bloody spider's web, crisscrossed the map, detailing the distances between significant locations—Dunbirlinn Castle, the pagan commune, the beach where Faye's body was found, MacVannin's croft, Ewan's cottage.

Angus walked over and stood at her shoulder. "Morning," he muttered, "hope I'm not distracting you."

She gave him a questioning squint. "Just something Crowley said," he explained. "Is that—" He pointed at a set of photographs that looked like those of Faye that had been stuck to Ewan's bedroom wall.

"Aye," Nadia said, "poor Vee and Boaby were up to all hours last night piecing the torn photographs together. Although I think Boaby enjoyed it. He likes jigsaws, apparently."

"And pies by the looks of him," Angus replied. He had yet to see DS Robert Dunbar without food in his paw.

"Hope you're not body-shaming, Angus?" Nadia said, eyes smiling.

"Me? Never." He moved his nose closer to the board and peered at one of the photographs. It showed Faye sitting on a flat rock, staring out to sea, the wind blowing strands of hair across her face. She wore a cornflower-blue dress and looked melancholy. Behind her was a small stone structure he recognised. . . .

"Briefing's about to start," Nadia said, nudging him on the side. Angus turned and plonked himself down on the nearest chair. Everyone else did likewise, whilst those without chairs perched on desks or stood awkwardly, unsure what to do with their hands.

"Right," Crowley said, without his usual preliminary banter, "what's the word on Ewan Hunter?"

"We've run down as many leads as possible after last night's appeal on the news," DC Ryan Fleet answered. "I'm not going to sugarcoat it, sir—we got bugger all. We've reviewed all the CCTV in the local area, which isn't much, but no sign of either him or the Nissan Pathfinder."

"Well, he can't have just disappeared," Crowley growled. "Doesn't he have any pals?"

"Not really," Vee answered. "He's a bit of a loner by all accounts. But on the plus side, sir, I spoke to the Procurator Fiscal and she says if the evidence we obtained from Ewan's cottage pans out, he is—and I quote—'totally screwed.'"

Crowley gave a wolfish grin. "When will the lab get back to us?"

"Later today."

"Excellent stuff, but let's not get ahead of ourselves. Hunter might be our top suspect, but he's not our only one."

"Another thing, sir," Vee said. "The lab did have some information for me this morning. I've good news and bad news. Which do you want first?"

"Hit me with the bad."

"The blood the sniffer dog detected on the altar stone up at the commune was common-or-garden O positive. Faye's blood is AB negative."

"If it wasn't Faye's blood, whose was it?"

Everyone suddenly seemed very interested in their shoes or notebooks.

"Rather dents the case against the pagans," Crowley said.

"Actually, sir," DC Fleet said, "I've been doing some digging on Christine Kelbie. Turns out she has a few run-ins with the police from years back. I spoke to a retired officer"—he glanced at his notebook—"a Constable McTaggart. He had dealings with her. He said Kelbie's originally from the Traveller community. Well, 'a dirty tinker' was how he actually phrased it."

Crowley reclined in his chair and crossed one ankle over the other. He wore scuffed leather boots but no socks, Angus noticed. "Why's this relevant, Rylo?"

"McTaggart said they frequently had to move Kelbie's caravans on from unauthorized campsites." He hesitated and dropped his eyes from Crowley's gaze. "He says Kelbie's mother—or grandmother, he couldn't be sure—placed a curse on him. And he swears, from that day on, he's suffered acute undiagnosed bouts of pain in his . . . erm . . . rectum. Had to take early retirement as a result."

Angus heard a few stifled giggles. He gave Nadia a sidelong look. She, too, was hiding a smile.

"Bum curses, Rylo!" Crowley boomed. "Really? My bullshit detector is tingling."

"Aye, maybe," Ryan said, trying to recover some dignity, "but the mention of curses put me in mind of the clay corpse. Could be that sort of lore was passed down from generation to generation."

"It's a bit thin," Crowley said. "But no harm in getting her in on a volley. In fact, we should reinterview all the pagans. Which reminds me, did forensics get anything from the camper van?"

"Nada," Fleet replied. "It's clean as a whistle. Well, apart from the odd strand of weed. They did have some information about the clay corpse. The hair that was glued to the doll's head is human."

"Faye's?"

"Err, no, but chemicals suggest it was dyed."

Crowley blew a raspberry. "Moving on: Vee, you promised me good news?"

"Aye, sir. Turns out the blood on the horse's flank was Faye's."

Crowley tugged at his bottom lip with his mutilated hand.

"So the killer bludgeons her, strangles her with a garrotte, then slings her body onto the horse to take to the deposition site. Risky."

"There were no hoofprints on the beach," Nadia said. "No footprints, either. We know that Faye's horse was a chestnut mare, but we've still not managed to trace anyone who is missing a white horse."

"Which means Bessie is still out there somewhere. Keep looking, but our priority remains finding Ewan Hunter."

Actions assigned by a croissant-munching DS Dunbar, the murder squad started to filter out of the village hall or return to their laptops and mobile phones. Angus stood for a few moments, staring at the pictures of Faye attached to the murder board. They weren't simply snapshots in time to him: he could hear the gurgle of the stream she sat beside in one photograph taken at the Fairy Pools; he could feel Bessie's warm flank as she hacked out from Dunbirlinn; he could smell the lush bracken as she sat by the ruined chapel.

His eyes fixed on the photograph he'd noticed earlier: Faye sitting on a flat rock with a stone structure in the background. The building was an old bothy known as Carlotta's Eyrie. Ewan had told him about the place, said he used to go there with his father.

He turned away from the board and spotted Nadia on her laptop. Rather than working, she seemed to be engrossed in a movie.

He marched across to her desk. "Busy, I see."

"Research," she muttered, without looking up.

"Aye?"

She had one earbud in, but he could still hear the warbling soundtrack to an old horror flick. On-screen, a scantily clad actress was fleeing a rabid army of the undead. Even for a pre-CGI movie, the thing looked pathetic.

The actress suddenly found herself at a dead end or, more accurately, a cliff edge. She was forced to turn and face the pursuing horde. Only then did he recognise a young Eleanor Chichester.

Nadia hit pause and flipped the earbud out.

"Hey! I was getting into that," he protested.

"It's only five minutes in, and she's the lead, so chances are she survives." She rolled her eyes at him then hit play. "I've been going through her filmography, such as it is."

On-screen, Eleanor drew what looked like spiky nunchucks and set about the zombies, who made it easy for her by attacking one at a time.

"I'm no Mark Kermode, but she can't act for toffee."

"What are you hoping to find?"

Nadia shrugged. "Nothing really. I'm finding it hard to sleep, that's all. Too bloody quiet. I miss the sirens and the Glasgow drunks fighting at three in the morning."

"Horror movies as a cure for insomnia? I'll have to remember that one."

"Do you sleep well, Angus?" she asked, suddenly serious.

He gave her a sidelong glance. "Aye," he lied.

"Maybe you were right."

"Eh? What d'you mean?"

"Moving here. Getting married. Settling down. Sleeping and stuff."

"It wasn't . . . I mean, that was never the plan."

Her head shot up. "No? Then what was the plan after Tulliallan, Angus?"

He tried to formulate a response, but the truth was wedged inside him. All he could manage now was a shrug.

After a long, awkward second, Nadia shook her head sadly. "Anyway," she muttered, "it hardly matters now." She closed the laptop with a snap, just as a gore-drenched Eleanor dispatched the last of the monsters with her nunchucks. "See, what did I tell you—she survives."

Angus could think of nothing to say to that, so he decided to tell her why he'd come to speak to her in the first place.

"Listen, Nadia, I've had a hunch," he said. "I think I know where Ewan is."

Angus drove them towards the village of Arisaig, the awkward silence punctuated by calls coming across the police radio, which he ignored.

"ZS calls NR 34A! Pick up, MacNeil, for God's sake!"

"Think you better answer that," Nadia said mildly. "Your boss sounds as if he's about to have a hernia."

Angus let out a long-suffering sigh and snatched up the radio. "Go ahead to 34A."

"About time, MacNeil! Where the hell are you?" Inspector Stout barked.

"Arisaig. Following a lead on Ewan Hunter."

"Aye, good for you. What's the update on the Knicker Snatcher? We need that scourge off our streets."

Angus squeezed the steering wheel, imagining it was Stout's scrawny neck. *Six months,* he told himself, *six months until the useless bastard retires.*

Beside him, Nadia tried—and failed—to suppress a laugh.

"I am kind of busy, sir," he protested.

"You'll find time," Stout replied, then cut the call.

Angus muttered a Gaelic curse under his breath. He gave Nadia a pained smile. "Welcome to the minor investigation team."

They pulled up in a secluded car park and set off on foot towards Carlotta's Eyrie. To begin with, a path sinuous with tree roots wended alongside a small stream, but soon they were climbing upwards through a murky wooded section of hillside, their footfalls muffled by moss and pine needles. Coal tits, siskins, and robins flitted between branches, but there were larger shadows too—hoodie crows that seemed to watch them pass with intense beady eyes. Their caws echoed around the canopy, the dry cackles an impenetrable language that somehow he recognised. He thought of James Chichester and heard again his bitter assessment of the human condition. *We've sacrificed a deeper, innate knowledge. We're now so far removed from our true selves that I fear there's no way back.*

A gloomy mood fogged his mind, one that did not dissipate until they left the forest behind and began the descent towards the secluded bay—named Camus Ghaoideil in Gaelic. Shingle crunched under their feet as they walked along the beach. Waves crashed onto the shore. Out to sea, gannets hung in the wind like white poly bags, then tucked their wings to their bodies and arrowed into the surf after the shoals of krill.

Carlotta's Eyrie was just visible in the distance, clinging to a sea stack like a limpet.

"Who's this Carlotta anyway?" Nadia asked, flicking hair out of her face.

"She was a trainee saboteur in the Special Operations Executive during World War Two," Angus said. "The SOE had several bases in the West Highlands. My dad used to say it was here the real battle against the Nazis was won. Agents were schooled in the dark arts of war—hand-to-hand combat, sabotage, espionage, explosives training, and how to live off the land."

"Do you think Ewan will be here?" Nadia asked.

"Aye. Ewan came here with his own father. It's a special place for him."

She didn't look convinced. "We checked his bank account. There's been no activity for a couple of days and Mrs. MacCrimmon said he was extremely upset about Faye."

"What are you getting at, Nadia?"

"Listen, Angus, you said yourself he's not coped well since the death of his dad. Sounds to me as if he's in a pretty dark place."

He understood now what she was hinting at. Ewan might well have decided to end it. However, there was another possibility, one he didn't feel like sharing with Nadia. Ewan could be lying in the heather, watching them through the scope of his hunting rifle, his finger on the trigger. Angus scanned the hillside, where drifts of dead bracken carpeted the lower slopes and scraggly trees sprang from fissures in the rock. There was no sign of movement, but that sense of being watched lingered until he reached the sea stack.

He paused, glanced up at the leaden sky, then skirted around the foot of the crag and began to climb. The path was steep but fairly well trodden down by sheep, and soon he reached the small, wizened trees that crowned the stack like coarse hair. From the rear, the bothy appeared deserted. It had been constructed with random-sized blocks, as if chiselled from the crag itself. A climbing rope was strung along the trees that fringed the building, and Angus used it for balance as he slithered down a slope to the bothy entrance. Past the rope was a sheer drop of some thirty or forty feet to the rocks below.

In the distance, the Moidart hills lay in the sea like a sleeping giant. Sunlight pierced the cloud blanket, throwing puddles of light on the waves. Slumped on a flat rock some twenty yards away—the place Faye had sat in the photograph—was Ewan.

Angus turned to Nadia. "Do you mind if I do the talking? If we come at him with cautions and arrests, he might spook."

"Aye, fair enough."

Ewan made no movement as Angus walked towards him, although he must have heard his approach. The ghillie faced out to sea, as if he were carved from rock. For a brief second he feared that Ewan had killed himself, but then he saw a slight movement. Ewan barely reacted when Angus walked past him and stood in his line of vision. The lad's eyes were haunted and red, and his stubble was fast becoming a beard.

"You're a hard man to find."

Ewan did not even look at him.

"You need to come with us, *a'bhalach*."

An old hunting rifle lay at Ewan's feet. The ghillie's eyes darted towards the gun.

Angus stepped forward and placed a foot on the barrel. "That's not how your dad would want his gun used."

The young man's shoulders began to shake. He hunched forward, hands covering his face as he sobbed quietly. Angus laid a gentle palm on Ewan's shoulder, just as he had in the hospital after John Hunter's death. "You're okay," he murmured, "it'll be okay," his words echoing the flimsy platitudes he'd used back then. Angus knew the unpalatable truth: Ewan was probably going to jail for murder.

CHAPTER 30

HALF an hour into the interview, Ruthven Crowley had still not asked Ewan about Faye or, indeed, anything remotely related to the case.

Angus sat on an uncomfortable office chair in the Silvaig Police Station observation room and watched the interview on a monitor. He was alone, Crowley having taken Nadia into the interview suite with him. Apart from a dishevelled Ewan, the only other person on-screen was the duty solicitor, Hamish McKeown, a grumpy borderline alcoholic who had once fallen asleep on his client when Angus was mid-interview.

To be fair to the solicitor, he was manfully keeping his eyes open as Crowley continued to quiz Ewan about hunting rifles and all aspects of deer stalking. Nadia sat with a notebook and a folder in front of her, but so far she'd not said a word, let alone made a note.

". . . you cannae go wrong with a Schmidt & Bender 8x56 Hungarian," Crowley opined, hands locked casually behind his head. "As good as any scope I've used. Point and shoot and unsurpassed light gathering, which means they're equally effective at dawn or dusk."

"Aye," Ewan said, nodding along, "they're no' bad for the price. Personally, I use a Vortex with my .243. Great in low light."

"What about bins?"

"Same: Vortex, although if I had the money, I'd go Swarovski or Zeiss. Best binoculars makers around."

Crowley grinned. "You'd love it in the States, young man. The hunting's out of this world. I've a buddy in Montana: ex–special forces, runs a hunting retreat in the Kootenai National Forest. I used to go up there two, three times a year. The game's incredible: mule deer, pronghorn antelope, Rocky Mountain elk, Shiras moose. . . ."

The DCI gazed up at the nicotine-yellow ceiling. "Then there's the big beasts—black bear, bison, mountain lion, wolves." He glanced suddenly at the ghillie. "I shot a wolf once. Big bugger. Me and my buddy tracked him for days, right out into the wilderness." He shook his head, and his tone became wistful. "You think the Highlands is vast, Ewan—you should see Montana. The Kootenai covers over two million acres. . . ."

He sighed. "Anyway, we tracked this wolf for three days, but the trail ran cold. My buddy, he's Native American as well as ex-army. Maybe it's in his genes, but he has this kinda sixth sense when it comes to wolves. He doubled back the way we'd come while I sat in camp. Guess what he found."

Angus watched Ewan on-screen. He could see Crowley had him hooked.

"That bloody wolf, Ewan, had been shadowing *us* for days." Crowley barked a laugh. "The hunters had become the hunted."

"What happened?" Ewan asked.

"My buddy told me to sit tight and keep my rifle locked and loaded."

"But how did he contact you?" Ewan asked.

"That's where us humans have the edge. Technology. He sent me a text message." Crowley grinned. "So I sat there and waited for the wolf to attack, which he duly did. . . ." The DCI paused, milking his captive audience.

"And?" Ewan asked, enthralled by the tale.

"I shot the bastard right between the eyes."

A slight smile tugged at Ewan's lips. Angus could only admire the way Crowley had set the ghillie at ease. Behind the laddish banter, Crowley clearly possessed a keen intelligence. Or base cunning, he wasn't sure which.

"So, who taught you to shoot, Ewan?"

"My old man."

"Is he a stalker too?"

Angus gave a small tut. Crowley knew fine well Ewan's father was dead.

"Was. He's dead," Ewan said.

"I'm sorry to hear that, Ewan. Lost my own da' about ten years back. He was a cop too." Crowley gave a sad laugh. "All I ever wanted to do was make him proud—know what I mean?"

Ewan nodded but did not answer. For a long time no one spoke.

"Listen, Ewan," Crowley said at last. "I don't think you're a bad guy. But I think you might have done something in the heat of the moment. I get it, man—we've all done and said stuff we wish we could take back. Yeah?"

When Ewan didn't answer, Crowley nodded to Nadia. She took a selection of A4-sized images from a folder and fanned them out on the scored table. "We conducted a search of your property yesterday, Ewan. We found these photographs on your bedroom floor, torn to shreds. We managed to piece them together, and the photographs are all of Faye Chichester."

McKeown shifted forward on his chair and peered at the photographs, then leaned towards Ewan and mumbled something in his ear.

Angus could guess what the solicitor was telling his client—say nothing. This was confirmed a moment later when Ewan muttered a "No comment."

"We have a witness who saw Faye slap you on the night she died," Nadia continued. "What was that about, Ewan?"

Even watching on-screen, Angus noticed a flash of anger in Ewan's eyes. He folded his arms and jutted out his chin. "No comment."

Crowley again folded his arms behind his head, as if he had all the time in the world. He gestured to Nadia, who reached into the folder and produced a series of photographs taken in Ewan's cottage. Angus could make out the messy kitchen, a close-up of the washing machine, and the evidence the SOCOs had discovered there: a balled-up bundle of bloodstained clothes. The proverbial smoking gun.

"Tell me about these, Ewan," Crowley said.

Ewan stared at the photographs, and put his head in his hands. "No . . . no . . . it's not what you think."

McKeown tried to intervene, but Ewan ignored him. "You've got this all wrong. That's deer blood, from a beast I gralloched out on the hill that morning."

"A doe?" Crowley asked.

"No. A stag."

"Royal?"

"Imperial!" Ewan spat.

Crowley sucked air between his teeth and gave an appreciative nod. "A real cracker, then? Just like Faye?"

Angus was glued to the screen, unblinking, watching for any sign that Ewan was lying. The ghillie bunched his hands into fists and scowled at the DCI. "I strung the deer up in Dunbirlinn. Go check if you don't believe me."

"We will, but that doesn't prove anything. You could have shot the deer anytime."

Ewan tapped an angry finger on one of the photographs. "If this was Faye's blood, do you honestly think I'd have stuffed the clothes in the washing machine and not turned it on? I'm not that thick."

Angus caught himself nodding along, and it hit him how desperately he wanted Ewan not to be the killer.

"We hear you like a drink?" Crowley said. "Maybe you forgot to turn the machine on? Maybe that's not all you forgot?"

Ewan shook his head, as if trying to dislodge the suggestion. "I hope you're a better hunter than you are a detective."

Crowley did not like that. The DCI stared at Ewan as Nadia flicked through her notebook.

"You claim that on the night of the thirty-first of October you stayed in a bothy at . . . Camus Ghaoideil," she said, consulting her notes. "Then on the morning of November the first you rose early to stalk deer in a nearby glen." She glanced up, seeking out Ewan's eyes. "Can anyone confirm that?"

"No comment."

"I'm trying to help you, Ewan. If someone could corroborate your where-abouts . . . well, it would put you in the clear. So I'll ask again, did anyone see you?"

The ghillie blanked her and clamped his lips shut.

"All this is hearsay and supposition," McKeown said, sounding bored. "As you clearly don't yet know whether the blood on these garments is the victim's, I suggest you either arrest my client or let him go, Detective Chief Inspector."

Crowley glanced casually at his thick gold watch. "We've still plenty of time left by my watch."

A blob of yogurt clung to the side of his father's mouth. He reached for a tissue and wiped the spot away. "That's us." Angus sighed, dropping the tissue on the tray beside the remnants of breakfast. His father, who used to have a healthy appetite, now ate like a bird. Anything solid made him choke, so the nurses pureed his food. Even after all these years it still felt wrong, a son feeding his father as if he were a weaning child. He wished he could be more like Gills, who was always cheery and full of banter, nattering away to Uisdean in Gaelic just as he always had. Angus smiled sadly—to hear Gills you'd think Uisdean was an active participant in the conversation, rather than some mute. His voice took Angus back to his childhood, the two friends arguing and laughing as he played on the rug with his Legos. Everything was vibrant and bejewelled in those memories: the sapphire-blue sea, lush emer-ald bracken, heather that shone like amethyst on the hillside. The cottage echoed with laughter and country music and smelt of caramelized apples from the tarts Mum baked.

He reached for a jug of water and filled a small plastic cup. He stuck a straw in the cup and raised it to his father's cracked lips. His wizened thrapple rippled as he drank.

"Do you remember Mum's apple tarts, Dad?" he asked softly.

His father's unfocused gaze on the painting of Ben Nevis mocked his efforts.

He placed his hand on his father's wrist. Fat veins bulged under his parchment skin, as if worms were crawling across his bones. "Do you hear anything I say?" he asked, a catch in his voice. Uisdean's eyes remained remote and unwavering; dark brown, like the fence in the back garden that they had treated with creosote one spring.

"I've been . . . seeing things again, Dad. Mum and the little boy and now this girl."

He heard in his voice an echo of a conversation they'd had almost two decades ago. He recalled his father's stern tone. *Listen, son, it's all in your head. Take the pills. Speak to the psychologist.*

But I want to speak to you, Dad.

No.

But why?

I can't, son. I just can't. Now, leave it at that.

He closed his eyes and felt the sting of splintered memories. Dad lying on the bathroom floor. Sobbing. Drunk. Bleeding. The softness of Sammy the Seal under his arm. Gills's calm voice: *Your dad's . . . a wee bit broken. But he'll mend. In time. We'll fix him, you and I.*

The sound of the door opening snapped him back to the present. He opened his eyes and saw Catriona walk into the room. She might not have been the friendliest nurse, but she was efficient. Gills suspected she was light-fingered, and he was right, but how else was he to get the little yellow pills? The internet was an option, but you never knew what you were buying, and he didn't want suspicious packages turning up on the doorstep for Ash to find.

She glared at him blankly, neither judging nor sympathetic, another thing he liked about her. Without a word, she took the pills from a pocket of the insipid lilac tunics all staff wore and placed the bottle on Uisdean's breakfast tray. He dropped two twenty-pound notes on the tray and lifted the bottle. "Thanks," he muttered.

Catriona gave a curt nod, lifted the tray, and swept back out of the room. Before he could take a couple of pills, Nadia phoned to tell him they'd finished interviewing Ewan, for the time being.

"He's sticking to his story," she said. "Until the lab gets back to us with the results of the blood analysis on the clothing we found in his washing machine, we don't have much to go on."

"What's your gut instinct?" he asked after a beat of silence. James Chichester had asked him the same question.

"Hard to say, although he doesn't seem the cold, calculating sort who could hold up under questioning. I can definitely see him killing Faye—there's rage enough in him—but that would more likely be a frenzied attack. Unplanned, spur-of-the-moment."

"Which doesn't fit with the elaborate killing method," he said.

"Aye, exactly. Which reminds me, Crowley wants you back at the village hall. We've got an expert coming in to talk to us about ritual killing."

"What expert?"

"Gills, of course."

The mobile almost slid from his hand. A vision, the same as before at the clootie tree, flashed through his head. He saw the rusted chain biting into flesh, but now he noticed more small details: a ring of purple bruising around the ankles; blue-veined feet, the toenails painted scarlet; brown fake-tan streaks on her skin. He blinked and the image disappeared, but only to be replaced with the same bloodied body he'd seen before. The corpse twisted in slow motion, ruby droplets of blood suspended in the air. Suddenly the body burst into flames.

CHAPTER 31

ANGUS stood at the sink in the village hall, staring at himself in the smeared mirror and trying to ignore the smell of piss that leached from the urinals. He threw a couple of yellow pills into his mouth and washed them down with water drunk straight from the tap. When he straightened up, Ethan Boyce was watching him from the corner of the toilets. He leant forward until his forehead rested on the glass. "Leave me be, *piollan*," he muttered. "For the love of God! Leave me be!"

He turned on the tap again and doused his face in icy cold water. This time he did not look in the mirror when he straightened up. Instead he grabbed a green paper towel from a shelf by the sink and slapped his face dry. He balled up the soggy paper and chucked it in the bin on the way out of the toilets. He thought of Eleanor Chichester and her insistence that everyone wore masks. How was his mask holding up? he wondered, slipping into the incident room.

Not well, he surmised.

He immediately spotted Gills, standing by the murder board and chatting to Crowley. He wore his good tweed suit with a salmon-pink shirt and an emerald-green tie. His burgundy brogues were buffed, but the laces didn't match, those on the right being multicoloured affairs salvaged from a pair of old hiking boots Angus vaguely remembered. His hair was the usual chaos, though—like spindrift blown from the crest of a wave.

Crowley called for everyone's attention, then introduced Gills as "an authority on Highland folklore and ancient customs." Gills gave a bashful smile, but when Angus caught his eye, his friend's stare was hard as granite. Behind Gills's head, Faye Chichester's picture on the wall stared at Angus with beseeching eyes.

You could have saved me!

He wanted to leave, but his legs acted of their own volition, propelling him to a chair beside Nadia. She glanced up as he sat, and smiled. "Perfect timing."

He nodded, not trusting himself to speak.

"The floor is yours, Dr. MacMurdo," Crowley said with a sweep of his arm.

Gills nodded his thanks. He appeared completely at ease, as if he spent every Monday evening addressing a roomful of Scotland's elite murder detectives. And Angus. He perched casually on the desk, thin legs sticking out in front, crossed at the ankles to reveal a few inches of white sports sock.

"Sacrifice, ladies and gentlemen, is what I'm here to discuss with you," he began. "We all have to make them." His eyes flicked to Angus, emphasizing the tacit rebuke. "But how many of you have made a sacrificial offering to a god or goddess? Not many, I'd wager, and those who have are keeping quiet about it, eh?"

Angus heard a few disembodied laughs.

"Sacrifice is how the ancients communicated with the divine. And the ultimate expression of that was blood, or human, sacrifice. Roman sources claim Celtic druids engaged widely in human sacrifice. Julius Caesar, writing in 44 BC, describes living humans being immolated in huge wicker figures."

Gills's silken voice catapulted him back to the Old Manse: to the smell of wet dog and whisky; to the tick of the grandfather clock; to the creak of leather as he squirmed on the retro armchair and described the horrors his mind had conjured.

He watched as Gills slipped off the desk and tapped a key on his laptop. A flat-screen monitor mounted on the wall behind sprang into life.

"Human sacrifice is a practice as old as the world itself. From the Inca to the Indians, the Egyptians to the Japanese, the power of human sacrifice was at once a near universally held belief. This poor chap here"—he tapped the image—"is about to be sacrificed by a Tahitian chief to the war god Oro. Captain Cook recorded the ritual during his exploration of the Pacific islands in 1774. The chief believed the human sacrifice would help him in his battle against the chief of a nearby island. And that, in essence, is what most human sacrifice is about—communicating with the divine. Just as Agamemnon killed his daughter Iphigenia to placate the goddess Artemis, and thus reach Troy to sack the city, sacrifice is a means to an end, usually to attain supernatural intervention."

Memories that Angus had long buried clawed their way to the surface as Gills talked. He saw himself as a skinny child, body convulsed in tears, as he tried to explain that first vision. He recalled his father's angry glare, those strong hands bunching into fists. *You'll never talk of this again! Do you hear me, boy!* Then suddenly he was pelting towards the Old Manse, tears burning his cheeks.

He looked up and found Gills staring at him with the same frustrated look he gave Bran when the dog tipped over the kitchen bin in search of scraps.

Angus closed his eyes and recalled the comforting earthy aroma of tobacco from the pipe Gills used to smoke, and the musty scent of aged books when he'd walked into the study in the Old Manse for the first time. In his mind's eye, he saw Gills plucking books off the shelves, as if he were picking brambles from the thicket that grew in the woods behind his house. He felt the weight of them in his arms. *Read this, and this . . . and old J. G. Campbell could help too.*

His eyes snapped up in time to see Gills tap his laptop. The image of Tahitian sacrifice vanished. "Sacrifice also spares followers from a deity's wrath," Gills declared. "Religions, from time immemorial, are based on fear. Take Christianity, for example, and the concept of Christ as the eternal sacrifice for the sins of mankind; or where sinfulness in life is punished by eternal damnation. So it was with pagan beliefs. The gods controlled our fates and had to be propitiated with appropriate offerings."

Gills tapped the laptop, and a photograph of a leathery-looking mummified corpse appeared on the screen. "Some of you will no doubt be familiar with bog bodies. These handsome fellows are found across Europe, preserved in bogs, with some of the best examples coming from Ireland. This charming chap is known as Clonycavan Man, recovered from a bog in County Meath. He suffered a gruesome demise, having been disembowelled and struck three times across the head and body with an axe. His nipples have also been cut off, which has led academics to theorize that Clonycavan Man was a failed king. In ancient Ireland, suckling a king's nipples was a gesture of submission: to have them severed would symbolically have made him incapable of kingship. In this era, rulers were profoundly associated with the land. If harvests failed, it was not the fault of the weather; it was the result of poor kingship. If harvests failed several years running . . . well, the king was not long for this world."

Memories flitted through Angus's mind, like the fledgling swallows that nested under the eaves of the Old Manse. He smelt the pine air freshener that dangled from the rearview mirror of Gills's Ford Anglia. He felt the summer breeze on his face as they flew past Eilean Donan Castle on the way to Kirkton to play Kinlochshiel in the cup. He saw Gills teaching him how to fly-fish in the hill loch above Glenruig. He pictured a patchwork of green fields and rugged tree-covered mountains from the top of Dunadd hill fort. He saw a footprint cut in the rock, and heard Gills telling him about the ancient kings of Dalriada who were inaugurated at Dunadd by placing their foot in the indent. He saw his own grubby Adidas Samba trainer, tiny when placed in the footprint. He recalled a biting cold that had spread up his legs, as if he'd stepped into a stream of energy stretching back to the beginning of time. Then Gills's hand on his shoulder, warm and solid. *Tell me what you see, young man. I'm not here to judge.*

A lump lodged in Angus's throat. All Gills had ever done was try to help him, but he'd turned his back on the old man. He felt the bottle of pills in his inside pocket, pressed against his heart—antipsychotics used to treat schizophrenia, bipolar disorder, and other major depressive disorders. He pictured himself standing in the kitchen of the Old Manse, dripping seawater onto the parquet floor, arms tired from pumping on Ethan's chest. Words ripped from his raw throat: *I'm done, Gills! No more! This is fucking useless!*

Please, Angus, you're not ill. This is a gift few possess. It's like a muscle: the more you use it, the stronger it becomes.

So if I don't use it, the muscle will wither away?

I don't—

Then that's what I'll do—I'll let it wither and die.

Angus tugged his mind back to the incident room. On the screen, Gills had brought up another warped-looking corpse. The body was well preserved, the face like a motion-blurred photograph, mouth agape as if he had been screaming for centuries. Angus saw Lewis Duncan, lips drawn back in a howl of agony as the flames carved his face.

"This is perhaps the most famous bog body: Lindow Man. He was found facedown in Lindow Moss in Cheshire. But he was no lowly pleb. His diet and manicured nails suggest he was of high status, perhaps a druidic prince. Around the first century AD, Roman forces had overrun southern Britain. The native Celts faced annihilation, their beliefs trampled under hobnailed boots. As religious leaders, the druids were seen as intermediaries between man and the gods. Lindow Man's sacrifice was, in this context, a last throw of the dice, a desperate plea to their gods for divine intervention."

Gills gave the officers a tight smile. "Lindow Man suffered a threefold death." He counted off the methods of violence on his fingers: "He suffered three stunning blows to the head, delivered with the sudden force of a thunderbolt. He was then strangled with a garrotte knotted in three places and made of fox sinew, his blood drained. Finally, after he was already dead, he was symbolically drowned. His third death."

Angus felt as if someone had opened a window to let the night in. He glanced around him. Even those who had at first appeared sceptical seemed to prick up their ears: the similarities between this ritual murder and Faye's killing were undeniable. He felt Nadia watching him, but his eyes were on Gills. His friend stared at him, an almost pleading expression on his craggy face.

Close your eyes and see.

"Why three deaths, Dr. MacMurdo?" Crowley asked.

"Because three was the Celts' sacred number," Gills replied. "It linked their tales, legends, and deities, and is a frequent motif across their art and literature. Many of their gods and goddesses have three aspects, and the vast vibrant Celtic pantheon is dominated by three mighty gods, each of whom have a thirst for human sacrifice."

He tapped the laptop and a triptych of gods appeared on-screen: a muscle-bound bearded man with a lightning bolt over his shoulder; a robed figure hacking a tree with an axe; and a fierce god with arms upraised, clasping two smaller human beings in his hands.

"Taranis, the thunder god, with his chariot wheel; Esus, the lord and master; and Teutates, the god of the tribe. They would have gone by different names locally, but this triad was worshipped across the Celtic world, from Ireland to Gaul."

"So they were the top dogs, like Zeus, Poseidon, and Hades?"

Angus glanced at DC Lockhart, who had asked the question. She sat with her legs crossed, notebook out, like an eager student in one of Gills's lectures.

"If you like," the old man replied. "Zeus, Poseidon, and Hades were the children of the Titans. Like the Greeks, the Highlands has its own Titan."

He jabbed the keyboard and another image appeared: a one-eyed crone with blue-tinged skin. She carried a staff and rode on the back of a wolf. Angus recognised the image from the lecture Gills had given to the German exchange students.

"This is Beira, Queen of Winter. The Bone Mother. Known in these parts as the Cailleach. She's the oldest deity we know of. Older than the Celtic people. Older than time, perhaps. She has three aspects—maiden, mother, and crone—which embody the cycle of life and death. Most tellingly, the Cailleach is said to rise on Samhain. Faye was killed on Samhain, which, for those of you who don't know, is the pagan festival that spawned Halloween. For the ancient Celts, it was a dangerous liminal time when the veil between this world and the otherworld was gossamer thin. Spirits and creatures from the realm of the dead could cross freely into our world."

The room was now eerily silent, nothing but the odd stifled cough and the *whish* of notes being taken to distract him from his friend's voice. Gills had his audience hooked. Angus thought of all the stories Gills had told him over the years, about old kings and queens, giants who lived in mountains and fairies who shape-shifted into animals. Myths and legends that the old man treated with reverence.

Crowley cleared his throat. "This goes no further than this room, Dr. MacMurdo. But there is a remarkable similarity between the death of this Lindow Man and Faye's murder."

Gills slapped the laptop shut and the monitor on the wall went blank. He linked his hand behind his back and looked down at his brogues, but appeared not to care about the mismatched laces. "Here's the thing, ladies and gents," he said, now looking up. "If we hadn't recovered Faye's body, the tide would have claimed her. Like Lindow Man, she was a high-status sacrifice, a laird's daughter. An offering to whom, I can't say. By whom is for you to determine. But what I can tell you is this: Lindow Man was not the only body pulled from Lindow Moss."

His eyes flicked to Angus.

Close your eyes.

"I fear Faye's murder might only be the beginning."

And see.

Angus slumped down on the monks bench and kicked off his boots. His brain had reached a saturation point but continued to churn. He closed his eyes but found no respite there, as images of mutilated bog bodies and Gills's pagan gods flickered through his head. He stood and walked across the hall. The living room retained a residue of heat from the woodburner, and a lingering hint of Ash's perfume. He opened the drinks cabinet and sloshed some Talisker into a crystal glass, spilling some on the worktop. "Bugger," he muttered. "Fucking-buggering-fuck!"

"Wow, someone's swallowed a dictionary."

He spun round and saw Faye curled on the couch, her legs tucked under her. She wore his old shinty hoodie, the one that Nadia used to wear. The sweatshirt was so large, it covered her knees. Her legs, the few inches he could see, were bare, the skin mottled.

"Your drinking is starting to freak me out," she said.

"I'm freaking *you* out?" He took a swig of Talisker but almost missed his mouth. Liquid dribbled down his chin, as if he were his father in the care home.

"I need you sober, Angus. With your wits about you."

He crumpled down onto an armchair next to Ash's clarsach. "I need you to leave me alone."

"They chose me for my royal blood," she said, ignoring him. "That's fucked up."

His fingers felt like sausages as he reached into his pocket and took out the bottle of pills.

"We're dealing with something out of the ordinary," Faye said. "Crowley and the other cops can't see that, but you can, Angus."

He unscrewed the lid and tipped out a handful of pills.

"Leave. Me. Alone," he growled.

"They do things in threes—that's what Gills said. Do you want two more murders on your conscience?"

Angus threw the handful of pills into his mouth and *chewed* them, welcoming the bitter, acrid taste. A powdery substance coated his mouth, but he continued to grind up the pills, eyes burning into Faye. The girl watched him. Disappointed. At length, he reached for his glass, took a gulp of whisky, swilled it around his mouth, swallowed. Choked. He folded forward, coughing and spluttering, his lungs burning. He tasted bile, a prelude to vomiting. Blindly, he staggered from the snug and reeled down the hall towards the bathroom. He shoved open the door and fell to his knees as his mouth filled with vomit. He grabbed both sides of the toilet, got his head over the bowl, and jackknifed, sending a torrent of undigested whisky, pills, and bile into the water. His back arched as he retched, again and again. With each spasm he saw the Dark One looming over Faye, thrusting a knee into her back. . . .

He whimpered, convulsed one last time, and slumped down on the cold bathroom tiles. His stomach felt like a wet cloth that had been wrung out. His eyes stung with tears. Suddenly the bathroom light flicked on, momentarily blinding.

"Angus, what the fu—"

Ash stood in the doorway in her nightdress, concern etched across her face. He hauled himself into a sitting position. "Something went down the wrong way," he said.

"Aye, whisky by the smell of it."

"What's that supposed to mean?" The question flew out, harsher than intended.

"Calm down, Angus. I was joking." She stepped forward and helped him to his feet.

"Sorry," he muttered.

"Come on," she said. "I'll make you a cup of tea."

"Nah. I just need to sleep."

She placed a gentle hand on his cheek, searching out his eyes. "Are you okay, *a chuisle*? You've had a darkness hanging over you recently. Like when we first met."

"I'm fine."

"You're not. Tell me what's bothering you?"

I can't! I just can't!

"Is it the case?" she asked. "It must be awful dealing with that. I understand, Angus."

No, you don't.

"I'm fine," he mumbled again. "Just tired."

A spark of anger flashed in her eyes. She let her hand drop to her side. "Tired. Right." She glanced away from him, a hint of irritation tainting her words.

He followed her through to the bedroom. A charged silence hung between them as he undressed to his boxer shorts and slipped under the duvet. Ash lay on her back, staring up at the ceiling. "You need to talk to me, Angus," she said. "This moody silence shit has to stop. I can't go through all that again."

It was Angus who now felt a surge of anger. "Give me a break. I've got a lot on my mind."

"Right, and I don't."

"I didn't say that."

"It's implied."

He bit his lip, rather than blurt out the curse that was on his tongue.

They lay for a long minute in simmering silence, each daring the other to speak.

It was Ash who threw the first punch. "Do you really want to have children, Angus?"

The question caught him off guard. "Where did that come from?"

She gave a quiet, despondent laugh. "If you don't know, then I'm not going to explain it."

"Christ!" he muttered. "Just speak plainly, would you?"

She sat up and twisted towards him, eyes blazing. "Your heart's not in this."

"It's not my heart that's the problem," he retorted.

"But it is, Angus. You've gone along with this for me, but you've never been fully committed."

"Ash, we're right in the fucking middle of IVF. How am I not committed?"

"Because I see it in your eyes every time we talk about the future."

The sadness in her voice shamed him, as did the truth of her words. He could not meet her glare. He grasped for some comeback that would make sense, but the words became clogged in his throat. All he could do was stare at the ceiling in mute self-disgust.

"Tell me something, Angus," Ash said, her voice cracking. "Is it just that you don't want children—or that you don't want them with me?"

It's you who shouldn't want children with me, he thought.

Angus willed the words out of his parched mouth, but they would not come. He felt as if a space were opening between them as they lay on the bed, a growing chasm that he had no idea how to bridge.

"You need to go to the spare room," Ash said in a pitiful whisper.

Angus sat up and went to put a hand on her arm, but she flinched away.

"Go," she said.

"Ash, wait . . ."

He reached for her again, but she slapped his hand away and whipped her head round. Her eyes shone with an incandescent anger. "Go!" she yelled. "Get the fuck out!"

He slid from the bed and stumbled from the room, the taste of bile and regret in his mouth.

CHAPTER 32

ASH thrust her arms back and forth like pistons as she ran along the narrow path by the sea. Waves crashed onto the rocks, sending great fountains of foamy water into the air. Last night's argument with Angus was raw and painful. She tore at the memory of it like a wolf at a carcass. There had been a moment when she'd felt an almost overwhelming urge to strike him. She thought she'd left that rage behind at Kintail House, but evidently it was still inside her, buried deep. She had been that angry, scared girl again. Alone and confused, her trust shattered.

From the minute she set off on her run, she'd been mentally composing a new piece of music, but the notes were off-key and jumbled. A knot of fear and sadness tightened across her chest. Did Angus really want to be with her? Did she want to be with him if he couldn't be honest with her about wanting children? Was this life she was grasping for another pipe dream, destined to be snatched away from her like everything else?

Something akin to panic rose inside her. She sucked in a lungful of cold air but couldn't seem to take a breath. Everything was crumbling, breaking apart until she was on her own again.

No! she thought, gritting her teeth. *Focus on the music, Ashleigh.* That's what Granny Beag had told her to do at Kintail House when the pain and loss threatened to overwhelm her. *Let the music wash all the bad stuff away.*

Ash closed her mind to the turbulent thoughts in her head and listened to the sounds all around her. The squawks of herring gulls and the staccato alarm call of a curlew segued into the pips and trills of chaffinches and blue tits as she left the shore behind and cut through the woods. Soon the path began to steepen as she reached the lower slopes of the hill. The sound of water was everywhere, not just from the stream that gurgled and spat down the mountainside. It dripped from the spiky needles of the Scots pines, squelched under the soles of her running shoes, swept across the hillside in sheets of rain that landed in rolling timpani bursts. Behind it all, the ever-present wind soughed a melancholy refrain through the naked trees.

Nature's music soothed her. It always had. She imagined the anger and fear sweating from her pores. If life in Kintail House had taught her anything, it was to build herself anew. And music was her foundation. Granny Beag had taught her that, too.

The symphony began to take shape as she pounded up the mountainside, flushing a pair of red grouse from the heather. The birds burst into the sky in a flurry of wings, croaking their displeasure at having been disturbed. The scarlet wattle above the male's eye looked like a splash of blood.

A memory flashed into her head: a cracked windscreen speckled with blood. Her dad slumped over the steering wheel. Water filling the car.

She throttled the memory before it could become fully formed and redoubled her efforts on the steep climb to the summit. As she neared the top, a wan dawn light permeated the mist illuminating the cairn. She checked her watch. She'd knocked almost a minute off her previous time. Just showed what a bit of anger could do. She slowed to a walk, hands clasped behind her head as she regained her breath. Her leg muscles burned, but she felt stronger now than she had when she set off. She wouldn't allow last night's argument to destroy five years of marriage.

Ash traced her fingers over the cairn, so solid and immutable, yet once it had just been a stone. Folk had built it—piece by piece, year after year, just as she had rebuilt herself after the Accident. The argument with Angus had shaken her foundations, but she was still standing.

CHAPTER 33

ANGUS again sat on his own in the observation room in Silvaig Police Station, eyes glued to the monitor. His back ached from sleeping on the hard sofa bed in the spare room. The argument with Ash reverberated through his head, filling him with self-loathing. She deserved so much better than him. He took a sip of vending machine coffee and winced. On-screen, Crowley sat with his arms folded, staring at Ewan, saying nothing. The ghillie was slumped on a chair in the interview suite, looking as if he hadn't slept a wink. Nadia flicked through her phone. Hamish McKeown, the portly duty solicitor, appeared to be sleeping.

Suddenly Crowley began to talk, taking everyone by surprise. "So that wolf I was telling you about, Ewan," he said. "That was all bullshit. I do have a mate who runs a hunting retreat in Montana, but we mainly go after bear and elk. And he's not Native American. I made that up too. Just to add colour. You believed me, though, didn't you, Ewan?"

The ghillie refused to meet Crowley's eyes.

"And that stuff about my father being an ex-polis. Made that up too. In truth, I don't even know my dad. He was a drunk who ran out on my mum when I was still in nappies. You see, Ewan, lying is an art form. I've learnt from the best, and you—buddy boy—are not one of the best. You're lower leagues, the Cowdenbeath of porky pies."

"Are you going somewhere with this, Detective?" McKeown asked without opening his eyes.

"That deer you say you shot, Ewan. We checked in the storeroom at Dunbirlinn last night, where you said it was hanging. Guess what—there was no deer."

Ewan finally looked at Crowley, his eyes wide in panic. "Bollocks! It must be there. I hung it myself. I did!"

Crowley shook his head, as if disappointed. "The Cowdenbeath of liars."

"I'm not lying!"

Crowley cocked an eyebrow. "The best lies contain a kernel of truth. I may not have shot a wolf between the eyes, but I am a hunter; I understand that primal instinct. You do too, don't you?"

Ewan's bottom lip stuck out as if he were close to tears. Angus had seen him like this as a child, on the shinty minibus when his teammates were making fun of him. Crowley reminded him of those boys now. No sympathy. No mercy.

"How do you feel, Ewan, when you have a Monarch stag in your crosshairs? Your finger poised on the trigger. The steady pump of your heartbeat. Every sense heightened."

The ghillie shook his head, still refusing to make eye contact.

Crowley smirked. "Oh, don't tell me! You take no pleasure in it? It's just a job?"

"It is," Ewan mumbled.

Crowley placed his elbows on the table and glared at Ewan. "Liar," he said in an almost-whisper. "Killing is all about power, Ewan. That's why we do it, you and I. In that moment, before our finger squeezes the trigger, we have the power of life or death."

Crowley leaned back and placed his hands flat on the scored table. "Did you feel powerful when you killed Faye, Ewan?"

Ewan's shoulders trembled. "I didn't kill her," he whined, tears beginning to flow. "I didn't . . . I wouldn't . . ."

The sound of Nadia's mobile phone ringing cut across Ewan's sobs. She glanced at the screen, then Crowley. Angus saw something pass between them. She stood and marched from the interview room, already tapping the phone screen.

Angus slid back on his chair, slipped out of the observation room, and clattered down a flight of stairs towards the dingy corridor that housed the interview suites, which were buried below the station. He found Nadia standing in a shadowy alcove, her mobile phone pressed to her ear. She was nodding forlornly at whatever the caller was saying. She muttered a thanks and then cut the call.

"Was that the lab?" he asked.

Before she could answer, the door to the interview room sprang open and Crowley barrelled out, looking pleased with himself. He shot Angus a frown, then turned his attention to Nadia. "So, don't keep us in suspenders, DI Sharif."

She shook her head. "Nae joy, sir. The blood isn't Faye's. It's from a deer, like he said."

Angus saw a flash of rage in Crowley's eyes, a hunter denied his kill. He turned away from them and stomped down the corridor, aiming a boot at a rubbish bin on the way past. The sound reverberated around the space. "Arse biscuits!" he yelled.

Angus and Nadia shared a look. "What now?" he asked.

She sighed. "We let Ewan go. Then we go buy something sugary. Then we start again."

DS Robert—aka Boaby—Dunbar dived on the box of sticky buns like the gannets Angus had seen yesterday at Camus Ghaoideil feasting on krill. Luckily, Nadia had had the foresight to buy three boxes from Nevis Bakery in Silvaig before they drove back to the village hall.

He lifted a Chelsea bun from the box and brought it over for Nadia. "Ta," she said, eyes glued to the screen of her laptop. A movie was playing—Eleanor Chichester again, this time dressed in a see-through black dress, concocting some kind of potion in a cauldron.

"What's this one called?" he asked.

"*The Suffering*. Could easily describe the viewers."

"Bad?"

"Truly terrible."

She lifted the bun and took a bite, murmuring appreciatively. A door thudded open and Crowley marched in, noticing that everyone seemed to be eating buns. He walked over to the discarded boxes and scowled. "Is that all you left me? Greedy bastards." He picked up the last cake—a glistening strawberry tart— and crammed it into his mouth.

"Right, everyone," he said, spraying crumbs, "gather round. I want progress reports."

Nadia snapped her laptop shut, and Angus found an unoccupied chair facing the murder board. As the rest of the MIT crowded round, he watched Crowley polish off the tart and suck red jam from the remaining fingers of his mutilated hand.

"Now, as you'll no doubt be aware, we've had to let Ewan Hunter go," Crowley said. "He's still very much a person of interest. Just because the blood on his clothes wasn't Faye's, doesn't mean he didn't kill her. So we keep on him. He's a drunk—if he did it, chances are he'll spill his guts to someone. Let's park him for the moment. Who's next on our hit list?"

DS Dunbar raised a hand, in which he held half a chocolate eclair. "Been going through the witness statements, sir." He dropped his hand and looked at the eclair as if he dearly wanted to take another bite.

"And . . . ?" Crowley asked.

"And the minister's wife is lying. Mrs. MacVannin told us her husband came home at eleven thirty on Halloween night. She remembered because a politics programme was starting on Radio Four. Only, it wasn't. Some crap with Nick Robinson was *supposed* to be on, but the schedule had changed. Nick Robinson was ill, so they put on something about Britain's finest waterways instead. Sounded quite good, actually."

"Good work, Boaby," Crowley said.

Dunbar acknowledged the praise by stuffing the rest of the eclair into his mouth.

"If Ruth MacVannin lied about her husband's alibi, that suggests he was out later than he claims," Crowley mused.

"Just a thought, sir," Vee Lockhart said, "but MacVannin will probably own black vestments. They'd look similar to the cloak worn by the mystery guy with the antlers from the Samhain footage."

"Aye, fair point. Maybe you can ask for a look at his vestments when you go to interview him? Hopefully he won't take it the wrong way."

He gave Lockhart a thin smile. "Moving on, and in light of Dr. MacMurdo's revelations, we need to look again at the pagans. The deer sinew clearly has ritualistic overtones. Either our killer is trying to cast suspicion on the pagans, or there's some religious mania at work here. Which reminds me." He turned to the murder board and picked up a marker. "At the start of this case, I said there were three motives for murder: lust, lucre, and loathing. But I missed one, as Dr. MacMurdo reminded us. When religious cults and maniacs are involved, all rational thought vacates the premises." He held up his mutilated hand and grinned. "As I know only too well."

Angus almost winced. You had to wonder about someone who made jokes about having his fingers amputated by a serial killer. Or was humour Crowley's coping mechanism?

The DCI daubed another heading on the whiteboard. "Sometimes this is the only explanation for murder." He tapped his pen against the board, where he'd written in block capitals the word "LUNACY."

"By this I don't mean our killer is some deranged escapee from a mental institution, although—" He glanced at Boaby.

"All nutters accounted for, sir. At least those we know about."

"Well, that's reassuring." Crowley gave a short cackle, the sound reminding Angus of a crow's caw. "Right, let's just say Faye was sacrificed to some old pagan gods as Dr. MacMurdo suggested. She was at a Samhain celebration on the night she died. Stands to reason that the killer is someone from the commune, right?"

"Seems a bit . . . obvious, and the blood wasn't a match," Fleet said.

"Aye, it does, Rylo," Crowley agreed. "But if it looks like a duck, quacks like a duck, etcetera, etcetera . . ."

He turned to the murder board and stared at the mug shots taken of the Teine Eigin residents—two rows of piercings, pleated hair, tattoos, and scowls. He tapped Chris Kelbie's picture. "What do we know about her, other than that she's from the Traveller community?"

"Indigenous Highland Travellers," Fleet said. "Apparently, they're a distinct group from your Romani Travellers and the showmen who go around the country with the funfairs. Kelbie had no formal education until she was twelve. Did a few years in Lochaber High School. Council records show she was living at a Traveller site near Spean Bridge. She left school at fifteen, though, and fell off the grid. She was known to authorities, but no criminal record."

"Has she any family?"

"Aye, the mother's local, although she's no longer a Traveller. I've an address for her, if you want us to interview her."

Crowley worked a crick out of his neck. "Might as well. Nadia, Angus, you take care of that, okay?"

"Yes, sir,"

The DCI turned to the suspect list. His pen hovered over the board for a second before he wrote Kelbie's name under the "LUNACY" heading, along with a plus sign and the word "PAGANS."

"Could they all be in on it, sir?" DC Lockhart asked. "Kelbie might be the Highland's answer to Charles Manson."

"Certainly possible, Vee," Crowley replied. "I worked a cult homicide back in the States, where the ringleaders were a respectable Massachusetts couple. Abe and Carol Zimmer were the least likely cult leaders you could imagine. He was the manager of a bacon-processing plant while she was a dowdy housewife who hosted Tupperware parties. Somehow, the Zimmers convinced folks they had spoken to aliens and knew how to evolve into a higher life-form. To join, followers had to give up their worldly possessions and, eventually, shed their mortal bodies. Aliens would then resurrect them at an undefined period in the future." Crowley chuckled. "It was batshit crazy, and at least five people were killed trying to reach alien nirvana, although it was probably more. Abe had access to an incinerator at his workplace, you see. We sifted through ash for days."

Crowley sighed, a smile playing about his lips, as if—Angus thought—he were reliving the good old days.

"Let's invite Christine Kelbie in for a wee chat. Any other business?"

"I've been trawling CCTV in Silvaig, boss," Fleet said. "Faye was in the town on Friday afternoon, a few hours before the Samhain celebration."

"Oh, aye? What was she doing?"

"I'll show you." Fleet scampered over to a PC and rattled his fingers over the keyboard. The monitor behind Crowley's head sprang to life, displaying grainy footage of Silvaig High Street. "Here she comes," Fleet said.

Angus watched as Faye's slender figure walked into the shot. Her hands were buried in the pockets of a knee-length sapphire-coloured coat with a fluffy collar. She wore a tartan scarf around her neck, and her hair fell in golden waves over her shoulders.

He clenched his teeth, eyes glued to the screen. Faye strode past Hutton's Butchers, a Ladbrokes betting shop, and Boyd's Chemist before turning into a small doorway. "Where's she going?" Crowley asked.

"Fancy dress shop," Fleet replied. "The manager told me Faye was there to pick up a green cloak." He scrolled the footage on until Faye reemerged, a mauve plastic bag with the shop logo on it held in her hand. Her face was tilted up at the camera, and there was a faint smile on her lips. However, as she continued along High Street, her expression seemed to Angus to become more sombre. Soon she was out of shot, but Fleet tapped a few keys to bring up footage from a camera positioned near the war memorial. It captured Faye walking past a Trespass store and turning down a small lane, which Angus recognised—Shaggers' Alley.

Fleet paused the footage. "That's all we got, sir. She doesn't reappear on CCTV."

"What's down that lane?"

"Nothing much. Laundrette, art gallery, ironmonger. You can cut through the alley to a taxi rank near the station. We think that's where she was heading."

Angus kept his mouth shut, but he had an idea where Faye was actually going.

CHAPTER 34

WITH half of Scotland's media camped across the road, Moira Anderson's shop was doing a brisk trade. As Gills took his copy of the *Herald* up to the counter, he noticed that the old shopkeeper had doubled the prices of confectionery and other items.

"Supply and demand, Gilleasbuig." She smirked.

"Daylight robbery more like," he muttered, folding the newspaper under his arm. He stepped outside and was surprised to find DI Sharif making a fuss of Bran and Sceolan, who were tied up nearby.

"Ah, Dr. MacMurdo," she said, rising. "Just the man I wanted to see."

Gills cocked a bushy eyebrow. "I'm at your disposal, DI Sharif. Shall we take a walk?"

He untied the dogs and put them on the leash until they reached the shore.

"So, what can I do for you?" he asked, setting the dogs free. They scurried away, tails whumping back and forth.

"There's a wee inconsistency with Faye's injuries and those you described as being part of a threefold death," she said. "It's probably nothing, but it's been bothering me."

"I see. And what might that be?"

"Faye was bludgeoned, strangled, then—as you suggested—symbolically drowned. Each of these methods had meaning. But her leg was also broken below the knee."

Gills gave a grim shake of his head. "A not uncommon practice, my dear," he said, "intended to prevent the spirit from walking away after death."

Nadia was silent for a long second. "Bloody hell," she muttered, her words whipped away on the wind. "Do you really think he'll kill again, Dr. MacMurdo?"

They paused by the water's edge. Bran splashed around in the shallows, chasing small fish. Happy and oblivious.

"I'm afraid so," Gills replied. "As I told the MIT, the Celts often did things in threes."

"Three is an important number in Islam, too," Nadia said. "Many sunnah acts are advised to be done in threes."

"The comparisons between ancient religions are manifold," Gills said. "Parallels can be drawn, for example, between Sufi dervishes, and the oracles of classical antiquity, or Japanese Itako and Siberian shamans, or the seers of Norse mythology and the seers of Celtic polytheism. There are ancient truths, my dear, that are common to all cultures." Gills met Nadia's warm eyes. "Why did you become a police officer?"

She glanced away from him, her smile fading. "I grew up wanting to be a doctor. Or at least that's what my family wanted. Cliché, right? The immigrant Glaswegian Pakistani family pushing their child to become a doctor?"

"So what changed?"

"Nothing, until my final year at uni." Her almond eyes had taken on a dark tinge, and Gills suddenly felt awkward.

"Apologies, my dear, it's none of my business—"

"No, it's okay. I just . . . don't speak about it often." She pushed a shiny strand of dark hair out of her eyes. "So, like I said, I was in my final year at Glasgow Uni. I was part of the rowing team. I was getting in some early-morning practice on the River Clyde, when I spotted something float-ing downstream. At first it looked like a mannequin." She gave a wry laugh. "My first thought was to retrieve it so I could play a prank on my flatmate. We were always doing dumb stuff like that. So I stretched out an oar and pulled what I thought was a shop dummy towards the boat. It was only then I realized it was a girl."

Nadia shook her head, as if reliving the moment. "She was so tiny. I remember holding her there, the current trying to drag her away. I felt if I let her go, I'd die, like she was a previous self and if I let the river take her, I'd simply vanish, as if I'd never existed."

Gills could hear raw emotion bleeding through in her voice. "Did they find out what happened to her?"

She shook her head. "The newspapers called her the River Angel. She'd been murdered and dumped in the Clyde, but no one was ever caught. Her parents were never traced. I couldn't accept that, so a few weeks after finding her body, I quit my medicine course at uni and joined the police."

The image of a little girl's body floating down the river stayed with Gills long after Nadia returned to the village hall. He pottered around the Old Manse for a while, before deciding a visit to the bookshop would cheer him up. When he got there, Lachy was not sitting in his customary position beside the heater, but he could hear the old bookseller behind the velvet curtain, apparently talking to himself. Numerous times whilst browsing in the shop, Gills had tried to peek behind the curtain but had never succeeded. Which was probably just as well: the mundane reality of what was stored there would hardly live up to his imaginings of other dimensions and wormholes in space and time.

He was a little worried about Lachy, though. The conversation the bookseller was having, although he couldn't hear exactly what was being said, appeared detailed, punctuated with pauses for the—presumably imaginary—other participant to speak. Ach! It was no different from the conversations he himself had with Uisdean in the care home. Those discussions could become heated, even though Uisdean was mute.

Gills tiptoed back outside the bookshop and reentered, giving the door a good slam that set the bell jangling. He sauntered past the piles of books, making as much noise as possible. Issy the cat extracted herself from her spot in front of the old gas heater and glided over to him, wrapping her warm body around his legs. "Afternoon, Issy!" he declared.

Lachy emerged from behind the curtain in a puff of cheroot smoke. "Christ on a bike, Gills! Do you have to make so much damned noise?"

Gills slapped his hands down on the counter and gave Lachy a wide smile. "Afternoon, old bean. And how are we today?"

"Fine until you showed up," Lachy grumbled.

"That's no way to talk to your best customer."

Lachy slumped down in his chair. "If I give you money, will you leave?"

Gills tickled Issy under the chin. "He loves me really, puss."

"He really doesn't," Lachy muttered. The bookseller stubbed out his cheroot in a glass ashtray that looked suspiciously like those used in the Glenruig Inn next door. He opened a small wooden box of Red Lions that sat on the counter and plucked out another cheroot, which he lit with a silver Zippo. "So, what can I do for you, Gills?" he said, blowing smoke into the air.

"I'm after all you've got on human sacrifice."

"If someone other than you asked me that, I might worry," Lachy replied. "What's your interest—another research paper?"

"Aye, something like that."

In truth, his presentation to the MIT last night had left him more concerned than reassured. It was clear Angus's mind was still fogged by those blasted pills. Behind the bravado, DCI Crowley seemed sharp, but Gills doubted even Scotland's best detectives were equipped to stop this . . . thing in their midst. Police officers, even the elite, were shackled to the parameters of their training. No doubt they talked at meetings about "thinking outside the box," but putting that into practice was more difficult. Theirs was not a world where the supernatural could coexist with objective reality.

Lachy pointed a nicotine-stained finger to a row of shelves next to the botany section. "You should find a few titles over there. I've got Patrick Tierney's *The Highest Altar*, Cat Jarman's *River Kings*, Shreeve's *Human Sacrifice*, and an assortment of other hack jobs."

"Much obliged."

Gills turned and, accompanied by Issy, walked over to the shelves. He was no stranger to the topic of human sacrifice in ancient cultures, but he was no expert, either. Who knew what small clue or detail could prove invaluable in forestalling further deaths? Most of the books had gruesome covers and titles, such as *Blood for Thought* and *The Sacred Executioner*. He flicked through a number at random, but most were hack jobs, as Lachy had warned. Not worth wasting his money on. After a few minutes, he was about to give up when his eyes fell on a book with a ripped cover and the title *Scotland's Last Druid*. The book's jacket featured a bearded figure holding an upraised staff, surrounded by supplicating followers. He wore what looked like a plaid, synonymous with Highland warriors. Gills took the book from the shelf and flicked to the front page, where he discovered the illustration was of Dòmhnall MacRuari. He was, of course, familiar with the chieftain, who had become one of the Highland's greatest bogeymen. But he had forgotten about Dòmhnall's association with human sacrifice, which in part accounted for his nickname—*an Draoidh*, the Druid. That his seat of power had been Dunbirlinn Castle was also . . . interesting.

Gills wandered back to the counter, reading the book as he went.

"You going to buy that?" Lachy snapped.

"What?" Gills asked, distracted. "Oh aye, sorry."

He placed the book down on the counter, then dug out his wallet. Lachy glanced at the cover and gave Gills a quizzical look.

"Have you anything else on Dòmhnall MacRuari?"

"*An Draoidh*," Lachy said. "No, you're out of luck. That's all I've left. All the books I had with even tangential references to Dòmhnall MacRuari were bought years ago."

"Really? By whom?"

"The laird, not that it's any of your business. I helped Chichester research his family tree. The Druid is his distant ancestor, on his mother's side."

CHAPTER 35

THE sea hurled itself against the Arisaig skerries like a rabid dog foaming at the mouth. Waves smashed onto the rocky coast and reared up, great spumy paws clawing an invisible foe. A cormorant veered overhead, black wings fighting hard to maintain its course inland. The sky was an avalanche of billowing clouds. Sleet slanted in from the sea, riding on angry gusts of wind. Angus raised an arm to ward off the assault, but icy needles dug into his exposed skin.

Ahead of him, Nadia picked her way across the shore towards what looked like an abandoned cottage floating on a lake of dying weeds and bramble bushes. Someone was in, though: grey tongues of smoke oozed from a teetering chimney before being scudded away on the wind.

Nadia marched up to the front door and gave it a swift rap with her knuckles, turned to Angus, and scrunched up her nose. "Is this what you'd call a fixer-upper?"

"More of a knock-down-and-start-againer."

"Aye." She gave the door another batter. "Come on, come on—"

He heard a key rattle in the lock, then the door creaked open an inch. Suspicious yellow-tinged eyes peered out at them from behind pink-rimmed spectacles. "Mrs Kelbie," Nadia said, pulling out her ID and thrusting it in front of the woman's eyeline. "Can we have a word?"

The set of eyes disappeared and the door swung open to reveal an odd-looking woman wearing mismatched golfing socks and a chunky knee-length cardigan. Her grey hair hung in matted hanks over her forehead, but the wool cardigan was a brilliant white, like the fleece of a freshly dipped sheep. She stood aside and he followed Nadia into the house, taking in the interior at a glance—peat fire smouldering in the hearth, low oak-beamed ceiling, rocking chair, sagging couch covered in moth-eaten throws, mahogany dresser festooned with jars and tins. The air was heavy with the scent of smoke and lavender, which almost masked a sickly sweet odour. Outside, the wind howled and raked at the window frames.

"What a day!" Nadia said, taking off her beanie hat and giving it a shake. Annie Kelbie shouldered the door closed and turned to face them. Her smile was a long, thin slash, like something a child would draw. "I was wondering when you would arrive," she said.

"Oh." Nadia frowned. "Why do you say that?"

Annie glided past, her feet hardly seeming to touch the wooden floor. "I hear the news, Detective," she replied. "It was only a matter of time before you zeroed in on my girl." She gestured to the couch. "Please, sit."

Angus lowered himself onto the couch, keeping Annie Kelbie in his line of sight the whole time. Despite her diminutive stature, she radiated a strange threat.

Nadia sat with her knees pressed primly together. "It's true, Mrs. Kelbie. Christine's name has come up in connection with our inquiry. However, I wouldn't say we've zeroed in on her."

"Then why are you here?"

Nadia's smile was tense. "Background."

Annie gave a girlish laugh and walked over to the rocking chair. Rather than sit, she leaned her forearms on the back of the chair and stared at them intently, as if examining curiosities in a museum. "Why don't you talk to her?"

"We're talking to you, Mrs. Kelbie," he replied, trying to keep the croak from his voice.

"And what if I don't want to talk?"

"I'd wonder what you had to hide?"

Her lips stretched into a grin. "That's rich coming from you, *Angus Dubh*."

"What are you talking about?" he asked. "How do you know my name?"

"You're the law around here, or so I'm told. Everyone knows the *handsome* local policeman."

Nadia coughed nervously. "If you don't want to speak to us, that's fine, Mrs. Kelbie—"

She turned her head slightly and her tongue flicked across her lips. "You're very pretty too, Detective Inspector. Such an attractive couple . . . No wedding ring either." She tutted, the sound like mud sucking at a Wellington boot. "Me and Christine's father were never married either. Not officially."

"Where is he now—Christine's father?" Nadia asked.

"He abandoned us when Chrissy was eight, and ran off to America."

"I'm sorry about that," Nadia said.

"Don't be. He occupied too much of me. I like space. Why else do you think I live out here in the armpit of nowhere?"

"Yet you used to be a member of the Travelling community?" he said.

"So politically correct, aren't we, Constable? Isn't it difficult—always trying to say the right thing, to hide in the shadows?"

He felt a cold tingle creep like a hand across his shoulders.

"Most people used to call us tinkers or gyppos or pikeys," Annie continued. "When I was a wee girl, I couldn't understand why everyone hated us so much. But it was obvious. We were different. We didn't conform, so they made us into bogeymen, scapegoats for all society's ills. A car is stolen—it was the tinkers. A girl is raped—it was the tinks. A man dies of an unknown disease—the tinks put the evil eye on him." Her mouth twisted into a sneer. "Folk hate what they don't understand."

"True—I grew up a minority within a minority myself," Nadia said.

"Why? What are you? Zoroastrian? Taoists? Alevis?"

"My parents were Sufis, but most of my friends were either conventional Muslim or Christians. I even went to a Catholic secondary school because it was the only one near my home that you could attend without fear of being stabbed."

"A mystic detective," Annie said with a smirk. "Must be a difficult circle to square?"

"How so?"

"The police force is built on a bedrock of science, evidence, empirical fact. But there's a sphere of knowledge beyond that, one that cannot be grasped through reason alone. Isn't that one of the key teachings of Sufism?"

Christ, she sounds just like Gills, Angus thought.

"Aye," Nadia said, "but a good police officer develops a keen intuition. For me, that's almost as important as DNA and fingerprints."

"Not in the eyes of the courts," Annie said.

Nadia conceded the point with a smile. "That's true."

"And in my experience, DI Sharif, most police officers lack any kind of imagination, let alone intuition."

"Maybe we can return to Christine?" Angus said. "When did she develop an interest in paganism?"

Annie walked across to the fire, nimble as a bird, and threw in another lump of peat, a wrinkled brown block that reminded him of Lindow Man's flesh.

"Chrissy was bullied at every school she went to. Not so much by the children—they were too scared, because she was handy with her fists. No, it was the teachers who were the worst. Sadists in ties and tweed two-pieces.

Then when she left school, no one would give her a job. The word 'Traveller' really puts the kibosh on a CV. She was a clever girl, too. Could have made something of herself."

"When was the last time you spoke to your daughter?" Nadia asked.

Mrs Kelbie stared into the fire, as if she hadn't heard the question. "She was always interested in preserving our culture. But our way of life was dying from before she was even born. Our community grew smaller and smaller. Folk took regular jobs. They moved into council housing. The young ones didn't want to live in caravans. They wanted mobile phones. Sky TV. Netflix. Designer clothes. They wanted to be the same as everyone else. Chrissy didn't want to conform."

"But why paganism?" Nadia persisted.

"A heady mixture of naivety, romanticism, and spiritualism," she sneered. "And she fell in with the wrong crowd: New Agers. Satanists. Hippies. Charlatans. They filled her mind with their claptrap. Like us all, Chrissy is searching for meaning. She thinks she can reconstruct an older, truer, more balanced way of life. She imagines an ancient utopia, full of golden-haired noble savages living off the land and spouting poetry. I told her she's chasing a myth. In every age we humans do the same—we spin these fables and fairy tales to glorify and vindicate our brutality. We're base creatures, Detective. Always were, always will be. Life has become a battle to repress these brutish desires. We cage them behind laws and science and religion. We build the bars of our cells with iron, without realizing the very walls of our prison are porous." She twisted her head slightly and looked Angus directly in the eye.

"Sooner or later we reveal our true selves."

He struggled to keep his face blank. He could almost feel Annie Kelbie's dirty fingers raking through his thoughts.

"My daughter," she continued, "is up on those mountains with her sheep and goats, flailing around like a blind woman. The truth is, I've not spoken to her in years. But once the scales fall from her eyes, I'll be here, waiting for her return. A mother never gives up on her child."

Outside, the wind howled in anguish. The peat fire spat and crackled. Angus fancied he could hear tiny feet scurrying under the floorboards.

Nadia spent a few more minutes asking Annie some general questions about Christine, but he could not concentrate on the answers. Their voices were muffled, as if he were hearing them from underwater. His head swam, jumbled thoughts and images crashing down on him like the waves on the shore outside. He saw his mother's fingers slide down a steamed-up car window. He felt coarse sand on his hands as he pumped on Ethan's chest. Faye toppled sideways onto the grass. He chewed the inside of his mouth and a bolt of pain chased the image away. Nadia glanced at him and indicated with a slight raise of her eyebrows that they were done. He sprang to his feet, eager to be out of the house and as far away as possible from this strange woman with the knowing eyes.

"Well, thanks for your time, Mrs. Kelbie," Nadia said. "You've been most helpful."

Annie wafted towards the door, like a snow cloud in her oversized white cardigan. The floorboards creaked under his boots as he followed her across the room.

Annie pulled open the door on the snarling wind and stepped aside. He was hit by a wall of sound: manic waves flagellated the shore; gulls like tenebrous wraiths shrieked across the sky; clumps of whin exhaled a death rattle. The wind was merciless.

Nadia tugged on her beanie and zipped her padded jacket up to the neck. She gave Annie a brief nod and then stepped outside. Angus went to follow, but before he could cross the stone lintel, Annie's hand shot out and grabbed his arm. She leaned in close and whispered in his ear. "Close your eyes and see, Angus. Before it's too late."

She flicked the matted hair away from her forehead to reveal an ugly, ragged scar. Then she shoved him out into the storm.

CHAPTER 36

DR Boyle's sporty silver BMW was parked outside Grant and Nualla's house at Ardnish. The modest two-storey property was perched on the hillside, a large front window affording views of the fish farms on Loch Ailort and the mountains of south Morar beyond. Ash drew up alongside the GP's car, climbed out, and retrieved the present for the new baby from the boot—cute little jumpsuits and a rabbit comforter. She also lifted a separate gift bag, stuffed with prosecco, chocolates, and flowers for Nualla.

The front door opened before she could reach it, and Dr. Boyle stepped out, still barking instructions to Grant. The GP was in her sixties, probably close to retirement, but had a youthful style that Ash had always admired. Today she wore jeans, green Converse, and a leather jacket over a striped nautical top. A black beret was perched jauntily on her head, streaks of silver-grey hair billowing from under the hat.

She smiled at Ash and pecked her on both cheeks. Originally from Normandy, she'd married a Scotsman decades ago but retained the French style of greeting, as well as the accent. "Apologies, Ashleigh," she said. "I must dash. No rest for thee wicked."

She scampered past Ash on a waft of expensive Chanel perfume and hopped into the BMW. She gunned the engine and powered away, tyres spinning on the gravel. Ash turned to Grant and raised a quizzical eyebrow. "She's some machine."

"Aye." Grant sighed. He looked tired, Ash thought, his skin pasty, beard thick and unkempt. The very picture of a first-time father.

"Come on in," he said, turning and leading the way into the house. She followed him through to the kitchen and placed her bags on the table.

"You look knackered," Ash said. "Rosie keeping you up?"

He nodded, but then his shoulders began to shake and Ash realized he was sobbing quietly. She walked over to him and placed a hand on his shoulder. "Grant, what's wrong? Is Rosie okay?"

"Aye, aye, she's fine, Ash," he said. "It's Nualla."

"Nualla?"

"She's . . . struggling. I mean, we both are, but Dr. Boyle thinks she might be suffering from postpartum depression. She's given me a prescription for some pills, so . . ." He shrugged, the sentence petering out.

"God, I'm sorry to hear that. Is there anything I can do to help?"

Grant shook his head, his eyes downcast. "The thing is, Ash, I'm due out at sea in a couple of days. You know what it's like—I'll be away for weeks. I don't want to leave her here on her own, but we need the money. Like, desperately."

Anger swelled in her. It wasn't fair that hardworking families were struggling to make ends meet. She knew they'd sunk everything they had into buying this house. It was nothing fancy but cost way over the odds because rich southerners had inflated the market by snapping up all the local housing stock for holiday homes or Airbnb.

"Right, here's what we'll do," Ash said. "You have work, there's no two ways about it. While you're at sea, either me or Ellen or Jan or one of Nualla's other pals on the community council will come round every day. I'll arrange a rota so she won't be alone for long. Even if it's just looking after Rosie for a few hours to give her time to herself. How does that sound?"

Grant swallowed, tears swelling in his eyes. "Aye." He sniffed. "Thanks, Ash. That would be great. That would be a real weight off my shoulders."

He rubbed his eyes with his sleeve then gave her a watery smile. "Do you want to come through and see the baby?"

She jabbed his arm. "Of course. Didn't come here to see you, ya big dafty."

He grinned, then turned and led them out of the kitchen and across the hall to the front room. Nualla was sat at the window seat, staring out across the loch. She wore jogging bottoms and a stained hoodie. Her skin was sallow, and her hair fell in lank skeins over her shoulders. Baby Rosie lay ignored in a Moses basket a few feet away, mewling softly.

Grant hovered awkwardly in the doorway. "Ash is here to see you, love."

Nualla continued to stare out the window. Grant glanced at Ash, embarrassed. He walked across to Nualla and gave her shoulder a gentle shake. "Ash is here," he said softly. Nualla glanced up. Her large dark eyes that had always reminded Ash of a seal were dull and listless, almost as if she'd already been medicated.

"Hi, hon. Come in, take a seat . . . if you can find one."

The room was littered with parts from an IKEA flat pack.

"Grant's battling with a changing table for the nursery," Nualla said.

"Aye, and so far it's winning," Grant said. "Here, Ash . . ." He shifted a half-built drawer from the two-seater sofa. Ash lowered herself onto it and shrugged off her coat. The room was stifling. She leaned forward and peered into the Moses basket. Rosie squirmed in a lilac sleepsuit, chubby arms held above her head, like a wrestler showing her muscles. She wore little mitts to prevent her scratching her face. "Oh, Nualla! She's beautiful."

She glanced up, but Nualla's smile seemed forced. "She's a wee toerag, that's what she is. Won't feed properly. Won't sleep . . ."

As if on cue, Rosie began to bawl. "Do you mind if I lift her?" Ash asked. Nualla shook her head. "Be my guest."

Ash slid her fingers under Rosie's small warm body and lifted her out of the basket, being careful to support her head. The child looked up at her with big round eyes, the same colour as her mother's. "Aren't you a wee belter," Ash crooned. Rosie seemed to smile at her, but then the baby's face scrunched up and she let out a plaintiff cry that reminded Ash of a bleating lamb.

"She's a fair set of lungs on her," Ash said, smiling at Nualla. She rocked Rosie gently, making little soothing sounds whilst pacing round the room. She started to sing a Gaelic lullaby her mother used to sing to her:

Hush, the waves are rolling in
White with foam, white with foam
Father toils amidst the din
But baby sleeps at home

As if by magic, Rosie quietened down. Ash sang another verse and for a second she was back in her childhood bed. The night-light cast a buttery glow on her mother's hair, which was the same colour as the autumn leaves on the chestnut tree at the bottom of their garden. The strands tickled her nose when she bent down to kiss her good night. She giggled, wound her little arms around her mother's neck. *Again, Mummy! Another song! Don't go!* A splintering sound shattered the memory. Blue flashing lights broke on the inky black surface of a loch. A dark figure emerged from the water carrying her mother's body. Ash heard herself scream.

She almost flinched, afraid she'd cried out loud, but then she realized the lullaby still fluttered from her lips. She dragged her mind back from the edge of the loch and the car crash that had taken her parents. The song petered out. She looked down at the tiny bundle in her arms.

Rosie's little hand curled around her finger. Ash gave a tremulous smile, imagining the dark thoughts being flushed out of her head.

"Right, I need to record you singing that," Grant said, only half-joking.

Ash glanced at Nualla, but she seemed to have forgotten anyone was there. Ash could see her ghostly reflection in the window, those big dark eyes staring at the sea as if she wanted it to swallow her up, to drown her.

CHAPTER 37

ANGUS'S head felt thick and woozy as he drove the Land Rover back towards the village hall, Annie Kelbie's parting words swimming in his mind.

Close your eyes and see. . . .

But he didn't want to see. That's why he took the pills, which reminded him: he'd wasted half the bottle last night, vomiting them down the toilet. A greater anxiety was the rift with Ash. She'd given up so much for him, but he'd taken a match to her dreams of a family. She now knew he didn't want children. But he couldn't tell her why.

Beside him in the passenger seat, Nadia was on the phone to Crowley, but he'd zoned out of the conversation. The wipers thrashed across the windscreen, struggling to clear away the icy deluge, but by the time they'd passed Arisaig, the sleety rain had stopped and patches of blue sky appeared between the clouds.

"Crowley is getting Christine Kelbie in on a volley," Nadia said, cutting the call. "He wants me as his sidekick, to "learn from the master.'" She rolled her eyes. "He isn't half as good as he thinks he is."

"Aye?"

"Ruthven's old-school, learnt interrogation in an era when suspects had a tendency to fall down stairs in custody."

"Folk were clumsier back then," he said.

She flashed him a faint smile. "Apparently."

Angus liked that he could still make her smile. "The incident with the Priest doesn't seem to have affected Crowley?" he said.

"He's a typical Scottish alpha male," she replied. "He would never admit to any weakness, but sometimes I wonder . . ."

"What?" he asked.

She seemed to shiver. "The Priest made his victims confess their sins as he tortured them. I just wonder what sins Ruthven confessed."

With Nadia preparing to interview Kelbie, Angus walked down Silvaig High Street and turned into Shaggers' Alley. Perhaps Faye had been taking a short-cut to the taxi rank at the station, as Ryan Fleet had surmised, but he suspected she might have had an appointment on route. A thin woman with dyed-blond hair and thick makeup stood outside Belle's Beauty Salon, sucking greedily on a cigarette. He recognised her as Geraldine MacAuley, a character he'd had several run-ins with in the past. As well as being a "beautician," she ran a stall at Silvaig's Sunday market, selling knockoff perfume, makeup, and "designer" clothes. Trading Standards were keeping a close eye on her.

She caught his eye and smirked. "Afternoon, Constable. Are ye here for a facial?"

"Not today, Gerry," he replied, striding past her.

"Ach, come one. I'll gie ye a discount."

He ignored her, walking on until he reached the gleaming black door of Glenda Wright Associates. He paused, glancing across at Ossian Fine Arts. Faye might have also visited the gallery to stock up on supplies. As far as he knew, Ossian was the only shop in town that sold quality artists' materials. If he was wrong that Faye had been visiting the therapist, the gallery was his next port of call.

The aroma of coffee oozed from the open door of Dr. Glenda Wright's office, fighting a winning battle against the pomegranate-infused candle. The therapist was reclined on a tan leather Barcelona chair by the window, engrossed in *Psychologies* magazine. He tapped the door to get her attention. "Cheers, Charlotte, just leave the report on the desk," she said without looking up.

He cleared his throat. "Sorry to bother you, Dr. Wright . . ."

She let the magazine fall to her lap and glared at him over her thick-rimmed glasses. "Oh, it's you, Angus. What's the matter? I don't see you for weeks, then you turn up twice in two days."

"It's not a personal visit."

He glanced over his shoulder out into the empty corridor. "Do you have time to talk?"

She checked her thin gold watch and sighed. "My next client's not due for fifteen minutes. Please, come in."

He shuffled into the office and closed the door behind him.

Dr Wright threw down her magazine. "So what's this about, Angus?"

"Faye Chichester," he said. "Was she one of your clients?"

Dr Wright held his stare, her eyes giving nothing away. She'd make a damn good poker player, he thought.

"I'd be well within my right not to answer that question, Angus."

"Come on, Glenda. I know patient confidentiality is protected, even after death. But this is a murder inquiry."

Still nothing from Dr. Wright.

"Look, I knew her, Glenda. Only a bit. But enough to know that she wasn't just some billionaire's daughter. This case is personal to me."

"And professional ethics are personal to me."

"Ach, for God's sake!" he growled. "Don't make me get a court order. Was she your client or not?"

He saw a flash of anger in her pale brown eyes. "I don't care for your tone, Angus. You can't waltz in here and threaten me. And besides, why should I help you? I've been your therapist for over a year, and you've given me nothing. You're bloody impenetrable. Sometimes I think I know you less well now than I did when we began."

He'd overstepped the mark. He sagged into the trendy chair beside her desk. "Sorry, Glenda," he said. "I guess I've not been exactly forthcoming in our sessions."

Her thin eyebrows shot up her forehead. "Understatement of the century."

"It's just . . ." He hesitated.

Tell her the truth, Angus.

"Just what?" Dr. Wright prompted.

Tell her about your visions. Tell her you're a seer.

"I'm *mollaichte*—that's Gaelic for "cursed.'"

Dr Wright's frown lines deepened. "Okay, that's not what I was expecting. Why do you believe you're cursed?"

He closed his eyes and saw his mother's hand sliding down the window of the Renault Scenic. Then, suddenly, he was in the car itself. Mum was driving him to school on a cold winter's morning. She was singing along to a pop song on Nevis Radio. He saw himself raise his index finger and draw a triple-spiral on the steamed-up window.

His eyes snapped open. Dr. Wright frowned at him over the rims of her spectacles. "Where were you there, Angus?"

"Remembering," he muttered.

"Remembering what?"

He stared into her eyes. "Better times. When my mother was alive."

Dr Wright nodded slowly. "Are you ready to talk about her?"

He was silent for a long second. "Aye," he said at last. "But not now."

"At our next session, then?"

He held her steely gaze, then gave a tiny nod.

Dr Wright checked her watch and gave a tired sigh. "Look, Angus, this isn't some kind of quid pro quo, but you're right—Faye was a client."

Angus felt neither triumph nor relief in the admission. "How long had she been seeing you?"

Dr Wright closed her eyes briefly, as if gathering her thoughts. "She first came to me in late June. I can check my diary for the exact date." She stood and walked around behind her desk. She pulled open a drawer, slid out a leather crocodile-print diary, and flicked through the pages with practiced fingers. "Here we are. Tuesday, June twenty-first, at two p.m." She slid the diary around so Angus could see.

"How often did she come? Weekly? Fortnightly?"

"Sporadically." She arched an eyebrow. "Like you."

"What did she talk about?"

Dr Wright steepled her fingers. "Lots of things, but primarily her mother's suicide. She felt a keen sense of abandonment and was struggling to cope with that."

"What did you make of her?" he asked.

Dr Wright's eyes softened, slight cracks appearing on the hard exterior. "I liked her, Angus. She was sharp and funny."

His throat felt as if it were full of pebbles. In his mind's eye, he saw Faye in the stables, humming gently as she teased the knots out of Bessie's mane with a comb. "She loved that horse," he said, as if to himself. "She didn't deserve to die like that, bludgeoned and strangled."

He blinked away the image and returned his gaze to Dr. Wright. The therapist's cheeks had gone a deadly shade of white, and the eyes behind her glasses bulged in shock. "Shit! I'm sorry, Glenda, I shouldn't have said that."

"Bludgeoned and strangled . . ." Dr. Wright repeated, her voice a breathy whisper.

"Aye, but please keep that to yourself. We haven't released those details and—"

She held up a hand to cut him off. "There's something you need to hear, Angus."

He watched, frowning, as Dr. Wright snatched up her phone and tapped a button. "Charlotte, can you drop everything you're doing and make a copy of my sessions with Faye Chichester?"

He could not hear the secretary's response, but Dr. Wright muttered a quick thanks and then returned the phone to its cradle.

"Glenda, what's the matter?"

"I recorded some of my sessions with Faye," she replied, as if to herself. There was a tremor in her voice and an uncertainty he'd never heard before.

"Did she say something that might help us catch her killer?"

"I . . . I don't know," Dr. Wright stammered. "It's a weird coincidence, that's all."

"Glenda, you're not making sense. What's a weird coincidence?"

The therapist glanced at him and seemed to shiver. "Listen to the recording of our last session, Angus. Then you'll understand what I mean."

CHAPTER 38

CHRIS Kelbie sat in the same chair in the same interview room that Ewan had occupied that morning. Watching her on the small monitor from the cramped observation room, Angus thought Kelbie looked just as uncomfortable as the ghillie had. She wore a lumberjack shirt, open at the neck to reveal a thin leather necklace decorated with colourful beads. She sat with her tattooed arms folded, Celtic knots, spirals, and mythological creatures coursing around sinewy forearms. He thought of the triple-spiral tattoo on the small of her back. Faye had probably seen it too, and that was why she had drawn it in her sketch pads. Why, though, had the symbol triggered some dim recollection?

Across the scratched table from Kelbie, Crowley lounged, cross-legged and nonchalant, beside Nadia.

"Cards on the table, Miss Kelbie," Crowley said. "I'm an atheist myself. Gods, demons, monsters—there's no such thing. But people do monstrous things. That I do believe, because I've seen the aftermath. Does that make people monsters?"

Kelbie responded to the question with a shrug.

"Here's what I think," Crowley continued. "We're not monsters. We're animals. We're driven by the same basic desires as the apes we evolved from millions of years ago. Food, shelter, reproduction. We invented gods and religion to bind us together, because in the beginning we were weak and alone in our tribes. This collective deception allowed people with nothing in common to unite and conquer the animal kingdom. But since we've clawed our way to the top of the food chain, our basic needs are now well catered for. So what do we yearn for next? I'll tell you—pleasure and power."

Angus thought he heard an echo of his father's cynicism—fatalism, even—in Crowley's reductive philosophy.

Is this really all we are? Mere animals?

"Which of these drives you, Christine? Pleasure? Power? Both?"

"I'm a member of a small Celtic Reconstructionist Pagan commune in the Highlands of Scotland,' she said. "I'm hardly Stalin or Chairman Mao or some power-crazed lunatic."

"So what is it you actually believe?" Nadia asked gently.

Kelbie looked bored by the question. "We're a polytheistic, animistic, religious, and cultural movement. We try to reconstruct aspects of ancient Celtic religions that were lost or subsumed by Christianity. Celtic identity is *not* based on genetics, as some so-called experts have wrongly suggested, but by being part of a linguistic and cultural group—Irish, Gaelic, Breton, Welsh, and Manx, for example."

"I see," Nadia said. "So you worship Celtic deities?"

"Well, yes, obviously."

"Such as?"

"There are loads, hundreds in fact. Irish and Scottish Reconstructionists might worship the Daghda or Brighid or Manannán Mac Lir; Welsh Reconstructionists, Rhiannon or Ceridwen. Most of us honour a number of deities but have an affinity with one in particular. Some have a subset of deities with whom they have a strong alliance, while still offering respect to the broader spectrum of spiritual beings."

"And which is your preferred deity?" Nadia asked.

Kelbie hesitated. "Look, how's that relevant?"

"Humour me."

"Well, I'm drawn to the Cailleach. She's—"

"The oldest deity there is," Crowley cut in, "pre-Celtic, worshipped by the first tribes, blah-de-blah . . ."

Kelbie looked at Crowley, surprised.

"She is particularly associated with Samhain, is she not?"

"Err, aye," Kelbie stammered. "She is said to rule the dark half of the year, which begins on Samhain."

"Do you make sacrifices to her, then?"

Kelbie, Angus thought, was doing herself no favours. She appeared evasive, petulant. But then again that was hardly surprising considering her upbringing, her fellow Travellers blamed for all society's ills.

A car is stolen—it was the tinkers.

A girl is raped—it was the tinks.

Close your eyes . . . and see.

"Look, sacrifice is a profound spiritual concept. I wouldn't expect someone like you to understand—"

"Too complex for my tiny brain to comprehend, is that what you're saying?"

Kelbie performed an eye roll Faye Chichester would have been proud of. "You're an atheist, Detective, and I'm fine with that. Just as I'd be untroubled if you were a Christian, a Muslim, or a frigging Jedi."

"What if murder were part of my religion? Would you be fine with that, too?"

"No, of course not," Kelbie snapped.

"But your gods demand sacrifice, do they not? Human sacrifice?"

"That's . . . unclear."

Crowley's lip curled. "No, it's not. Celtic Reconstructionists are obsessed with re-creating authentic pagan rites and practices. Certain Celtic gods were honoured and appeased with human blood. Of that there is no doubt."

"Obviously, there are certain things we don't do," Kelbie mumbled. "Do you think Christians follow the Bible to the letter? Of course they don't."

Crowley punched a fist into his palm. "That, right there, is what really gets on my wick. You shouldn't get to pick or choose which parts of a religion you like. Either you believe it all or none of it. So which is it, Christine? Do you believe human sacrifice is justified, in certain extreme cases?"

"Of course not," Kelbie spat. "Look, this is getting ridiculous. We would never consider sacrificing a human being. The idea is preposterous."

"It does happen," Nadia said mildly. "Do you recall a child's torso was found in the Thames a few years back? Adam, the police called him. Killed by a witch doctor as part of a muti ritual sacrifice."

"I did not kill Faye," Kelbie said, voice wobbling. "None of us at the commune would do something like that."

"Yet the method of her death parallels, almost to the exact cut, a ritual carried out to honour your gods. That's one heck of a coincidence." Crowley leaned across the table as if he wanted to grab Kelbie by the neck, and stared into her eyes. A muscle in his jaw twitched. His gaze was like a scalpel. Kelbie's eyes were downcast, partially hidden behind her braids. "I've been a detective a long time, Miss Kelbie. And I've learnt that the old adage is true—if it walks like a duck and quacks like a duck, chances are it's a fucking duck. Faye was killed in a *pagan* sacrificial ritual. She was last seen alive at a *pagan* celebration. I mean, come on! Doesn't take a genius to work out that you and your fellow cultists had something to do with it."

Kelbie's chin wobbled. She seemed on the verge of tears. "I came here voluntarily because I wanted to help you catch whoever killed Faye. But it's clear this is a stitch-up job, so I'd like to go now."

For a long moment nobody spoke. At length, Crowley shot Kelbie a wolfish grin. "Of course," he said with forced joviality. "Police Scotland appreciates your cooperation in this matter. But before you go, I'd like you to consider one thing, Miss Kelbie."

She flicked the braids out of her face and met the detective's eyes. "What's that?"

"How well do you know your friends from the commune? You've gathered waifs and strays from all walks of life there: What do you really know about their pasts? Who they are? What are they capable of?"

"We're a family," Kelbie replied.

"Families turn on each other in moments of crisis. I've seen it countless times. If the killer *is* amongst you, I can guarantee one thing: he—or she—will not hesitate to drop you in it."

Kelbie scraped her chair back and stood, a belligerent set to her jaw. "I'm going now."

Crowley sprang upright, smiling. "Fair enough." He ushered Kelbie towards the door like a good host. "Please, think about what I said, Christine. Folk would sell their granny to avoid prison." He yanked open the door and stood aside.

"Some might even sacrifice her."

CHAPTER 39

WITH Nadia and Crowley still picking over the aftermath of the interview, Angus had time to listen to the recording of Faye's session with Dr. Wright. He slid the flash drive Glenda's secretary, Charlotte, had given him into a PC. A dialogue box popped up and he selected the open folder option. The folder contained three audio files, each dated. He was about to click on the most recent, when someone behind him cleared their throat.

"Ahem! Did I give you permission to listen to that?"

He spun around, startled. Faye stood by the door of the observation room. She wore the same sapphire coat with the fur collar that she'd had on in the CCTV footage. The tartan scarf dangled from her neck, revealing the ugly gash inflicted by the garrotte. Her hair was limp and wet, as if she'd been caught out in a storm.

"You're dead," he said. "I don't need your permission."

She stepped farther into the room, her Converse squelching.

"Why are you so wet?"

"Me and Ethan had a water fight."

He flinched at the name. One of the police reports had mentioned that, on the day of his death, Ethan's mother had bought her son a new water pistol.

"He doesn't blame you, Angus. He's too young and innocent to hold a grudge."

"Why does he torture me then?" he asked.

Faye gave that weird off-key laugh. "Try being smashed on the head, then choked with a garrotte. That's torture, Angus."

"Sorry," he muttered, "I didn't mean to sound self-pitying."

"Yeah, whatever. And yes, you can. I allow you."

He gave a confused frown. Her eyes retained a trace of green, but the colour was dim, like a T-shirt that had been washed too many times.

"The recording of my sessions with Glenda. You can listen to them. I've got nothing to hide. Can you say the same?"

"I don't know what you're talking about."

Faye wrapped the tartan scarf around her neck, covering the wound. "Go on, then," she coaxed. "Hit play."

He stared at her for a long moment, then turned back to the PC and clicked on the audio file. Her voice cut through him like a knife. Unlike the girl who haunted him, this Faye's voice crackled with vitality, a hint of a Highland accent creeping into her American twang. He smiled faintly. "You're starting to sound like a native." When he glanced over his shoulder to gauge her reaction, Faye was gone.

He turned to face the monitor again. A small dialogue box on the screen showed a pulsing line of audio waves as Faye and Dr. Wright spoke. He listened to the first few minutes of small talk, inconsequential chat about the weather and horse riding, clearly Glenda trying to put Faye at ease. Laughter punctuated Faye's sentences and he sensed a real warmth between Dr. Wright and her client.

"Have you been shopping?" the therapist asked. Angus recalled the mauve bag from the fancy dress shop that Faye had been carrying in the footage.

"Samhain costume," Faye said. "Do you want to see?"

"Sure."

He heard the rustle of bags. "Got this fairy princess kinda vibe, don't you think?"

"Wow, very smart. Where's the party?"

"At the pagan commune I told you about. Samhain's a big deal for them. They're planning all these cool rituals to honour the old gods. I'm going to ride up there on Bessie—make an entrance."

"I'm sure you will." Angus could hear the smile in Glenda's voice. She never sounded like that with him. "What is it you like about the commune? When you talk about it, your eyes always light up."

Faye was quiet for a long second. "This might seem weird, but I feel close to Mom there. For a long time after she killed herself, I was so angry with her. You know? *How dare she leave me? Was I not enough?*"

"The rage prevented you from grieving?"

"Aye, exactly."

Angus's lips twitched upwards at her use of the word "aye."

"I wasn't just angry, though. I felt guilty, too. I thought if I'd been a better daughter, if I'd loved her harder, then she wouldn't have done it. I couldn't stop thinking about all the bitchy things I said to her, all the times I'd behaved like a spoiled brat. Like, on my tenth birthday, I was really mad at her because she bought me the wrong handbag. I wanted this blue crocodile Hermès Birkin, but she got me python by mistake. It cost, like, a hundred k, but it wasn't the one I wanted, so I . . . made a scene." She laughed without humour. "I'm mortified even thinking about it now. I told my friend Ewan that story, and he said Mom should have given me a good slap."

Angus chuckled—he could hear the ghillie saying that.

"He was right," Faye continued. "But of course Mom would never have done something like that. She was . . . a gentle soul. Fragile, like a little bird."

"Your parents divorced when you were young?"

"Yeah, when I was, like, five. They had joint custody, but because Dad was so busy, I was with Mom in New York most of the time."

"She had mental health issues?" Dr. Wright asked.

"She did. It's only really since I started spending time at the commune that I've come to terms with that."

"That's a great start, Faye," Dr. Wright said. "Unfortunately, when people are in a dark place like your mother, it's often impossible to pull them out. It's natural for loved ones to blame themselves. But there's nothing you could have done. You're not to blame."

Angus closed his eyes and felt Gills's tender hand on his fevered forehead after he'd woken from another nightmare. *You're not to blame, wee man. It's not your fault.*

He swallowed down the lump in his throat and focussed on Faye's voice. She was talking now about the people at the commune.

"They accept me for who I am. They don't care who my dad is or how much my handbag cost." Her laugh was tinged with irony. "I auctioned that dumb Hermès bag for charity. It went for double its value." There was a brief pause in the conversation. Angus could almost see Dr. Wright watching Faye over her thick-rimmed glasses. "Don't get me wrong, I still like nice things," Faye said at last. "But the days of one-hundred-thousand-dollar bags are gone. The people at the commune have no luxuries, but they're happy. I think of my friends back in New York, and none of them were really, truly happy."

Faye went on to talk for a long time about her life in the States, which seemed to consist of parties, holidays in exotic locations, and a string of teenage dramas. She described these times with self-effacing humour, as if she were talking about a different person.

"You've made so much progress since our first session, Faye," Dr. Wright said.

"I know, right? I couldn't even talk about my mom then without breaking down. You've helped me so much, Glenda, but I think discovering the commune, and learning about their beliefs, has helped too."

"In one of our early sessions, you said you were an atheist?"

"Yeah, I've kinda changed my mind about that. Something lives on after death, I'm sure of that. Sometimes when I'm at the commune, I just sit and talk to Mom, and she listens. Sounds crazy, right?"

"Not at all."

"I'm starting to see it's a cycle, you know? Life, death, rebirth." For the next few minutes, Faye talked about the various people from the commune, but like her prolonged discussion about her friends' love lives, Angus got the impression she was tiptoeing around something.

Dr Wright clearly felt so too. "I'm glad you're making friends, but we're here to talk about you, not them," she said. "There's something else, isn't there?"

A long silence followed. Angus stared at the thin line on the dialog box, tiny blips marking Faye's breathing.

"What's the matter, Faye?" Dr. Wright asked gently.

"I've . . . been seeing things?"

An icy shiver shot across his shoulders.

"What kind of things?"

He heard Faye give a shuddering sigh. "I suppose they're, like, visions—nightmares, except I'm awake, and, well, they don't come at night."

"And what do you see in these visions?"

"I see this crooked old tree. And there's a burning corpse hanging from one of its branches."

Angus's body went rigid, as if the blood in his veins had frozen. His eyes flicked to the date of the recording. Two full weeks before he'd seen the burning corpse, Faye had experienced the exact same vision.

"But that's not all," she continued. "I also see a girl kneeling on the ground. This . . . thing in a deer-skull mask stands behind her. I can feel the wetness seeping through her clothes. I smell smoke, too, as if the thing is made of ashes."

Faye's voice had become taut and sharp, like barbed wire. "Then I hear this horrible wet crunch and the girl falls forward. And then I'm above, looking down, as if I'm a bird watching this. I see the thing loop this, like, piano wire or something around her neck. It jams a knee in her back and yanks. There's blood everywhere. Her head jerks back and it's only then I see the girl's face. . . ."

The final words, before Faye broke down in tears, seemed to rip from her throat.

"It's me, Glenda. I watch myself being murdered."

CHAPTER 40

THE graveyard was silent and empty when Angus arrived, weathered tombstones poking up from the wet earth like broken teeth. Mature oak and beech trees overhung the drystane perimeter wall, like old men bowing their heads in mourning. Over their topmost branches, the towers of Dunbirlinn lurked like a stalker.

He walked past a crumbling mausoleum for the MacRuari clan, and a recumbent monument of what was reputed to be a Templar knight. The warrior was still just about visible, lying on his back clasping a broadsword. His mother's grave marker was less fancy and less worn by time. It sat in a secluded spot underneath an ancient sprawling yew in a corner of the graveyard.

Crows and magpies chattered in the branches of the tree as he stooped and yanked out some weeds from the base of the gravestone. He stayed there, crouched, and ran his fingers over the words etched in the stone:

CAITLIN MACNEIL

LOVING WIFE AND MOTHER

Apart from the dates representing her short time on this earth, that was it: his father, no doubt, had resisted any kind of sentimental flourish, such as a line of poetry or a profound epithet. Yet she'd loved poetry. He could still hear her reading to him, beautiful lyrical verses by Màiri Mhòr nan Òran and Duncan Bàn MacIntyre. Folk had a tendency to lionize those who had died. Curmudgeonly old bodachs suddenly became great wits of boundless compassion when the whisky began to flow at their wake. But his mother *was* one of the good ones.

He bent forward until his head rested on the coarse granite headstone, but when he closed his eyes, he saw her hand slap on the steamed-up window of the Renault. He thumped his head gently against the stone, forced himself to stay with the vision. He saw the dark shape looming behind her. Saw her head yanked back to reveal the pale white skin of her neck. Saw pure fear in her eyes. Saw the flash of a blade, a spurt of blood then . . . nothing. The vision ended abruptly, like a candle snuffed out. No matter how hard he tried, he could not see what happened next. He could not see his mother's murderer.

"I'm sorry," he muttered, tears stinging behind his eyelids. "I'm so sorry. . . ."

He heard Dr. Wright's professional voice, telling Faye she was not to blame for her mother's suicide. The girl seemed to have accepted that. Why couldn't he?

Angus gave his head one last thump against the headstone and then stood. The crows and magpies had fallen silent, but he felt them watching him from the branches of the yew. A robin flitted between the lichen-encrusted gravestones, a whirring crimson flash.

Two of the others he couldn't save were buried here too. Ethan Boyce and Barbara Klein. Lewis Duncan had been cremated, which had seemed to Angus like a sick joke. He wondered what would happen to Faye's body, which was still in the mortuary. She hadn't lived in Scotland long. Did she have a lair waiting for her back in the States? A plot next to her mother, perhaps?

"You know I can't rest until you find whoever did this?"

Her voice came from behind him, but he did not turn around. "I know," he whispered, no longer surprised by her appearances.

"Then stop feeling sorry for yourself and do something."

Anger fizzled in his chest. Who was she to tell him what to do? He spun around, a few choice words on his lips, but nothing was there apart from the robin, perched on the arm of a Celtic cross. The bird cocked its head to the side and studied him with twinkling intelligent eyes.

"Just . . . leave me alone." He sighed.

A sudden blare from his mobile phone shattered the stillness of the cemetery. He glanced at the screen, saw Nadia's name, and answered. "There's something you need to see," she said. "Can you meet me? I'm in a café in Silvaig, down by the harbour."

"The Jac-O-bite?"

"If that's the one someone's vomited tartan over, then yeah. Does a mean scone, though."

"Give me ten minutes."

Angus pushed open the café door and was smacked in the face by the smell of coffee, home baking, and recirculated damp air. He was greeted by a six-foot-high replica of a Jacobite warrior, kitted out in tartan and wielding a round targe and claymore. The figure reminded him of the painting of Dòmhnall MacRuari in Dunbirlinn Castle, although the replica lacked the portrait's unerring glare.

He found Nadia sitting in a booth at the rear of the café, her laptop on the table in front of her. "I ordered you a scone and coffee," she said, pointing to a plate.

He slid into the booth opposite her. "Thanks." He took a sip of the coffee and got to work spreading butter and jam on the scone. "So what's up? You sounded a bit squirrely on the phone."

She spun her laptop round so the screen was facing him. "Watch this."

He placed his knife down, frowning at the urgency in her voice. On-screen, the same movie she had been watching earlier was playing. "Still *Suffering?*"

"Aye, now shoosh your mouth and watch."

He shrugged and took a bite of his scone. Nadia was right, they were good. He washed down the sweet crumbly mixture with a mouthful of coffee, eyes on the laptop. The scene was some dark chamber, lit by flaming torches in wall sconces and large church candles. The set looked about as realistic as the fiberglass Highland landscape in Dunbirlinn. Eleanor stood at the top of some stone steps, again wearing some see-through black number. The camera lingered on her thighs, moving slowly up her body, pausing again on her chest, before eventually focussing on her face. She leered, pink tongue darting over moist scarlet lips, then the camera panned out, following Eleanor as she crept, catlike, down the steps and over to a stone tomb.

She laid a small object on top of the tomb. Angus moved his nose closer to the screen, a tingle of apprehension prickling the hair on his forearms. The shot cut to a close-up of Eleanor's face, eyes wide now, lips slightly parted, as Faye's had been when he'd found her on the beach. She began to mouth a guttural incantation in a language he did not understand. Spliced with a jagged soundtrack, the invocation became faster, louder. Eleanor writhed and bucked like a tormented animal, her performance climaxing with a piercing cry. He glanced at Nadia over the laptop.

"Keep watching," she said.

He took another bite of scone and dropped his eyes to the screen, just as the annoying soundtrack abruptly ceased, as if someone had decapitated the musicians. Eleanor's panting was now the only noise. They were in a booth, but he hoped the other customers couldn't hear. He could almost see the headlines: "Local Cop Caught Watching Porn in Café." He caught Nadia's faint smile as he tapped mute. On-screen, Eleanor was again licking her lips for some reason. Her hair was plastered to her forehead. Beads of sweat trickled down her cheeks and neck. The camera panned downwards over her heaving breasts.

Angus took another bite of scone, growing impatient. Eventually the lens fell on the object she had placed on the tomb.

He stopped chewing and stared at the laptop. "Fuck," he said, spraying crumbs across the table. "That looks—"

"Aye, it does,"

"But she said—"

"Aye, she did."

He hissed out a breath between his teeth.

"Think we should pay Lady Chichester a wee visit, don't you?" Nadia asked.

Mist rolled in off the sea and smashed on the jagged coastline, grey fingers fanning outwards to probe the pine-studded banks and lower slopes of the glen. Angus swung the Land Rover past a knot of protesters outside the gates of Dunbirlinn. Ash was not amongst them. They were mainly middle-aged, or older folk, wrapped up in hats and scarves. Some held placards reading "PEOPLE BEFORE WOLVES, GIVE US OUR LAND BACK" and "CHICHESTER, F**K OFF!" Above the protesters, the wolf on the billboard advertising Wild West Highlands glared down at them as if they were lunch.

"Ten years ago, before Chichester bought the estate, there was a bid for community ownership," Angus said. "They had all sorts of plans for sustainable housing, ecotourism, and other business ventures. They were pretty sure the buyout would be approved, but then Chichester breezed in. Paid four times the asking price, and paid a few sweeteners, too, if you believe certain folk."

"Do you?"

"Maybe. Probably." He gave a one-shouldered shrug. "Wouldn't be the first time a rich foreigner has carved out a personal Highland fiefdom."

The Land Rover splashed past Ewan's cottage and skirted the stable block. Up ahead, Dunbirlinn Castle lurked into the gloom like a scaly demon. Inside the courtyard, Faye's Merc sat next to the mustard Range Rover, an abandoned beauty. Angus parked next to Chichester's Aston Martin and climbed out of the Land Rover. Mrs. MacCrimmon appeared in the shadow of the portico and glared at him, mouth a thin line.

"I hear you came to your senses and let Ewan go," she said.

"Aye," Angus said, scuffing up the castle steps. "Didn't have enough evidence to charge him."

"Good, because he didn't do it." The housekeeper gave Nadia an unfriendly smile.

"How do you know?"

"Och! I just do."

"Er, okay," Angus said. "Actually, Mary, we're here to speak to Lady Chichester. Is she around?"

"Aye, she's in the drawing room enjoying an *aperitif*." She puckered her lips at the word. "Come on, if you hurry, you'll catch her sober. Well, sober-*ish*."

Mrs MacCrimmon spun around and led the way into the castle. Nadia cocked an eyebrow at Angus and then followed. Their footsteps echoed around the cavernous lobby as they walked towards the west wing of the castle. The corridors became tighter, more claustrophobic, the farther into Dunbirlinn they ventured. He again thought of Dòmhnall MacRuari's adulterous wife, bricked up in the secret room somewhere in the bowels of the castle. Madness seeping into her brain like mould. Knuckles bloody from pounding at the walls of her prison.

He shook his head to dislodge the thought as Mrs. MacCrimmon rapped on the door of the drawing room. She shoved it open and ushered them inside. "Police to see you, Lady Chichester."

Eleanor stood in a finger bone of light to the right of an arched window. She wore a black bell-sleeve dress, low cut and cinched below her chest with a silver belt. Her hair was pulled back in a tight bun. Cruel diamonds glinted from her earrings and necklace. Her mouth was a red slash of lipstick. In one hand she clutched the stem of an ornate cocktail glass.

"Officers," she breathed. "To what do I owe the pleasure?"

Nadia slapped on a smile. "Sorry to call unannounced, Lady Chichester. We have a couple of follow-up questions. Routine stuff. Nothing to worry about."

"I'm not worried."

Her dark eyes flitted over Angus, the tip of her tongue darting across wet lips. She teetered towards them on six-inch black stilettos. "Mary, be a darling and fix these detectives a drink?"

"No, thanks," Nadia cut in. "On duty."

"What about you, Angus?" Eleanor said. "You look like you could do with a Scotch."

A dram didn't sound like a bad idea, but he shook his head.

"Shame. Oh well, as you're here, you might as well fix me another Manhattan, Mary."

The housekeeper looked as if she wanted to punch Eleanor, but she did as she was told.

"Come in, sit down," Eleanor said, gesturing to the seating area in front of the fire. "I suppose you're wondering why I'm so glammed up?" She struck a pose, pouting like a starlet on the red carpet.

"Err . . ." Nadia stammered.

She dropped the act, her red lips twisting into a frown. "It's our wedding anniversary," Eleanor muttered, before either he or Nadia could respond. "Eight years. Seems like a lifetime." She lowered herself into an armchair and crossed one sheer black stockinged leg over the other. "Traditionally, gifts of bronze are given on the eighth anniversary, symbolizing the durability of the marriage bond." She gave a humourless bark of laughter. "But of course James has forgotten."

Angus lowered himself into an armchair as Nadia unslung her laptop bag from her shoulder.

"In the laird's defence, he has had a lot on his plate," he said.

"Hmmph! Just like men to stick together." She took a sip of her cocktail, then gave him a frank stare. "James has taken a shine to you, Angus. Perhaps you're his new pet project."

"I doubt that."

"Lady Chichester, there's something we'd like to show you," Nadia said.

The smooth skin on Eleanor's forehead wrinkled ever so slightly as Nadia flipped open the laptop and turned it towards her.

"Do you remember making this movie?" she asked. "It was called *The Suffering?*"

Eleanor's mouth puckered, as if tasting something off. She took another sip of her cocktail and appeared to swill it around her mouth. "Yes, vaguely. Panned by the critics, if I remember correctly. Forbes Forbisher was the director." She gave a slight shudder. "He of the wandering hands. Forbes fancied himself as an artist, but the amount of heroin he was shooting in his veins back then, it was a miracle we ever got the movie made."

Mrs MacCrimmon placed a fresh drink down on a low coffee table in front of Eleanor. "Just a second, Mary," Eleanor said, downing her current cocktail and handing the housekeeper the empty glass.

Mrs MacCrimmon snatched it off her and stomped away, not quite slamming the door on her way out, but making her feelings felt nonetheless.

"You were saying," Nadia prompted, "about the movie."

"Was I? Ah yes, it bombed at the box office, but c'est la vie. Look, what's this all about? I don't see how my movie from over thirty years ago can have any bearing on your hunt for my stepdaughter's killer."

"There's one scene in particular. If you'll take a look, all will be revealed."

Eleanor cocked a thin eyebrow. "You sound like Hercule Poirot, DI Sharif."

"Miss Marple, more like."

Angus watched Eleanor's reaction as the tinny soundtrack echoed around the drawing room, soon to be replaced by the laboured breathing. She wore a faint smile that didn't quite reach her eyes.

"What am I looking at?" she asked, taking another swig of her cocktail. "Other than some rather excellent acting."

"Wait for it. . . ." Nadia said. "Ah, here we go." She tapped pause and the racket ceased. On-screen, the young Eleanor froze, her hand held aloft as she prepared to ram pins into a small effigy. Angus snapped back to the beach, and saw Gills lifting the *corp creadha* from the sand. It looked almost identical to the doll frozen on the screen: lumpy figure, straw-coloured hair, pouting lips, and shards of glass for eyes.

Eleanor glanced up from the laptop. "And?"

"Well, I'd have thought it was pretty obvious, Lady Chichester? At our last meeting, I showed you a picture of a clay corpse. It was found in Faye's possession when she died." She tapped the laptop. "It looks remarkably like this doll, yet you told us you'd never seen anything like it."

A ripple of confusion, or perhaps fear, flitted across Eleanor's face. But then the barriers came down. Her eyes hardened and her lips tightened like a wound closing.

"What are you suggesting, Detective? That I killed my stepdaughter? And this . . . voodoo doll proves it?"

"Not at all," Nadia replied. "We only want to know why you didn't tell us about this doll. It is rather distinctive."

She raised her head haughtily, the sinewy cords in her neck pulling tight. "Do you know how many movies I made back then? Dozens. How am I supposed to remember specific scenes, let alone the props?"

"So you have no recollection of this scene?"

"None. Hardly surprising, I was stoned for most of the nineties."

"Might you have taken the prop as a souvenir?" Angus asked. "Perhaps Faye found it?"

Eleanor reached clumsily for her cocktail glass but only succeeded in knocking it over. The thin bowl shattered, sending blocks of ice and ruby liquid streaming across the coffee table. "Now look what you've made me do!"

Nadia pulled out a wad of tissue and dabbed at the spillage.

"Leave it," Eleanor barked. "Mary can take care of it." She stood and teetered towards the door, yanked it open. "Mrs MacCrimmon! Mrs. MacCrimmon! Some assistance, please!"

She turned and glared at them.

"You never answered my question," Angus said. "Could you have taken the doll as a souvenir?"

"No!" she replied, voice like a whipcrack. "The only souvenir I took from *The Suffering* was an unwanted pregnancy, courtesy of Forbes fucking Forbisher!"

Eleanor clamped her mouth shut, as if she immediately regretted the admission. Angus gave Nadia a brief glance. "I . . . didn't know you had a child?"

"I don't," she snapped at him. "Forbes made me get rid of it." She stuck her head out of the door. "Mrs MacCrimmon! Mrs. MacCrimmon! For God's sake! Where is she?"

Muttering under her breath, she veered across the drawing room towards the drinks cabinet and began mixing another cocktail. She glanced over her shoulder at Angus, her eyes glassy and bitter. "You and Miss Marple can fuck off now," she slurred. "If you want to speak to me again, contact my lawyer first."

CHAPTER 41

EWAN Hunter barrelled out of the off-license, the bottles of Bell's he'd bought clinking as he slithered up Davies Brae. He passed shops selling the tartan tat his father had hated—tea towels, Highland cow T-shirts, Nessie soft toys. *The Highlands has lost any sense of itself, son*, he'd say. *We've thrown on a kilt and sold up for the price of a box of fudge and a fluffy West Highland terrier.*

Ewan hadn't really understood what he meant at first. But then he'd started to read the books his father had given him and the scales fell from his eyes. Highlanders like him were history's whipping boys. For centuries they'd been under systematic attack from English imperialists and their Lowland Scottish lackeys.

Cultural genocide, son. It's nothing short of cultural genocide.

His eyes flitted to the window of the Army Careers Centre as he passed. The poster was still there—a guy wearing military fatigues and a stupid beret, "BE THE BEST" emblazoned in block capitals above his head.

Imperialist bastards, he thought, recalling the smarmy recruitment officer he'd spoken to that day. Wee English twat with a Hitler moustache: *Oh no, Mr. Hunter, you can't just be a sniper. First you need to apply to join an infantry regiment. Then you need to qualify for your marksman badge. Only then can you put yourself forward for sniper training. And of course not everyone can cut it. Incidentally, I noticed Tesco is recruiting at the moment.*

That *sneer* on the little twat's face. As if he thought Ewan were something to be scraped off his shoe. The same look his teachers used to give him when he didn't hand in his homework, even though it was in his schoolbag, completed days previously.

He glanced in the window of the Steam Inn, the pub he'd gone to after his humiliation at the Army Careers Centre. In a flash, he was back in the dingy, sweaty atmosphere, whisky coursing red-hot through his body. His mother's new boyfriend laughing at the bar. Drinking, not a care in the world whilst his father lay in the cemetery. He remembered ripping the bastard from the barstool. Next thing, he was in the street. Fists coated in blood. Only, it was no longer his mum's boyfriend he was smashing. It was the little twat with the Hitler moustache.

Snow again started to fall, like cold wet kisses. He thought of his attempt to kiss Faye, and cringed. The irony of it was he didn't even fancy her *that way*. He recalled a trip to Glenfinnan earlier in the year, and the leering group of bikers parked near the monument. *Give her one for me, big lad!* one of them had shouted as they walked past. Only Faye's hand on his arm had stopped him knocking the prick out. His love—and it was love—was pure, untainted by lust. The idea of pawing at her was almost sacrilege, like defiling a great artwork. Why then, had he tried to kiss her?

Ewan worked up a mouthful of saliva and spat, as if disgorging the memory. The Pathfinder lurked at the top of the hill in a small rectangle reserved for church parking. The Good Lord could go fuck himself, Ewan thought, fumbling in the pocket of his stained combat pants for his car keys. What had God ever done for him?

"D'you hear me!" he shouted. "You can go fuck yourself!"

There was no reply. The churchyard was still. Beyond it, the arm of Sleat on the Isle of Skye lay dark and rigid amidst a gleaming sea. Like a wolf on the prowl.

He slid inside the jeep, revved the engine loudly, then backed out of the car park, narrowly avoiding a lamppost. He crunched the car into gear and powered out of Silvaig on the coast road, the rear of the Pathfinder fishtailing in the snow. Dunbirlinn was some half an hour away, but at this time of night the road was empty, which was just as well, as he was driving like a maniac. He stamped his foot down on the accelerator, swinging the jeep around the tight bends, hardly caring if he slid off the road and plummeted into the sea.

His thoughts lurched to the deer hanging from the hook in the storeroom. He remembered how warm her coat had felt. But the detective had said there was no deer. He'd lied. He was nothing but a goddamn liar. They all were. He'd slaughtered hundreds of animals, but he'd never have hurt Faye. He'd been at the bothy when she'd died, drinking whisky. Sure, he couldn't remember the *whole* night. . . . He often had blackouts when he was on the *deoch*.

"I'm the apex predator!" he yelled. "I'm the fucking apex predator!"

Through the trees, he glimpsed the blackened walls of Dunbirlinn, the ramparts like rotten teeth in a decaying corpse. A light shone from the room at the top of the tower. What was the laird doing up at this hour? Probably couldn't sleep. Whisky was the best remedy for that. Enough to render you unconscious. Ewan would get started on the Bell's soon enough. But first he had a job to do.

His father's old rifle bounced against his shoulder as he walked around the perimeter of the wolf enclosure. The spot he'd chosen wasn't far, a wooded area where the fence ran close to the pines. Some of the branches overhung the enclosure, providing cover from the snow. Cover, too, for the task at hand.

He propped the rifle against the fence and took the wire cutters from his pocket. He stood for a few minutes, listening intently. Across the moor, he heard the throaty, repetitive call of a ptarmigan and the whistle of the wind in the branches above his head. He sniffed, but all he could smell was damp pine needles. The feral stink of the wolves was absent.

He gripped the wire cutters and hunkered down beside the fence. His previous attempts to sabotage the nature reserve had been pointless, he saw that now. The petulant acts of a child. Burning down the shed with the GPS trackers inside, slashing tyres on the heavy machinery—it had been an irritant to Chichester, nothing more. The wolves were the root cause of his problems. They were a threat to his livelihood, and just as his famous ancestor Roderick had done, he would wipe them from the land. Eradication was the only answer.

He had been trained in the procedure to follow if the wolves escaped. The first priority was preserving human life. Wolves were designated Category I animals, defined as those likely to cause serious injury or be a serious threat to life. Once they were in a public space, lethal force was permitted.

But first he had to set the wolves free. Only then could he track and kill them.

CHAPTER 42

ANGUS woke from a fitful sleep plagued by nightmares. He sat bolt upright, disoriented, still in that otherworld of unconsciousness. In his head, he was sprinting through a dank forest, pursued by some unknown terror. He heard the ominous bass note of a hunting horn. The sound seemed to come from all around him. The unearthly din reverberated in his chest and seemed to convey something worse than death. He fled from the noise, plummeting blindly through thick briars and stinging undergrowth. Thorns raked his body, flaying the skin from his face and arms. Blood seeped from a hundred lacerations. It flowed into his eyes and mouth, making him choke. His heart thrashed, but he could not outrun his pursuer. He felt its hot breath on his neck. . . .

"It's not real," he hissed. "It's not real."

Slowly, the nightmare faded, leaving nothing but a lingering sense of unease. He reached for his phone and checked the time. Not yet seven.

He rose from the sofa bed, groaning in pain. Ash had already been in bed when he'd returned home last night. He'd suspected she wouldn't want him anywhere near her after the row, so he'd decided to sleep in the spare room again.

He padded into the kitchen and filled the kettle at the sink, staring out the window. Dawn was still a promise on the horizon. The hill behind the cottage was silhouetted against a charcoal-grey sky. Fresh snow had fallen overnight; he could make out a thin white layer on the top of the woodshed.

As the kettle boiled, Angus retrieved the memory stick of Faye's sessions with Dr. Wright from his coat pocket and then powered up his laptop. He took his time making coffee, putting off the moment he would hear her voice again. He was only delaying the inevitable. Sighing, he slumped down at the kitchen table and slotted the memory stick into the laptop's USB port. Despite being prepared for it, her voice made his stomach twist. The coffee tasted acrid in his mouth. Faye sounded as if she were in this very room, sitting across from him. She was upset, a wobble in her voice as she responded to Dr. Wright's questions.

"Tell me more about this vision, Faye. Was this the first one?"

"Yeah," she mumbled. "I've had, like, nightmares before. Who hasn't, right? But this was different."

"You said you were awake when it happened?"

"I was in the stables, taking off Bessie's saddle. We'd been out for a hack in the hills—"

"So you were tired?"

"Not really. My legs were a little sore, but I wasn't sleepy or anything."

"Do you suffer from epilepsy or any other neurological illness?"

"What? No."

"Are you a daydreamer, Faye?"

"It wasn't a dream, Glenda." Angus heard a hint of annoyance in Faye's voice. "It seemed so real. I could feel the wet grass seeping through my clothes. And there was this faint smell of smoke. Not a bonfire or wood-smoke. More like the big Cuban cigars my dad used to smoke. What do you think it means?"

Dr Wright was silent for a long second. "Hallucinations are often brought on by alcohol and drugs," she said at last.

Faye laughed softly. "You think I've been on shrooms? Or stealing my dad's whisky?"

Angus smiled at her quick-witted response.

"Only natural for girls your age to experiment with drink and drugs."

"Been there, done that," Faye replied.

"You've taken drugs?"

"Of course. My best friend from school went into rehab at thirteen. Seeing her in that state kinda put me off drugs, though. Haven't smoked since. And I don't drink."

"I see. Well, another explanation for your hallucination could be stress. In a previous session, I recall you mentioning a row with your stepmother over education?"

"Yeah, she's sending me to a stuck-up finishing school in Switzerland."

"But you want to go to art school, right? Could this be making you anxious?"

"I'm pissed about that, Glenda. But strung out? I don't think so."

Angus's mobile lit up. He checked the screen and saw an unknown number. He frowned. Who would be calling at this hour? He raised the device to his ear and answered with a gruff hello.

"Angus, is that you?"

He recognised the Texan drawl immediately, but why the hell was James Chichester phoning him?

"Mr Chichester. What can I do for you?"

"Apologies for calling you so early. Mrs. MacCrimmon gave me your number." The laird's voice sounded tense.

"No problem. What's up?"

"I need your help. Someone has released my wolves."

The snow was falling again, a gentle flurry, the flakes like eiderdown from a torn pillow. James Chichester stood on the viewing platform overlooking the wolf enclosure, motionless, as if frozen in ice. He had been there for some time, judging from the layer of snow that had settled on the shoulders of his long wax jacket. Angus took a deep breath and walked towards the laird. Chichester appeared not to realize he was there, but then he suddenly spoke. "Do you think grief has a scent, Angus?"

He frowned, wrong-footed by the question. "Yes," he said eventually. "It has a scent, and taste. It even has texture."

Chichester turned his head slowly and looked at him. "How do you know?"

"Observation."

"Observation," Chichester repeated quietly. "Yes, I believe you're right. Perhaps if we observed more, consumed less, we'd be worth saving."

He turned back to stare across the snow-covered landscape. "Wolves mourn when they lose a member of the pack. I remember hearing about an alpha female from Yellowstone who for six weeks kept returning to the same spot her mate was shot, searching for him. The area was just outside the reserve. Inevitably, she ended up being shot herself. Afterwards, the pack scattered. Her store of knowledge was the glue that had held them together. Without her, they were doomed."

Chichester's gloveless hands rested on top of the barrier that curved around the viewing platform. "My daughter, now my pack, has gone," he said, sorrow—not self-pity—cracking his words. "I look around and I wonder: Was it worth it? Will this suffering be enough?"

The laird did not look well. His jaw was peppered with coarse white stubble. His cheeks were sunken, and there were dark bags under his eyes, as if he hadn't slept.

"You said the wolves have escaped?"

Chichester, though, was lost in his own thoughts. "Ten thousand years ago man arrived here," he said. "He was gifted an unspoiled wilderness: a great Caledonian pine forest full of deer and elk; crystal-clear rivers teeming with salmon and trout; lofty mountains, home to eagles and osprey, a fastness for lynx and cave lion; the valleys below lush from the receding ice, grazed by aurochs and bison.

"These hunter-gatherers shared in the bountiful harvest. They lived and died in harmony. Like wolves, they gained knowledge and passed it down from generation to generation. Their lives were short and tough, of course, but rich and meaningful in a way ours have ceased to be."

Chichester's hands, Angus noticed, were turning white. "How will history remember my daughter? A spoiled heiress—remarkable only for the manner of her death, salacious fodder for the masses. It makes me sick to the stomach!"

"Not everyone is so callous. You shouldn't give up hope."

Chichester's eyes never wavered from a point on the horizon. "We are irredeemably lost, Angus Dubh."

The certainty in his tone struck Angus to the core: it brooked no dissent. "I'm sorry," he whispered, although he'd no idea what he was apologizing for.

Chichester turned and patted him on the shoulder. "You're a good man, Angus. Come on, I'll show you where the wolves left."

He reached for his wolf-headed walking stick, and together they descended from the viewing platform. Chichester turned right and led the way around the perimeter of the enclosure. They passed a ten-foot-high padlocked metal gate. A red sign attached to the gate read "Authorized Personnel Only." He felt suddenly vulnerable. If the wolves had been set free, they could still be in the vicinity.

Chichester seemed to read his thoughts. "Don't worry, Angus. My wolves prefer deer to man. They shun humans, and would only attack when threatened."

Angus nodded, but he could smell their musky feral spoor in the air. The scent tripped something deep within his consciousness, a warning as effective, its meaning as obvious, as the sign attached to the gate.

"Wolves have learnt to fear humans," Chichester said. "We're ecological serial killers, after all, our evolution—our so-called progress—achieved by slaughtering everything in our path. It can't go on, Angus Dubh—it simply can't go on."

They left the path and followed the fence as it ran along the edge of a pine forest. After a hundred yards or so, Chichester paused and pointed. Angus crunched across the snow and bent to examine the fence. It was immediately obvious it had not been damaged accidentally, by the wind or a tree falling against it. The steel wire mesh had been sheared in an inverted L and then rolled away to create a gap some two meters wide. Fresh snow had fallen, but vague paw marks were still just about visible on the ground. He followed the tracks into the pine forest, but with no snow penetrating the canopy, the trail petered out.

"They'll be shot," Chichester said. "Ewan Hunter and a group of marksmen will track the pack down, by helicopter if need be. They'll eradicate them like the hunters of old."

"Won't they try to recapture them first?"

Chichester shook his head sadly. "I'm well aware of the rules around escapee wolves. If there's any threat to people, they'll be shot."

"What's the alternative, sir?" he asked. "We have to inform the public."

The laird slumped down onto a nearby rock. "I suppose you're right."

Angus dug his hand into his pocket. His fingers fell on the hip flask Chichester had given him in their previous encounter. He took it out and handed it to the laird.

Chichester took the flask with a wan smile. "The English drink tea in a crisis; the Scots whisky. That's why I like this country." He unscrewed the cap and took a swig. Then another. "Everything I love has been taken from me," he said, as if to himself. "If only I'd known . . ."

It struck Angus that the escape of his wolves had cut Chichester as deeply as the death of his daughter.

Again, the laird seemed to read his thoughts. He glanced up at him. "I know, they're only animals. The thing is, it's taken years of planning, lobbying, and kissing ass to get the nature reserve to this point, not to mention greasing a few palms. It was my dream, but now it's shattered. Do you know how that feels, Angus?"

"Aye," he croaked. "I do."

Chichester sat in silence for a long minute, staring at the pine needles that carpeted the ground.

"Faye would have been seventeen next week," he said eventually. "I forgot her birthday last year. And probably would have done so again if Elle hadn't mentioned it yesterday. Guess I wasn't a very good parent." He took another gulp of whisky, his Adam's apple bobbing as he drank.

Chichester turned back to stare at the forest. "Wolves really are incredible," he said. "They live in complex social units, but unlike us, they all work for the betterment of the pack. They form friendships, nurture the sick, and collectively care for the young. Crucially, they pass on knowledge from generation to generation. In fact, it's greater than knowledge; it's a whole culture, a matrix of myth and lore that binds the pack together, just as the oral storytellers and bards of the Highlands glued society together in their stories and verse. We used to feel part of something. We had faith, not the mumbo jumbo espoused by the likes of Reverend MacVannin, but something more profound, grounded in nature and our relationship with her.

"Where did it all go wrong, Angus Dubh? That's what I want to know."

He had no answer to that, nor, he suspected, did Chichester expect one.

CHAPTER 43

GILLS hummed along to a tune on Radio nan Gàidheal as he drove around the head of Loch nan Uamh. The sea had been sucked out by a spring tide, a brown crust of seaweed on the rocky coastline marking where the water usually sat. The view was spectacular—the knobbly little snow-coated islands poking out of the loch, the great thrust of mountains, the huge flotillas of clouds moving lazily across the sky.

Some hardy Japanese tourists were taking photographs at the Prince's Cairn, which was built on the spot Bonnie Prince Charlie was said to have embarked for France in 1746, after his ill-fated attempt to seize the crown for the Stuarts. Many believed this sorry chapter in Scottish history marked the beginning of the end of the Highlander, but in truth the Gaelic language and culture had been under attack well before the Jacobite's capitulation in the decisive Battle of Culloden. But did the exact sequence of events really matter? Certainly that was not what had brought these Japanese visitors halfway across the world to visit an unremarkable cairn in a small corner of Europe. No, they'd come because of the stories—romanticized tales of derring-do and tragic defeat. They came here chasing a myth.

Gills swung the Anglia inland, and wound through a landscape of sturdy Scots pine, roaring cataracts, and cliff faces. The dogs were thrown around in the boot, which earned Gills a reproachful scowl from Sceolan when he glanced in the rearview mirror. "Sorry, boys," he said.

They climbed for another couple of minutes before the road snaked back towards the sea and the village of Arisaig. Just outside the village, he saw the blackened remnants of the house where Lewis Duncan and his mother had lived. The ruins lurked in a small overgrown plot by the roadside, choked with ivy and bramble thickets. Gills remembered the tidy property it had been. A swing had hung from the thick bough of a beech tree in the garden.

Often, when driving to or from work in Silvaig, Gills would see Mrs. Duncan outside pushing her son back and forth, or watering the flowers in her window boxes. The swing was gone now, although a length of frayed rope was still wrapped around the branch.

A "For Sale" sign stood askew in what had once been a neatly tended lawn. Despite the huge demand for land to build holiday homes in the area, the old Duncan property had still not sold, many years after the fire. Gills had heard that a banker from London had agreed to buy it having viewed it on the internet, but backed out of the deal when he came to visit the site in person. Folk whispered that the place was cursed.

His good mood evaporated. In his mind's eye, he saw Angus sitting at the kitchen table in the Old Manse with his head in his hands, shaking and dirty, his clothes stinking of smoke. The lad had made it as far as the front porch of the Duncan place before the flames had beaten him back. He pictured himself dabbing Germolene on Angus's burns and then wrapping his hands in bandages. The antiseptic cream had soothed his wounds, but Angus had been inconsolable, rambling. It had taken Gills fifteen minutes to get the gist of what had happened.

The fire, he recalled, had been started early on the morning of the May Day bank holiday. The university had been shut; otherwise, he himself might have been driving past as the blaze took hold. Funny how this detail had only now occurred to him.

Something nagged at the back of his mind as he drove through Arisaig and Back of Keppoch. The camper vans that clogged the narrow coastal road in summer were mercifully absent. Traigh golf course shivered under a layer of snow. The Small Isles lay like roadkill in the sea. But Gills, deep in thought, gave the scenery only a passing glance.

He was so distracted, he missed the turnoff. The Anglia's rear tyres slithered on the icy surface as he broke sharply. Luckily, no other vehicle was behind him, so he reversed and turned down the brae that led to Camusdarach Beach. For once, the car park was empty. He killed the engine. The dogs scratched at the boot, excited to get out. "Walkies time!" Gills chirped, climbing from the car and popping open the boot. Bran and Sceolan leapt out of the car and scurried towards the sand dunes like greyhounds released from the traps. They didn't need a fake rabbit to chase, though: there were plenty of the real animals to be found in the gorse that flourished in the lee of the dune system.

Gills lifted his walking stick from the boot, pulled on his thick green parka, and followed the dogs, only at a more sedate pace. A narrow path ran around the foot of the dunes and then followed the course of a small spluttering burn down to the beach. A brisk wind hit him as he emerged onto the long curving expanse of sand. Gulls wheeled overhead, squawking insults at him as he picked his way down the beach, heading for the firmer sand, which was easier to walk on. He glanced over his shoulder and saw the blurry shapes of Bran and Sceolan atop the dunes, nosing through swathes of marram grass, tails whumping back and forth, pink tongues sticking out. He chuckled, but the smile died on his lips when he looked out to sea and remembered the tragedy that had occurred here. That was the one that had really done it for Angus. The wee boy. Ethan. Drowned at this very spot by his own father.

Gills plodded along the beach, head down. That nagging sensation was back, a mounting frustration, like when he was writing a research paper and knew he'd forgotten to include some vital piece of information. His mind travelled back to the day of the boy's murder. It was the first of August, a beautiful summer evening, and he'd been mowing the lawn when Angus turned up. Unlike with Lewis Duncan, he'd been strangely detached, emotionless as he explained what had happened. *I can't take this anymore, Gills. To be so close . . . it's agony.* Looking back, he realized this was when Angus had decided to self-medicate—to deny the seer in him. Gills could still see the lad standing in the garden, dull-eyed, his face pale as a sheet, a dark shadow—

Gills stopped abruptly, the hair on his forearms standing on end. Ethan had been killed on August the first. Lewis had perished in the fire on May Day. Why had he never noticed the coincidence of the dates until now? His heart was beating ten to the dozen. Using his walking stick, he scratched the names Lewis and Ethan on the sand. Below, he wrote Barbara, Caitlin, Faye, and Eleanor, as well as the dates of their murders.

He stood back and stared wide-eyed at the list of the dead carved in the wet sand. What he had missed all these years now stood out in stark relief.

"A Mhoire Mhàthair!" he breathed.

CHAPTER 44

INSPECTOR Stout was not entirely happy when Angus told him a pack of wolves was on the loose.

"Jesus H. Christ," he muttered, voice crackling from the Land Rover's police radio. "I knew something like this would happen. There's a reason wolves were hunted to extinction—they're dangerous buggers. I suppose you've alerted the relevant authorities?"

"Aye, although it might be prudent to put a bulletin out on radio and social media, maybe contact the local schools?"

He heard Stout sigh. "I'll contact the media twiglets, get them to knock up a statement, and post a twit, or whatever it is they do. Why the fuck couldn't all this have happened six months later, eh, MacNeil? I'd be happily retired by then. Nothing to do but fish and work on my golf game."

Stout hung up before he could reply. Angus was about to fire up the engine when he heard a rap at the window. He gave a slight start, and glanced to his right. Mrs. MacCrimmon stood in the courtyard, her pale face and rouged cheeks giving her the look of a newly embalmed corpse. He wound down the window and greeted the housekeeper in Gaelic.

"Her Ladyship would like to speak to you," Mrs. MacCrimmon said.

"What about?"

"She's hardly going to tell me, Angus."

Against his better judgement, he found himself climbing from the Land Rover and following Mrs. MacCrimmon into Dunbirlinn.

"She's in the library," the housekeeper said. "You know the way, yes?"

It was more statement than question, but he nodded anyway.

"Good, then you don't need me. I've things to be getting on with."

She spun on her heel and marched away, her footsteps echoing even after her figure faded into Dunbirlinn's shadows.

Angus glanced up at the portrait of Dòmhnall MacRuari. He stared into the chieftain's fierce dark eyes and shuddered.

Once he reached the library door, he knocked and waited. When there was no answer, he gently pushed the door open and stepped inside. A log fire crackled in the hearth, and a shaft of daylight arrowed into the room from the window that overlooked the small courtyard. Eleanor sat on the leather couch, legs drawn up under her body, engrossed in a book.

He stepped farther into the room and cleared his throat. Eleanor glanced up, startled. She was dressed casually in tight jeans and a cable-knit jumper. She wore neither jewellery nor makeup, and the eyes that met his were dull and washed out, the corners ribbed with crow's feet. Her hair was tied in a loose bun, but he could see strands of silver in the dyed blond.

"Mrs MacCrimmon said you wanted to see me?"

She placed the book she was reading on a coffee table. The cover showed a powerful robed woman with three heads. She held a spear and a flaming torch in her upraised hands. One of her faces stared out at the reader, whilst the other two—a girl and an elderly woman—were in profile. *Maiden, Mother, Crone* was the title of the book.

"Angus," she said, with none of her usual flirtatiousness. "Thank you for coming."

He walked across and sat on a wingback chair next to the couch. "Is everything okay, Lady Chichester?"

"I . . . wanted to apologize for how I behaved yesterday," she said haltingly. "James had stood me up and I was . . . not quite myself."

"No apology needed." He gestured to the book. "Some light reading?"

Eleanor wrinkled her nose. "I chanced across it this morning. The title struck a chord—it seemed to encapsulate my life to a T."

"How so?"

She stared unfocused at the flames, a faint smile on her lips. "When I started out in Hollywood, I was young and beautiful and in demand. You should have seen me then, Angus—I was a little firecracker. Casting directors showered me with gifts; actors brought me out to exclusive nightclubs; executives took me for lunch at fancy restaurants and promised me I'd be the next Michelle Pfeiffer."

She gave a sad laugh. "All I was to them was fresh meat, a naive plaything blown in from some dying little town in rural Wisconsin. Once I'd lost my maidenhood, they lost interest. There was no MeToo movement back then. You had to develop a skin so thick, it was like armour. Either that or die."

She glanced across at Angus. "You think I'm exaggerating, but you've no idea the number of my contemporaries who committed suicide. My roommate when I first moved to LA opened her wrists in the bathroom of the Continental. Three actresses I worked with on one production took their own lives, all within weeks of each other. Others gave up on their dream and headed back to their poverty-stricken hometowns to drink themselves to death.

"And drugs were everywhere. When I said yesterday that I was stoned for most of the nineties, that was no lie. Then, after you'd left, I forced myself to think about that movie—*The Suffering*." She chewed the words as if they were gristle.

Angus gave a slight nod of encouragement but resisted the urge to intervene. Whatever Eleanor wanted to say, she would do so in her own time.

"That was the one that tipped me over the edge, Angus. The set was . . . bacchanalian, and not in a good way." She scrubbed her hands across her face, as if trying to scour away the memory. "And then, of course, I got pregnant. Forbes Forbisher told me if I ever wanted to work in Hollywood again, I'd have to get rid of it. He even drove me to the abortion clinic. I remember how terrified I was. In my heart, I wanted to keep the baby. I was raised a strict Catholic, and although by then I wasn't going to confession, I knew that what I was about to do was a sin."

She closed her tired eyes for a long second, as if the pain of looking into the past were too much.

"That must have been very tough," he said softly.

She nodded, eyes still closed. "When we reached the clinic, there was this group of protesters outside—pro-lifers—all waving placards with pictures of aborted foetuses on them. I wouldn't leave the car." She opened her eyes and gave him a wan smile. "But Forbes wouldn't have that. He got out of the car and practically dragged me towards the clinic doors through this throng of people, all of them snarling and spitting at me, calling me a murderer. Funnily enough, I can't remember the procedure itself. I simply went numb. But I can still hear those people shouting at me—*Child killer! Burn in Hell! Die, bitch!*"

"I'm sorry," he said. "That sounds awful."

Eleanor's eyes were moist. She swiped away her tears, as if annoyed with herself, then lifted the book from the coffee table. She stared at the image of the three-faced goddess on the front cover. Suddenly she stood and walked to the open fire. "That was my chance at motherhood, and I let some arrogant *cunt* of a man take it from me." With a sudden flick of the wrist she threw the book into the fire. It landed on top of the burning logs. Flames licked the book, tasting it.

Eleanor watched the book burn. "I thought Faye might be my second chance, but we know how that ended."

She turned and stared at Angus, eyes now dry and hard. "My maidenhood was taken too soon, and my motherhood died before it was even born. All that's left now is this old crone you see before you."

Angus shook his head. "You're not—"

Eleanor held up a hand, cutting him off. "I'm not fishing for compliments or sympathy, Angus. I'm merely trying to explain my emotional state at the time when *The Suffering* was made. I should probably have gone to see a shrink, but instead I blocked out that period of my life. I shoved all those memories into a room in my head and locked the door—do you know what I mean?"

Only too well.

"That's why I couldn't recall ever having seen that horrible little doll you showed me yesterday. I'd buried the memory."

"But now you do remember?"

"Yes, but I have no idea how something like that ended up in my stepdaughter's possession. I can only conclude that someone's trying to set me up."

"They'd have to be familiar with your movies, and confident we would make the connection. A crazed fan? A jilted lover perhaps? Was there anyone from back then, a—"

"No," she interjected. "There was only Forbes. Sure, I got the odd piece of fan mail, but nothing that rang alarm bells. If I had a stalker, they didn't reveal themselves."

"Where was the film made?" he asked.

"We shot on location in Scotland, some big old castle in the middle of nowhere." She seemed to shudder. "I remember it being so cold. Every morning when I woke, there was a film of ice on the panes of my bedroom window. When James said we were moving to a castle in the Highlands, my first reaction was 'over my dead body.'"

"What happened to change your mind?"

"When my husband sets his sights on something, he's like a landslide. You either go with it or get flattened. He also promised we wouldn't live at Dunbirlinn all year-round. But now he refuses to leave. He seems to prefer this cold, rainy climate to the south of France or the Caribbean." She turned and glowered down into the flames. "Why would anyone want to stay here, after what's happened?"

He shifted awkwardly in his chair. "To return to *The Suffering* for a moment: Can you remember who made the doll?"

"It was thirty years ago, Angus."

"Even so . . ."

"Christ! I wish I hadn't stopped smoking. I don't suppose you . . ." She tore her gaze away from the fire and gave him a penetrating look. "No, you don't have the look of a smoker. But you have other vices, right?"

He held her stare but kept his lips pressed shut.

Eleanor glared at him for a long second, then gave a thin smile. She turned back to the hearth, lifted a wrought-iron poker, and jabbed at the flaky remnants of the book, grinding them into the fire. "The prop and costume department doubled as a kind of pharmacy. Cocaine was the drug of choice for many, but they could get you anything—acid, amphetamines, LSD, benzos. Forbes had a penchant for opium, which I always thought was a pretension, an attempt to cultivate a mysterious, sophisticated air. He projected a certain image, that of the troubled outsider, the tortured *artiste*, but it was all an act." Her grip on the poker tightened as she spoke. "He was a grifter. When the veneer wore off, there was nothing underneath but an emotional void. He was the most selfish man I ever met."

Her knuckles were turning white as she squeezed the poker, her wrist rigid.

"Do you remember anyone who worked in the prop department?" He could check the movie credits later, but there was no harm in asking, especially as it might distract Eleanor from her dark reminiscences of this Forbes character.

She glanced at Angus and her shoulders slumped. Her grip on the poker loosened. "It was run by a sleazebag nicknamed Hawkeye, after the character in *M*A*S*H.*" She gave an involuntary shudder. "Hawkeye was . . . not a good guy. He and Forbes were thick as thieves."

She half-turned, her eyes returning to the flames, as if they contained absolution.

"So he would know where the clay corpse came from?"

"Possibly."

"Is he still alive?"

Eleanor was quiet for a long time. The glow from the flames flickered across her face. For a brief second Angus saw her as the young starlet, then as the actress in her prime, before her expression was contorted in pain and sadness, transforming her face into that of a crone. She twisted her head towards him. Her eyes were puckered puncture wounds.

"I hope not, Angus. I hope Hawkeye died a slow, painful death."

Crowley watched the dungeon scene from *The Suffering* on Nadia's laptop with an amused glint in his eye. "This sort of thing isn't good for my old ticker. What are you trying to do, Nadia, give me a heart attack?"

Angus saw Crowley's eyes harden as the scene reached its crescendo. "Ahhh," he breathed, "now I see what's got you pair in a tizzy."

"She claims the doll was made by the prop department," Nadia said.

Crowley snapped the laptop shut and sat for a long moment, staring up at the ceiling. At length, he slapped his hands down on the table and stood. "It's an odd coincidence, I'll grant you that. Could someone from her past be trying to set her up? A spurned lover, some crazed stalker?"

"I asked her that, but she can't think of anyone," Angus said.

"Then are you suggesting this doll points to Eleanor's direct involvement?"

"Err—"

"Because I can't see her killing her own stepdaughter. The only motive would be money, and I'm reliably informed Eleanor will be well taken care of in Chichester's will. Even if she'd had to share the filthy lucre with Faye, she stood to inherit more than she could ever spend."

"She could have some motive we've not considered," Nadia said.

"Aye, maybe," Crowley said. "Although CCTV proves Eleanor was in the castle the night Faye died, so . . ."

Nadia was about to speak, but Crowley held up a hand to stop her. "Yes, I know the idea of a hit man has been floated, but I'm not convinced by that theory. Look, if you can track down who made the doll, great. But don't waste too much time on it. Besides, Rylo has dredged up some grade-A dirt on our pagan chum."

He gave them a crooked smile. "You're going to love this. When Christine Kelbie was in her early twenties, she fell in with a group of occultists. They squatted in an old hunting lodge on the shores of Loch Ness, near Boleskine. Soon after, pets and livestock started disappearing from the local villages and farms. Police raided the lodge and found a mound of charred and decomposing carcasses, apparently slaughtered in satanic rituals."

Angus recalled that unguarded look on Kelbie's face when they first interviewed her, and a chill crept across his shoulders.

"The ringleaders of the cult were charged, but Kelbie avoided prosecution, hence her lack of criminal record," Crowley said. "But anyone who's involved in butchering cats and dogs has a deviant mindset."

CHAPTER 45

EWAN traipsed through the wild landscape of south Morar, his father's old hunting rifle clasped to his chest. The mountains weren't particularly high, but the snow and poor visibility made conditions tough. His absolutely stonking hangover didn't help. At least he remembered what he had done last night. He didn't regret setting the wolves free one bit. So, despite the thumping headache, he was in a pretty good mood. *In fine fettle*, as his dad used to say.

He crouched beside a swollen mountain stream and dooked his head under the icy cold water. For a second he was back at the Fairy Pools with Faye, diving down, his lungs on fire as he tried to retrieve a stone from the bottom. There was a moment then, when he'd had the rock in his hand and he'd kicked for the surface—Faye's wobbly image floating above him—that he'd thought he was going to die. But from the panic he'd summoned some last vestige of oxygen, enough to see him to the surface, where Faye, giggling, had called him a "big eejit." He'd recently taught her the phrase, and she'd taken delight in using it.

Something clawed at his chest, as if a frightened bird were trapped there. He stood and wiped water from his eyes. Then he snatched out a hip flask from his inside pocket, took a deep draught of Bell's, and lifted his rifle.

A team of marksmen had been scrambled to hunt down the wolves, but the poor visibility meant a helicopter couldn't fly. The others were scouring the mountains around Glenruig and the Rough Bounds, but he had headed farther afield. Wolves could travel vast distances quickly. His hunter's instinct told him they would have made for this mountain fastness.

He continued to swig from the hip flask as he walked, the warmth of the whisky counteracting the increasingly biting wind. He kept his eyes peeled for footprints, but so far all he'd spotted were deer and sheep.

By mid-afternoon his legs were getting heavy. The rain had kept up a steady downpour, turning large swathes of the hillside into a sodden mossy morass that sucked at his boots, as if the ground were trying to pull him under. As he climbed higher, the rain progressed to sleet and snow. He knew from the distinctive shape of a crag, seen through the mist, that he was near Rowan Beag bothy. He lifted the hip flask to his lips, but only a dribble came out. He frowned. The flask had been full when he'd left that morning. Thankfully, he had another half bottle of Bell's tucked away in his rucksack. He would crack that open when he reached the bothy.

Ewan sat on dusty floorboards covered in mice droppings, his back against the wood-panelled wall. On the opposite wall of the bothy, a stag's skull leered down at him. He reached for his rifle and pointed it at the skull. It seemed to split apart until three sets of dark eye sockets were staring at him. His vision went blurry, and when he regained focus, he saw his own head mounted on the wall, where the stag's skull had been. He blinked away the hallucination.

"Hell's bells, I'm pissed," he muttered. He lifted the bottle of Bell's and squinted at the finger's worth of amber liquid left in the bottom. He downed the rest of the whisky then hurled the empty bottle at the skull. Missing by several feet. The bottle shattered into a thousand pieces. He smiled stupidly, then slid down onto the floor, the gun cuddled to his chest like his old teddy. He stroked the walnut stock as if it were a kitten. The bothy spun. He was at the ceilidh dancing with Faye. Her green eyes sparkled. Beads of sweat glistened on her forehead. Her smile was joyful and genuine, infectious. Her golden hair whipped around her face as she twirled, but with each rotation, her features twisted and warped until she'd morphed into the deer he'd killed, spinning around in the dark with its stomach splayed open. He chased the image away, only for it to be replaced by his father lying in the heather, gasping like a beached trout. He placed his hands on either side of his skull and squeezed. "Arrrgh! Get out of my head!"

It did not help. He was mugged by memories. Defenceless against their onslaught. He scrambled into a sitting position and lifted the rifle, spinning it around so the barrel pointed at his face. He opened his mouth and swallowed the cold metal. With shaking fingers, he reached for the trigger, but in stretching he pushed the barrel too far down his throat. He gagged and instinctively pulled the barrel from his mouth. His eyes watered, but he wasn't sure if he was crying or choking. Both, probably. He imagined his brains splattered over the blistered wood panelling. He pictured matted hair; slithers of skull and grey brain matter; thick, viscous blood dribbling onto the floor. It was a calming thought, and soon he was asleep.

A low growl woke him from his slumber. He jerked awake, his hands gripping the rifle. In his dream, two huge wolfhounds were chasing him. Their jowls were drawn back, red teeth bared, strings of mucus drooling from their maws. He scrambled to his feet and pressed his back against the wall. Shadows danced and flickered. Someone was in here. Someone or something. He could feel a presence.

The noise came again. A throaty growl.

He shuffled along the wall and peeped around a rotten doorframe into the bothy's kitchen area. His arm was shaking so much, he could hardly keep the gun steady. An elongated rectangle of light jutted onto the floor. The door to the outside world was open, and in that shaft of light there stood a large wolf. Ewan recognised the thick blue-grey coat of the alpha female from Chichester's pack. A gust of wind shrieked through the open doorway, bringing with it that musky feral stink of wolf. This was no dream. Ewan's legs turned to mush. His whisky-bloated bladder felt close to bursting.

The wolf turned her regal head and fixed him with a cruel amber glare, the black-rimmed eyes reminding him of an illustration of Cleopatra in one of his father's old encyclopaedias.

"I'm the apex predator! I'm the apex predator! I'm the apex predator!" he muttered, bracing the butt of the rifle against his shoulder. His finger trembled as he cocked it around the trigger. He found it nearly impossible to keep the barrel straight, but he could take down a deer at five hundred meters in flat light and a blowing gale. He should have no problem hitting a wolf twelve feet away.

"I'm the apex predator!" he yelled, and squeezed the trigger.

Nothing happened.

He glanced down at the rifle. The safety catch was off. He squeezed the trigger, but again nothing happened. The rifle was old, and he'd not been meticulous in its upkeep lately. "Oh Christ," he sobbed, backing away from the wolf. An image of his father flashed into his head— the old man cleaning his gun in the kitchen. *Keep your weapon clean, son. Dirt can cause it to jam.*

The wolf padded towards him, teeth drawn back from fleshy pink gums. Only an hour or so ago he'd thought about blowing his brains out, but now, faced with being torn apart by a wolf, he'd do anything to live.

Slowly, he lowered the rifle, then launched it at the wolf. In almost the same movement he slammed the door shut and braced his back against it. He felt a thud as the wolf threw itself against the other side, heard it clawing at the wood, frantic to reach him. Suddenly a panel of the door splintered and a bolt of pain shot up his arm. He looked down and saw teeth marks on his forearm, blood already flowing. Through the hole in the door a set of bright eyes glared at him—emotionless, cruel. The real apex predator.

Again the wolf charged at the door. Dust puffed out from the ancient rotten timber. He knew it would not hold much longer. His eyes darted about the room. He felt cornered, trapped, like a rabbit in a snare. Outside, the wolf would run him down, but at least he had a chance. He could climb a tree, or find a weapon to defend himself. At the far end of the room there was a small window, his only hope of escape. In here, he was as good as dead.

He chanced a peek through the hole in the door. The wolf had backed up as if readying another assault. But that was not what scared him the most. Because there wasn't just one wolf, now—there was the whole pack.

"Fuck it!" he growled, and sprinted for the window. Arms up to protect his head and face, he dived through the window. Shards of glass tore at his flesh, but he hardly felt the pain. Then he was tumbling down the hillside, the taste of snow and blood in his mouth. He slammed into a bank of heather, and lay there, winded, gazing up at the clouds. Gingerly, he got to his feet and swiped blood from his eyes. More blood oozed from the bite mark on his forearm.

He glanced back up the hill, and froze. The wolves stood in a line by the gable wall of the bothy. The alpha female spotted him and let out a high-pitched howl that made Ewan want to cry. Then they came, flying down the hillside like streaks of smoke.

Ewan turned and ran, blindly, without hope. His breaths caught in his throat as he sprinted, hardly aware of where he was going. All around him were towering crags, lichen-encrusted rocks, wizened trees, and rushing cataracts. Never in his life had he felt *less* of an apex predator. This was the primal terror of the hunted. This was what he'd seen in the bulging eyes of the animals he'd killed.

I'm sorry! I'm sorry!

Tears stung his eyes as he pounded around the foot of a rocky bluff. Perhaps there was a cave where he could hide? Somewhere he could climb until he was out of reach? He rounded the rock face, but the trail he was on soon petered out, and he found himself standing on the lip of a precipice. He peered over the edge. The cliff was sheer, tumbling a hundred feet or more to the valley floor.

Behind him, he heard a low mucusy growl. He thought of Faye spinning on his arm at the ceilidh. Those beautiful green eyes that had shimmered like emeralds. Her golden hair a halo around her head.

Then Ewan turned to face the wolves.

CHAPTER 46

CORKY and Lorna were going at it hell-for-leather when Angus pulled up in the police Land Rover. A pack of wolves might be on the loose, but that wasn't going to get in the way of the old lovers and their feud.

He was about to climb from the Land Rover when his phone warbled, an unknown number flashing on the screen. He raised the device to his ear and answered with a gruff hello.

"Constable Angus MacNeil?" The man's voice was like a rustle of dry leaves, the accent faintly American.

"Speaking?"

"My name is Gregory Stewart. I believe you have been trying to contact me?"

After his conversation with Crowley, Angus had spent much of last night trying to track down the cast and crew of *The Suffering*. This had proven a more difficult task than he'd imagined. The company that had made the movie had long since gone bust. The director, Forbes Forbisher, was dead, as were two executive producers, the director of photography, the editor, and the locations manager. The actors who'd starred alongside Eleanor had faded into obscurity. Stewart had been one of a handful of writers, and had gone on to achieve modest success in the industry.

"Thanks for returning my call, Mr. Stewart."

"Well, I was intrigued. I was just thinking about that movie the other day."

"That's an odd coincidence."

"Not really. The murder of Eleanor's stepdaughter has blanket coverage on some channels here in the US. We're a country of ghouls." He cleared his throat, which turned into a coughing fit.

"Apologies, Constable," he spluttered. "A lifetime of pipe smoking has left my lungs as black as a defence attorney's heart. And all so I could look like Arthur Conan Doyle."

"That's okay," Angus said. "This might sound odd, but I wanted to ask you about a specific scene in *The Suffering*. It's the one where Eleanor places a hex on someone using a kind of voodoo doll."

Stewart gave a gravelly chuckle. "Sure, I remember that scene. Forbisher made it more pervy than in the script. He claimed his influences were art house, but really his creative thrust was more John Holmes than Jean-Luc Godard."

Angus did not recognise either name, nor did he care. "It's actually the doll I'm interested in."

"Ah yes, the clay corpse."

"How did you know about them?"

"Research, Constable. The House of Stewart ruled Scotland for centuries. I've a deep interest in the history of your islands. When I was in better health, I'd travel across every year to Edinburgh for the Clan Stewart Gathering."

"I see. So you created a storyline involving a clay corpse?"

Stewart sighed deeply, lungs crackling. "*The Suffering* was one of my first gigs. Not my finest work."

"Do you remember who made the doll?"

Stewart suddenly sounded suspicious. "Why are you asking about this?"

"I'm sorry, Mr. Stewart, I really can't say. My boss would have my guts for garters."

"Fair enough," he rasped. "The clay corpse would have been made by one of the guys in the prop department."

"Hawkeye?" Angus asked.

Stewart fell silent, but Angus could hear the man's heavy breathing. "There's a name I haven't heard in a while," he said at last. "No, his skill set was more in the acquisition of narcotics."

"How many people worked in the prop department?"

"About ten or twelve maybe. I'm afraid I can't remember any of their names, although—"

Angus squeezed the phone, willing Stewart to talk. "Yes?" he prompted.

"One young guy was Scottish. Christ! What was his name . . . ?"

Angus could almost hear the cogs turning as Stewart fumbled in his memories. "Nope, sorry, it's gone," he said at last. "But I tell you what, I'll phone around a few of my old associates from back then, see if I can get you a list of names."

He thanked Stewart again and then cut the call. Crowley had been right: this lead was a waste of time. He couldn't picture Eleanor in the dead of night, waiting in the shadows to ambush Faye on her return from the pagan commune. The killer had jammed their knee in Faye's back and yanked with such force that two of the girl's ribs had cracked. Eleanor looked like she worked out, but would she have the power to do that? She would also have had to lift the corpse onto Bessie's back. No, she couldn't have killed Faye herself, so did that mean the clay corpse link was a coincidence? He rubbed his temples in frustration.

The snow had started to fall again, but Corky and Lorna were too busy arguing to care. He climbed from the Land Rover, shrugging on his jacket, and tramped towards the rowing pair.

That morning, Crowley had concisely summed up the state of play with regards to suspects. "It's either the wicked stepmother who stands to inherit a fortune, a lovestruck gamekeeper who can't take rejection, a Free Kirk minister with a grudge, or some lunatic pagans honouring their gods."

When asked about her false alibi, Ruth MacVannin had claimed she had simply mixed up her dates. She hadn't been listening to the radio after all that night. She'd been reading. The Bible, naturally.

As Angus trudged closer, he saw that Corky held a shotgun, cocked open in the crook of his arm, but that didn't bother Lorna. She jabbed a finger at the wee crofter, then pointed at something lying on the ground. They stopped their bickering as Angus approached. Lorna strode towards him, her face like a thunderstorm. "Look what this bastard has done now! I want him charged, Angus. This has gone too far."

Only then could he make out the object lying on the ground, which appeared to be the source of the argument. A dead chicken.

"Ach! Will you shut your cakehole, woman?" Corky said. "It's just a hen. I didnae see her. And if you didn't let the bloody birds run amok, it wouldnae have happened."

"You saw her all right, Charlie Corcoran. You reversed over her on purpose."

"I did nothing of the kind."

"I saw you from the kitchen window. Angus, I saw him. He did it intentionally."

"For the last time, woman! I. Didn't. See. Her. Can you no' get that through your thick skull?"

"You're calling me thick. Pots, kettles, and black!"

Angus stared down at the chicken, the sound of the old couple's row fading into the background. The bird was a mess of matted dark feathers, its innards spilling out onto the pristine snow. He felt a sharp pain slice up his arm. Then a series of images flashed through his head, as if he were looking at a child's flip-book. Blood dripping onto snow. The hungry amber eyes of a wolf, the alpha female from Chichester's pack. Racing clouds scudding across the sky. The obsidian eye of a crow. Someone standing on the edge of a cliff. He heard a low throaty growl. The figure turned, picked out against the bruised sky, and he knew then who it was, just as he knew, with absolute certainty, what was about to happen.

"No," he muttered. "No!"

Corky and Lorna stopped arguing and stared at him. He glanced up from the dead chicken, seeing confusion ripple across their wrinkly faces.

"I need that," he said, grabbing Corky's gun.

"Hey!" he protested, but Angus was already on his way, sprinting back towards the Land Rover. He crunched the vehicle into gear and powered away. A voice in his head told him it was futile, but he ignored it and slammed his foot down on the accelerator.

Ewan's Nissan Pathfinder lurked in the Forestry Commission car park at the foot of the trail. *Doesn't mean anything*, Angus told himself, dodging past it and pounding into the forest. His father's voice kept a running commentary in his head as he jinked around dark pines and splashed through freezing bogs.

It's all in your head. It's all in your head, it's all in your head. . . .

Take the pills, son.

He burst from the forest and hurdled a rotten stile that bridged a barbed-wire fence. New images flashed through his head. A mountain stream. A callused face of rock. A structure he recognised. The nagging voice kept up its refrain, but the words had changed.

You're too late! Too late! You're always too late!

"Shut up!" he howled. "Shut up!" His cries were swallowed by peat bogs and heather, absorbed by scree and mossy rocks. The path became steeper, sapping the strength from his thighs. Dread twisted like a blade in his stomach. He hoped he was wrong. He hoped he was going mad, but then he heard waves crashing on the shore and he was back on the dunes, watching the dying kicks of a young boy, too far away to intervene. Why hadn't he trusted his instincts and walked into the sea? Floated away to Tír na nÓg.

His father's voice cut above the din. *It's the hope that kills ye, son.*

"No!" he yelled, the word ripping from his throat.

Now he was back in the woods, crouched over Barbara Klein's broken body. Her neck was spattered with blood. It felt warm when he touched her, checking in vain for a pulse.

It's the hope that kills ye.

"Not real!" he snarled. "Not real!"

Yet even as the words spilled from his lips he saw the bothy from his vision. He pictured Ewan sprawled on the ground, wolves tearing at his limbs. He heard the awful sounds of rending flesh, cries of agony, snarls, and the crunch of bone.

It's all in your head!

Angus staggered through the bothy door, gasping for breath. The first thing he noticed were footprints on the dusty floorboards, as well as paw marks: large, clawed. The second thing he noticed sent a bolt of fear through him—Ewan's rifle, the one he'd inherited from his father, lying on the floor. The door to another room hung from its hinges, the wood splintered. Droplets of blood glistened on the doorframe. Heart thrashing, he laid a finger in the blood. It was still warm, like Barbara Klein's.

See, Dad! There is hope!

He dashed from the bothy and ran around to the rear. Shards of glass from a broken window lay on the snow. He saw more paw prints, disappearing down the hill into the murk. He clutched the gun tight, then, with his arms out for balance, slithered down the hillside, leaning back slightly to prevent himself toppling over. At the bottom, he saw more droplets of blood. More paw prints, too. Lots of them.

He tried to regulate his breathing as he ran, but the cold seemed to tear at his lungs. *Keep going! Keep going! Don't stop!*

Every few meters he saw more spots of blood in the snow. Head down, he followed the macabre trail around the foot of a rocky bluff. He was close to exhaustion now, gasping for breath, but as he inhaled he caught a scent in the air. Musky. Feral. Unmistakably wolf.

He thought of Ewan, a small boy bullied on the bus to shinty matches, fighting back his tears, refusing to show his pain. Then he pictured Ewan sobbing into his shoulder when John Hunter had died.

He slowed to a walk, eyes on the ground. He could still hear his father's voice, but it was fainter now, the words jumbled.

Head . . . kills . . . late . . . hope . . .

Suddenly the words were drowned out completely by another sound, like a small-engined motorbike ticking over. A growl. He lifted the gun to his shoulder and crept around a great pillar of fluted granite.

His sense of déjà vu was palpable. Ewan stood on a slab of rock that jutted out from the cliff face. The wolves surrounded him, blocking the way to a scree slope that slid down the mountainside. One of the wolves slunk towards him, crouched low, ready to pounce. The others mirrored her movements, teeth bared and snarling.

Angus sucked in a great lungful of air and yelled, "HEY! OVER HERE!"

The wolves turned as one, and half a dozen sets of eyes burned into him. He raised Corky's shotgun and took aim at the nearest animal. He wasn't much of a shot, but his arm was steady as he squeezed the trigger. The sound echoed around the mountainside like a clap of thunder. The butt of the rifle kicked into his shoulder, as if he'd been punched. The wolf let out a high-pitched yelp, took a couple of steps towards him, then collapsed.

The rest of the pack scattered, melding like grey shadows into the rocks.

Ewan fell to his knees and began to sob.

CHAPTER 47

IT was late by the time he pulled up outside Ewan's cottage. The Land Rover's headlights probed the darkness, like the yellow eyes of a wolf. Angus balked at the thought and turned the engine off, but Ewan continued to sit there, massaging the bandage on his arm. The ghillie's wound had been treated at Silvaig General and he'd been given a tetanus shot to prevent infection from the bite. Angus had sat in the drab A&E waiting room amongst the other injured patients and worried family members as he'd tried to process what had happened up on the mountain. He ought to have felt ecstatic—his vision had led him to Ewan, and he'd saved the young man's life. But as he slumped in the uncomfortable scratched plastic chair, a black weariness had come over him. Shadows lurked at the edge of his consciousness, just out of sight.

Eventually Ewan broke the silence. "I'm sorry, Gus," he muttered. "About . . . everything."

"Aye, I know. I know."

He heard the ghillie swallow. "There's something you should know. It was me who set the wolves free."

Angus twisted in his seat. "Why would you do that?"

"Chichester told me the wolves would keep down the deer numbers. I'm . . . What was it he said . . . 'surplus to requirements.' I thought if I freed them, then I could kill them. . . ." He petered out. "Stupid. I've been so bloody stupid."

Angus placed a gentle hand on his shoulder. "Aye, but don't worry about that now. Go inside. Get some rest. Stay off the *deoch*."

Ewan nodded but still made no move to leave the Land Rover. "I didn't kill her, Gus," he said. "I'd never do that to Faye. I . . . I loved her."

Angus squeezed his shoulder. "I know. I believe you."

Ewan finally looked at him. His eyes were that of the child Angus had taught to block and cleek on the shinty pitch.

"Thanks," he mumbled. Before the tears could come, Ewan reached for the door handle and winced out into the night. Angus watched him hobble towards the front door of his cottage, which had already been fixed up after PC Devine destroyed it with the Big Red Key. Ewan pushed open the door and disappeared inside. A shadow of a smile flitted across Angus's face. There was still no euphoria, but perhaps all the suffering, those long hours spent with Gills trying to hone his gift, had not been in vain.

"Sleep tight, *a'bhalach*," he murmured, then fired up the engine. The headlights flicked on automatically, and Angus jumped as if he'd been butted by an angry bull. His hands clenched the steering wheel as his body went rigid with shock. There, standing in the twin beams of the headlights, was the terrifying horned figure of Donn Fírinne.

Every hair on his body prickled.

The thing seemed to stare straight at him. Its eyeholes were two dark voids. Cracked teeth jutted from the creature's jawbone as if it were grinning. The skull was spattered with dark material. Mud or blood, he couldn't be sure.

For what felt like a long time, neither moved. Angus relaxed his grip on the steering wheel. Was this thing real or yet another delusion?

He leaned forward and squinted at the figure. It seemed to pull back, edging away from the headlights and into the darkness. Angus crunched the Land Rover into gear and stamped down on the accelerator. The thing turned and ran. He drove towards the fleeing shadow, teeth gritted.

It's just a man in a bloody costume!

The figure darted off the track and bolted towards the forest, so fast that it appeared to be flying. Angus slammed his foot on the brakes and grabbed a flashlight from the glove compartment. His eye fell on Corky's shotgun.

He snatched up the gun and leapt out of the Land Rover.

He sprinted after the figure into the forest, his muscles protesting. The pine canopy was so thick, it blotted out the stars. He flicked on the torch and trained the beam on the forest floor. No snow lay here under the branches. The ground was carpeted in moss and pine needles, but he saw no sign of tracks. A primal fear flared in his chest. A thousand irrational terrors, the monsters and demons from his childhood nightmares, flitted through his head. All the tales that Gills had told him over the years now took on new meaning. Was *Crom Dubh* waiting for him in the shadows? Or the *nuckelavee*? Or the *baobhan sith*? Was the Celtic hellhound, the *cù-sìth*, stalking him, biding its moment to pounce?

He heard a twig snap, and his head whipped around, the torch beam casting sinister patterns on the skeletal branches. Every rustle was amplified in the darkness, as if tree and thicket were swarming with malevolent creatures. He raised the shotgun, the torch braced against the walnut forestock. His arm shook slightly, but a mounting anger doused the burning fear inside him. Whatever that thing was, it had killed Faye. It had butchered her like a deer carcass.

He heard another snap, somewhere in the distance, deeper into the woods. He ran in the direction of the sound. Twigs and thorns whipped and scratched his face, but he almost welcomed the pain. Teeth gritted, he careered through the forest, stopping every twenty yards or so to listen. Time seemed to warp and twist. He didn't know whether he'd been chasing the figure for five minutes or thirty. Time was nebulous under the dark canopy, the forest itself a shadowy maze. Fear rekindled in his chest. He was disoriented, lost. Had he slipped into some dread otherworld? A place of ghosts and hungry spirits? He paused, listening intently. He heard his own shallow breathing and the faint whisper of running water. He lowered the shotgun and stumbled in the direction of the sound, cursing silently. The wave of terror subsided, but a burning anguish filled the space where it had been. He'd let Faye's killer get away.

He stumbled onwards through the darkness, teeth clenched in frustration. Soon he found himself on the edge of a narrow fast-flowing burn. The canopy was less dense here, and a thin covering of snow lay on the ground. Still no sign of footprints. He squinted. A faint eerie glow danced in the distance, slashes of light flickering between crooked branches. He followed the course of the spitting stream towards the glow, a fizzle of apprehension at the base of his spine.

It might be nothing, he told himself. Teenagers camping and having a few ciders by the fire.

But as he drew closer, he saw that the fire was not on the ground. Rather, it appeared to rage in midair.

He emerged from the forest into an open glade covered in a blanket of shimmering snow. At once he recognised the gnarled shape of the clootie tree. He gripped the shotgun tighter. Whatever was on fire, it hung from one of the tree's branches. Angus realized he'd seen this tableaux before, two nights ago when he'd been bent over the toilet bowl being sick. It was the same vision Faye had described to Dr. Wright.

He let the shotgun fall to his side. "No . . ." he whimpered. "Please. No."

His legs felt numb as he walked towards the clootie tree. The smell almost turned his stomach: acrid, sulphurous, meaty. He could feel the heat from the fire on his face. The flames crackled and roared as they devoured a human form.

Angus sank to his knees in the snow and looked in horror at the burning chrysalis. A chain had been wrapped around the body's ankles and looped around a stout branch. The body dangled over the stream, so that although most of it was alight, the head was submerged underwater. The torrent swirled downstream, tugging at the body, and for a brief second a pale face emerged. Illuminated by rabid flames, the face seemed to transmogrify, at once a young starlet, a woman in her prime, and a crone. He'd seen this optical illusion before. In Dunbirlinn Castle.

It was Eleanor Chichester.

CHAPTER 48

ANGUS lay on his back and watched snow curl down from the clouds. His steel pillow felt like a block of ice pressed against the back of his head. If only the cold could numb his senses, but his mind continued its churn. What should he do with his hands? Lay them by his sides? Across his body like a vampire in a coffin? Behind his head as if relaxing on the beach? It hardly mattered. None of it did.

He wondered what time it was, but he wasn't wearing his watch. Neither did he have his phone. Both lay on the embankment fifteen feet away, alongside his police ID, wallet, and car keys. For some reason, he'd also decided to take off his jacket. Doing so had seemed appropriate. Part of a ritual as old as time, not as elaborate as Faye's murder, but a ritual nonetheless.

He closed his eyes and saw Faye sitting on Bessie as she trotted into the courtyard of Dunbirlinn Castle. A smile as wide as the Skye Bridge. Then he smelt the salt on the wind as he bent by her broken body on the beach.

The image faded, but the taste of salt lingered. He was back in Tulliallan with Nadia. They clung to each other in the half-light as she told him about the River Angel. His lips feathered her face, kisses imprinted in his memory with the tang of her tears. His mind lurched to Ash, and the first time he saw her onstage in the village hall, her hair a tumult of oranges, golds, and reds. The sweet strains of her clarsach had thawed the ice in his heart. She'd shown him another life was possible, one full of light, music, and happiness. He'd wanted to grasp that life, but the shadows wouldn't let him. He'd tainted her goodness. She would be better off without him.

"That doesn't look very comfortable."

Faye's face appeared above him, her hair hanging in long curtains over her cheeks. "What *exactly* are you playing at?"

He closed his eyes. "Leave me alone."

"Eh, no-o!" He could almost hear the eye roll in her voice. "Seriously, get up. You look ridiculous."

"No."

"So you planning to end it all, yeah?"

"That's the idea."

"Why here?"

"First place that came to mind." Which wasn't exactly true. After killing his son, Jonathan Boyce, Ethan's father, had lain down on the tracks at this exact spot.

"Gills said the killings come in threes. You're just going to let someone else die?"

"I can't stop it."

Always too late!

"Maybe if you stopped taking those pills . . ."

"No! It doesn't matter what I do!"

"You saved Ewan."

"But Eleanor still died!"

The first rumblings came to him then, splitting the darkness like an anguished cry. Like the sound of the Unforgiven Dead, coming to feed on his soul.

His body quivered.

"Right, this isn't funny anymore," Faye said. "Get up!" The rumble grew louder, like an approaching thunderstorm. His chest heaved. Each breath ragged and painful. His fingers scrabbled across the loose stone chippings in between the sleepers, as if searching for something buried there.

"Angus!" Her voice was frantic now. "Get up! I need you to find whoever killed me!"

His metal pillow began to vibrate. His legs began to twitch. He imagined death would be peaceful, but he'd been wrong. Death took whatever form it wanted. His lungs crackled, fit to burst with the cold air he was sucking into them. Yet he struggled to breathe. Splintered images of all those he could not save flashed through his brain. Barbara Klein butchered in the grove. Lewis Duncan screaming in agony as the flames carved his face. The sodden weight of Ethan in his arms. His mother's bulging eyes.

"Get up! Get up, you fucking coward!"

The distant rumble became a throaty growl, then a roar. Snow slid from metal as the tracks trembled, as if in fear. His heart clawed at his rib cage. Snowflakes fell like tears on his face and forehead. All his fears, his pent-up anger, his regrets and guilt coalesced into a writhing mass in his stomach. The vortex swept up his body and funnelled through his parched throat. His skull would explode if he did not let it out.

"You owe it to us!" Faye screamed. "You owe it to me! You owe it to your mom!"

He twisted his head to the side. Two hundred tonnes of panting, snarling metal was hurtling towards him through the snow, so close that he could smell its rancid diesel breath. Two white orbs of light shone from its face. The cold, dispassionate eyes of a killer.

He sucked in one final, shaking breath, taking the cold deep into his lungs. Then he shrieked his pain and anguish into the juggernaut.

ACT IV

"In every age there are individuals
who are spectre-haunted. . . . When a person
was about to die, especially if his death was to be by
violence or drowning, his wraith or phantom was seen by
those who had the Second Sight."
—*The Gaelic Otherworld*, J. G. Campbell, 1902

CHAPTER 49

RED wax crumbles from the crayon and clots his picture. From the playground comes the dull thump of a football being driven against a wall, happy cries and laughter. Miss Marshall has left the classroom. He can hear her sniffling in the corridor. Next to the blackboard, on which their grammar lesson for the day is written in chalk, a policeman talks to Gills in hushed tones.

"The wee lad's in shock. He doesn't seem to understand what's happened."

He sees rain hammering off the roof of his mum's Renault Scenic. Puddles quiver as he walks through them towards the car. Water seeps into his polished shoes. His blue polo shirt sticks to his body. The school badge chafes his skin. There's a tree behind the car: leafless, dead, its branches like bleached bone. Three crows are hunched on a wizened bough. He feels their dark eyes on him. Suddenly a hand slaps against the window of the car. He hears the ugly squeak as her fingers slide down the misted-up glass. In the cleared patch, he sees his mother's face. Her eyes are wide and pleading.

The crayon snaps.

"Where's his father?"

"A conference in Inverness. I'm his godfather."

"You can take care of him, aye?"

"Of course."

"Maybe get him checked over by a doctor. He's said some weird stuff—"

The policeman's voice fades and he sees smoke from his father's cigarette curling into the cool morning air. Dad sits on the front step of the cottage, wearing an old checked towelling robe.

The smoke catches in his throat as he sits. He glances at his father's face, doesn't like what he sees. His skin is sallow. Coarse grey hairs pepper his chin and cheeks. The bags under his eyes are like rain clouds. He smells of stale whisky.

He's told him the truth already, but his father only ignored him, as if the words had never reached his ears.

"Dad. I saw what happened. I was sitting in class, and Miss Marshall was droning on about adverbials, and I . . . I saw . . ."

His father's hand shoots out and grabs him by the upper arm. His fingers are like a vice.

"You didn't see anything." His grip tightens. "Death plays with your mind."

"No! I saw what happened!"

"That's impossible, Angus! Now away you go and let me smoke in peace."

Hot, frustrated tears prickle behind his eyes.

"Why won't you believe me!"

Dad stares at him, eyes like the glowing tip of the cigarette held in his shaking fingers. His voice quivers. "Enough of this nonsense! Do you want the men in white suits to take you away? Don't ever speak about this again!"

Dad raises his hand as if to slap him. Angus flinches, closes his eyes, anticipating a blow that never arrives.

When he opens his eyes again, he is no longer on the front step of the cottage. He is running down the gravel road towards the Old Manse, his vision blurred by tears. Dad's words play on a loop in his head: Don't ever speak about this again!

He thinks of the lies he's told in the past, like breaking the shed window with a shinty ball, then claiming a bird flew into it. Dad had found the ball in the shed amongst the shards of glass. Is that why he doesn't believe him now?

The wrought-iron gate shrieks as he yanks it open. He is shaking like the stray lurcher he and Mum found last winter near the graveyard. The dog was emaciated, its ribs visible under matted fur. It limped over to them, broken and wounded as he is now. Part of the dog's jaw had been ripped off. Blood and pus oozed from gashes that crisscrossed its flank and neck, as if the animal were a zombie dog, risen from the nearby cemetery.

He collapses against the door of the Old Manse, just as the dog had flopped down at his feet. Mum told him not to touch it, but he couldn't stop himself. He'd crouched and laid a hand on the dog's shivering head. He wanted so much to save the dog, but Cruikshank shook his head. The vet told them the lurcher had been savaged by another dog. Probably an organized fight. The tinks—sorry, the Travellers—did that sort of thing, and this wasn't the first dog he'd seen in this state. Beyond saving.

Angus had looked into the dog's bloodshot eyes and seen only despair and defeat, the same wretchedness as he'd seen in his father's expression.

He hammers his fist against the door of the Old Manse. It swings open and he stumbles into Gills's arms, buries his face in his thick woollen sweater. It smells of woodsmoke, fresh leaves, and wet dog. He forces out a muffled sentence: "Dad says men in white suits will take me away."

Gills crouches down until they are face-to-face. His eyes are deep blue and kind. He smiles faintly. "Ach, that's nonsense. No one's taking you anywhere."

"Dad doesn't believe me."

"No, but I do, wee man. I do...."

Thick flakes of snow tossed and turned on the wind, like the blizzard of memories he had fought to hold back. His lungs crackled as he ran headlong through the sparse forest. The smell of charred flesh and diesel fumes clung to his skin. He felt like that child again, running for the sanctuary of the ivy-coated house. His clothes were wet and soiled. Through the trees, a buttery light glowed from a window of the Old Manse.

An image of the savaged dog flashed into his head as he stumbled through the gate, then staggered up the path towards the front door of the house. He recalled the look of utter desolation in the dog's eyes. "No," he muttered. "No."

His voice sounded feeble, as if he were still that wee confused boy. He saw the child raise his fist to hammer on the door, just as he was doing now.

The sharp thuds jolted him back to the present. He waited, melting snow dripping from his hair onto the front step. From the rear of the house he heard Bran and Sceolan barking, then the hall light flicked on. The door swung open and Gills was there, real and substantial. He wore the fur-lined moccasin slippers and a dressing gown over tartan pyjamas that reminded him of Faye's scarf.

Words spurted from Angus's cracked lips. His throat felt raw from that feral scream as he lay on the railway tracks.

He sniffed and the dam of tears finally broke. Gills pulled him into a tight embrace.

"Too late, Gills . . . I was too late."

CHAPTER 50

ANGUS stood in front of the sink in the bathroom of the Old Manse, a thick towel wrapped around his waist. The scalding hot shower had thawed his bones, but his body still felt alien, his muscles drained. He replayed the moment over and over: the crackle in the air, the dazzling bright lights, the thrum in his chest. He'd felt the abject terror of death's hot breath on his neck. And in that split second he'd been granted a reprieve. Faye was right—he owed it to them.

He shrugged on the fresh towelling robe that Gills had hung on the hook of the bathroom door. He padded through to the kitchen, to the sound of the kettle boiling, the whirr of his clothes drying in the machine, and Gills whistling tunelessly. Bran and Sceolan scampered over to him and pressed their warm flanks against his legs.

"Ah, there you are," Gills said. "I'm making us hot toddies. I reckon we could do with them, don't you?"

He accepted the glass with a nod of thanks. A toast didn't seem appropriate, so he simply drank.

Gills took a sip of his toddy. "What you described, the body hung upside down, is another Celtic threefold death ritual. Gormla of Borve, the prophetess I told you about, met a similar fate at the hands of Dòmhnall MacRuari. There are other examples from Celtic mythology, but the triple death is not just a motif. Roman sources claim followers of the Celtic god Esus suspended sacrificial victims from trees before killing them."

He rummaged under a newspaper with Faye's picture on the front and pulled out a leather-bound tome. "This is the Carntyne manuscript where Gormla of Borve's prophecies are recorded. Listen to this. . . ."

He flicked to a page full of tight, looping script. "'When the Royalty Stone falls on a church, the MacRuari line will end and the land will be overrun by ministers without grace and women without shame. Glad am I that I will not see that day, for it will be a time of slaughter. The wretched will make bargains with demons and, thus possessed, make blood sacrifices to slake the thirst of the old gods.'" Gills paused. "It sounds prettier in the old Gaelic, of course."

He cocked an eyebrow and continued. "As our genealogist friend Lachlan discovered, James Chichester is a descendant of Dòmhnall MacRuari. With Faye's death, the first half of this prophecy has been fulfilled. The second part of the prophecy, about ministers without grace and women without shame, well . . ." He shrugged, a slight smile on his lips. "Many would say that is already the case in the Highlands."

"And the final part?" Angus asked.

"Quite clearly suggests that our killer is acting under the influence of another entity. That he—or, indeed, she—is possessed. That we aren't necessarily hunting a 'who,' at least not entirely."

The old man stood and walked around the table. He crouched and placed a hand on Angus's shoulder. "That thing you chased tonight—you called it the Dark One? Where did you hear that?"

"From Chris Kelbie. That same cloaked figure was at the Samhain celebration the night Faye was murdered. Kelbie said he was dressed as a Celtic god of death."

"Donn Fírinne?"

Angus nodded.

"Makes sense. The Cailleach brings death with her, and Donn Fírinne is a Gaelic reaper. It follows that the killer would have adopted his visage."

Gills squeezed Angus's shoulder.

"What I'm telling you is real, old bean. You knew that, once. Prophecies, myths, and folklore are not mere stories. They are a link to an archaic system of knowledge that we've all but lost. The ancients were not crazy. Aye, they couldn't make a combustion engine or send a rocket to the moon, but they had a deeper understanding of the cosmos. They thought in terms of parallel realms—the spiritual, the physical, and the celestial—existing independently, yet able to impact on their physical world. The veil between these worlds was porous, especially at certain times of the year, such as Samhain."

"What if it's just a man in a costume, Gills?"

The old man squeezed his shoulder. "Think of what you've gone through, Angus, what you've seen. There is no rational explanation for *dà-shealladh*. But by God, the Sight is real! As real as this house. As real as you and me."

Silence hung between them. He heard the faint whisper of his father's voice. *Don't listen to that old baolastair, son. All that learning's kiboshed his brain.*

Gills's earnest blue eyes bored into his. "Angus, it's not in your head. None of it. And it never was." He held up the bottle of yellow pills, which he must have found in Angus's pocket. "You don't need these, old bean. You are proof that"—he lifted the weathered Gaelic manuscript—"that this isn't some pile of horseshit written in a savage tongue, trod upon by the Church, stomped on by the Crown, and cast aside by a society with no goddamn interest in anything other than its obsession with the rationale."

"There's just one problem about your theory, Gills," he said. "If the killer is possessed, it could be anyone. Hell, they might not even know they're the killer."

Gills shook his head. "No, old bean. They have volition—as the prophecy says, they made a bargain. They agreed to make these sacrifices. We just don't know what the killer was promised in return."

Gills stood and walked to the sink. He unscrewed the bottle and tipped the pills into the waste disposal.

Gills padded from the kitchen and down the hallway to the study. He pushed open the door and flicked on a light. Angus hesitated, then took a deep breath and stepped across the threshold into what he'd long ago come to regard as the room of the supernatural. His pulse quickened as he glanced around. The number of books had multiplied since he'd been here last. Piles of them sat on almost every available surface, overflowing the shelves and cascading onto the floor.

Gills walked to his writing desk and flicked on a banker's lamp. The desk had been pushed into a corner to make space for the familiar retro brown leather armchair. How many hours had he sat in that chair? It faced the only wall not given over to bookshelves.

Gills had created his own murder board.

Like the one in the incident room, it featured a large map of the area, but rather than crime scene photographs, the wall bristled with drawings of mythological creatures and articles cut from newspapers, magazines, and journals. Red string attached to pins joined points on the board, the links meaningless to Angus.

A sudden draught ruffled the seemingly hundreds of yellow Post-it notes stuck at random around the board, making the wall quiver like a giant bird. A picture of Faye crimped from the front page of the *Herald* was pinned near the top of the board. Underneath was a magazine portrait of a younger James Chichester perched on the edge of a lavish teak desk. He looked a couple of stones heavier than he was now and wore a pin-striped three-piece suit. A gold watch glinted from his wrist. The eyes that peered out from his fleshy face held an arrogant forthrightness. Behind him, the thrust of the Manhattan skyline shimmered with pride. "Master of All He Surveys," read the headline above the photograph.

Next to Chichester's picture was a shot of Eleanor, again cut from a glossy magazine. She smiled coyly at the camera. Clearly, she'd practiced the look—it was the same one she'd given Angus in Dunbirlinn.

His eyes drifted across the wall and stopped at a familiar photograph. He let out an involuntary gasp. It was his mother. He stared at the image, a twisted knot of wire in his throat. Below the photograph were several more pictures he knew well: Lewis Duncan, Barbara Klein, and Ethan Boyce. Beside each of the victims was the date of their murder in brackets, and another word written in block capitals. "SAMHAIN," "IMBOLC," "BELTANE," and "LUGHNASADH."

"Gills, what the hell is all this?"

He heard the swish of Gills's moccasin slippers as the old man walked over to him. "I noticed a pattern," he said. He pointed to the picture of Faye Chichester. "Faye was killed on Samhain, as we know. But what I hadn't noticed was the significance of the other dates. Angus, they were all killed on the dates of the ancient Celtic fire festivals." He tapped Ethan's picture. "August the first corresponds with Lughnasadh, and marks the beginning of harvest season. Barbara Klein was killed on Imbolc, February the first, while Mr. Duncan died on Beltane."

"And Mum died on Samhain, too," Angus murmured.

Gills cleared his throat. "Yes, I'm afraid so."

Angus let his eyes wander over the wall, with its smiling pictures of Faye and Eleanor, James Chichester and Dòmhnall MacRuari.

"What about Eleanor?" he asked suddenly. "She wasn't killed on any of these dates."

"That's not strictly speaking true, old bean. Yes, dates are traditionally attached to these festivals, but they were a movable feast, literally. Also, they could last quite a bit longer than one day. In the *Ulster Cycle*, for example, there's the story of *The Sick Bed of Cúchulainn*, in which the ancient tribe of the Uliad celebrate Samhain with drink, fighting, and sacrifice. The debauchery lasts a whole week. The party has not ended yet, it would seem, for our Dark One."

Angus slumped into the retro chair. His fingertips brushed the cracked leather armrests, the sensation recalling his father's parchment skin. "These dates must be a coincidence," he said. "Lewis, Barbara, Ethan—their killers all committed suicide. They can't be involved."

"Well, quite," Gills replied. "But we need to look closer at these cases. There will be a common denominator between the killers, a thread that links them to the Chichester murderer, I'm certain of it. Whatever this is, it didn't start with Faye."

CHAPTER 51

THE rags hanging from the clootie tree danced in the raw morning wind, the bright, cheerful dabs of colour a stark counterpoint to the blackened corpse still dangling from the branch. Angus stood with his hands buried deep in his jacket pockets and watched the white-suited forensics officers crawl around the crime scene like fat grubs over a carcass. More SOCOs kitted out in wet-suits waded through the stream, some looking for evidence, others preparing to recover the body. Intermittent flashes from the photographer's camera only heightened the sense of surrealism he felt watching the scene play out. Had he really been here last night? In the cold light of dawn he had almost convinced himself it was a nightmare.

Nearer to the clootie tree, Nadia broke off from her conversation with Orla Kelly and tramped towards him through the snow. Her cheeks, and the tip of her nose, were flushed from the cold.

"What did Orla say?" he asked.

"Not much. Difficult to examine a body when it's . . . where it is. Going to be a while before they get her down."

She gave him a tight smile, then frowned at the scratches on his face. "What happened to you yesterday? I called about a hundred times."

"Aye, sorry about that. Got tied up with a few cases."

"Did they involve being attacked by an angry cat? Because that's what it looks like."

"Nah, had to chase some wee ne'er-do-well from the undergrowth."

She nodded, losing interest in the conversation, as he'd hoped she would. "Come on, we have to go to Dunbirlinn and take a statement from James Chichester."

"He's been informed, though, right?"

"Aye, and he hasn't spoken a word since."

James Chichester sat on a fiberglass rock amidst the wildlife exhibit in Dunbirlinn's new museum, watched by the lifeless eyes of stuffed animals. In his hands he cradled a silver object, which Angus recognised as the Fairy Horn of the MacRuaris. The glass cabinet that displayed the ancient horn yawned open. Angus's and Nadia's footfalls echoed around the hall as they approached. He glanced warily at the stuffed wolf, which reminded him of the animal he'd shot yesterday with Corky's shotgun.

They stopped a few feet from the laird, and Angus cleared his throat.

"Ah, Angus Dubh," Chichester rasped. "At last, someone I actually like."

Angus tipped his head in sad acknowledgement. "James Glas. This is my colleague, DI Sharif. I don't believe you've met."

Chichester gave Nadia a fleeting glance. "Detective," he said, with a slight incline of his head.

"We're sorry for your loss," Nadia said. "I know that always sounds trite, but it's true."

Chichester, however, appeared not to hear her. "Our ancient ancestors believed, at the end of time, the sky and stars would collapse upon the earth, and the earth would crash into the ocean. Other historians have a different theory—that the Celts, like the Norse, believed the apocalypse comes in the form of a great wolf that devours everything: the sun, the moon, the earth, and all living things. . . ."

Gills's prophecy echoed through his mind.

The wretched will make bargains with demons and, thus possessed—

Nonsense, son, his father's voice nagged. *Look at this man! Does he look possessed to ye?*

Angus looked into Chichester's greenish-blue eyes, but all he saw was grief and despair.

"What do you believe, DI Sharif? How does it all end?"

"I was raised a Sufi Muslim, Mr. Chichester. The Quran teaches us that life is merely an amusement and diversion; the real life is in the hereafter. Sufis still hold the traditional Islamic view of the Day of Reckoning, though, where all life will be annihilated before the resurrection, when we will be judged upon our deeds in life."

"And if you've led a bad life?"

"Jahannam—Hell—awaits."

The laird nodded slowly. "Perhaps, but if there's one thing I've learnt, it's that much in life is beyond our control." He turned the fairy horn over in his hands, his fingertips tracing the intricate spirals. "I used to think one's importance was directly proportional to their bank balance. Which made me very important indeed. Made me think I had my own sort of superpower, that I was special. I'd click my fingers, and people would scurry around doing my bidding. I had world leaders on speed dial. I could bring down governments. With a few choice whispers in the right ears, I could raise a man up or cast him down. There were times when I felt godlike." His face twisted into a sneer. "And now I'm paying for that hubris."

"We need to ask you a few questions, James. About Eleanor."

Chichester's cool glare slid over Angus. "Very well."

"When did you last see your wife?"

"Yesterday evening. She was in the drawing room, passed out drunk. The same as the night before, and the night before that."

"You left her there?" Nadia asked.

He nodded. "Draped a blanket over her and went to bed. Mrs. MacCrimmon had gone home for the night, so must have been after ten."

"Do you have any idea why she would have gone outside after that? Could she have met someone, or gone for a walk?"

Chichester shook his head. "Impossible. Elle doesn't walk anywhere if she can avoid it, especially not in this weather. And who would she meet at that time of night?"

"Fair point," Angus said. "Did she have any visitors yesterday?"

He shook his head again. "She meets her girlfriends for lunch and gets a manicure at some health spa on Wednesdays. Usually returns home around five, in her best performance of sobriety."

"Did you see her come home?"

"No, I was out with the search teams, looking for my wolves. Mrs. MacCrimmon will know more, perhaps."

The laird, groaning, got to his feet. "Do you know the story behind this artifact, DI Sharif?" he asked, holding up the horn. "It was a gift from the fairies to my ancestor Dòmhnall MacRuari. His is the portrait hanging in the entrance lobby. Dòmhnall was a colourful character, by all accounts. Anyhow, if the horn was blown in battle, no matter the odds, the MacRuaris would emerge victorious." He gave a bark of laughter. "Didn't do Dòmhnall much good in the end."

"How so?" Nadia asked.

"Dòmhnall and his men murdered the son of a rival chieftain of the MacLoughlin clan. As a reprisal, MacLoughlin launched a surprise attack on Samhain as the MacRuaris were celebrating. Those who were not butchered, including Dòmhnall and his family, escaped and hid in a cave. But MacLoughlin tracked them down. Rather than go in after them, he had a bonfire built across the mouth of the cave. MacLoughlin decided he would leave the final decision to God's will: If the wind blew from the sea, the fire would be lit. If there was a land breeze, the people would be spared."

Angus watched Chichester place the fairy horn back on its stand. Chichester turned and caught Angus staring at him. He gave a thin smile. "Dòmhnall was reputed to follow the old gods, hence his moniker—*an Draoidh*, the Druid. What do you know of druids, Angus?"

"Very little," he lied.

"Druidism fascinates me," Chichester said. "Their training was intense, but we have no idea of the breadth of their learning because they never wrote anything down. They fell into three classes: the druids themselves, who were philosophers, teachers, and judges; the bards, who sang the songs and stories of the tribe; and the ovates, which is a Latin word equivalent to the Irish *filí*, or seer."

Angus maintained his blank face. Chichester was just a man wishing to drown himself in stories, anything to distract himself from the loss that now surrounded him on all sides.

"Long ago, those with the gift of prophecy were part of a privileged caste," Chichester said. "They drew their lore from the natural world and the old deities, as did my ancestor, I believe. The MacLoughlins, though, were Christians. You might think a Christian god would show mercy, but no—the wind blew in from the sea and the fire was lit. Dòmhnall and most of his kin suffocated. The incident went down in legend as the Glen Màma Massacre."

Chichester looked at his brogues, then up at Angus. "That cave, Angus Dubh, was the same one in which I took refuge." He swung the door of the glass cabinet closed. "Magic horn, my ass," he muttered, the end of the sentence disintegrating into a sob.

Angus gave Nadia a sidelong glance. He padded across to the laird and placed a gentle hand on his shoulder. "We'll find who did this, sir. I promise you."

Chichester placed his own leathery hand on Angus's and gave a brief squeeze. "I know you will."

Angus let his hand drop to his side. "With your permission, we'd like to see the CCTV footage from last night."

"Of course. Mrs. MacCrimmon will give you all the assistance you need."

As if from nowhere, the housekeeper appeared. Angus wondered if she'd been there the whole time, listening in on the conversation.

"Follow me, please," Mrs. MacCrimmon said.

Angus locked eyes with Chichester and gave a brief nod. The laird leaned towards him and said in a low whisper: "Know what I reckon, Angus? We're bit-part players in an epic game as old as time. We're nothing but pawns. And sometimes pawns are sacrificed."

Angus was still mulling over Chichester's cryptic comment when Mrs. MacCrimmon showed them into a narrow room that might have been a prison cell in a former life. Now it was an office, with a bank of monitors showing footage from all the cameras perched around the walls of Dunbirlinn.

"When was the last time you saw Lady Chichester?" Nadia asked the housekeeper.

"Just before ten. I poked my head into the drawing room to tell her I was done for the night."

"Did she say anything?"

"No, she was too busy dancing by herself. I left her to it."

"Would it be unusual for her to leave the castle at that time of night?"

"Unheard of."

Angus listened as Nadia asked Mrs. MacCrimmon a few more questions, but his eyes were glued to the monitor in front of him. It showed footage from the courtyard played at high speed, Faye's Merc and Eleanor's mustard Range Rover parked side by side. Nothing much was happening until another vehicle appeared.

"Here we go," he said to Nadia. She leaned forward, peering over his shoulder, so close that he could smell her fresh perfume. He slowed down the video as the car—a gleaming BMW—trundled to a halt. "Who's that?" Nadia asked.

"Taxi," Mrs. MacCrimmon replied.

"Bit fancy for a cab."

"Diamond Cars," the housekeeper said. "A cab firm for folk with more money than sense. Eleanor used them when she was going to drink."

As if to prove the point, Eleanor emerged from the taxi and stumbled up the castle steps, clearly drunk.

"Five minutes past five," he said, glancing at the time stamp on the screen.

Using a trackpad, he again sped up the footage, watching as daylight faded and security lights flicked on in the courtyard. At just after six, Chichester himself returned to the castle and trudged up the steps. Angus scrolled on, hours passing in minutes, but still no movement.

"When Eleanor left the castle, she would have to go this way, right?" Nadia asked.

"There's a servants' door," Mrs. MacCrimmon said, "but she'd still be on that camera walking across the courtyard."

Angus returned to the point in the footage when Eleanor had arrived in the taxi. Then he fast-forwarded again. By the time he stopped the video, dawn was breaking in the sky above the ramparts.

They'd been through the entire night, but Eleanor had not reappeared.

CHAPTER 52

CAMERAS flashed and questions were lobbed towards Angus and Nadia as they drove past the scrum of reporters outside the village hall. Their numbers appeared to have swelled in the past couple of hours, like flies drawn to the scent of decay. Angus spotted Alice Seaton smoking a roll-up under a large sycamore tree. The local reporter didn't look happy about the blow-ins.

Inside the incident room, the atmosphere was less febrile but more tense. There was none of the usual good-natured badinage from Crowley as he assembled the team for afternoon briefing. The DCI's face looked pinched, his deep-set eyes like two smouldering embers as he plucked Eleanor's photograph from the "suspect" column, and pinned her under the "victims" heading.

Angus's mind returned to Gills's *bòrd-murt*, so similar to Crowley's in some ways, but with four additional "victims." His eyes scanned the photographs of all the suspects the MIT had so far considered. MacVannin glared at him with his bulging eyes. A man of Christian cloth, would he really make a bargain with demons, as Gormla's prophecy suggested?

Then there was the scowling Kelbie, her braids partially covering her eyes. The woman who believed in blood sacrifice, if the traces on the altar stone were anything to go on. When he and Nadia had spoken to Annie Kelbie, she'd hinted at a deep confusion and anger festering inside her daughter. What was it Annie had said about Chris? *My daughter is up on those mountains with her sheep and goats, flailing around like a blind woman.*

Perhaps it was no stretch of the imagination to see a woman like that making such a deal—by Kelbie's own admission, she and her followers were Reconstructionists who sought to replicate ancient rituals. And what ritual could be more potent than blood sacrifice?

Ach! Wise up, would ye! his father's voice hectored in his ear. *These pagan folk may be deluded, but they're no' possessed. Not any more than MacVannin's possessed by the Holy Spirit.*

Nadia quickly explained about the CCTV apparently showing Eleanor returning to Dunbirlinn but not leaving again that night.

"Must be another way out," Ryan Fleet said. "Secret tunnel or something."

"Agreed. Otherwise, how did she end up dangling from a chain burnt to a crisp? Rylo, sort out a team. I want every inch of Dunbirlinn Castle searched. Dogs, GPR, the works."

"Maybe we'll finally find out if the legend's true," Vee said.

"What legend?" Crowley asked.

"I've been reading up on Dunbirlinn's history. A certain nasty chieftain supposedly bricked up his cheating wife behind a wall. Alive. You can still hear her ghost scratching at the walls of her tomb."

"Aye, thanks for that, Vee," Crowley said, rubbing his temples. "This case is a horror show as it is, without the ghost stories. But speaking of horrors: Nadia, can you and Angus interview Reverend MacVannin again? We'll see if his wife can come up with a more compelling alibi this time."

"Nae bother," Nadia said.

"Okay, what were Ewan Hunter's movements last night?" Crowley asked.

Angus was about to speak up but clamped his mouth shut. Better not to leave a thread to pull on.

"Took a statement from him earlier, sir," Vee said. "He was in A&E last night after being bitten by a dog. He was discharged around half ten, so I suppose he could have made it back and killed Eleanor, bearing in mind his cottage is not far from the crime scene. But I spoke to the doctor who treated him. He said Ewan would have trouble lifting anything heavier than a pint glass. No way he could have hauled Eleanor up that tree."

The gruesome image of Eleanor hanging head down from the branch was seared into Angus's brain. He saw again the pink and purple blistered skin, the yellowish rendered fat. The roots of her dyed-blond hair were grey, which suddenly reminded him of the *corp creadha*. Whoever had made the clay corpse had used human hair.

"Which leaves us with the pagans," Crowley said. "It makes sense given the nature of the killing. I don't need Dr. MacMurdo to tell me I'll find similar accounts in the Big Book of Celtic Sacrifice. The weather's forecast to clear later, so we can get the chopper up to the commune. But let's get the dogs out again too. Kelbie and her lot don't have access to a helicopter. They'd have had to get to Dunbirlinn on foot, abduct Eleanor without being picked up on

CCTV, and kill her in front of this sacred tree. Then they'd have to get back to the commune. Bound to leave a trail."

"In normal circumstances, aye," Nadia said. "But it was snowing last night. Any footprints were covered."

"Don't piss on my parade, DI Sharif," Crowley said, his spirits much restored. "Scour the forests. Scour the hills. We'll find something. When's the PM?"

"Orla's going to do it for us this afternoon," Nadia replied.

"Good of her."

Nadia ignored the sarcasm. "She did warn not to expect much in the way of DNA evidence."

"Okay," Crowley said. "Anyone got anything useful to add?" His eyes flitted around the group.

He did.

Angus cleared his throat. "Sir, the hair on the clay corpse was dyed blond. I think it might have been Eleanor's, which would mean the killer was telling us their next victim all along."

CHAPTER 53

A JCB lurked like a vulture beside the rubble of John MacVannin's church, its bucket drawn up as if ready to feast. The twisted corrugated iron roofing, shattered timber, and blocks of stone had been pushed to the side, and a space cleared for the foundations of a new church, farther away from the mountainside this time. Angus wondered if the *Clach Rìoghalachd*, the Royalty Stone that Gills had talked about, lay amidst the debris. Perhaps it would be reused in the new church walls. The idea appealed to him.

He climbed from the Land Rover and picked his way across the churned-up ground towards the crofthouse, Nadia not far behind. His mobile phone pinged—a text message from Inspector Stout, three words all in block capitals: *KNICKER SNATCHER UPDATE.* Followed by a line of question marks. Angus shoved the phone back into his pocket.

The clang of someone hammering metal sounded from the rear of the crofthouse. "Try round the back first," Nadia said.

Angus walked around the side of the property, which was clad in an unappealing grey harling. The windows were cheap plastic and out of character with the rest of the building. Not that the house had much character, unless you counted meanness of spirit. The back garden wasn't much better—a small patch of lawn, neglected flower beds, and a gnarled crab apple tree that looked as if it had been struck by lightning. A rickety old shed with a lean-to for storing logs festered amongst overgrown bushes at the end of the garden. The shed's doors gaped open, and it was from here the hammering was coming.

"Charlie Dimmock would have her work cut out here," Nadia commented, ducking under a sagging clothesline. "I've seen demolition sites with more charm."

The clanging intensified as they reached the open shed doors. MacVannin was inside, dressed in a grubby boilersuit, bunnet, and steel-toe-capped boots, hammering at a metal object. It took Angus a second to realize it was the cross that had been mangled in the rockfall. The minister was hunched over, beating the iron with such fury, he hadn't heard them approach.

"Reverend MacVannin!" he yelled, fighting to be heard over the hammer blows. "Reverend MacVannin!"

The minister suddenly stopped the assault, the hammer raised above his shoulder. He turned towards them and curled a blubbery lip. His bulbous eyes looked as if they were about to burst from his sweat-streaked face. "What dae youse want?"

"You might have heard, Reverend—there's been another murder," Nadia said.

MacVannin lowered the hammer and pulled himself up to his full height, just shy of five five.

"'And the sea gave up the dead who were in it,'" he said. "'Death and Hades gave up the dead who were in them, and they were judged, each one of them, for what they had done. Then Death and Hades were thrown into the lake of fire.'" He glared at Nadia. "Revelation 20:13–14."

"And your point is?" Nadia asked.

"It's begun, the Great Tribulation."

"Let me get this straight—you think we're living in the End of Days?"

MacVannin snatched the farmer's bunnet from his head and wiped the sweat from his brow. "I don't *think*. I know. Our fall from grace is almost complete."

"Well, there's a cheery thought. . . ."

"Mock all you like," MacVannin spat. "They mocked Noah, too." He threw down the hammer. "So, who was it got themselves killed?"

Angus struggled to maintain his composure in the face of the minister's apparent indifference.

"Lady Chichester," Angus said, "and she didn't *get herself killed*. Someone did it to her."

MacVannin barely reacted. Had the minister been so callous twenty years ago when he heard of his mother's murder? Angus wondered. Probably. He stared into those bulbous eyes and saw nothing but an intransigent instrument of a jealous god, one that bore more than a passing resemblance to Kelbie's wrathful deities. This man was no druid, no interlocutor to a higher power, only a little turd in black vestments.

"Where were you last night?" Nadia asked.

"Here."

"In this shed?"

"No! Here, on the croft."

"Don't tell me, your wife can vouch for you, just like she did the last time?"

"Aye, but I can do better than that."

Nadia folded her arms and cocked a questioning eyebrow.

"That pagan bitch was here last night."

Angus gave Nadia a sidelong glance. Her smile was incredulous. "Why on earth would Kelbie visit you, of all people?"

"She wasnae visiting. I caught her trespassing on my land."

"Why didn't you report it?"

MacVannin stuck the bunnet back on his misshapen head. "No point wasting my time. Anyway, I caught her clambering through my field when I went out to check the cattle."

"What was she doing?"

MacVannin sighed. "There was a shrine down by the river, the other side of the common grazing."

"Shrine to whom?"

"I don't know, some pagan goddess. They say she protects the glen." He sneered. "Superstitious nonsense."

"What time was this?"

"Back of ten."

"And did you have words?"

"Aye, of course. Wasn't going to let trash like that gallivant over my field. I tellt her the truth—that her soul was possessed by the anti-Christ."

"Did you prevent her from visiting this shrine?"

MacVannin's smirked. "Didnae have to—there is no shrine. I followed the advice in Leviticus and smashed it."

"You did what?"

MacVannin placed a hand on the cross. "And I will destroy your high places and cut down your incense altars and cast your dead bodies upon the dead bodies of your idols, and my soul will abhor you." Scotland, Detective, is a *Christian* country."

"How did Kelbie react?" Angus asked.

The minister's smirk broadened. How Angus longed to wipe that smile off his face.

"Like someone had pissed in her porridge."

"So she was angry?"

"Livid. She would have killed me if she could. Don't be taken in by all that tree-hugging nonsense she spouts, Angus. There's a demon inside Kelbie. I saw it in her eyes last night. A beast, fighting to get out."

"He did what!" Gills exclaimed, sending biscuit crumbs flying from his mouth. "That's . . . that's cultural vandalism! Surely you can charge him with something? That's our heritage he's destroyed. That shrine has been there for hundreds of years."

Sceolan, who was lying in front of the Aga in the kitchen of the Old Manse, glanced up, alerted by his master's indignant tone.

"Easy, *a'bhalach*," Angus said.

"Can you tell us about the shrine, Dr. MacMurdo?" Nadia asked.

Gills let out a long sigh. "It is—*was*—dedicated to the Cailleach."

"The goddess you told the MIT about?"

"Indeed. It's not much, really, just a small shieling with a turf roof. Three stones outside represent the Cailleach; her husband, the *Bodach*; and her daughter, *Nighean*. The legend goes that the Cailleach and her family were sheltered by the folk of the glen during a snowstorm. The Cailleach was so grateful for the hospitality, she left the stones at the house she occupied—with the promise that as long as they were cared for, the glen would prosper."

"There's a tradition that the stones are taken out of the shieling at Beltane on May first, and placed back inside for the winter at or around Samhain."

Gills shook his head. "John's always been a wrong 'un. Sure, he's a minister, but before he found God, he was an awful man for drinking and fighting." He glanced at Angus. "Me and your dad used to hang around with him when we were kids. I remember once we were playing shinty and found a bird's nest that had blown down from that big oak beside the field. There were three chicks in the nest, still alive. Me and your da' were discussing how to get the nest back in the tree when John ran over and whacked it with his caman."

Gills stared into his coffee cup, as if looking into the past. "I'll never forget the look on John's face as he clubbed those poor chicks to death. He was . . . thrilled." He shuddered. "Myself and Uisdean did our best to avoid him after that."

"When did MacVannin find God, as you put it?" Nadia asked.

"Och! Must have been twenty years ago."

"What did he do before that?"

"He was even an odd-job man at Dunbirlinn for a while, before he started working for his uncle Billy MacLoughlin, who had a construction company."

"MacLoughlin," Nadia mused. "The same clan that wiped out the MacRuaris."

"Aye," Gills replied, frowning. "John's mother was called Julie MacLoughlin. But how do you know about the Glen Màma Massacre?"

"James Chichester mentioned it," Angus said.

"The laird seems a tad obsessed with Dòmhnall MacRuari," Gills mused. "Lachy told me Chichester bought every book he stocked about the MacRuaris."

"But don't you think Reverend MacVannin's hatred of Chichester is out of all proportion?" Nadia cut in. "I mean, what's the laird really done? Let some folk establish a commune on his land. Founded a nature reserve. Big deal?"

"What are you getting at?" Angus asked.

"From what Chichester said, the MacLoughlins were warrior Christians. Their goal was to wipe out the pagan MacRuaris. They didn't manage that."

Nadia glanced from Gills to Angus, her eyes narrowed. "What if Reverend MacVannin thinks he's finishing the work his ancestors started by annihilating Chichester's bloodline?"

CHAPTER 54

ELEANOR'S charred corpse lay on the slab in Silvaig mortuary, the sight made all the more gruesome because her head was relatively pristine, having been under the water. Angus had slathered his upper lip with Vicks, but the smell of roasted flesh was so strong, he could almost taste it. Beside him, he heard Nadia mutter a string of curses.

What did this to you, Eleanor?

"I know, it's not pretty," Dr. Orla Kelly said. "But you'll be glad to hear she was dead before she was set alight.

"The flames have destroyed much of the physical evidence. However, I was able to recover a tiny section of material from inside the wound on her neck." She took a pair of tweezers and lifted a strip of thin fibre. "It's sinew."

"So she was strangled with a garrotte, like Faye," Nadia said.

You saved Ewan. Hold on to that.

"Aye, and that's not where the similarities end." She pointed to a lesion on the side of her head. "She was bludgeoned, too. Probably knocked unconscious. And her leg is also broken below the knee."

Angus could almost hear the sound of bone shattering, the brutality made all the more raw after Gills planting the seed in his head that all this . . . this madness could be connected to his mother's murder.

Nadia blew a breath of air. "We're looking for the same killer, then?"

"We never released the details of Faye's killing, so yes. Definitely."

"Any idea on the time of death?"

"Difficult to be precise, what with the burning, the cold temperatures last night, and the fact her head was submerged in water. I'd say between ten p.m. and two a.m. That's about as best as I can do."

"Any idea what was used as an accelerant?"

"Synthetic isoparaffinic hydrocarbon. More commonly known as naphtha—"

"Or lighter fluid," Nadia added.

"Indeed," Orla said with a faint smile. "Could be your killer's a smoker. I also compared a hair sample taken from the creepy doll with Eleanor's."

"And?"

"It's a match."

"You were right, Angus," Nadia mused. "They were telling us who their next victim was all along."

Ruthven Crowley sat in the interview room with his arms folded, hooded eyes fixed on Christine Kelbie. Vee Lockhart occupied the chair next to the DCI, prim and proper in a Peter Pan–collar blouse and black skirt. She sat with her back rigid, like a schoolteacher about to deliver a grammar lesson. In contrast, the duty solicitor, Hamish McKeown, was slouched in his chair as if recovering from a weekend on the sauce. In fact, he might have been sleeping again. Kelbie herself looked pale and drawn, Angus thought. Her lank braids hung over her face, as if she were hiding behind them.

Beside him in the observation room, Nadia exhaled loudly. It was the third time she'd sighed in as many minutes. "Oh, get on with it, Ruthven."

"Does he do this often?" Angus asked, glancing at a clock on the wall. Crowley had been trying to stare Kelbie out for a good ten minutes.

Suddenly the duty solicitor appeared to rouse himself from his slumber. "Do you intend to question my client at any point, Detective Chief Inspector? Only, if not, we've all got better things to do."

Crowley ignored him and continued staring.

McKeown gave a loud tut, half-stood, and began to gather up his papers. "Okay, I've had enough—"

"Sit down!" Crowley's voice was like a whipcrack. The solicitor slowly lowered himself back into his seat, grumbling, but the DCI's eyes never left Kelbie. "Why were you on the MacVannin croft last night, Christine?"

"If you know I was there, then you know why," she answered.

"Yes, but I'd like to hear your version."

Kelbie flicked the braids out of her eyes. "There's a shrine on the other side of his croft. I was planning to visit it."

"At that time of night?"

"The moon is important in our belief system. Last night there was a waxing gibbous. Coming before the full moon, it symbolizes the concept of final steps."

Crowley gave a thin smile. "Final steps of what?"

"Could be anything—a project, spiritual growth, something you've strived for. It's a . . . difficult time of the month. Often I seek solace and guidance from the goddess."

"Ah, so that's why you were there? Seeking guidance?"

"I would have, if that arsehole hadn't destroyed the shrine."

"Reverend MacVannin has his own made-up gods to serve, I suppose."

A muscle in Kelbie's jaw twitched, but she didn't rise to the insult.

Crowley ran his hands over his face. "Okay, take me through everything you did, from the run-in with MacVannin onwards."

"Not much to tell," Kelbie replied with a shrug. "I returned to the commune."

"What time did you get back?"

"Half past eleven or thereabouts."

"And no doubt you've a cast of alibis willing to testify to that?"

"Several folk were still up . . . so, aye."

"Convenient."

"Nothing about this is convenient," Kelbie replied.

"Look, Christine," Vee said in her teacherly tone, "we've got a team of forensic officers going through your hut as we speak. These guys are good. You might think you've been careful, but they can detect specks of blood or fibres unseen by the human eye. We've already found all sorts of literature that link you to these crimes."

"Tell me about this satanic cult you were part of," Crowley said suddenly.

Kelbie's mouth hung open, face frozen in surprise. McKeown gave her a sharp glance, his expression like a man caught with his trousers down. "That . . . that was a long time ago," she stuttered.

"Ten years? I've socks older than that."

Lewis Duncan had been killed ten years ago, Angus thought. His mother twenty. During much of that decade gap between the killings he'd been taking the pills, like his father had told him. What had he not "seen"? Could there be other deaths linked to all this? Missing person cases? Homicides attributed to domestic violence?

"I . . . I was a different person back then . . . easily led," Kelbie stammered.

Crowley gave a cruel laugh. "Aye, you know you're running with the wrong crowd when sacrificing dogs to Beelzebub constitutes a good Saturday night."

"I never participated."

"No? So you were in procurement or something?"

"What? No!" Kelbie spat.

And why had he foreseen only these murders? Angus wondered. Sure, the pills maybe had something to do with it, but they hadn't prevented the visions of Faye and Eleanor. He knew the effectiveness of some drugs waned over time. Perhaps the seer in him simply became stronger than the pills. Seers' visions were usually related to death, and the more violent the circumstances, the stronger the hallucination.

Crowley shook his head, sucking air between his teeth. "All those poor wee family doggies lured from their back gardens and burned alive. Pretty sick stuff."

Kelbie flicked the braids out of her face. Her eyes radiated hatred. "I had nothing to do with it," she hissed. "I was just a stupid kid! You're wasting your time, and while you harass innocent people, the real killer's still out there."

Angus ground his teeth, as if drawing on Kelbie's anger. Faye's and Eleanor's murders could hardly have been more violent. So, too, his mother's. But Kelbie couldn't have had anything to do with that—she would have been a child when his mother was murdered. Unless she was embroiled in some death cult going back decades . . .

"Innocent? Tell that to the wee girl whose pet pooch you stole and butchered."

"I didn't steal anything. . . ."

"You must have watched, though? Drank the dog's blood or something?"

Suddenly Kelbie slammed her palms down on the table, making her solicitor jump.

Angus noticed his own hands were balled into fists. He uncurled his fingers.

"So smug in your certainties, aren't you, Detective?" Kelbie growled. "I've met so many men like you—arrogant, patronizing pricks. You wear your lack of belief like a badge of honour, not realizing how weak it makes you. There's a hole inside you where faith should be, and you fill it with hate and spite and cynicism—"

McKeown placed a hand on Kelbie's shoulder, but she shrugged him off and glared at Crowley. "You don't care about dogs, and I doubt you give a shit about Faye, either! All you care about is your ego. At least I have faith in something."

"Aye, a pagan death cult," Crowley said with a satisfied smirk.

Once more, Gormla's prophecy rang through Angus's mind.

The wretched will make bargains with demons and, thus possessed—

"I've seen it before," Crowley continued. "Killing's like a drug: you need the hit it brings. It starts with birds or mice, then dogs and cats. But that doesn't satisfy you for long, so you progress to something a bit more substantial—a goat maybe, or a horse. That might sustain you for a while, but eventually you crave more, you yearn for the ultimate high. . . ." Crowley hunched forward, teeth bared. "The only way to feed that hunger is by killing another human being, by watching as life drains from their eyes—"

"No," Kelbie muttered. "Death isn't the end. Death is the centre of a long life, merely a passing between realms, part of a cycle of life, death, and rebirth. We believe the soul is immortal and treat life as sacred."

"Even when you're taking it?"

Kelbie's eyes blazed with an incandescent fury. "Yes!" she yelled, spittle flying from her lips. "Even when we're taking it!"

Her outburst shocked everyone, even Crowley, into silence. Angus glanced at Nadia, but her eyes were glued to the monitor. McKeown leaned across and whispered urgently in Kelbie's ear. He turned to Crowley and cleared his throat. "My, err, client, would like to clarify that her previous comment was not an admission of guilt—"

"Sounded like one to me," Crowley said mildly.

"Well, it wasn't!" Kelbie hissed. "I didn't kill Faye or Eleanor, so—"

McKeown slapped a hand down on her forearm. The fire in Kelbie's eyes flickered, then went out. The braids again fell across her face. This time she didn't brush them back. Nor did she say another word.

CHAPTER 55

MRS MacCrimmon glowered at the search teams traipsing through Dunbirlinn's draughty halls and recesses, her mouth an angry slash, powdered cheeks tinged pink.

"Is this really necessary, Angus?" she asked. "I've worked here for over forty years. I know every inch of this castle, and there are no secret exits or entrances."

They were standing in a tight stone corridor with arched windows that connected the north watchtower to the chapel, with its vaulted ceiling and fluted pillars. A couple of SOCOs in Tyvek suits squeezed past them, one pushing a device that looked like a cross between a lawn mower and a fancy golf trolley. "'Scuse me, coming through—"

Angus and Mrs. MacCrimmon flattened themselves against the wall. "What in the name of the wee man is that?" the housekeeper asked.

"Ground penetrating radar," he said. "It can be used to identify underground tunnels—"

"Of which there are none—"

"Then how did Eleanor leave the castle without being picked up by CCTV?"

"Perhaps someone . . . fiddled with the tapes."

Nadia suddenly appeared behind him. "We have considered that, Mrs. MacCrimmon. Our experts have examined the tapes and found no evidence of . . . fiddling."

Mrs MacCrimmon stuck her nose in the air. "Well, I'm still not happy with this. . . ." She wafted a hand in the air. "Not happy at all."

"We'll be out of your hair before you know it, Mary," Angus said.

Mrs MacCrimmon fixed him with a watery stare. "Och! Fine then." She turned on her heel and clopped away.

"Do you think she has something to hide?" Nadia asked.

"Mrs MacCrimmon? She's protective of her territory. This place must feel more like her home than Chichester's. She's lived here most of her life."

"She hated Eleanor," Nadia said.

"Everyone hates their boss." He thought of Stout hounding him about the Knicker Snatcher. "I know I do."

They turned and followed the search team towards the chapel. "I don't hate Crowley," Nadia said. "Although sometimes I'd gladly wring his neck." They scuffed down a small set of steps, the stone in the centre of the blocks worn down by the hundreds of feet that had passed this way over the centuries.

Angus watched as the technician slowly trundled his golf-trolley-cum-lawnmower down one side of the chapel. Small recesses were carved into the wall every couple of meters, and would probably at one time have held religious statues. Now, however, the alcoves were empty. In fact, the chapel contained very little Christian iconography. A large reredos behind the plain altar appeared to have been intentionally defaced, the stone carvings on the screen hacked off.

Angus placed a hand on the altar. It was carved from one great block of stone, almost as if from the very rock on which the castle sat. He walked slowly around it, fingers tracing the edge of the cold slab. Angus saw the technician with the GPR machine out of the corner of his eye. He'd reached the end wall and was wheeling the machine towards the reredos, whistling tunelessly. He paused a few feet away, in front of the reredos, and stared down at the screen on his GPR machine. "Hold up! Think I've got something here!"

His voice echoed around the chapel. A couple of other techies in white Tyvek suits appeared from behind pillars and rustled towards them. Angus was closer, but when he peered down at the grid screen, he saw nothing but a series of wavy coloured lines that meant absolutely nothing to him. "'Scuse me," one of the techies said, elbowing him aside. "What have you got, Ken?"

"See the lighter section," he said, jabbing a finger at the screen. "That's an anomaly, right?"

The other techie squinted at the screen, then turned to Nadia and Angus. "There's definitely something down there. Could be a burial, like a tomb or a vault or something. It's too big for an air pocket."

"Or a tunnel?" Nadia asked.

"Could be. Can't be sure yet. We'll need to go over this whole area."

"Right, we'll get out of your way."

"Probably a false alarm," she said as they walked away. "I worked a missing gangster case a few years back. We got intel that he'd been executed by a rival and buried in some waste ground in Clydebank. We went over every inch of the place with the GPR. Turned up old sewers, a mine shaft, dead animals, even an unexploded bomb from the Blitz."

"No dead gangster, though?"

"Nah. The intel was bogus. The gangster was in the Costa del Sol, working on his tan."

While Nadia made a phone call to Crowley, Angus slipped outside Dunbirlinn for some fresh air and found himself wandering towards the stables. He went inside and leaned against Bessie's stall. The white horse ambled over and let him stroke her muzzle.

"She likes you," came a voice from the shadows.

Angus gave a slight start. Faye sat on a hay bale in the corner of the stall, watching him and Bessie with sad eyes.

"So what is it, Gus? Are we chasing a who or a what? You don't mind me asking, do you? I'm rather curious . . . you know, as the blood sacrifice."

"I don't know."

She appeared to accept his answer.

She stood and walked across to Bessie. The horse seemed to shudder when Faye stroked her flank. "I can't feel her," she said. "But I think she knows I'm here."

Angus swallowed the lump in his throat. "Aye, she knows."

He stared into Faye's vacant pale green eyes. "I never thanked you," he said.

"For what?"

"For saving my life."

"Maybe that's all I was here for." She gave him a faint, watery smile, and then was gone.

Angus stood there for a long minute, his hand caressing Bessie's warm neck. The sound of his mobile phone ringing shattered the silence. He slid the phone from his pocket and answered. "Angus, you'd better get back here," Nadia said. "They've found something."

He clattered down the steps and into the chapel, which had been transformed into a hive of activity. Nadia spotted him and gave a brief wave.

"You've got to see this." She grinned, gesturing him over to her.

He edged past a cluster of portable crime scene lamps, which had been arranged around the altar, their beams pointed at the reredos on the back wall. The carved ornamental screen sat at an odd angle, and only when he got closer did he see why. A large panel of the screen actually swung outwards, and behind it was a small arched doorway.

"This is a false wall," Nadia said, tapping the brickwork. "Take a look."

Angus stuck his head through the arched doorway, breathed in the damp, musty air. Another lamp had been set up in here, illuminating a narrow room. He stooped inside, half-expecting to see a woman's skeleton, straggly hair still attached to her scalp. The room, though, was empty. But a gaping hole in the floor revealed the first few steps of a rough staircase winding down into darkness.

Angus's heart fluttered in his chest. A rank-smelling breeze came from the mouth of the hole.

"Amazing, isn't it?" Nadia said, shuffling into the room beside him.

He worked some saliva into his parched mouth. "Where do the stairs lead?"

"No one's been down. The SOCOs want a safety assessment before anyone ventures any farther."

Angus pulled a flashlight from his jacket. "Bugger that."

Nadia grabbed his sleeve. "Angus, wait. What if the whole thing collapses?"

"Clearly, whoever abducted Eleanor entered this way. It can't be that dangerous."

He flicked on the torch and set foot on the top step.

"Famous last words," Nadia mumbled, but he sensed her at his back as he began his descent.

Her voice was swallowed by the walls. Angus kept his torch pointed at the stairs as he crept downwards. The staircase seemed to twist like the body of a snake. The beam revealed a long tunnel, apparently hacked out of the rock, supported every few meters by rotting timber.

He set off again, gripping the torch tight in his right hand. From the darkness came the sound of tiny scurrying feet.

"What the hell's that?" Nadia hissed.

"Mice probably."

Was Eleanor already dead when the killer carried his blood sacrifice through here? he wondered. No, that final act would have taken place at the clootie tree.

They walked on in tense silence, for what seemed like several hundred yards, although it could have been more. Suddenly the torch beam fell on another staircase. Angus quickened his pace, practically bounding up the stone steps. But when he reached the top landing, he was met with a dead end. "No, no," he muttered, "there must be some way out." He scanned the space with the torch, the beam falling on a dark patch on the flagstone by his feet. He crouched and rubbed it with his fingertips. "Blood," he said. "Whoever took Eleanor must have laid her down here." He handed the torch to Nadia. "Here, take this. Shine it on the wall." He stepped forward and worked his fingers along the section of wall where the stone met the ceiling, then down the side. Halfway down he felt something, like a metal lever. He squeezed it and to his amazement the wall began to move.

He jumped back, colliding with Nadia. "Bloody hell!" he gasped.

With a sound like grinding bone, the wall slid to the side. Nadia grabbed a fist of his jacket, and together they edged out, not into light, but a murky darkness, a twilight zone. "Angus, where are we?" Nadia asked in the voice of a frightened child.

"I'm . . . not sure," he croaked. His mind flashed back to Gills's tales of caves that led to the underworld. He tried to dismiss the thought, but it lodged, like a stone in his shoe. Nadia scanned the space with the torch. The beam fell on shadowy recesses, long shelves cut into the walls. Some contained crumbling tombs; others, stone effigies almost worn smooth by time.

And suddenly Angus knew where they were. "There's a graveyard in the woods not far from Dunbirlinn. It's where my mum is buried," he murmured. "The chiefs of clan MacRuari are interred there too." He ran his hand along one of the stone effigies. "We're in their crypt."

Angus crouched by his mother's grave and howked out a couple of dandelions growing by the headstone. The forensic operation around the MacRuari mausoleum was in full swing, but he was hidden by the ancient yew tree's twisted limbs and dense prickly leaves. It felt good to be out in the clean, fresh air after the suffocating dank of the tunnel and crypt. He stood and stuffed his hands into his pockets. In his head, he heard the words of both Gills and Annie Kelbie.

Close your eyes and see, Angus. Before it's too late, close your eyes and see.

He did exactly that, squeezing his eyes tight. As expected, he was met with only darkness. His gift—his curse—didn't work like that. If he hadn't seen who killed his mother back then, he wouldn't see them now. He spun around and found Nadia standing a few feet away, watching him.

"Sorry," she said, "didn't mean to sneak up on you." Her eyes flicked to the headstone. He watched the frown creep across her face, followed by the dawning realization. "Is that—"

"Aye."

"You never spoke about her, back in college."

"No."

"Do you mind if I ask what happened?"

"She was murdered."

Nadia's mouth fell open. She stepped forward as if about to hug him, but something in his eyes must have stopped her. "Oh, Angus, I'm sorry. I . . . I never knew."

He sniffed, felt the tears nipping at his eyes. Sympathy was always the most difficult emotion to deal with. "S'okay," he replied. "Long time ago."

"Did they, you know, ever catch anyone?"

He ground his teeth, shaking his head. He was grateful that Nadia did not probe any further. She knew what it was like, of course. The case of the River Angel was still unsolved all these years later.

They turned and walked back towards the MacRuari crypt.

"This changes everything, of course," Nadia said. "The killer has to be someone with an intimate knowledge of Dunbirlinn."

Angus understood what she was saying. "James Chichester?"

"We have to consider him a suspect now, Angus."

He nodded, but the possibility that Chichester, a man he'd grown to like and respect, could murder his wife and daughter was almost too perverse, too vile to contemplate.

"MacVannin used to work at Dunbirlinn as an odd-job man. He could have stumbled upon the tunnel?"

Nadia pursed her lips. "It's possible. There's also a scenario where the killer is someone we haven't even considered yet. Either way, unless the killer swiped Eleanor's hair for the clay corpse from her hairdresser, they must have had access to the castle. That way they could collect it from, say, her hairbrush."

"Aye, makes sense," he said. "The castle's undergone a fair amount of renovation over the years. A workman could have discovered the tunnel by chance, or a housemaid or a cleaner."

"Mrs MacCrimmon seems the fastidious type," he mused.

"Aye, she does," Nadia said, flashing him a quick smile.

"I bet she keeps records of anyone ever employed on the estate."

"Let's go and ask her," she said.

CHAPTER 56

ASH found Granny Beag up a ladder, wearing an ancient green parka, trainers, and neon-pink rubber gloves.

"Granny, what on earth are you doing!" Ash exclaimed.

The old woman gave her a brief scowl, then reached forward and scooped a handful of dead leaves from the guttering. She dropped the soggy brown ball onto the ground, forcing Ash to take a step back. "I'd have thought that obvious, Ashleigh."

"Don't come crying to me if you fall and break your hip again."

Granny Beag tutted and scraped another wad of dead leaves into her rubber-gloved hand.

"Couldn't you at least have waited until the snow thawed?"

"Wheesht your whining. I'm done now anyway."

Ash held the ladder steady as Granny Beag climbed down.

"So tell me, how's the wee lassie getting on with my old clarsach?"

"Good," Ash said. "Actually, I'm heading to Kintail House now. Just thought I'd pop in and see how you were." Her face clouded over. "You'll have heard there's been another murder?"

Granny Beag yanked off the rubber gloves, then gave a deep sigh. "Aye, I heard."

Suddenly she pulled Ash into a surprisingly tight hug. Ash smelt the mustiness of dead leaves mixed with lavender soap, and felt a catch in her throat. Granny Beag held her for a few seconds, then released her. Her face set into a frown. "You look like you've been crying, *a luaidh*?"

"I'm fine," she said.

Granny Beag stared at her for a long second. "Have you time for a cup of tea?"

"Aye."

Granny Beag shuffled inside the house and skooshed some water in the kettle. "Have you thought about what I said, Ashleigh? About being a candidate at the local elections?"

"Ach, no! Not this again."

Granny Beag pointed to a pile of papers on the kitchen table. "I printed you a nomination form. All you have to do is fill it in and get it witnessed."

"You don't give up, do you?"

"I am persistent."

"Stubborn, more like."

Granny Beag clicked on the kettle and turned to face her. "You're a great public speaker, love. And you've a way with folk. . . . They listen to you."

Ash lifted the form and flicked through the sections. "I don't respond to flattery, you know that." She folded the form in half and stuck it into her pocket. "But I'll think about it. As long as you promise not to go climbing any more ladders."

Granny Beag cracked a wide grin. "Deal."

A snowman lurked on the lawn in front of Kintail House. It seemed to stare at Ash with eyes of coal as she walked towards the entrance. Smaller lumps had been used for the mouth, arcing upwards in a black smirk. Together with the bent carrot nose and misshapen head, the snowman was a dead ringer for Reverend MacVannin. Ash glanced around to make sure no one was watching, then gave the snowman the middle finger. "Spin on it, you dirty old sod," she muttered.

Her heart rate was higher than normal as she jogged up the steps and into Kintail House. She couldn't be sure why. Having been a runner since her late teens, she was particularly sensitive to changes in her body's rhythm. Perhaps she was coming down with a cold?

The beginning of a new song she had composed for Lilly fluttered in her head. The piece was easy enough for a beginner like Lilly to learn, yet there was something beautiful in its simple sliding scales, like falling rain.

Big Mo glanced up from behind reception, a dusty blue bonbon halfway to her mouth. She popped the small round sweetie into her mouth. "How are you today, hen?"

"Ach, you know, a wee bit shook up."

"I hear you. One was bad enough, but two . . ." She sooked at the sweetie, creating deep hollows in her chubby cheeks. "You must get the inside track from your hubby. Who do they think done it?"

"Angus doesn't discuss his work at home," she replied.

"I heard Faye was killed in some weird ritual. If that doesn't point to one o' they *pagans*, I don't know what does."

Ash shrugged. "You could be right."

Mo popped another bonbon into her mouth, clearly disappointed not to get any juicy gossip.

"How's Lilly?" Ash asked. "Are those boys still harassing her?"

"Not that I've noticed." She rolled the bonbon around her mouth. "The thing is, Ash, Lilly has a tendency to make things up. All the kids in here had tough upbringings, you know that, but Lilly's was particularly severe. I can't go into specifics, but she's suffered a history of abuse, most of it real, but some of it definitely imagined. You should treat what she says with a pinch of salt."

"Noted," Ash said, irritated. "But I'm only here to teach her the clarsach, Mo."

"Absolutely." Mo beamed. "And she's been practicing away. She'll probably be in the glasshouse now waiting for ye."

Ash left Mo to her bag of sweets and walked through the familiar drab corridors. Her chest still felt tight. She was surely coming down with something. Probably caught a chill running, or contracted something from one of her sniffly students. It was cold-and-flu season, after all.

What certainly wasn't cold was the glasshouse. The heat, when she pushed the door open and stepped inside, was stifling. Her clarsach sat in the middle of the room surrounded by tropical ferns and trees, but no Lilly.

Ash waited a few minutes before returning to reception. The piece she'd composed for Lilly had taken on a life of its own. From nowhere, a low register arpeggio was repeating in her head. Big Mo had polished off the bonbons and was flicking through a copy of *Vogue*.

"Have you seen Lilly? She's not in the glasshouse."

"She's probably in her room," Mo replied. "You can go on up."

"Which one is it?"

"Yours." Mo said. "She stays in your old room."

Ash's heart again fluttered. She wasn't sure she wanted to see that room again. It had always felt like a jail cell.

"I can fetch her, if you like?" Mo said.

"No, no, it's okay. Thanks."

She turned away from reception and walked through the lobby, stopping at the foot of the wooden staircase. She remembered Keira sliding down the banister and landing in a heap on the floor. She had sprained her ankle once. Had to get crutches. Ash shook away the memory and began to climb, the song in her head rising with her, creaking almost, just as the stairs groaned under her feet. Years of Mo stomping up and down must have taken their toll.

She reached the landing and walked past three doors, remembering their occupants: Claire, who'd once tried to kiss her; Tanya, who'd tried to strangle her; and Keira, who'd taught her how to jimmy a lock and hot-wire a car. Life skills.

The last door on the left was her room. Well, Lilly's now. The repeating arpeggio was now smothered by a descending glissando, but the normally beautiful slide of notes became a jagged rip that made it hard to think. She could still see a slight indent on the door where she'd punched it all those years ago. Thinking back, she couldn't remember what had caused the outburst. She'd punched lots of things back then: mirrors, walls, pictures. Tanya's face . . .

Now she raised her fist and gave the door a gentle tap. When there was no answer, she knocked again, louder. "Lilly! It's me, Ash!"

She placed her ear to the door, sure she could hear the faint sound of running water, but not sure if it was the tinkling song in her head. Lilly was probably in the shower. She'd come back later. She turned away, but something was troubling her. Her heart was beating too fast, and now the hair on the nape of her neck was standing up. Glancing down at her feet, she saw the threadbare carpet was wet. Water had seeped through the gap at the bottom of the door.

"Oh fuck!" Ash slammed the flat of her hand on the door. "Lilly!" she yelled. "Lilly! Are you in there!" She grabbed the doorknob, but it wouldn't turn. She gave it a rattle, then took a few steps back and ran, ramming her shoulder against the door. The wood groaned but held firm. She backed up again, and this time drove the sole of her boot against the door. She heard a cracking sound, so hit it again and again, harder this time, channelling all her power into her foot. On the fifth kick the wooden frame splintered and the door cannoned inwards, slamming against the wall.

The room was filled with steam. Ash stepped inside, her feet squelching on the carpet. The door to the en suite was open. She covered the ground in three quick strides. She skidded into the bathroom, almost sliding in the pool of water that covered the tiled floor. "Oh God, no!" she whimpered, raising a hand to her mouth.

The old freestanding bath where she used to enjoy blissful moments of peace was full to the brim. The taps were still running and water cascaded over the side of the bath and onto the floor. Lilly lay in rose-tinged water. One pale arm dangled over the side of the bath.

A blood-stained razor lay on the wet floor.

The glissando shattered inside her head, mutating into one long shrill banshee wail.

CHAPTER 57

IT wasn't often Mrs. MacCrimmon ate humble pie. Angus could tell the taste wasn't to her liking. "Nobody's been down to that old chapel in years," she muttered. "How was I supposed to know there was a hidden tunnel there?"

Angus bit his tongue. *I thought you knew every inch of the castle?*

"No one's blaming you, Mary. We only want to know what the chapel was used for during your time in service."

The housekeeper stuck her nose in the air. "Like I said, it hasn't been used for years."

They were sat at the big oak table in the staff kitchen. Behind them, the vast fire roared and spat. The last time he'd been in here the fire had been unlit, and Stout had been stuffing down scones like there was no tomorrow.

"Has the chapel undergone renovation work, anything like that?" he asked.

"No," she replied, "but that reminds me: It was used for restoration work for a short period. Must be five, six years ago, Mr. Chichester thought some of the old paintings in the castle were losing their lustre. He had them taken down and put in the chapel. I hired a local firm of art-restoration specialists, and they did their work in the chapel."

"What was the name of the firm?" he asked, a faint bell ringing in his head.

"Och! I can't remember, but I'll have a record of it. I keep detailed accounts going back years."

"We were counting on that," Nadia said with a smile. "May we see them?"

Mrs MacCrimmon sniffed. "Fine, but don't mess them up. I can't abide things put back out of place."

Angus was not surprised to discover that Mrs. MacCrimmon had resisted the move to digital. The room she led them to contained a long row of slate-grey filing cabinets, an antique desk, a leather chair, and little else. Daylight filtered into the room from an arched window high up on the wall.

"This may take some time," Nadia muttered, glaring at the filing cabinets.

"Do you have a separate personnel section, Mrs. MacCrimmon?" Angus asked.

"Of course, but only for staff employed directly by the estate. I keep invoices from all our suppliers, too. A vast amount of paperwork, as you can imagine."

"Aye, I'll bet," he replied. Mrs. MacCrimmon showed him where the personnel records were kept, then left, repeating her previous warning: "Don't mess things up!"

Once she was gone, Angus and Nadia stood in silence staring at the line of filing cabinets. Angus hauled one drawer open and pulled out an invoice at random. It was from 2014: "Twelve filet steaks, three pounds of sausage meat, six pheasants, and four haggis. All from Hutton & Sons butcher in Silvaig," he said aloud. "Two-hundred and fifty-nine pounds seventy pence. Plus VAT. It'll take years to go through all this." He slammed the drawer shut. "And what are we looking for anyway?"

"You're right," Nadia said. "Let's just take the personnel records back to the incident room and divvy them up. All we're looking for is a name that jumps out. Someone who used to work at Dunbirlinn and might have known about the tunnel."

"This is scut work, isn't it?" he muttered.

She grinned at him, apparently enjoying herself. "Abso-fucking-lutely."

Angus shook his head and got to work emptying the personnel files. They were divided into separate folders and went back decades. However, there weren't *that* many. They would be able to carry them out to the Land Rover in one trip.

"Hope Mrs. MacCrimmon doesn't catch us," Angus muttered as they snuck through the lobby with the files. The painting of Dòmhnall MacRuari glared down at them, his savage eyes bright and alive, the colours on his plaid fresh and vibrant. No doubt this was one of the paintings Mrs. MacCrimmon had referred to, which had been restored in the chapel. Something about that still nagged in his mind. There couldn't be many fine-art specialists locally. Once he was back in the incident room, he would track them down, if only to satisfy his curiosity.

Only, he never reached the incident room. He was in the Land Rover when Ashleigh called.

CHAPTER 58

ASH sat at the clarsach, the side of her face resting on the finely decorated body of the instrument as she plucked desolately at the strings. The notes echoed around the snug room, plaintive and haunting. She looked up and gave Angus a watery smile. Track lines ran down her cheeks. Her sleeves and the front of her sweater were stained in blood.

He walked across the room and dropped to his knees beside the stool on which she sat. Her hands fell from the strings, and she threw her arms around him. He stroked her thick russet hair and tried to ignore the metallic scent of blood. "I was so scared, Angus," she mumbled into his shoulder. "I thought she was dead."

"I'm sorry, *a ghràidh*," he whispered. "I'm sorry for everything." He'd heard Ash talk about Lilly but hadn't paid much attention before. Like Chichester, he'd been so wrapped up in his own affairs, he'd neglected the people closest to him.

"How is she?" he asked.

"Alive," she murmured. "That's all that matters."

Eventually Ash told him what had happened, how she'd turned up at Kintail House to give Lilly a clarsach lesson only to find her in the bath, her wrists cut.

"I should have done more for her," Ash said.

"Don't torture yourself, love. It's not your fault. We're not responsible for the actions of others."

"But if I'd only—"

"No," he soothed. "It's not your fault, okay?"

She held his gaze, then gave a slight nod. "Perhaps not," she mumbled then. "My head feels like it's going to burst. I think I'll have a lie-down." She stood, swaying woozily from the shock. "Thank you," she said.

"For what?"

"For coming home." She offered him a tepid smile. "For listening to me . . ."

He stood and pulled her into a hug.

"I love you," she whispered, her breath warm on his neck.

"Me too," he replied. "Me too."

After a moment she gently pushed him away. "Now go. You have work to do."

He shook his head. "I can stay."

"There's no point in you hanging around here while I'm sleeping. I'm okay now. Honestly."

She brushed her lips against his and shuffled from the room. He heard the bedroom door open and shut.

He rubbed his hands across his face. Ash had been forced to deal with so much in her life. She hid her scars well, but, like him, she was damaged.

His thoughts were interrupted by his mobile phone ringing. He saw Nadia's name flash up, and answered. "There's been a couple of developments," she said. "Can you come down?"

"Err, sure." There was a coldness to her tone that put him on edge.

"Don't go to the village hall, though. Meet me in my room at the Glenruig Inn."

She hung up without waiting for a reply. Angus stared at the phone screen. Alarm bells pounded in his head.

Angus gently rapped on the door of Nadia's room, then dug his nails into his palms as the door swung open.

"In you come then," Nadia said, barely glancing at him. She was barefooted, dressed casually in leggings and a loose-fitting cream Henley top. Her hair was damp, as if she'd just come out of the shower. He stepped into the warmth and took in the room at a glance: stylish and cosy, with a double bed, built-in wardrobe, dressing table, drinks cabinet, and armchair. The walls were hung with landscape paintings by local artists. The odd flash of tartan was dotted around, on pillows and throws, but the room didn't stray into the twee.

He shrugged off his jacket and slung it over the back of a chair. It was only then he noticed the scattering of photographs stuck to the wall. He homed in on the image of a little girl, lying on her back on a riverbank. Her eyes were closed, hair falling in rivulets around her perfectly oval face. She could have been asleep, but the paleness of her skin told another story. This was the River Angel.

Angus felt Nadia's eyes on his back. "Still no closure, eh?"

"For me, or the case?"

"Both."

"No." There was an edge to her voice. There had always been a determination, but there was a bitterness on the fringes he hadn't recalled.

He turned to face her. "What about the van that was spotted near the river?"

This mysterious van had been one of the main lines of inquiry. An early-morning dog walker had spotted a man taking something from the back of the Transit and throwing it in the Clyde, not long before Nadia had found the girl's body when she was rowing.

"I'm surprised you remember that," she said.

"You told me all about the case when we were at Tulliallan." He tapped his head. "The details are stored in here."

She held his gaze for a second, then sighed. "The van man was a dead end. I tracked him down. He was fly-tipping. What the dog walker saw being flung in the river was a rolled-up rug."

"What about—"

"Look, Angus," she said, cutting him off. "I didn't ask you round here to discuss the River Angel." She folded her arms and glared at him. "Where were you on Wednesday night?"

The question caught him off guard. "Tying up a few of my own cases. I told you."

"Sure, you were away all day, but what did you do after clocking off?"

He tried not to look like a schoolkid caught truanting. "Why do you ask?"

"Crowley asked me to check if any patrol cars had been in the vicinity at the time of Eleanor's murder. Your Land Rover's fitted with GPS, Angus."

A bead of sweat dribbled down his spine. He forced out a laugh. "And you think I was running around killing Eleanor Chichester?"

Nadia let her arms fall to her sides. "Of course not," she tutted, eyes softening a little. "But what were you doing there?"

"I was leaving Ewan Hunter back home," he said. "He couldn't drive after being bitten by the dog, so I collected him from the hospital in Silvaig."

"Why didn't you mention this?"

"Ach, I don't know," he said irritably. "It had nothing to do with the case."

"So you didn't see anything suspicious?"

"Nadia, if I'd seen anything, I'd have told you," he replied, injecting a slither of indignation into his tone.

She held his stare, then gave a hollow laugh. "Sorry, I had to ask. But you have to admit, you've been a bit secretive the past couple of days."

"Well, you'd know all about that." Instantly he wished he could jam the words back into his throat.

"Whoa! What's that supposed to mean?"

"Nothing. It doesn't matter."

"No. Out with it, Angus."

He held her gaze. "Do you remember that time your dad made an unannounced visit to Tulliallan? And I had to climb out the window so he wouldn't see me?"

A faint smile touched her lips. "Aye, and . . ."

"That's when I realized I would always be your dirty little secret."

"Come on, Angus. No girl wants to be caught in flagrante by her father." He smiled despite himself. "True, but that wasn't the only occasion. Remember when your sisters turned up? You wouldn't even introduce us. Ach, admit it, Nadia—you were ashamed of your white teuchter boyfriend."

"Angus, you're being a dick. I wasn't ashamed of you, quite the opposite actually. But introducing you to my family was a big step. My dad in particular was very traditional in his beliefs. You risked nothing going out with the brown girl; I risked being disowned by my whole community."

She took a step towards him, the gold flecks in her eyes like tiny embers. "I would have, though. I'd have risked everything for you, but you never hung around long enough to find that out."

She walked to the drinks cabinet and snatched a miniature bottle of Gordon's from the fridge. "Everything happens for a reason. Isn't that what they say?" She twisted off the cap and poured the gin into a glass.

"Do they? Not sure I believe that."

She reached for a bottle opener and wedged off the lid from a tonic water.

"Me neither," she said as the water fizzed into the glass. She glanced at him. "Do you want something? There's gin, vodka, or whisky."

"No . . . thanks. I'd better be getting home."

"Wait," she said. "I didn't just ask you over here to grill you about the Land Rover and dissect our past."

"No?"

She squeezed a slice of lime into her gin and tonic and took a long drink. "I wanted to tell you that Christine Kelbie's done a Thelma and Louise. Without the Louise."

"She's gone?" he exclaimed.

"Aye. Left shortly after we interviewed her. The communal camper van is missing. One of the residents said Kelbie was scared of being fitted up. Crowley sees it a different way, of course. He thinks she felt the net closing in and decided to disappear."

"In an easily identifiable camper van?"

Nadia swirled her G&T around the glass. "She might have ditched it by now."

"Aye, maybe." He turned away from her and studied the photograph of the River Angel. The image was in black and white. A few plainclothes detectives were caught in the shot, half in, half out of the frame. They all wore trench coats and bleak expressions. One had a cigarette dangling from the corner of his mouth. In the background, beyond the river, a row of brutal tenements and high-rise flats thrust upwards into a drab Glasgow sky. All eyes, but that of the camera, were directed away from the little girl, as if they couldn't bear to linger on her pitiful rag doll form.

What sort of person could do that to a wee girl? He thought of Kelbie and that unguarded anger that had burst from her in the interview room. What was it she'd said?

We treat life as sacred. Even when we're taking it.

Angus flipped open the dog-eared case file and tried to switch into professional mode, as Orla Kelly did when "processing" a body.

He placed all the newspaper reports on his mother's killing to one side. Gills the historian had told him all about source material: the police reports and interviews were intrinsically more valuable than whatever the hacks had written for the tabloids at the time.

He longed for a glass of Talisker, but Faye's warning about his drinking had hit home. He needed a clear head for this. Instead he took a sip of sugary tea and got to work.

He started with the autopsy report, reasoning that it was better to get the worst over and done with. His mother's injuries were described in detail, the medical jargon doing little to soften the impact. Like Faye, she had died as the result of asphyxia caused by ligature strangulation. Unlike in Faye's case, a length of cable had been used rather than sinew. A long discussion of the type of cable followed, the conclusion being that it was of a common type used in the construction industry, and also available from hardware stores up and down the country.

His mother's other injuries were described, including a wound to the head inflicted with a heavy metal object, possibly a hammer. However, the inconsistencies with Faye's and Eleanor's murders were as stark as the similarities. His mother had put up a fight. Her body was covered in bruises and the pathologist had found skin under her nails. Presumably, this was the killer's, but there had been no DNA matches in the database. She'd been killed in a car, unlike the others, which had led DI Hood to surmise that Mum had known her killer. Either that or she'd picked up a hitchhiker. There was no hint that she had been symbolically drowned and her leg was not broken below the knee.

Angus finished reading the autopsy, then sat with his head in his hands for a long time. So much for professional detachment. He reached for his cup of tea, but it had long gone cold. A word the pathologist had used in the report kept coming back to him. She'd said the murder was "disorganized." So not frenzied, just . . . incompetent. Angus recalled the textbooks on serial killers he'd read back at Tulliallan. They often started by playing out their fantasies on animals, as Crowley had alluded to in the interview of Kelbie. Their first murders, though, still tended to be untidy.

Disorganized.

Because they had not yet perfected their craft.

CHAPTER 59

THE next morning, they took Ash's Clio and drove into Silvaig. His wife looked wan, her eyes red and sore, as if she were suffering from hay fever. She stared out the car window for the whole journey, but he could tell from her reflection in the glass that she was not taking in the scenery. Several times he opened his mouth to speak, then stopped, unsure what to say. Small talk about the weather seemed inappropriate. Besides, he didn't feel overly jaunty himself. He'd been up half the night rereading his mother's case file, then playing over scenarios in his head until he was in a fankle, as his dad used to say. Why had he "seen" these murders in particular? The dates certainly suggested some sort of connection. Perhaps his visions had not been random either? There was one massive stumbling block—it simply could not be the same killer.

The clinic was a short walk from the esplanade, so Angus parked the Clio in the harbour car park. The CalMac ferry was disgorging passengers from Skye onto the new pier as gulls arced overhead. Several fishing boats were moored alongside the old wooden pier, crewmen flitting about the decks like canaries in their yellow oilskins. Angus recognised one of the boats as the *Silver Darling*, and sure enough there on deck was Grant Abbot.

He killed the engine and they sat in silence for a long second. "Listen, about the other night . . ."

She placed her hand on top of his. "It's okay, Angus. We don't have to go there. . . ."

"No, I need to explain, Ash. I'm scared, that's all. Scared our child will inherit my bad genes."

She gave his hand a slight squeeze. "Just because your dad has that horrible disease doesn't mean our child will suffer too."

Angus chewed his bottom lip.

She leaned over and kissed him lightly on the cheek. "Come on. Let's get this over with," she whispered.

He stepped out of the Clio and into a salt-scented wind. Ash slipped her arm through his as they walked along the esplanade to the shriek of gulls and the crash of the waves against the seawall. Up ahead, watching the *Silver Darling* prepare to leave for the fishing grounds of the Faroe Bank, was Nualla Abbot. She stood with a baby stroller, her dark hair whipping around her face.

She didn't look around until they were almost beside her. "Nualla," Ash said, placing a hand on her arm.

The woman flinched, as if awoken from a trance. "Ash! God, sorry. I was miles away."

Below, on deck, Grant noticed them and gave a brief wave. Both Angus and Ash returned the gesture. "Good luck, *a'bhalach*!" Angus yelled.

Grant grinned and gave him a thumbs-up.

"Don't worry, Nualla," Ash said. "The time will fly past, and me and the girls will be there. If you want us to look after Rosie or run errands or drink prosecco with you, we're here, okay?"

Nualla sniffed, close to tears. "Thanks, Ash. You're a good pal."

"Don't mention it," Ash said, leaning into the stroller to get a glimpse of baby Rosie. "Ach, she's sleeping, the wee mite."

"Aye, for once," Nualla muttered.

Ash straightened up and gave Nualla a brief hug. "Look, we have to go, but I'll pop in later, okay?"

Nualla's smile looked forced. "Great. I'll see you then."

They left Nualla to her lonely vigil and walked towards the underpass that led to High Street. Angus leaned in towards Ash and kissed her briefly on the cheek. "You're amazing, you know that, right? Even after what happened yesterday, you're still thinking of other people."

"Stop, Angus, you're making me blush." She glanced up at him and smiled for the first time that day. "Ironic, isn't it?" she said. "Here's us on the way to a fertility clinic, and there's Nualla with a beautiful baby girl, but miserable."

Inside the clinic, a receptionist directed them straight to Dr. Morrow's office. She was a no-nonsense sort of woman in her mid-forties with a dry sense of humour that Angus liked a lot. Ash was gripping his hand so tight, it hurt when they entered the office. Dr. Morrow greeted them with a warm smile and directed them into a couple of seats on the other side of her messy desk.

Before she even opened her mouth, Angus knew the procedure had not worked. He'd done enough death knocks to know the signs—the slightly hunched posture, the way sympathy worked on facial muscles. Dr. Morrow clasped her hands on the desk in front of her. "The news is not good, I'm afraid. Fertilization has again been unsuccessful."

CHAPTER 60

"HOW could Christine Kelbie find out about the tunnel? That's what I want to know." Crowley glanced around the police officers assembled in front of the murder board, grey-flecked eyebrows twitching. "Anyone?"

Angus's eyes darted around the room, looking for Nadia. It was unlike her to miss briefing.

Ryan Fleet cleared his throat, but Crowley cut him off before he could speak. "Rylo, if you're going to talk about bum curses again, you can save your breath."

A few of the detectives shared surreptitious glances, trying not to laugh.

"Err, no, that wasn't exactly where I was going, sir."

"Good, then tear away."

"So, we know that Kelbie is originally from the Traveller community. I've looked into their history, and when the clan system dominated the Highlands, they were known as *Ceardannan*, which meant 'smith' or 'craftsperson.' They basically went around fixing weapons and other metal objects. They were highly respected and their skills were no doubt in great demand amongst the warring clans—"

"Aye, thanks for the history lesson," Crowley said. "Any danger of you getting to the point soon?"

"Err, sorry, sir. My point is, the *Ceardannan* were a kind of guild, or a secret society, a bit like the Freemasons."

Boaby Dunbar rolled up the leg of his trouser. "Watch it, young man."

"Let's leave Masonic rituals out of this, Boaby." Crowley grinned. "And I see what you're saying, Rylo. This tunnel could have been secret knowledge passed down for generations. The whatsits"—he clicked his fingers—"the *Ceardannan* might even have helped construct the tunnel. Kelbie could then have used it to sneak in and steal Eleanor's hair for the clay corpse, before coming back to abduct her days or even weeks later."

"Exactly," Ryan said, disappointed Crowley had stolen his thunder.

"There's another possibility," DC Lockhart said. "Kelbie doesn't know about the tunnel because she didn't do it. The hair could have been taken by anyone who knew where she got her hair cut."

Angus thought of the connection Gills had unearthed between the Chichester murders and the others. Kelbie would be well aware of the significance of the dates, but she would have been only a child when the first murder had occurred. Perhaps she was mixed up in some cult linked to the *Ceardannan* that had sacrificed humans to the old gods for decades, only no one had spotted it until now.

"Then why has she run?" Crowley asked, throwing his hands out.

"She's scared of being made a scapegoat."

Crowley tugged at his bottom lip. "Of course, we should keep an open mind. But let's find Kelbie, eh? Get her photo out to the press, Vee."

DS Lockhart nodded. "Will do."

"Where's DI Sharif, by the way?"

"Visiting Dr. MacMurdo," Boaby Dunbar said. "Wanted to pick his brains some more about these old gods and goddesses." He shrugged and took a slug of Diet Irn-Bru.

Angus's expression did not change, but his heart seemed to skip a beat.

"Fine." Crowley sighed. "Right, Boaby's got all your actions. Away you go. We'll reconvene this evening, by which time I want Kelbie in custody."

A lichen-encrusted dyke wandered around the garden of the Old Manse, the stones grizzled and haphazard, a bit like Gills himself. Angus skidded the Land Rover to a stop next to it, beside Nadia's black Audi. He clambered out and yanked open the gate. Ghostly footprints in the snow wended up the garden path towards the front door, which lay slightly ajar.

He followed the footprints but hadn't taken more than a few paces when he heard the sound of barking behind him. He turned and saw Bran and Sceolan tear out of the woods, followed a few seconds later by Gills.

His heart plummeted into his boots. Gills gave him a jaunty wave as the dogs bounded through the gate. Bran pounced up on Angus, affording him a hot blast of dog breath. He disentangled himself from the collie, calming him down with a cursory scratch under the chin. "Where have you been?" he asked Gills.

The old man frowned at the curt tone. "Just out for a wee dander."

"Did you forget to close the door again?"

Gills's eyes flicked to the front of the house. "That's a distinct possibility."

Angus puffed out a frustrated breath. *"Gills!"*

"What? Have I been burgled?"

"No, but that's Nadia's car."

Gills's bushy eyebrows shot up his forehead. "Oh . . . fiddlesticks!"

"Aye, *fiddlesticks*, indeed. Don't suppose you locked the study door?" He was clutching at straws.

"Err . . . no."

Angus closed his eyes and cursed under his breath. Gills slapped a warm hand down on his shoulder. "Don't worry, old bean. DI Sharif will understand."

He gave Angus a tight smile then trudged towards the front door.

Angus turned and followed. "No, she bloody won't," he muttered.

His stomach churned as he crossed the threshold and stood in the eerie stillness of the hall. The dogs had caught Nadia's scent and scuttled into the house past him, nails scratching on the parquet floor. Angus smelt a hint of her perfume, too, the light feminine aroma a counterpoint to the scent of woodsmoke, leather, and wet dog.

The collies made straight for the open door of the study, yipping excitedly. Angus placed a hand on Gills's arm. "Let me go first," he whispered. The old man gave an almost imperceptible nod. Angus brushed past him and walked towards the study on rickety legs. He worked some saliva into his dry mouth, then entered the room.

Nadia stood with her back to him, hands on her hips, ignoring the attention of the dogs. She was staring at Gills's supernatural murder board.

After what felt like an eternity, but in reality was probably less than a second, she turned and stared at him.

He opened his mouth to speak, but she got there first.

"Angus, what the actual *fuck* is this?"

"I . . . can explain," he stammered.

"This better be good, Angus."

Sceolan looked up at him expectantly with his mismatched eyes.

Before he could formulate a response, Gills breezed into the study. "Ah! DI Sharif, what a lovely surprise!" He shrugged off his jacket and threw it aimlessly at a coat stand behind the door, then unwound the checked lambswool scarf from around his neck. "I see you've discovered my *bòrd-murt*. Not bad for an amateur sleuth, eh? Granted, it doesn't have the polish of Detective Chief Inspector Crowley's, but then, he is a professional."

He gave Nadia a wide, dazzling smile. "There really is no cause for concern, my dear. Like Angus said, we can explain everything."

"Where did you get the crime scene photographs? As if I need to ask."

"Would you believe me if I told you I moonlight as a hacker? Mild-mannered academic by day, feared black hat by night."

She glanced at the ancient Apple Mac hunkering on his desk. "On that thing—you couldn't order pizza, never mind hack a police database."

"I shared everything we have on the Chichester case with Gills." Angus sighed. "I thought he could help us."

"I *can* help."

"We'll see," Nadia said. She let out a long, ragged breath, releasing some of the tension in her shoulders. She turned to the *bòrd-murt*. "Okay, the first question I have is this: Why, when only two people have been murdered, do you have six photographs under the 'victims' heading?"

"An excellent question, DI Sharif. Angus, do you want to take this one?"

Angus walked across to the murder board and stood next to Nadia. He pointed at the little boy. "This is Ethan Boyce. He was drowned in the sea near Morar on August the first, five years ago." He traced his finger up the wall to the photograph of the Strangled Woman. "Barbara Klein from Silvaig: killed in some woods on the first of February, six years ago."

His finger moved to the wheelchair-bound man. "Lewis Duncan, a twenty-one-year-old from Arisaig. Died in a house fire on May Day ten years ago."

His hand shook as he pointed at the last photograph. His mother wore the wide-brimmed hat that now mouldered in his attic, dusty and moth-eaten. She stared candidly at the camera, a half-smile on her lips. "Murdered by persons unknown twenty years ago, also on Samhain. Caitlin MacNeil. My mother."

Nadia took a half-step forward and stared at the photograph for a long second. "She has your eyes. Were there ever any suspects?"

He shook his head, the details fresh in his mind from reading the case file last night. "You remember, about six years ago, a guy was killing women in Ayrshire and dumping their bodies in lay-bys?"

"The M74 Ripper?"

"Right. The MO was similar, but it turned out he was living in the States when my mother was killed." He gave a frustrated shrug. "The best the police came up with at the time was some drifter, or a tourist."

Angus decided not to mention the insinuation from the detective all those years ago.

Maybe you should be looking closer to home, son.

It was nonsense anyway. His dad had been away in Inverness when it happened.

"We—Gills and I—think there's a link between these murders and the Chichester case," he said. "All of these victims, including Eleanor and Faye, were killed on important dates in the old Celtic calendar—Samhain, Imbolc, Lughnasadh, and Beltane."

Nadia turned back to the murder board and studied the images, eyes narrowed. "Are you saying the same person is responsible for all these killings?"

Angus turned from the wall, unable to stare at the faces any longer. He slumped down in the retro leather chair. "No," he croaked. "They can't be. Lewis was disabled. His mother was his carer. The consensus was she couldn't cope with looking after him anymore and burned the house down with both of them inside. She had also recently lost a legal case against Agri-Scotia."

"About what?" Nadia asked.

"Agri-Scotia made fertilizers and animal feed. They had a plant near the spring that fed the Duncans' water supply. She claimed Agri-Scotia had let illegal waste seep into her water, and this caused her son's birth defects. The company disputed this and their lawyers got the case tied up in so much red tape, it took years to untangle."

Nadia squinted at the small picture of Elizabeth Duncan, pinned up next to her son. "Poor woman. Losing that case would be enough to push anyone over the edge." She tapped the picture of Barbara Klein.

"What about this one?" "She was killed by her husband, a guy named Joseph Carver," Angus said. "He was last seen getting on a ferry at Ullapool. He didn't get off at Stornoway. His body is somewhere in the Minch. And Ethan was drowned by his father in the sea at Camusdarach." In his head, he saw wild thrashing in cobalt-blue water. He tasted the brine. . . .

"His dad, Jonathan Boyce, was a mild-mannered and well-respected local artist," Gills said, taking up the story. "No one had a clue why he did it. And the police couldn't ask him, because after killing Ethan, he lay down in front of the sleeper train from Glasgow. Similarly, Lewis's mother, Elizabeth, or Betty to her friends, was a kindhearted soul who wouldn't hurt a fly. No one saw it coming."

"Joseph Carver had married Barbara weeks before he killed her," Angus added. "His friends said they were deliriously happy. And there was no suggestion one or the other had cheated. God knows why he did it."

"Jesus," Nadia hissed. "Bloody tragic."

They were silent for a long time, all staring at the faces stuck on the wall.

"The dates are an odd coincidence," Nadia mused.

"And the MO," Gills said. "We have victims who were burned, drowned, or strangled. Now, I've not read their autopsies, but I'm willing to bet they suffered other injuries consistent with a triple death, just like Faye."

Angus met Nadia's stare. "I can check that," she said.

Gills nodded, a faint smile on his lips. "A thread links all these cases, my dear," he declared.

Nadia chewed her bottom lip, again staring at the *bòrd-murt*, as if her eyes were drawn to it. "If there's no way the same person committed all the murders, that could mean two things. One: we've got a copycat, but that seems unlikely, as they'd need to be familiar with the details of the cases, which won't be in the public domain. Or two: Mr. Boyce, Mrs. Duncan, Mr. Carver, and whoever killed your mother, Angus, were all members of some pagan death cult. And so is whoever killed Faye and Eleanor."

CHAPTER 61

LILLY was on the same ward where Angus had recuperated after the knife attack last year. As Ash stepped out of the elevator and walked pass the nurses station, she relived that awful moment when Archie Devine had phoned to say Angus had been injured in the line of duty. She'd thought it was happening all over again, that she was destined to have everyone she loved die. Archie had managed to calm her down a little, but she could still remember that drive to Silvaig General, the currents of despair and anger swirling inside her, bringing all those dark memories to the surface. Memories of the Accident. Blood in her eyes. Dad slumped dead over the steering wheel. Mum trapped like the rabbit Ash had once found caught in a snare. It wasn't until she had seen Angus sitting up in bed that the black dread had subsided.

Likewise, today, it wasn't until she saw Lilly propped up on a mountain of pillows that the tightness in her throat eased. The girl gave Ash a wan smile. She wore a baggy blue hospital gown. Her face was makeup free, making her look much younger than the girl she'd met at Kintail House. Her eyes were red-rimmed but bright. Alive.

Ash placed a box of chocolates and some magazines she'd bought in the hospital newsagent on the cabinet next to the bed. Her eyes flitted to the bandages on Lilly's wrists then back to her face. She smiled and brushed a stray lock of hair behind Lilly's ear. The girl's chin wobbled, tears pooling at the edges of her eyes. "I'm sorry, Ashleigh. I—"

Ash took her gently by the hand. "Shhh!" she soothed. "It's okay. You don't have to explain."

Ash lowered herself into the visitors chair. "How do you feel?"

Lilly glanced away. "Weak," she mumbled.

"That's to be expected. But your strength will return. The doctors—"

"I don't mean physically," Lilly cut in.

Ash searched out her eyes. She understood Lilly's sense of hopelessness, because she had worn that cloak too. Her response had been to lash out, to blame other people, or when her anger couldn't be personified, to blame the world or fate or God.

"I've been where you are, Lilly," Ash said. "I wanted to smash everything to smithereens. So I'm not going to sit here and tell you everything's going to be easy. Life isn't easy. But you have to fight, Lilly."

Ash took a handkerchief from her pocket and dabbed Lilly's eyes. "Because believe me, Lilly, if you do, then one day—in ten, fifteen years—you'll be lying on a beach somewhere, or launching your own company, or . . ."

"I don't know if I'm strong enough, Ash."

"Neither do I. But I believe in you, Lilly. There's a fire inside you."

Like there was inside me.

Ash squeezed her hand. "And I'll be here to help you. I promise, okay?"

Lilly gave a tremulous smile, sniffing back tears.

"And the first thing I'm going to do is get you some decent clothes from Kintail House."

Lilly gave a hiccuppy laugh. "And maybe some makeup?" the girl said.

The carpet in Lilly's room squelched under Ashleigh's feet as she entered, a small suitcase gripped in her hand. The door to the en suite hung open, the tiled floor now dry and mercifully free of bloodstains. She stared at the big freestanding bath where Lilly had lain. In her head she saw Lilly's pale face, the skinny arm dangling over the side of the bath. Her fingernails had been painted bubble-gum pink, the lacquer chipped and flaky. The cuts on her wrist had been a deep crimson.

Ash choked back tears, not just for the pain Lilly must have felt, but for the children she would never have. After the news from the clinic, she had felt hollow inside, like one of the pumpkins she had watched the schoolchildren carve at the fayre in the village hall a week ago. A simulacrum of a human being.

Of course, she would slap on a brave face. Christ, she'd been doing that her whole life. She was a strong, independent woman—wasn't that what Granny Beag always told her? Why, then, did she feel so insubstantial? As if she could melt away like the snowman on the lawn outside Kintail House.

At length, she turned away from the en suite and placed the suitcase on Lilly's bed. The mattress was softer than the one she had lain on, but the bed frame looked to be the same. She wiggled the bed out from the wall a few inches and examined the back of the timber headboard. Sure enough, the words she had carved with a knife stolen from the canteen were still there: "FUCK THE WORLD."

Hardly the most original statement, but it had neatly encapsulated how she'd felt back then. Ash shoved the bed back against the wall and lowered herself onto the mattress. She'd overcome that sense of hopelessness, but every so often she had what Granny Beag would term "a wobble."

She shook the thought from her head and stood with a sense of purpose. She flipped the case open and packed a selection of comfy clothes, underwear, socks, and pyjamas. Next she walked to the en suite, her gaze directed away from the bath, and lifted Lilly's toothbrush, a makeup bag, and a hairbrush.

The case full, she took one last look around the bedroom and left. The corridors of Kintail House were quiet as a morgue. A sense of shock seemed to hang in the air, so tangible that Ash could almost taste it. She could still smell the copper-pennies scent of blood. She quickened her pace, suddenly claustrophobic, as if the insipid mint-green walls were closing in on her.

By the time she reached the lobby, a sheen of cold sweat clung to her forehead. Big Mo was hunched behind the reception desk, a large tub of Cadbury Celebrations at her elbow. The warden's face did not scream "celebration," however. Her eyes were underhung with saggy dark bags of flesh. Chocolate wrappers were scattered around her like shrapnel from an exploded bomb. She glanced up at Ash and gave a sad smile. Her teeth were coated in chocolate. "How are ye, pet?" she asked.

She lowered the case to the floor. "I'm okay," she lied.

"Aye, you were always a tough wee cookie."

"Why did she do it, Mo? She seemed like a sensible girl."

The warden tore open another chocolate and stuffed it into her mouth. "Ach, who knows? She had a terrible start in life. Maybe it's too simplistic to blame the parents, but they have to take some responsibility, in my mind. They were both heroin addicts. The father left and the boyfriend who replaced him was a right bastard—used to beat up Lilly and her mum. The police thought he was pimping her out for drug money. Turned out, it wasn't just Lilly's mum the men were coming to see."

Ash gritted her teeth, anger coursing through her body. "Jesus Christ! How could you do that?"

"The world's full of sickos," Mo said, chewing morosely. "Most of them are men, although us women aren't entirely innocent. But you'll know that better than most."

"What's that supposed to mean?" Ash said, bristling.

Mo glanced up, a miniature Twix halfway to her maw. "Och, I don't mean you, pet. I just mean that it can't be easy, knowing your own mother abandoned you."

At first Ash wondered if she'd heard the warden correctly. "You've got that wrong, Mo. My parents died in a car crash."

Big Mo's face blanched. She looked at the Twix held between her thick fingers, then back at Ash. "Aye, that's right," she said, popping the chocolate into her mouth.

"So why did you say I was abandoned?"

Big Mo concentrated on masticating the Twix, but her eyes darted around furtively, unable to meet Ash's glare.

"Mo, what did you mean?" Her voice was almost a growl.

After an unbearable pause, the warden looked up. Her sympathetic smile mirrored the doctor's at the clinic the previous day. "Your mum and dad did die in a car crash, but they were your adoptive parents."

Ash gripped the lip of the reception desk. Her legs felt wobbly, as if she'd been sitting in the pub drinking all afternoon and had then tried to stand. "So who were my real parents?" she said, her voice barely audible.

Big Mo's mullet hardly moved when she shook her head. "No one knows. You were a foundling, pet. Your mother abandoned you in the ruins of Cille Bharra chapel on the island of Barra. Some tourists found you lying in front of the Kilbar Stone. You'd been left there overnight. In winter."

Big Mo reached forward and placed a big paw on Ash's hand. Mo's fingers were warm and sticky, and Ash had to resist the temptation to snatch her hand away.

"It's a miracle you survived," Big Mo said.

A scummy film had settled on the mug of tea that sat untouched on the coffee table in front of her. The woodburner roared, the flames casting dancing fingers of light on the walls of the snug room. Ash was on the couch, legs drawn up, arms wrapped around her knees. She stroked the smooth skin of her left wrist with the pad of her right thumb, as if trying to reassure herself that she existed. The origin story she'd told herself growing up—the idyllic loving family snatched away from her—was a myth. She'd never had a family. She'd simply emerged, a miracle child, as if from the earth itself.

She heard Angus pull up in the Land Rover, the glow from the vehicle's headlights strobing around the darkened room. A surge of relief shuddered through her. She did not want to be alone tonight. She slid off the couch and flicked on a table lamp. She caught a glimpse of herself in the mirror above the fireplace and almost flinched. She hardly recognised the woman staring back at her. She raised a hand to her pale cheek and traced the contour of her jawline, then brought a fingertip up to her bottom lip. She pressed the pliable flesh against her teeth, then let her hand fall to her side. She stared into her unfathomable greyish-blue eyes. "Who the fuck *are* you?" she asked.

The sound of the door opening cut short her moment of self-reflection. She turned away from the mirror as Angus entered. He walked over to her and took her in his arms. She closed her eyes and breathed in his smell, which always reminded her of the outdoors—of gorse, oak moss, and the sea. He kissed the top of her head and gently massaged the small of her back. "How are you, *a ghràidh?*"

Her automatic response—that she was fine—died in her throat. She felt something dislodge in her stomach, like the dead leaves Granny Beag had scraped from the guttering of her house. Tears began to flow. All the anger, grief, and frustration of the past week gushed out of her in a torrent of great racking sobs. She clutched onto Angus as if he were a tree trunk in a flood, her hands gripping his clothes and twisting them into her fists. He held her tight, cradling her in his arms and murmuring gently to her as she wept.

Ash did not know how long they stood there, entwined, like victims of the Pompeii volcano, frozen together by the thermal shock. At length, she peeled herself off his chest and glanced up at him with glassy eyes.

"I went back to Kintail House today," she said.

"Ach, Ash. Why put yourself through that?"

"I wanted to get some clothes for Lilly."

"I could have done that, love."

"I know, I know. . . ." She squeezed his hand and gave a watery smile. "I found out something when I was there. About myself. And it kind of freaked me out."

His eyes never left her face as she told him what Big Mo had said.

When she was done, he brushed a stray strand of hair out of her eyes and kissed her gently on the lips. "So you're a Barra lass." He smiled. "Could be worse—you could come from Eriskay," he said. "They're a bunch of six-toed knuckle draggers according to my grandad Alec."

She pulled him towards her and pressed her lips to his. "I love you, Angus," she murmured. "You're all I have."

CHAPTER 62

A haar had drifted in from the Atlantic, clinging to the rugged coast and making it look as though Dunbirlinn were floating on mist. Like the giant's castle in *Jack and the Beanstalk*. His mother used to read him the fairy tale in bed as a child. He smiled faintly, remembering how she would put on all the different characters' voices, and how she'd pounce on him and tickle his ribs when the giant thundered the famous line—*I'll grind your bones to make my bread!*

It was strange to think Ashleigh was from Barra. He wondered if his mother had known about the baby discovered in the ruined chapel, or whether it had been covered up. Surely the authorities on the island had tried to find Ashleigh's birth mother? The population of Barra was only 1,700. In a small community like that, keeping a pregnancy secret would be difficult but not impossible. Or was Ashleigh's mother from the mainland? Perhaps, like the plot of some Victorian novel, she had travelled to Barra to have her child in secret and hide her family's shame. No wonder Ash had been distraught. It was such a cruel irony—after being told she could not have children, she'd discovered her own parents had left her for dead as a baby. Ash, though, was strong; she'd had to be, growing up. After the tears of last night, she'd seemed renewed somehow this morning, like a bud appearing after a torrent of rain. They would try again with the IVF. Ash would never give up.

He eased his foot off the accelerator as the gates for Dunbirlinn emerged from the mist. A small knot of protesters still held vigil outside, placards clutched in gloved hands. He felt the familiar flutter of apprehension in his chest as he drove through the gates. The laird had not yet been grilled about the tunnel. That morning Crowley had assigned them the unenviable task of asking him, ever so delicately, if he'd had anything to do with Eleanor's murder.

In the passenger seat, Nadia was flicking through the old case files for the murders of Lewis, Barbara, Ethan, and his mother.

"So, do they contain anything interesting?" he asked.

"Didn't have time to read them all last night," she said. "But I did take a look at the postmortem reports on all four victims. To cut a long story short, I think you and Gills might be onto something. Lewis Duncan's body was too badly burned to draw any conclusions, but Barbara Klein fits the pattern. She was killed next to a river: struck on the head, then strangled, and her hair was wet, as if her head had been submerged. They didn't make anything of it at the time."

She glanced at Angus, suddenly hesitant.

"It's okay," he said. "I can handle it."

"The cause of your mother's death was definitely strangulation, but she was also bludgeoned. That said, the differences are as notable as the similarities. I suppose the pattern could reflect a fledgling killer perfecting his technique."

"Aye, that's what I thought."

She frowned a question at him.

"I have a copy of the case file, Nadia. Of course I do."

"Aye," Nadia murmured. "Anyway, these deaths weren't obviously ritualistic to the officers investigating at the time, so it's easy to see how strangulation or blunt force trauma didn't take on any special meaning."

He nodded, eyes staring dead ahead into the mist.

"Which only leaves the wee boy," Nadia said, moving on quickly. "Angus, why didn't you tell me you were there? That you tried to save him?"

He squeezed the steering wheel, saw one hand on top of the other, pumping at the boy's chest. He felt a brief, yet sharp, desire to share everything with Nadia, to do now what he should have done in Tulliallan—to let her into his secret. "It's still raw, even after all these years. I still see him in my . . . dreams. He begs me to save him. I keep going back over everything I did that day. What if I'd taken less time in the shower? Or if the queue at the shop hadn't been so long? Or I hadn't stopped to chat with Grant Abbot? Precious time wasted."

"You can't think like that, Angus," Nadia said softly. "It'll drive you mad. You did save him from what could have been a triple death."

"How do you mean?"

"I checked the inventory of Jonathan Boyce's possessions. Before he lay down on the railway track, he took off his coat for some reason."

Just as I had, Angus thought.

"In his pocket they found a knife and a ligature. They were both photographed, and the ligature looks exactly like the one the killer used on Faye. It was even knotted in three places."

"Jesus!" Angus hissed. "Was it ever analysed?"

"No, presumably, the SIO decided there was no point, as it was never used in the crime. But what's the bet it was also made of sinew?"

"We can test it, right? It's still in storage somewhere?"

Nadia grinned. "Already on it."

"Have you mentioned any of this to Crowley?" Angus asked.

Nadia shook her head. "If the lab comes back and tells me the ligature found in Jonathan Boyce's pocket is sinew, then I'll go to Ruthven. In the meantime, we try to find a link between the killers."

"Which reminds me," he said. "I finished going through the personnel files from Dunbirlinn last night. It was a waste of time, but there was one coincidence: Lewis Duncan's mother—Betty—worked here, at Dunbirlinn. According to the records, she was employed as a cleaner for almost two years."

He clattered the Land Rover through the gatehouse and into the courtyard. He pulled up next to Chichester's Aston Martin.

"Did Joseph Carver or Jonathan Boyce have links to Dunbirlinn?" Nadia asked.

"Not that I know of. Their names weren't in the personnel files. Betty's been dead ten years. Even if she had discovered the tunnel while working here, she couldn't be involved in Eleanor's murder."

"True. Anything else in the files?"

"Nah, like I said, waste of time. A contractor undertook the renovation work years ago. Trying to track down all the tradesmen who worked here would be almost impossible."

"Speaking of renovation," Nadia said, "I tracked down the art-restoration company that Mrs. MacCrimmon mentioned—the one that used the chapel? It was a local firm called Ossian Fine Arts."

"Aye, I know it," he said. "Didn't know they did art restoration, too. They have a gallery in Shaggers' Alley."

Nadia laughed for the first time that day. "Shaggers' Alley?"

"Frequented by amorous couples after the disco," he explained, grinning. "It might be worth a visit—the gallery that is, not the alley."

Nadia gave him a playful punch on the arm. "Aye, after we speak to Chichester."

The smile fell from his lips. "You don't think Chichester—"

"I don't know, Angus," she said, cutting him off. "He was here when Eleanor was snatched. We only have his word for it that he left her lying passed out in the drawing room before he went to bed."

They climbed from the Land Rover and walked towards the great iron-studded door. Before they reached them, the doors cracked open and Mrs. MacCrimmon shooed them inside with a tired grimace. "The laird is in the library," she said. "Please don't upset him. The poor man's been through enough, don't you think?" The housekeeper worried at the silver wolf-headed broach on her lapel as she led them across the lobby.

"Don't worry, Mrs. MacCrimmon, we'll be gentle," Nadia said.

"I'm concerned about him. Usually he's running around like a man possessed, but since yesterday he's just been sitting there in front of the fire. Refuses all food. Barely drinks."

They passed under the unerring gaze of Dòmhnall MacRuari, *an Draoidh*. Angus felt the chieftain's eyes follow him from the painting as they left the lobby and snaked through the passages and corridors of Dunbirlinn to the library. Mrs. MacCrimmon knocked. Then, when there was no answer, she tentatively pushed open the door. She cleared her throat. "DI Sharif and Constable MacNeil here to see you, Laird," she said.

Chichester was slumped in a wingback chair, staring into the dying embers of a log fire. He twisted his head slightly and locked eyes with Angus.

"Thank you, Mary," he rasped.

The housekeeper turned, flashed Angus an anxious look, then left. He followed Nadia across the library, eyes taking in the rows and rows of books. Had Chichester read them all? The MacRuari family tree, he noticed, had been taken down. A ghostly pale rectangle on the wall marked where it had once hung. He returned his attention to the laird. Despite his slumped posture and all that he'd gone through, Chichester still looked robust. The hands that gripped the armrests looked strong, and his skin retained that healthy tanned complexion Angus had noted on their first meeting. His eyes, though, looked washed out, the verdigris colour fading to an algae-green patina.

"Angus Dubh, good to see you."

He gave a polite nod. "James Glas."

"And DI Sharif. Please sit."

He lowered himself onto the antique sofa next to Nadia. "How are you holding up, sir?"

"About as well as can be expected in the circumstances, Angus."

"Mrs MacCrimmon is worried about you."

Chichester barked a humourless laugh. "Mary thinks she's my mother."

"We just wanted to . . . update you on what we found," Nadia said.

"I heard. A tunnel leading from the chapel to the MacRuari crypt. Quite remarkable."

"We think this is how your wife's abductor managed to snatch her while evading the CCTV cameras out front."

Chichester's eyes returned to the glowing embers in the fireplace. "Seems a natural conclusion."

"We have to ask," Angus said. "Did you know about the tunnel?"

Chichester appeared not to hear the question. "Legend has it this castle is haunted by the ghost of my ancestor, the Druid," he said. "Sometimes I fancy I hear him striding through the corridors, barking instructions to his servants in a strange language. I've read about a Gaelic-based cant that has since died out. Perhaps that was his native tongue? Lost now, like so much . . ."

Angus glanced at Nadia, who cocked an eyebrow. "Mr Chichester . . . James," he said, "did you know about the tunnel?"

"What secrets the walls of Dunbirlinn must have heard over the centuries," Chichester continued, again ignoring the question. "Betrayals, rebellion, illicit affairs—all history in the making. But the powerful always fall in the end. Always."

Angus reached forward and placed a tentative hand on the laird's shoulder. Despite sitting in front of a roaring fire, Chichester was cold to the touch. "James, we were asking you about the tunnel. Did you know about it?"

The laird seemed to snap out of the trance he was in. "Ergo, did I kill my wife?" he muttered.

Angus removed his hand from the laird's shoulder, but his eyes remained on Chichester. James Glas turned his head slightly and stared straight at Angus, the movement somehow reminding him of the way the alpha female had glanced up at him from the wolf enclosure. But rather than the wolf's cold feral glare, Angus again saw only loss and despair in the laird's eyes.

"No," Chichester said simply. "I had no clue about the tunnel. And I did not kill my wife."

Angus held his stare. "I'm sorry, James. We had to ask."

Chichester gave a slight nod.

"One other thing," Angus said. "Do you remember a woman named Elizabeth Duncan, known as Betty? She used to work as a cleaner at Dunbirlinn."

Chichester dismissed the question with a wave of his hand. "Mrs MacCrimmon deals with all that."

"Fair enough," he said. "What about the name Joseph Carver or Jonathan Boyce? Ring any bells?"

Angus watched Chichester's expression intently but saw no flicker of recognition in his eyes. "No. Should they?"

"Probably not." He glanced at Nadia and together they stood. "We're sorry for disturbing you," she said.

Chichester nodded, his gaze sliding back to the embers in the fireplace.

"We'll show ourselves out," she said.

"Not sure that got us anywhere," Nadia said as they settled back inside the Land Rover. Angus slid the key into the ignition. The engine gave a frustrated growl as he reversed out of the parking space and powered across the courtyard.

"I believed him," he said. "I don't think he knew about the tunnel. And he didn't recognise those names either."

"Or he's an accomplished liar."

He was about to respond when Nadia's mobile phone rang. She snatched it up and glanced at the screen. "Crowley," she told him, before answering. "What's up, sir?"

Angus watched her out of the side of his eye as he drove out of the grounds of Dunbirlinn. A few protesters lingered at the gates, shivering.

"Okay," Nadia said. "That's good, right?"

Angus could not hear what Crowley was saying, but a smile crept across Nadia's face.

She cut the call, and turned towards him. "Christine Kelbie's been spotted by a member of the public in a Co-op on Skye. She left the shop and got into a beat-up camper van, heading north out of Portree. Local plod are on her tail. In the meantime, we might as well check out this gallery. Could do with a nice painting for my flat."

The bright front window of Ossian Fine Arts was hung with paintings and crafts by local artists. Only now did he notice a smaller sign advertising "top-quality art-restoration services."

He glanced at the discreet black door of Glenda Wright Associates. He'd hated going there, but strangely he was now almost looking forward to his next session with the therapist. His mind ran to Ash. She was unmoored from her past and her hopes for a future with children of her own dashed. He didn't like the idea of her seeing the same therapist, but surely speaking to someone would help. Perhaps Glenda could give him a name of someone for Ash.

A bell above the door jangled as they entered the gallery, reminding Angus of the bookshop in Glenruig. That, however, was about the only comparison to Lachlan Campbell's disordered and cramped store. Ossian Fine Arts was as bright as a summer's day, the white walls hung with colourful paintings of the west coast in varying styles, from realistic to abstract. A wrought-iron staircase spiralled up to a mezzanine level, where shelves of artists' materials were on display: blank canvases, sketch pads, brushes, pastels, easels, and tubes of paint.

A small counter seemed to float in the air towards the rear of the shop. Behind the counter a raffish-looking man of around fifty perched on a stool, eyes glued to a MacBook. He glanced up when Angus and Nadia approached, treating them to a flash of expensive dental work. He slid off the stool and came out from behind the counter. He wore a plum-coloured suit, a natty Paisley shirt open at the neck, and shiny leather loafers with a double buckle, the type of shoes his father used to refer to as "brothel creepers."

"Afternoon, just in for a browse?" he asked in a faux posh accent.

Nadia flashed her warrant card. "Are you the owner?"

"Indeed. Rob Cunnigham-Graham, at your service." He gave a slight bow, complete with hand flourish.

"DI Sharif, and this is my colleague Constable MacNeil."

Angus gave the man a blank-faced nod.

"We'd like to ask you about some restoration work you carried out a few years ago on paintings at Dunbirlinn Castle."

"Ah yes! Quite the commission for our modest business."

"How did that come about?"

"The laird himself came into the gallery one day and asked if we'd be interested. His offer was . . . generous, shall we say."

"Did you undertake the work yourself?"

"Oh gosh, no!" Rob said, pressing a hand to his heart. "That's way too technical for me. No, my talents lie in sales and marketing."

"So who carried out the actual restoration work?"

"I have a team of specialists that I call on as and when needed. Some are artists in their own right who do restoration as a sideline, while others only do restoration. If I remember correctly, we had three people on the Dunbirlinn job. I can check."

He returned behind the counter and began tapping the laptop, his fingers lightning fast. "Ah yes, here we are," he said. "We restored twelve paintings. The majority of the work was done by Susie and Guido van Cleef, a delightful couple from Edinburgh. One painting was restored by . . . oh, of course! JoBo!"

Nadia raised a questioning eyebrow. "JoBo?"

"The infamous Jonathan Boyce," Rob said, smile faltering. "JoBo was how he signed his paintings, in a futile attempt to replicate Jolomo. His work was derivative, too. Although it sells for a fortune now after . . . well, after what he did—"

Angus glanced at Nadia, but her face was still.

"You do know what he did?" Rob asked.

"Aye, we know," Angus replied.

The gallery owner shuddered. "People can be so ghoulish. One of his paintings that used to hang in this gallery came up for auction a couple of years ago. Went for a six-figure sum. I sold it for ninety-five pounds. Can you believe it? Ninety-five pounds!"

But you're not bitter, Angus thought. "Did you know Jonathan Boyce well?"

"Fairly. He was something of cliché—the *tortured artiste* whom nobody understands. He suffered from bouts of depression where he moped around drinking whisky, without washing or shaving, let alone painting. These sometimes lasted for weeks, but then, all of a sudden, he'd snap out of it and start on another project with manic intensity. I'd go into his studio and find him dashing paint on a canvas, his eyes bright as buttons. *This is the one, Robbie*, he used to say. *This is the one that will make them sit up and notice me.* It never was, though. Unfortunately, his talent didn't match his expectations."

Rob gave a sad shake of his head. "Jonathan was obsessed with gaining acceptance from the establishment. He wanted not just to belong, but to be feted and adored. He lurched from bombastic overconfidence to paralyzing self-doubt and insecurity. In many ways, he was like a child showing off. He demanded constant reassurance that he was a great painter. No, not just great—brilliant. A once-in-a-generation talent."

The gallery owner rolled his eyes, as if he'd met this type of character too many times to count. "Like the vast majority of us, Jonathan was distinctly average. When I heard what he'd done to his poor child, I was shocked but not really surprised. For someone like Jonathan, infamy would be infinitely better than obscurity."

The wretched will make bargains with demons. . . .

"Did Jonathan ever mention being part of something, like a secret society?" Nadia asked.

Rob looked at her as if she'd suggested JoBo could walk on water. "No, why do you ask?"

Nadia gave an innocent shrug.

"You said Mr. Boyce only restored one painting at Dunbirlinn," Angus said. "Do you have a record of which one?" Rob glared at them both for a second before returning his eyes to the laptop. "Yes, here we are. It was a large portrait entitled *an Draoidh*."

He looked up at Angus and gave a white-toothed grin. "Whatever the heck that means."

CHAPTER 63

ANGUS was creeping past Stout's office in Silvaig Police Station when he felt a tap on his shoulder. Heart sinking, he turned, but rather than Stout, Archie Devine stood there, smirking. "At ease, Gus," the big man said. "Inspector Useless is away fishing." He clapped Angus on the shoulder and stomped away.

Angus scuttled over to his workstation and booted up his computer. Stout could still be back any minute to hassle him about the Knicker Snatcher, so he had to work quickly. Thankfully, violent death was rare in the Highlands. Only two murders had occurred in the ten-year period between his mother's death and Lewis Duncan's. One was committed in a drunken fight outside a nightclub in Silvaig, whilst the other was a domestic—a wife stabbing her abusive husband in the heart. Neither had ritualistic overtones.

As Angus accessed the missing persons database, he pondered the limitations of his task. If the nascent victim of a threefold death had, for example, ended up in the sea, they might never be found. Alternatively, their injuries could be explained as the work of a ship's propeller, or their body might be so badly decomposed that no conclusion could be drawn.

Putting his doubts aside, Angus again adjusted the search options to show only people who had vanished in that ten-year window. Looking back, he thought how dark that period of his life had been. He gave a bitter laugh. Since his mother's death, there'd only been shades of black. Those teenage years, though, had been particularly tough. His father's grief and rage had galvanized into a kind of nihilism, poisoning his mind before early dementia had completed the job.

The results of his search appeared almost instantly. Only twelve people had disappeared and, reading between the lines, he discovered that three of them were young men who had almost certainly taken their own lives. Angus was well aware the Highlands had one of the highest suicide rates in Scotland. A couple of days ago he'd almost become a statistic himself.

He shook away the thought and concentrated on the other nine missing people. Two he discounted straightaway, both visitors from down south who had disappeared whilst hiking. The mountains didn't always give up their dead. As Gills said, they were home to giants.

Another couple appeared to be classic examples of teenagers running away to London, whilst a further case had all the hallmarks of a young thug fleeing a drug debt. That left four people—two men, two women, each disappearance approximately two years apart. Of these, one case in particular sent a shiver down his spine. It concerned a twenty-one-year-old apprentice mechanic named Arthur Gillespie. He'd been missing for twelve years. His parents had always maintained he would never run out on them, and his partner at the time—a Simon Cooper—had been so distraught, he killed himself. That coincidence was reason enough for Angus to sit up and take notice, but then he saw the date of Arthur's disappearance—November the first. Samhain.

The lunchtime rush had passed, leaving the Jac-O-bite almost empty, tables strewn with used plates and cups. Angus and Nadia sidestepped the replica of the Highland warrior and slid into a window booth opposite Gills, who had come into Silvaig to meet them for coffee.

"Scones?" he asked.

Nadia shrugged off her coat and hung it on a peg at the end of the booth. "Aye, and a bucket of coffee."

A waitress bustled over and took their order. Angus wiped his sleeve against the window, clearing a patch in the condensation. Across the street from the café, a queue was forming outside Hutton & Sons, the butchers who had supplied Dunbirlinn Castle. He saw the pink meats glistening in the window and looked away.

"So, I have a theory about the white horse," Gills said.

"Shocker," Angus remarked.

Gills ignored the sarcasm. "Now, I'm not surprised DCI Crowley would conclude the horse that you discovered at the pagan commune was a different animal to Faye's horse. Stands to reason. Brown horses don't suddenly turn white. Although there is such a thing as Marie Antoinette syndrome. Either of you heard of it?"

Both Angus and Nadia gave him a blank stare.

"The French queen's hair supposedly turned white before her execution in 1793. Something similar occurred before Mary, Queen of Scots, was beheaded a couple of centuries earlier, or so an eyewitness account testifies. Now, this may just be a literary trope, but it's one repeated in various Highland folktales. Interestingly, it is often a horse or dog that turns white in these folktales. The cause, invariably, is the animal being subjected to some momentous supernatural terror."

Such as seeing her owner butchered by someone possessed by a demon.

Gills's bristly eyebrows twitched upwards, giving him the look of a wise old owl. "However, rather than the horse's coat turning white, it was the fact she was covered in blood that got me thinking. It *was* Faye's blood, correct?"

Angus glanced at Nadia. "Aye."

"Clearly, this suggests that after the first part of the ritual was enacted, Faye was placed on horseback," Gills said. "I believe this initial phase would have occurred at a sacred site, probably the clootie tree. After this, Faye's body would have been lashed onto the horse and led to the shore on a predetermined, processional route. There's a distant echo of this in a local folk custom called the Riding of the *Banrigh Dubh*. It involved the effigy of the Black Queen being rode through villages while inhabitants jeered and threw stones and rubbish at her. Later, the Banrigh Dubh was replaced with an unjust lord, but the ancient roots are all too clear—the Black Queen is a scapegoat character. She is an aristocrat upon whom the people place all their misfortunes and who is then ritually killed as a divine victim. Oh, and here's the clincher—the custom took place around Samhain."

"That could also explain why there were no footprints in the sand around Faye's body," Nadia said. "The horse could have been led around the headland. Time it right, and the body could have been deposited on the beach with the killer and the horse standing in the shallows. They would then have returned using the same route, all the while walking in the water to avoid leaving traces."

The conversation was interrupted by the waitress appearing with their coffee and scones. As Nadia set about spreading her scone with butter and jam, Angus filled Gills in on what he and Nadia had discovered—the echoes of threefold death in the historic cases: the garrotte found in Jonathan Boyce's possessions, as well as the fact that Lewis Duncan's mother had worked in Dunbirlinn, and Boyce had restored the picture of Dòmhnall MacRuari.

"Chichester told us he sheltered from a storm in the exact cave where the Druid and his kin were trapped and suffocated," Angus said. "He was delirious with the cold, and had this epiphany."

"What sort of epiphany?"

"That he would reintroduce wolves."

"Interesting," Gills said, eyes narrowing.

"What did this Druid character do to earn such a bad rep?" Nadia asked.

Gills appeared lost in thought.

"Gills?" Angus said, raising his eyebrows.

"What? Ah yes, the Druid. Well, it's difficult to separate fact from legend, but they say he liked to flay his rivals, or boil them alive in huge vats of oil. Some sources even claim he ate prisoners, like a West Highland version of Sawney Bean. Even allowing for a deal of exaggeration, Dòmhnall was a feared and brutal warlord. Then, of course, there are his associations with the old gods, which gave birth to his moniker—*an Draoidh*."

Gills grinned at Nadia, warming to his theme. "Dòmhnall was a semidivine figure, my dear, like the Irish warrior Cú Chulainn or the Sumerian king Gilgamesh or Hercules or the pharaohs of ancient Egypt."

"Aye, but to return to the matter at hand," Angus said. "I've been looking for other cases that we could have missed."

"Other murders?" Nadia asked.

"Yeah, but there aren't any. Unlike Glaswegians, we're not lawless savages up here." He gave her a thin smile. "But there are a few missing person cases that gave me pause for thought. One in particular—a young guy called Arthur Gillespie who disappeared without a trace twelve years ago. His partner killed himself soon after."

"Sounds familiar," Gills commented.

"Aye, and so will the date of Arthur's disappearance. November the first."

"Samhain," Gills said.

They were silent for a long minute. "That's another eerie coincidence," Nadia said eventually. "But without a body, it's complete speculation."

"True," Angus replied, "and here's another piece of speculation—could Dunbirlinn be the common thread between the killers? Betty Lewis worked there; Mr. Boyce worked there. Which only leaves Joseph Carver. The case file said he worked as a delivery driver. Did they say what he delivered?"

Nadia shook her head.

"Inspector Stout would know," Angus said. "He's a pain in the proverbial, but he's worked in this town for thirty-odd years. He knows everyone."

"Give him a call then."

He hesitated. Stout would only harangue him about the Knicker Snatcher and other trivial cases. "Fine." He sighed, taking his phone from his pocket. He placed the call and waited as it rang and rang. Eventually Stout picked up. "Ah, if it isn't the myth, the legend, Angus MacNeil! I'd almost given up on you."

"Aye, well, as you know, I've been working the Chichester case."

"Told you to leave that to the big boys. What's happening with the Knicker Snatcher?"

He closed his eyes and resisted the urge to lob his phone across the café. "It's in hand. Listen, sir, I'm calling because I need your help. Your knowledge of Silvaig is second to none."

He raised an eyebrow at Nadia. Nothing wrong with buttering up the inspector.

"I was wondering if you remember a case a few years back—guy called Joseph Carver, killed his wife then disappeared."

"Took a swan dive from the Stornoway ferry, didn't he?"

"That was never confirmed, but aye, that's the case I mean."

"What about him? Has he turned up?"

"No, nothing like that. I was just wondering if you recall what he worked as?"

"He was a delivery driver."

"Aye, but what did he deliver?"

Stout sucked air between his teeth. "Now you're asking. Fish maybe, or chickens . . . no, hang on a minute—he worked for a butchers."

Angus felt as if someone had opened the café door, letting in an icy wind. "Which butchers?" he asked, already knowing the answer.

"The only decent one in Silvaig—Hutton & Sons."

A thin man wearing a hairnet and a grubby bloodstained apron hacked at a hunch of beef with a seven-inch cleaver. Around him, other workers traded banter as they produced sausages and filled crates with orders for nearby restaurants—piles of burgers, chicken Marylands, and thick sirloin steaks. The smell of blood and raw meat hung in the air.

"That's him there," said a young counter assistant, pointing Angus and Nadia towards the thin man. As it was police business, they'd left Gills in the café across the road.

"Gordy! Hey, Gordy!" the assistant yelled.

The butcher turned round: pointy cheekbones, dimpled chin, and a Burt Reynolds moustache. Darting, suspicious eyes.

"These detectives want tae ask you about Joe," the young lad said.

Gordy buried the cleaver in the chopping board with a deft flick of his wrist. He folded his arms. "Oh, aye?"

Angus glanced at the cleaver. Slithers of flesh clung to the blade.

The wretched will make bargains with demons. . . .

"Is there somewhere private we can talk?" Nadia asked.

Gordy gave her a once-over, a bit too obviously for Angus's liking. 'C'mon then."

He led them up a tight flight of stairs, past rooms where hot food was being prepared, and into a storeroom-cum-staff-room.

He grabbed a plastic chair, spun it round, and straddled it, muscled forearms wrestling on the back. "So, you want to know about Joe? After all these years?"

"We asked around downstairs," Angus said. "They say you and Joseph Carver were best pals?"

"Aye, we stayed in the same block of flats. Went to school together, played fitba together, did pretty much everything together."

"And you worked here together too?"

"Aye, but it was only a temporary gig for Joe. He wasnae like me—he was clever, wanted to start his own business."

"Doing what?"

"Whisky tours." Gordy grinned. "I'm mair of a vodka man myself, but Joe loved his whisky. What he didn't know about a malt wasnae worth knowing." His smile faded, and Angus noticed a flicker of emotion in his eyes. "Joe's plan was to create a whisky trail, a luxury trip all around the island and the West Highland distilleries—Skye, Tiree, Jura, Tobermory. A bespoke experience, as he called it. The Yank and Japanese tourists would have lapped it up. Barbs and him had it all worked out. They'd drawn up a business plan, and had got funding from Highlands and Islands Enterprise."

Gordy examined his bloody fingertips. "That's what I never understood. Joe and Barbs were solid. Not long married. Never argued. And the business was going places." He glanced up at Angus and Nadia. "So why did he do it?"

Angus cleared his throat. "Gordy, we believe Joe delivered to Dunbirlinn?"

"Aye. As it happens, it was the laird who got him into fancy whisky."

"Chichester?" Angus's voice shot up an octave. "Are you sure?"

"Aye. He met Chichester while delivering and they got round to discussing whisky. After that he was always dropping into conversation that he was pals with the laird. It was all *James says this* and *When I was up at the castle with James. . . .*" Gordy shook his head in disgust. "I used to rip the pish out of him about it, but Joe always was a social climber. He hated that he came from a rough housing estate, hated having nae money and a mum who cleaned toilets for a living. Joe thought too much. You have tae make the best with what you've got, eh?"

His eyes darted between Angus and Nadia, as if daring them to contradict him.

"Anyway," he said, when no challenge was forthcoming, "I mind Joe telling me that the laird took him into the castle once and let him try this really expensive malt. Cannae remember what it was—"

"Macallan 1926 by any chance?" Angus muttered.

Gordy's brow scrunched into a frown. "Aye, that's the one. Joe said it cost a million quid a bottle. I think that's what sparked the whisky trail idea. A million quid a bottle—who wouldn't want a taste of that? But the funny thing is, it wasn't just the price of a dram that interested him. He became a whisky connoisseur." He rolled his eyes, just as Rob Cunnigham-Graham had earlier. "He used to bore the arse off me, talking about subtle flavours and peaty finishes. The water of life—that's what he said whisky was called in Gaelic. Kept banging on about how it was an elemental life force or some bollocks." Gordy laughed, but there was a sadness to the sound. "He tried to convert me, but I says, 'Joe, pal, they all taste the fucking same tae me.'"

"Did he say anything strange, or do anything out of the ordinary in the days before the killing?"

"Other than rattling on about whisky, no."

"So he didn't seem distracted or worried about anything?"

"You lot asked me that at the time," he said. "And my answer hasnae changed—he was the same old Joe." Gordy unfolded his arms and stood. "Look, I need tae get back to work."

Nadia flashed him a smile. "Of course. Thanks for talking to us, Gordon."

"Aye, nae bother." He took a few steps towards the door, then hesitated. He turned, and Angus saw his eyes were glassy. "Sometimes I wonder if Joe really did kill Barbs. I'm no' into all these mad conspiracies, but maybe someone set him up. They never did find Joe's body, did they?"

A stiff wind was hurtling down High Street when they emerged from the butchers. Shoppers hurried past, heads down, hoods and anoraks flapping. The sky overhead had turned a spoiled-meat grey.

"Why would Chichester lie about knowing Carver?" Nadia asked.

"Perhaps Chichester didn't know him as Joseph?" Angus suggested. "He could have known him simply as Joe—the delivery driver who liked whisky."

"Aye, that's possible. Damn, we should have shown him a photograph of Carver."

"We still can."

"Either way, we now know a link between Betty Duncan, Jonathan Boyce, and Joe Carver."

Angus stared at the stringy piles of mince and glistening cuts of meat in the window. "Dunbirlinn," he muttered.

The castle seemed to scowl as they drove under the iron teeth of the portcullis for the second time that day, as if its patience were wearing thin. So far, Dunbirlinn had accepted the presence of the police and the forensic teams with sullen compliance, but Angus still sensed that malignant force lurking behind the stone facade, as if any minute the very walls could turn on these invaders and devour them.

Mrs MacCrimmon was equally unwelcoming when they found her on her hands and knees in the drawing room, scooping ash from the fireplace. Scrunched-up balls of newspaper and a pile of kindling lay on the hearth, ready to be used to light the fire. The housekeeper groaned to her feet, the heat rising to her cheeks, evidently mortified to have been found in such an undignified position. "What are you pair doing here?" she demanded, hands on hips.

"Apologies, Mary," Angus said. "We need to ask the laird a few more questions."

"Don't you think he's been through enough?" she snapped.

He gave a slight shrug but held her frosty glare.

Mrs MacCrimmon glanced away. "Anyway, he's not here."

Angus cocked a questioning eyebrow. Chichester's Aston Martin was parked in the courtyard, as was his late wife's Range Rover and his daughter's Merc. "Where did he go?"

"Och! I don't know. I'm not his mother. But if I were to hazard a guess, I'd say he was up in the helicopter, looking for his wolves."

"When will he be back?"

"Your guess is as good as mine."

Nadia dug a photograph of Joe Carver out of her pocket. "Do you recognise this man?" she asked, shoving the picture in front of the housekeeper's face.

Mrs MacCrimmon gave the picture a fleeting look. "Aye. That's Joe Carver. He used to deliver meat to us before . . ." The sentence petered out.

"He killed his wife," Nadia finished for her.

The old lady's thin lips stretched tight.

"Joe and Mr. Chichester spent time together, we believe?"

"They did. He was a good lad, Joe. Clever. The laird was supportive towards him."

"In what way?"

"He helped him get his business venture off the ground. Connected him to the right people."

"I see." Nadia gave Angus a quick glance. "What about Betty Duncan? Were she and the laird close?"

Mrs MacCrimmon frowned, her face crumpling like the scrunched-up newspaper on the hearth. "What's that got to do with the price of fish?"

Angus took a half-step towards the housekeeper. "Probably nothing, Mary. Just something we need to tidy up."

"Before she was employed here in Dunbirlinn, I knew Betty through the bowling club," she said.

"Like ten-pin bowling?" Nadia asked.

An improbable image of Mrs. MacCrimmon launching a ball at some skittles popped into his head, then instantly dissolved under the housekeeper's withering glare.

"No, lawn bowls, of course." She glanced down, and when she next spoke, her tone was wistful. "Betty had one of the best wick-and-plant shots you'd hope to see. She used to take Lewis along to watch us play. He loved that. Used to sit there in his wheelchair, eyes never leaving the game." She smiled sadly. "I can still see him with a tartan rug over his knees, clapping when someone made a good shot."

Mrs MacCrimmon blinked rapidly, as if fighting back tears. "Betty did everything she could for that boy, but the legal case against Agri-Scotia broke her. It's them I blame for what happened, not Betty."

She looked up and fixed them with a frank stare. "Betty became obsessed with getting justice. She told me all the twists and turns in the case. It was never reported in the papers, but Agri-Scotia wanted to settle out of court. They offered Betty over a million pounds, but she refused because they wouldn't accept liability. She was a principled woman. Aye, she wanted recompense, of course she did—but more than that she wanted Agri-Scotia's management to admit what they'd done. They wouldn't do that, so the case dragged on. That took its toll on Betty's health. If it weren't for the laird, she'd have cracked long before she did."

"Why? What part did Chichester play in all this?" Angus asked.

Mrs MacCrimmon raised her head, the sinew in her neck tightening. "The laird heard of her predicament. This was never made public, but it was Mr. Chichester who paid for her legal case."

CHAPTER 64

A high spring tide had crept up the beach, choking the river mouth and transforming Glenruig bay into a wide sheet of burnished metal. The ranks of press outside the village hall seemed to have swelled too. Technicians swarmed around the outside broadcasting units, fiddling with lighting equipment and cables, whilst reporters prepped for pieces to camera, makeup crews flitting around them like birds around a feeder. There was a sense of frenzied activity. Angus nosed the Land Rover through the scrum of reporters, almost running over the foot of Alice Seaton, who gave him a look that could have frozen the Minch.

He parked the car around the side of the hall, his senses tingling.

"Should we tell Crowley what we've found?" he asked.

Nadia gave a slight shake of her head. "We need more, Angus. We have zero evidence." Her eyes looked tired, the gold flecks lacking their usual spark. "But if a thread connects these cases like Gills said, it's James Chichester. He told us he didn't know Joe Carver, but now we find out he actually befriended him and introduced him to his business contacts. He also said he didn't know Betty Duncan, despite the fact he bankrolled her legal case against Agri-Scotia. And it was Chichester himself who ordered the paintings be restored. Boyce was in the castle for weeks. Surely the laird would have taken an interest in the work, and the artist."

Angus instinctively felt a need to defend the laird. "He's just lost his wife and daughter, Nadia. Who knows where his head's at?"

She gave a contemptuous sniff. "Establishing a pagan commune on your land gives you a perfect scapegoat," she mused. "It's brilliant."

They sat in silence for a long minute. "We still need evidence," she said at last. "You don't take a shot at someone like Chichester without lots of ammunition. He has political clout. He can afford the best lawyers. And he owns half the media."

They climbed from the Land Rover and walked towards the entrance of the village hall, where Constable Devine stood sentry. "How's form, Archie?" Angus asked.

"Living ma best life, Gus," he replied, stony-faced.

"Aye, me too." Angus sighed. "What's going on? Why are the press pack foaming at the mouth?"

"Haven't ye heard?"

Something cold rippled across his shoulders. "No, what's happened?"

"Our prime suspect's brown bread."

"What!" he exclaimed. "Kelbie's dead?"

"As a doorknob."

"How? What happened?"

"Crashed her camper van into a loch." He gave Angus what passed for a smile. "Case closed."

Angus glanced at Nadia. Her eyes were wide, mouth hanging open in a parody of surprise. Without a word, they sidestepped Constable Devine and marched into the village hall. Angus held open the door to the incident room for Nadia and then followed her inside. The atmosphere in the room was bordering on giddy. Boaby Dunbar sucked from a can of Tennant's whilst Ryan Fleet and Vee Lockhart were perched on Crowley's desk, demolishing a bottle of prosecco.

The DCI himself looked up from his mobile phone and spotted Angus and Nadia.

"Ah, the wanderers have returned!" he boomed. "Come into the body of the kirk. Angus, grab yourself a beer." He jabbed a finger at an open case of Tennant's next to the coffee machine. "There's gin over there too, DI Sharif."

Nadia gave Crowley a what-the-fuck look, but he only smiled.

"Go on," he said. "Fill your boots."

The last thing Angus wanted was a drink, but Crowley wasn't so much asking as telling. They walked to the table on which the alcohol had been laid out. Angus slid a yellow can out of the case and popped it open. Nadia decanted a small amount of prosecco into a plastic cup.

"Cheers," he said, voice dripping sarcasm.

"Aye, *slàinte*," Nadia replied.

"Right, gather round, everyone," Crowley shouted above the din. The officers and support staff shuffled forward and stood in a semicircle around Crowley. The DCI gave them a paternal smile. "First off, I want to congratulate you all on your sterling work over the past ten days. It's not been easy, but not one of you has let me down. Even you, Rylo."

Angus glanced around him at the laughing faces, and felt a strange sense of dislocation. He was not one of these people. Perhaps he never would be.

"However," Crowley continued, "we've still got work to do. Now for the absence of all doubt, and because some of you haven't heard all the gory details, I'll walk you through the sequence of events that led to Christine Kelbie's untimely demise."

He raised a finger on his mutilated hand. "Firstly, and it's not often I say this, we have the public to thank. An upstanding member of the community saw Kelbie in a Co-op in Portree at approximately half past four. Local police were alerted and Kelbie's camper van was spotted heading north on the A855 towards Staffin. They tailed her at a distance, to a remote crofthouse by the side of Loch Leathan. Boaby, we need to find out who owns that property."

"Yes, boss."

"The decision was taken to arrest Kelbie, but there was, frankly, a bit of a cock-up. In short, Kelbie battered a couple of uniforms—who were big strapping lads, or so I'm told—and made a bid for freedom. The local lads set off in pursuit along one of these shitty twisty wee roads that are the absolute curse of the Highlands. It had not been gritted. Either Kelbie hit a patch of black ice or she swerved to avoid some sheep. The camper van ended up in the loch. She hadn't put on her seat belt and suffered catastrophic head injuries. Probably died instantly. Now, I don't mean to sound callous, but that's saved the taxpayer a shitload of money. If she'd survived, this case would have gone to trial. Some morally bankrupt lawyer would have taken Kelbie's case and tried to weasel her out of it. But let me be clear—the evidence is incontrovertible. Hidden in that camper van we found another garrotte knotted in three places."

"But didn't forensics search the camper van, sir?" Ryan asked.

"Yes, they did. Before Eleanor was killed. Arses are getting kicked as we speak. Clearly, forensics did a piss-poor job, but don't be surprised if no one gets fired—the chief constable is determined the press doesn't catch wind of this"—he raised his fingers to make quotation marks—"'little faux pas.'"

Angus leaned across and whispered in Nadia's ear: "Bit convenient?"

"I was thinking the same."

Crowley gave them a sharp glance. "Something you want to share with the class, DI Sharif?"

"No, sir. Nothing important."

"Good. Now, we need to get a press conference set up. The sooner we get that done, the sooner these journalist bastards will fuck off back under the rocks from which they crawled."

The tide had receded, leaving a shiny damp residue on the shingle. The wind suddenly dropped and the sea became calm, the surface reflecting a milky-white moon and a scattering of stars. Everything was still and slightly foreboding—the waves that lapped the shore like a dog licking flesh from a bone; the rustle of the wind through the gorse; the odd cackle of crows from their roosting place in the woods surrounding the village hall.

Angus's fingers curled around the hip flask that Chichester had given him, which was still in his coat pocket. Was this the same whisky that had turned Joe Carver into the lunatic who had strangled and beaten his wife? He took it out and angled the flask so the moonlight glinted off the swirling patterns.

Don't be an eejit, he heard his father say. *It's just expensive whisky.*

"Bugger it," Angus muttered, then unscrewed the lid. He put the flask to his lips and tipped his head back. The Macallan slid down his throat, the liquid slightly syrupy, the flavours of peat, cedar, and oak so evocative, it was as if he were drinking the land itself. The whisky burned its way down his throat and settled like a ball of heat in his stomach. He closed his eyes and savoured the warm sensation. His senses were lulled by the murmur of the waves on the shore.

Suddenly the moment of tranquillity shattered. A sharp pain shot through his body, from the base of his spine to the tips of his ears. His legs gave way and he collapsed to his knees on the shingle. Images flashed through his head—a bloodstained hammer, white hair attached to the head; a clay corpse spinning in the air and exploding in a cloud of dust; a bound body plummeting head down into the sea.

He gasped for breath and his eyes snapped open. The hip flask was still clutched in his hand. He sprang to his feet, adrenaline pulsing through his body. A slight wind ruffled the sea, as if something writhed, unseen, just below the surface. He replayed the images in his head, saw again the body drop into the waves, headfirst. The victim had a shock of white hair and as he hit the water, Angus had seen his face.

It was Gills.

ACT V

"When roused to anger, Beira was as fierce as the biting north wind and harsh as the tempest-stricken sea."

—*Wonder Tales from Scottish Myth and Legend*, Donald A. Mackenzie, 1917

CHAPTER 65

HIS mobile phone felt like a brick as he raised it to his ear. But before he could place a call, the phone sprang to life. He flinched, and the phone almost slithered out of his hand. He grabbed the device and glanced at the screen, saw the name GILLS flash up. Relief flooded through his body. He jabbed at the screen.

"Gills! Where are you? Are you okay?"

He heard the old man chuckle. "Never better, old bean. But you don't sound too chipper."

"Where are you?"

"Err, at home," Gills replied, now sounding a wee bit concerned.

"I'm coming over."

"Good, because I've found something out—"

Angus cut the call before Gills could finish. He turned away from the sea and ran towards the Old Manse, a familiar mixture of dread and panic churning inside his stomach. The vision played on a loop in his head. He tried to focus on the details. Gills's wrists and legs were bound with the same coarse rope that had been used to tie up Faye. His face was speckled with blood. He wore odd socks, one a diamond pattern, the other plain and maroon.

Almost before he knew it, he was standing on the front step of the Old Manse, breathing heavily. He reached for the brass handle and pushed the door open. *Why the hell does Gills never lock the door?*

He barged into the house, calling the old man's name.

"In here!" came the shout from the study.

Angus scampered down the hallway and yanked open the study door. Gills was reclining on the retro leather chair, staring at the *bòrd-murt*. He twisted his head and gave Angus a wide grin. "Ah good, just in time." He raised an empty whisky glass. "Care to do the honours?"

Angus wiped a sheen of sweat from his forehead. Gills's bristly eyebrows scrunched together. "Have you been running?"

A bottle of Talisker languished amidst the books and papers on Gills's desk. Angus lifted the bottle and sloshed the amber liquid into the old man's glass. "Whoa!" Gills said. "That's a hefty dram, even for me."

"You'll need it," he muttered.

The creases on Gills's forehead deepened. "Why? What's happened?"

Angus walked back to the desk and rummaged in a drawer for another glass. There were none, but he found an old chipped mug that would do the job. He poured an equally large dram for himself and then turned to face Gills.

"I had another vision." He lifted the mug and took a gulp of whisky. He swiped his hand across his mouth and the words tumbled out. "I saw you, Gills. You were trussed up and you were falling headfirst into the sea. I saw you hit the water and go under. I saw you die."

Gills stood and walked over to him. He placed his hands on Angus's shoulders. "That is excellent news."

Angus glared at the old man as if he were mad.

"Forewarned is forearmed, old bean."

"Gills, you need to take this seriously."

"Oh, don't worry, I will. But don't you see? This shows that those pills were stifling your gift. For the first time, you're seeing properly, Angus." Gills gave his shoulders an encouraging squeeze. "Now, tell me again what you saw. Slower this time."

Angus sat in the chair recently vacated by Gills and took him through the sequence of events. He described the vision with as much detail as he could, but there were no clues pointing to where Gills was when he was thrown into the sea, nor who had done it.

"I was scared I was already too late," Angus said, finishing the dregs of his whisky. The bottle of Talisker appeared at his elbow, as if by magic.

Gills poured him another dram. "You can't get rid of me that easily. You saved Ewan. You can save me, too, old bean."

He walked back over to his messy desk and lifted a book. The cover showed a bearded figure in a plaid holding an upraised staff. Around him, supplicating followers lay prone on the ground. "Now, let's put my impending demise to one side for the moment. Like I tried to tell you on the phone—I've found something interesting. I've been reading up on Chichester's ancestor Dòmhnall MacRuari."

Angus wasn't in the mood for another history lesson, but the hint of excitement in Gills's tone piqued his curiosity.

"This book claims Dòmhnall established a unit of elite warriors to act as his personal bodyguard. They were known as *na Sgàilean*. The Shadows."

"Like a Praetorian Guard?" he asked.

"Exactly. Charlemagne had his Paladins, Genghis Khan the Kheshig, the Ottomans had the Janissaries—Dòmhnall MacRuari had his Shadows. Although, now that I think about it, the Norse berserkers is perhaps a more fitting analogy. Like these feared Viking warriors, the Shadows worked themselves into a frenzy before battle, then charged into the carnage impervious to fear or pain. Interestingly, the mythological hero of the Ulster Cycle—Cú Chulainn—was possessed by a similar bloodlust in battle. The ancient chroniclers even had a name for it—*ríastrad*—which has been translated as 'warp spasm.'

"Now, becoming one of these esteemed warriors conferred status and privilege, but that came at a price. As well as brutal training, a would-be Shadow had to demonstrate his loyalty." Gills took a sip of his dram.

"And how did he do that?" Angus asked.

Gills fixed him with a piercing stare. "By sacrificing one of his kin to the old gods. But that's not all. Dòmhnall himself is said to have led by example. He had one of his own children slaughtered as an offering to the Bone Mother."

CHAPTER 66

ANGUS drifted in the liminal space between slumber and wakefulness as dawn crept across the sea and roused the crows from their roosting spot high in the branches of the beech, elm, and sycamore trees surrounding the Old Manse.

He woke to the cawing of the birds and sat bolt upright, glancing around wildly. It took him a second to find his bearings. Gills had insisted he should go home last night, but instead he'd sat awake in the Land Rover keeping vigil. At some point during the long night he must have fallen asleep. He rubbed his gritty eyes and checked the time on his phone—just after seven o'clock.

He opened a Web browser on his phone and typed "survival rates for pancreatic cancer" into the search engine. He was directed to a page of links to cancer charity websites. Eleanor had said Chichester's cancer was distant, meaning it had spread to other parts of the body. It didn't take Angus long to confirm what he already suspected. When pancreatic cancer was as far advanced as Chichester's, it simply did not go into remission. Patients could cling on for a year or so, but after two years the survival rates were zero. It seemed the laird was a medical miracle.

Yawning, he clambered out of the Land Rover and stretched his arms above his head, wincing at the ache in his back. It was a brisk morning, a biting northerly wind bringing with it the threat of more snow. A robin sat on the garden dyke, its feathers puffed out, as if it had gorged on worms. Cobwebs bejewelled in frost shimmered from the branches of bushes and shrubs.

He heard barking coming from the house and figured Gills was up and about. He rolled a kink from his neck as he walked up the garden path, but before he reached the front door, it opened and Gills appeared. He was dressed for hiking in plus fours, gaiters, and leather walking boots that looked like something Edmund Hillary might have worn. Bran and Sceolan wriggled past him and began running excited rings round the garden. Gills slung a rucksack over his shoulder, an ancient thing that wouldn't have looked out of place in a museum. His gloves, however, were newish and Gore-Tex, and his walking poles lightweight aluminium.

Angus gave his outfit a once-over. "Where are you going? To scale K2?"

The older man grinned. "Be prepared. Scouts motto."

"Seriously, though, where are you going?"

"Where are *we* going, you mean." He squinted at Angus. "Wait . . . you haven't been out here all night, have you?"

"No," Angus replied, without conviction.

Gills gave a frustrated sigh and stood aside. "In you come. We'll get some breakfast into you before we go."

"Okay, but where are we going?"

Gills tapped the side of his nose. "Cave hunting."

Angus parked the Land Rover in the shadow of an eight-arched viaduct that spanned the northeastern shores of Loch nan Uamh. Easily mistaken for its bigger and—because of the Harry Potter series—more famous cousin some sixteen miles east at Glenfinnan, the viaduct was a popular spot for camera-toting tourists. Today, however, Angus and Gills had the run of the place, aside from a few black-faced sheep, who eyed them suspiciously as they climbed from the Land Rover, then bolted when they saw Bran and Sceolan.

"Now will you tell me where we're going?" he asked.

Gills shouldered his ancient rucksack. "To find the site of the Glen Màma Massacre. When you mentioned Chichester told you he was once trapped in the cave, it got me thinking."

"Aye?"

He clapped Angus on the shoulder. "I'll tell you on the way."

Gills got the dogs on their leads and then set off down a rough track that led past a sturdy farmhouse. Once they'd crossed a wooden bridge over Allt a' Mhama, he untethered the dogs, who shot off into the undergrowth. As they climbed, the burn, swollen by meltwater, surged down the wooded glen, a torrent of peaty water glimpsed through dripping branches of Atlantic oak. The rich scent of moss, rotting wood, and decaying leaves lingered behind the crisp freshness of the mountain stream, a bracing smell that chased away Angus's tiredness.

Gills set a good pace for a man of nearly seventy. Angus smiled affection-ately at the old man—with his walking poles jutting out like extra limbs, Gills resembled a big stick insect. The smile died when he thought of the vision he'd seen on the shore last night. Whatever happened, he couldn't let Gills near the sea until this was over.

Soon the trees thinned and the path opened onto a bleak moorland dotted with the skeletons of dead oak. Towering mountains glared down on them as they wended their way through the heather.

"Up until thirty or so years ago, academics disputed whether the Glen Màma Massacre had actually occurred," Gills wheezed. "Sure, it had a basis in reality—the MacRuari clan *was* annihilated by the MacLoughlins; numer-ous sources attest to this. The detail about the cave, though, was considered far-fetched, a literary motif used by the chronicle writers. But then some potholers exploring the cave system of the glen stumbled across piles of human bones. They called the police, erroneously believing the bones were recent. For a time, rumours of a serial killer's lair swirled around, until the bones were radiocarbon-dated to the sixteenth century. Archaeologists later discovered charcoal deposits and evidence of burnt bone a foot or so down. The remains were from men, women, and children, which all but clinched the deal—here was the physical evidence of the massacre referred to in the ancient manuscripts."

They walked around the shores of a small dark lochan, then struck off the main path, following what was little more than a sheep trail around the base of the crags.

"The exact location of the cave was kept secret by authorities to deter trophy hunters," Gills said.

"Then how do you know where we're going?"

"Myself and the lead archaeologist on the dig were friends. He told me where to find the cave." He paused and turned to Angus. "And here's a curi-ous thing: the cave is known in Gaelic as *Uamh na Caillich*."

An icy tingle fluttered across Angus's shoulder blades. "Cave of the Cailleach," he murmured.

"Another odd coincidence, eh? It's almost as if Dòmhnall and his kin made the ultimate sacrifice to the Bone Mother." He gave Angus a tight smile, then pointed to a narrow cleft between two great slabs of ice-encrusted schist. "The cave is on the other side of these rocks. Watch how you go, though."

"Just concentrate on yourself, *a'bhalach*," he said.

Using his poles for balance, Gills picked his way down the steep slope, the dogs a few paces in front. Angus slithered after them, heart hammering as he fought to keep his footing. He passed between the two slabs and found himself hemmed in on three sides by sheer cliffs. Tiny scraggly trees sprouted improbably from cracks and fissures in the rock. Clumps of moss and grass clung to the crags like patches of hair on the face of an old man. Water streamed down the rock face, as if the mountains themselves were crying.

Angus shivered, sensing some malevolent presence in this remote, lonely place. The collies appeared to feel it too. Their hackles rose as they glared at the gaping black maw in the mountainside. Bran let out a low, throaty growl. Sceolan crouched, as if ready to pounce, his mismatched eyes bright and fierce.

"Easy, boys, it's just a cave," Gills said, voice betraying a hint of nervousness. He unslung his rucksack, took out a couple of torches, and handed one to Angus. "You fit?"

"Aye," he muttered.

They walked to the cave mouth and stood for a few seconds, peering into the murk. A faint fetid-smelling wind arose from the darkness, as if the cave were sighing. Angus screwed up his nose at the rank sickly sweet scent of decay. Gills clicked on his torch and padded into the cave. Angus licked his cracked lips, then glanced back at the dogs. Bran paced back and forth, but would come no closer. Sceolan stood as if frozen, his front paw in the air, eyes fixed on the cave mouth. Angus flicked on his own torch and followed Gills into the dank cavern.

Daylight illuminated the first few meters, revealing green-tinted granite and rock worn into ribbons and flutes by centuries of dripping water. The cave floor was covered in loose boulders, smoother slabs and a thin layer of vegetation and soil. Ten feet above his head, the callused roof was pock-marked with toothlike stalactites and dark patches the colour of rust.

"Quite remarkable," Gills breathed, the beam from his torch darting around the cave.

Angus did not trust himself to speak. In his mind's eye, he saw a mass of bodies pressed together in the darkness. He heard the pitiful wails of children, bleak curses, and the anguished cries of women as the cave filled with smoke. He smelt the acrid stench of damp wood and heather burning. It masked the reek of piss and shit as the condemned loosened their bowels and coughed up their lungs.

"There is a certain . . . malignant aura, as if the events of the past have been scorched into the walls. That's why I wanted us to come here."

"What do you mean?"

"'The wretched will make bargains with demons and, thus possessed, make blood sacrifices to slake the thirst of the old gods.'"

"That's the prophecy."

"Aye, and like you, I've been thinking about what that might mean . . . more practically."

"You've been thinking about what possession by an entity from the Celtic otherworld according to an ancient manuscript might mean . . . more practically?"

"Aye." Gills's craggy face was uplit by the torchlight. "Will you humour me for a second, old bean?"

"Gills, I've been humouring you my whole life."

The old man chuckled softly. "Quite. Well, then. Gormla didn't live in our world, with its car parks and microcomputers. She lived in this world—the natural world. It thus occurred to me that the answer might be in the natural world, Angus. So I'd like to tell you about the humble horsehair worm."

"Ok-ay . . ."

"These worms mate in the water and when their eggs hatch, the tiny larvae settle on the bottom of streams and rivers, where they are eaten by the larvae of other insects, like midges or mosquitoes. When the midges metamorphose, they emerge from the water, fly about a bit, and are inevitably eaten by other insects such as crickets." Gills strobed the torch beam around the roof of the cave, eyes narrowed. "But the cricket doesn't know the midge has a stowaway on board. Once inside the cricket, the worm larva begins to grow, sometimes up to a foot long. Outwardly, the cricket appears unchanged, but here's the good bit"—his eyes flitted to Angus—"the worm produces large amounts of neurotransmitters that make the cricket act in ways it normally wouldn't. For example, it stops the cricket chirping."

Angus frowned. "But why?"

"Because chirping alerts predators. The worm doesn't want the cricket eaten, for obvious reasons. It has basically hijacked the cricket's brain, and when the worm is ready to emerge, it does something else quite remarkable. Crickets avoid water, the dangers of fish and drowning being great. But crickets infected by horsehair worms think they're Tom Daley. They seek out the nearest pool and dive in kamikaze-style. By now the worm has bored a porthole in the cricket's exoskeleton. As soon as the insect hits the water, the worm squirms out of its host and goes off to find a mate. And so the cycle begins again.

"The cricket, incidentally, if not eaten by a fish, does not necessarily die. It hops away, a great hole inside it where the worm used to be."

Angus glared at Gills, waiting for him to continue. "And your point is?"

"I'd have thought that obvious, old bean. I think when James Chichester was trapped inside this cave, he was, in a sense, infected. He became a host, not for a horsehair worm, but for some ancient entity, perhaps the spirit of his ancestor *an Draoidh*. Dòmhnall MacRuari was not just a follower of the old gods; he was an emissary between them and his people. He drew his power from them, but when Chichester stumbled into this cave, that power was all but gone. To become strong again, *an Draoidh* therefore needed to strengthen the gods."

"Through human sacrifice?" Angus croaked.

"Indeed, blood is the currency of the gods. *An Draoidh* needed Chichester as much as Chichester needed him. So they made a bargain. In fact, Chichester almost told you as much, Angus."

"Did he?"

"He told you he made a pact, remember?"

"Aye, to reintroduce wolves."

"Wolves and the Cailleach have a symbiotic relationship. She represents the natural order on which they subsist—this place before damned motorways and fish farms arrived. And they, in turn, preserve the natural order that *is* the Cailleach."

He pictured Chichester, sweeping his walking stick across the landscape as they stood on the platform above the wolves.

This is make-believe, an artificial creation of man, first branded by the Victorians and flogged to death by successive governments ever since. No landscape can truly be called a wilderness when its top predator has been eradicated.

"Think about everything the Cailleach represents. She is the summer and the winter, the harvest and the frost. She is life and death—not as we know it, but as a continuum, as a sacred circle of renewal. And so is the wolf. It is the apex predator that in creating death preserves nature and thus life."

He thought of Chichester, his eyes narrowed to slits, like the arrow loops in Dunbirlinn Castle.

In ten years' time—if the reintroduction project is allowed to progress unhindered—the view from here will be quite different. . . .

Wolves have a symbiotic relationship with nature, Angus. . . .

She is the missing link in the chain.

"Angus, the murders of Eleanor and Faye are blood sacrifices to honour and sustain the goddess."

"But what does she want?"

"What all deities want—to be worshipped. Chichester—or whatever's left of him—is the spider at the centre of this web. Like Dòmhnall MacRuari, he has *na Sgàilean*, his Shadows. Betty Duncan, Joe Carver, Jonathan Boyce. All of them, out of the blue, brutally murdered people close to them. They were sacrificed, Angus. And the thing inside James Chichester compelled them to do it."

"My mother, too?" Angus asked, voice little more than a whisper.

Gills shook his head. "Your mother was taken from us before Chichester ever set foot in the Highlands, let alone this cave. No, Chichester had nothing to do with Caitlin's murder, but I believe it is connected."

"How?"

"By you, Angus. Your visions. They are not random. In fact, they're the opposite. Even when you weren't taking those pills, lots of people died. Road accidents. Drownings at sea. But you foresaw none of those."

Angus peered into the darkness and tried to still the thumping of his heart. What Gills said had a kind of logic, but something still bothered him.

"Why not kill them himself?" he asked. "Why drag in someone else?"

"I believe Chichester is the living embodiment of his ancestor Dòmhnall MacRuari. *An Draoidh* was considered a semidivine figure. He had devotees, just as Chichester now has whoever is garbed as Donn Fírinne. Ask yourself this, Angus: Who is more powerful, the hangman who places the rope around a condemned man's neck, or the king who ordered the execution? Dòmhnall straddled the divide between the sacred and the profane. He was an intermediary between the gods. His followers had to prove themselves."

"But how does that even work?" he asked.

Gills released his arm and sighed. "That, I don't know. My guess is some kind of Faustian bargain. In one lurid historical account, Dòmhnall makes just such a pact with the Devil. He gains his heart's desire—dominion over his enemies—but in doing so, everyone he loves is, eventually, slaughtered. The story is a Christianised version of a much older tale, with the Devil transplanting some other supernatural being, quite possibly a Celtic deity."

"Eleanor told us her husband had been diagnosed with pancreatic cancer," Angus said. "She said it was at a distant stage, meaning the cancer had spread to other parts of his body. The doctors gave him eighteen months to live, tops. I looked up the survival rates online. For men of Chichester's age, with his type of cancer, and at such an advanced stage, he simply could not survive. Yet he's still in robust health a decade later. Either he's a medical miracle—"

"Or something else," Gills said, finishing Angus's thought.

"Aye."

Angus swept his torch beam over the moist walls of the cave and tried to still the shake in his arm. He thought of that brief glimpse of something feral in the laird's eyes when they'd spoken at the wolf enclosure. Phrases from their strange, rambling conversations seemed to echo around the cave:

I fell into this trancelike state of hyper-awareness. . . .

There were times when I felt godlike. . . .

Angus tried to banish the laird from his head, but that reedy voice continued to reverberate.

And now I'm paying for that hubris. . . .

Will this suffering be enough . . . ?

We are irredeemably lost, Angus Dubh. . . .

And suddenly it hit him, like the force of the Steall Waterfall. Chichester had been confessing to him the whole time. It hadn't just been grief Angus had seen in the laird's eyes. It had been guilt.

CHAPTER 67

ASHLEIGH sat on the small, padded stool at her clarsach and gazed, unseeing, out the window. Dusk was beginning to fall, a scattering of stars appearing in the north sky. She leaned forward and rested her head against the neck of the clarsach. At her bare feet sat the forms Granny Beag had given her, ready to be sent to the electoral office. After the devastating news at the clinic, she had made the decision to run at the local elections in the New Year, only a couple of months away. There was more to being a woman than raising children; Granny Beag had taught her that. And besides, she heard the old woman say, *You're young yet; you've still got options.* Angus had insisted they could save up and try IVF through a private clinic. Or they could adopt. Why then did she feel so utterly despondent? Why, beside that measured, reasonable voice in her head, was there another? A sneering, hectoring voice that told her she was worthless, told her to tear everything down and burn it.

FUCK THE WORLD.

Suddenly she heard the low purr of an engine as a car pulled up in front of the cottage. Then silence. She waited, heard the sound of a car door slam and the creak of footsteps walking towards the front door. A delivery driver, she thought, although they hadn't ordered anything recently, and besides, it was Sunday. Jehovah's Witnesses perhaps, offering to save her soul, just like Reverend MacVannin.

She rose from the stool and walked into the hall. She could see the dark shape of someone—a man, judging from the height—behind the frosted glass on the door. Despite this, she jumped when the doorbell rang.

She closed her eyes and muttered a near-silent curse. If it was the Jehovah's, they were going to get short shrift. She marched to the door, undid the chain, and hauled it open. Her mouth fell open in surprise. Standing there in an immaculate dark coat and charcoal suit, a trilby on his head, was James Chichester. He clutched a cane with a wolf-headed handle in his leather-gloved right hand, and his tanned face wore an expression of light amusement.

"Finally, my nemesis, in the flesh," he drawled. "It's nice to meet you, Mrs. MacNeil."

Ashleigh folded her arms across her chest, painfully aware of her casual attire—old jogging bottoms, thick woolly socks, and a loose-fitting sweater. "What can I do for you, Mr. Chichester?"

"I'm sorry to drop in unannounced, but there's something I'd like to discuss."

"You'd better come in then." Reluctantly, Ash stepped aside.

Chichester stamped the snow from his Oxford brogues on the doorstep and walked into the hall. Ash felt the chill follow him into the house. He propped his cane against the wall, then removed his hat and placed it carefully on the monks bench. Then he pulled off his leather gloves—first the right, then the left—and laid them on the bench next to his hat.

He turned and fixed her with a stare that seemed to strip her bare.

"I'm . . . I'm sorry for your loss," she stammered. "I can't imagine how that must feel."

A ghost of a smile tugged at his lips. "Losses."

Ash felt a flush creep up her neck. "Anyway, please come in."

She showed him into the snug room. "Can I get you a drink? A dram? My husband has a bottle of Talisker in here somewhere." She was rambling, and she knew it. She'd never met Chichester, and he had a kind of aura that was unsettling.

"I've met your husband," he said. "In fact, I'd go as far as to say we've become friends."

Ash frowned. First she'd heard of it.

"He is a remarkable man."

"Aye, he's not a bad sort," she joked, but Chichester did not smile. Instead he observed her with an intense stare.

"If you've come about my opposition to the nature reserve, there's not much to discuss. I won't stop. People are more important than wolves. I'm all for rewilding, but it has to be done in tandem with initiatives that benefit the local community as a whole. Our young folk need affordable housing and decent jobs so they aren't forced to move away from the area."

As she spoke, Chichester strolled around the room, examining the ornaments on the fireplace and the books on the shelves. He paused by the clarsach and ran a hand across the instrument's neck, the touch tender. It made her skin crawl.

"Look, I know you believe in what you're doing, but you can't bend nature to your will. Highlanders are tired of rich foreigners coming over here and patronizing us, telling us what's best for ourselves and our families. No offense, but you're just another one of these green lairds that seem to be all the rage. How long before you're planting huge swathes of trees and selling carbon credits to multinationals so they can *offset* their emissions and carry on polluting? Land prices are skyrocketing. The Highlands are again being sold from under the feet of local people."

Chichester plucked a couple of the clarsach's strings. "I admire your passion, Mrs. MacNeil, but this has never been about the money. I have money enough for a thousand lifetimes."

Ash was beginning to feel deeply uneasy. Her stomach churned, from fear or anger, she couldn't tell. "Look, what do you want?"

Chichester reached into the inside pocket of his dark coat and took out a letter. He clasped it between thumb and forefinger and held it out to her. The envelope was textured and pearlescent. Her name was written on the front in a fountain pen, the script beautiful and sinuous. Instinctively, Ash jammed her hands into her pockets. "What's this?"

Chichester's lips twitched upwards. "Please, take it. You'll like what's inside. I promise."

Ash stared into his strange, milky turquoise eyes, and almost against her will she withdrew her hands from her pockets and took the envelope. She turned it over and found it sealed with red wax, like a droplet of blood. Using her fingernail, she broke the seal and plucked out the letter. The paper was thick and textured like the envelope, adorned with the ghost of heraldic crests. At the top of the letter, in the same swirling script, it said, *The Last Will and Testament of James Percy Chichester.*

Ash glanced at the laird. He gave her an encouraging nod. "Read it aloud."

She held his gaze for a second, then her eyes dropped to the letter. Her throat felt dry as she started to read. "'I, James Percy Chichester, being of sound mental health and possessed of full mental capacity, hereby declare this document and all its contents and provisions to be my complete and legally binding last will and testament. I hereby revoke any and all wills, testaments, and codicils made prior to this last will and testament.'"

"Skip to the good part." Chichester grinned.

Ash scanned down the page, her confusion mounting, then let out a small gasp. She reread the sentence, her voice little more than a croak. "'I hereby declare that my lands of the Kilcreggan Estate shall be bequeathed to the Glenruig Community Trust. . . .'" Ash shook her head, a small laugh bubbling from her lips. "What is this? What game are you playing?"

"No game," Chichester said. "I had my lawyer in Silvaig draw this up this morning. You'll find everything is in order."

"But . . ." Ash found herself at a loss for words. "Why?"

"It's what you want, isn't it?"

"Well . . . yes," she stammered. "But I don't understand. There must be a catch?"

Chichester stuck out his bottom lip. "No catch."

Ash again read the salient points. It appeared true—Chichester was just giving them the estate. "No," she said, shaking her head, "you want something. Men like you always do."

The laird cocked an eyebrow. He stepped away from the clarsach and gestured for her to sit. "All I ask is that you play something for me."

Ash gave a nervous laugh. "What?"

"Please, play something. Anything."

"I'm not . . . Look, I've not had the best couple of days. Tell me what you want."

"They say you're very good. Could have been one of the best."

"I—"

"Come on, Mrs. MacNeil. One short tune to make an old, pitiful man happy."

Ash shook her head but found herself walking towards the clarsach against her will. She settled herself onto the stool and placed Chichester's will on the carpet at her feet. Her hands reached for the strings.

"I . . . I don't know what to play."

She felt Chichester's presence behind her, looming, palpable. "Play anything," he murmured. "Just close your eyes, and play."

Her fingers shook violently as she brushed the strings. She found herself closing her eyes, doing exactly what Chichester said. The first notes were clumsy and weak, but soon she relaxed into the familiar rhythms. The tension in her shoulders eased, and she found herself swaying in time to the music. Her foot started to tap. Without her registering it, Chichester had placed his hands on her shoulders.

"So sweet," she heard him whisper. "So sweet." It took her a second to realize he'd spoken in Gaelic. There was no trace of his Texan accent. The reedy voice that whispered in her ear was that of an old man. No, not old. Ancient. It had a timbre and texture that was not of this world. The Gaelic, too, was unfamiliar. She could hardly understand the hushed words that seemed to worm their way inside her ear. Yet she was transfixed, utterly terrified, but unable to stop playing, her fingers flying across the strings, conjuring runs she never thought possible.

And still he muttered in her ear, filling her head with this eerie Gaelic that had taken on the rhythm of an incantation. The words squirmed inside her, burrowing down and latching on like a newborn calf to its mother's teat. She felt her defences breaking down. She wanted to scream, to turn away from the clarsach and rip his eyes out. Instead she played faster. Icy beads of sweat coursed down her face and long-buried memories simmered to the surface.

Cracks bloom on a car windshield, like a bloody spiderweb. She hears the sound of shearing metal and her mother's screams. Her father's head rests on the steering wheel, as if he's fallen asleep. His window's open because he'd been smoking a cigarette and Mum doesn't like the smell. Freezing water pours into the car. Mum's trapped by the front console, which had closed around her like a vice on impact. She unbuckles her seat belt and tries to pull Mum free. She's sobbing, begging, so scared, she wets herself. It doesn't matter because she's already soaked. Through the window she sees the rain-spattered surface of the loch, and then the car sinks under. She hears Mum splutter: "Go, my darling!" She takes her small hand and squeezes tight. "Mummy loves you. Now go!" But she stays, even after Mum rips her hand free and yells at her. She stays until the water covers them. Mum's hair billows around her face. Air bubbles shoot from between her lips. Her eyes are two terrified white orbs. When they go to the swimming pool, they have competitions to see who can stay underwater for the longest. Mum lets her win. She knows this, because adults have big lungs that can hold more oxygen. Her heart feels as if it's exploding, like the frog a horrible boy from her school named Bradley had blown up with a firecracker.

She lets go of Mum's hand and swims out the window. She's screaming inside, but when she breaks the surface, she's lying on her back in the grass. Stars sparkle in the night sky above her. Something tells her this is her first memory. Cold lips press against her forehead. A warm tear falls on her cheek. A presence looms over her, but then it's gone and she is all alone. A gimlet-eyed moon watches over her. An owl hoots. A shadow passes in front of the moon—a crow, with feathers as black as ink. The bird lands on an ancient standing stone covered in mysterious symbols. It glares at her with beady eyes infused with a strange glow. She hears a murmuring Gaelic voice. At first she thinks it's the crow, talking to her, but then she realizes this sound is not part of the memory. It's Chichester, and he's pouring poison into her ear.

Her memories shattered like old, brittle bone.

"You can have what you've always wanted," Chichester rasped.

"No!" she growled. "No!"

"A child of your own."

She clawed at the clarsach strings with a manic fury. From the instrument came a hideous shriek, like a child being flayed alive. Behind her eyelids, Ash saw a raging fire and the silhouettes of people being devoured by flames. She succumbed to the voice in her head. Her spine arched. She threw her head back and screamed. She screamed until her throat was raw. Her hands fell from the strings and she toppled backwards off the stool.

She lay there for a long time on the carpet, no sound but that of her laboured breathing. Eventually she opened her eyes. The ceiling swam in front of her. She raised her hands and saw they were crimson, the fingertips torn and bleeding.

Only then did the pain hit: a throb that began at her ruined fingers and shot up her arms and across her shoulders. Using her elbows, she levered her body into a sitting position. Gradually the room stopped spinning. She saw the fancy envelope and letter lying a few feet away, and suddenly remembered—James Chichester had been here, in this house. What had he done to her? She recalled those cold hands on her shoulders. Had he drugged her somehow?

Her legs almost gave way when she tried to stand. Her muscles felt incredibly weary, as if she'd run a tough hill race. Trembling, she stumbled into the hall and saw herself in the full-length mirror. She looked like a wraith, her hands those of a butcher.

She glanced at the wall by the door. His wolf-headed cane was gone, so, too, his hat and gloves. She limped to the door and pulled it open a crack, a stab of pain again pulsing up her arm. Outside, the wind hissed through the trees. Clouds scudded across the sky. There was no sign of Chichester's car.

Ash slammed the door shut and fumbled with the chain. Eventually she managed to slide it into place, then she turned and pressed her back against the door. She slid to the floor and buried her head in her arms. Her whole body shook. Her fingers throbbed. She tried to scream, but her throat was like sandpaper, and the only sound that came out was a dry whimper.

Her tears, when they came, smelt like ashes.

CHAPTER 68

THE Sunday market was in full swing, rows of stalls set out along the length of Silvaig High Street, selling everything from crafts and clothes to vegetables and secondhand "antiques." The striped awnings of the stalls added a splash of colour to what had become a cold overcast winter's day. Jaunty pop music warbled from a stall selling toys and helium balloons in the shape of dinosaurs and Peppa Pig. In the background, like a conscience, Angus heard a familiar voice preaching to the shoppers. He glanced along High Street and spotted Reverend MacVannin standing on the steps of the war memorial, microphone in hand. Flanking the minister was a white-haired elder, Bible clenched in arthritic fingers, and Raymond the Waver, his head bobbing. MacVannin's eyes bulged as he spat his venom into the microphone. He'd become a fixture in front of the war memorial since the town council had agreed to allow a Sunday market. A squad of cackling youths walked past. One made an explicit hand gesture in MacVannin's direction, but otherwise the minister was roundly ignored. His voice trembled as he berated the shoppers.

Angus and Gills shared a look, then the old man pushed open the door of the Jac-O-bite. Only when they were ensconced in a window booth with coffee and steaming bowls of Cullen skink in front of them did Angus's cloying sense of anxiety begin to lift.

He glanced out the window and frowned. A familiar figure in a padded coat and teal beanie stood beside a jewellery stall. Nadia glanced up and their eyes met. She raised a gloved hand and waved, a wide smile on her face. Angus raised a hand in response.

"Shit, it's Nadia," he said. "She's coming over. What do we tell her about Chichester?"

"The truth," Gills replied.

"What!" Angus hissed. "She'll think we're mental."

"Then we stick close to the truth—Chichester is a madman, the leader of a secret pagan cult linked to Dunbirlinn. He believes an ancient goddess cured his cancer, but for his continued survival he must give tribute in the form of human sacrifice. These offerings are made at regular intervals, and on the dates of Celtic fire festivals. There's no need to mention anything not of this earth."

"Perhaps that's true?"

Gills leaned across the table, keeping his voice low. "How can you say that, after all you've seen? Your visions, all these murders going back to your mother's—none of it is happenstance. You're destined to stop these crimes."

Gills held his stare for a long second, then his expression softened. "Besides, I have a vested interest in getting to the bottom of this case, if your latest vision is anything to go by."

Angus felt something twist inside his stomach. "I told you not to joke about that."

"What else am I supposed to do? Live in fear? Lock myself in my house? Sleep with a carving knife beneath my pillow?"

The door of the Jac-O-bite swung open and Nadia entered. Angus plastered on a smile. "Might not be a bad idea," he said between gritted teeth.

Nadia edged past a pair of young lovers enjoying hot chocolate and walked over to Angus and Gills's table. "Fancy meeting you here."

"Please, join us, DI Sharif," Gills said.

She slid into the booth alongside Gills. "Thanks, I could do with a coffee and something covered in sugar. I'm a teensy bit hungover."

Nadia gestured to the waitress with the blond bob, who scampered over to them, smiling. Nadia ordered coffee and a Belgian bun, then, when the waitress had left, frowned at Gills's attire. "Where have you pair been? Scaling the Eiger?"

"A gentle stroll, nothing more," Gills replied with a grin. "And you?"

"Recovering."

Gills cocked an eyebrow. "Celebrating the resolution of the case?"

She stifled a yawn. "It's resolved to Crowley's satisfaction."

"And that of the top brass," Angus said. "There's no physical evidence against Kelbie. Apart from the garrottes found in the camper van."

"Clearly, someone planted the garrotte in the camper van," Gills said, trying to keep his voice down.

Nadia glanced at Angus. "Aye, we did think that was a bit convenient. It wouldn't have been hard to do. The camper van's door didn't lock."

The waitress returned with Nadia's order. Nadia immediately took a bite of the bun and let out a moan of satisfaction. "So good."

"I was up half the night thinking about this," Gills said. "Running through all the permutations in my head."

"And?" she asked.

"And I wish this coffee were whisky."

Nadia gave his arm a gentle punch. "Your liver must be shot."

"Hardly, I only drink the good stuff. It cleanses."

"Aye, right." She tore off a piece of bun and popped it into her mouth. She chewed thoughtfully, the smile slipping from her lips. "I think we have to go to Crowley with what we've got," she said. "The more I think about it, the more convinced I am that these historic cases are linked. The dates can't be a coincidence."

Angus gave Gills a quick glance. "We've discovered another coincidence," he said.

"Aye?"

"You tell her, Gills. You're the historian."

Gills pushed his empty bowl of soup aside. "Chichester's ancestor Dòmhnall MacRuari, I've been reading up on him. According to certain sources, he established a band of elite warriors called *na Sgàilean*. The Shadows. To become a Shadow you had to complete a rather horrific initiation—you had to sacrifice one of your kin to the Cailleach."

Nadia's eyes darted to Angus. "That's a helluva coincidence." She groaned, rubbing at her temples, as if trying to massage away her hangover. "It has to be Chichester behind this, right? He's obsessed with this Druid guy. Maybe he thinks he's Dòmhnall's reincarnation or something?"

Angus shot Gills a surreptitious glance. "Aye, that's what we were thinking too."

"So he forms a cult at Dunbirlinn and creates his own Shadows," Nadia said, warming to her theme. "He picks folk he can manipulate, men like Jonathan Boyce with a history of depression, or Joe Carver, who he can dazzle with his money and knowledge. Then there's Betty Duncan, who's at her wits end with Agri-Scotia."

She took another bite of her bun and chased it down with a sip of coffee. "I can't sit back and let Kelbie take the rap for something orchestrated by some rich guy. More to the point, whoever murdered Faye and Eleanor is still out there, and they might kill again."

Will kill again, Angus thought.

He glanced out the window and saw a young mother browsing the perfume and clothes stalls outside the café. She held a double buggy, and a couple of chubby little faces stared out from under blankets. Both babies wore woolly hats: one blue, one pink. He thought of Ash. The latest IVF failure had hit his wife hard, only compounded by Lilly's attempted suicide and the revelation that she was a foundling. No wonder she had been withdrawn the last couple of days. He smiled faintly as one of the babies appeared to wave a fat little hand at him. The smile did not linger. Ash deserved better than him. She deserved a husband without secrets. She deserved a proper family, that which she never had growing up.

He glanced at the infants' mother. She was mid-twenties and wore skinny jeans, Ugg boots, and a black leather biker jacket. Thrift-shop trendy. She plucked a garment from a rack and ran a critical eye over it.

It was a leopard-print top.

Angus rose from the booth, eyes still on the woman. "Wait here a second," he muttered.

He slipped out of the café and walked towards the clothes stall. MacVannin droned on in the background: *"Do not love the world or the things in the world. If anyone loves the world, the love of the Father is not in him. . . ."*

The young mother hung the top back on the rack and moved on. He watched her go for a second, then reached up and checked the label on the garment. It was from Monsoon, the same shop where Corky had bought a leopard-print top for Lorna.

He turned to the stallholder, a bleach-blond woman in her late twenties drinking tea from a Styrofoam cup. It was Geraldine MacAuley, the beautician who worked in Shaggers' Alley and was on the radar of Trading Standards.

"I see you have some new stock, Gerry," he said.

The stallholder froze, cup halfway towards her thin, crooked lips.

"It's all legit, Constable MacNeil."

"Even that top," he said, jabbing a thumb over his shoulder at the leopard-print monstrosity. "Because it matches one stolen from a clothesline at High Cross farm."

The woman tried to look offended, but when that didn't work, she launched her cup at him. Hot tea hit him like a slap across the face. "Jesus! What the fu—"

He swiped a sleeve across his eyes, in time to see Geraldine disappear from the rear of the stall.

"Gerry! Don't be stupid!"

He spat a Gaelic curse, then pelted after the Knicker Snatcher.

Gerry was already twenty yards ahead, legging it down High Street, pushing shoppers out of the way. She shouldered a wee woman with a Scottie dog on a lead, sending her spinning against a shop window. MacVannin kept up his tirade.

"For all that is in the world—the desires of the flesh and the desires of the eyes and pride in possessions—is not from the Father but is from the world. . . ."

He gritted his teeth and sprinted, leaping over the small dog as it snapped at his ankles. Gerry disappeared down Shaggers' Alley. Raymond the Waver did what he did best, and waved at Angus as he pounded past the war memorial. He skidded into the alley. Gerry was outside Belle's Beauty Salon, frantically yanking the door handle, but, being Sunday, the shop was closed. Gerry gave the door a frustrated kick, then bolted away again. Angus tore after her, past Ossian Fine Arts, where Rob Cunnigham-Graham was fussing over a window display. MacVannin's voice chased him into the shadows.

"And the world is passing away along with its desires, but whoever does the will of God abides forever!"

He darted between the buildings and spilled out onto the lane that ran behind the shops. Lines of bins were stationed along the lane. A winding set of steps led away from the town centre into a residential area.

He bounded up the steps three at a time, his thighs burning after that morning's hike. When he reached the top, Gerry was nowhere to be seen. He glanced both ways along the street, panting. Rows of bland terraced houses with privet hedges. Where the hell had she gone?

He walked along the street, peering over hedges and walls into front gardens. It didn't take long before he spotted her, hunkering behind a large hydrangea.

"Gerry." He sighed. "I can see you. Come on out."

The woman burst from behind the overgrown shrub and sprinted around the side of the house.

"For Christ's sake!" He hurdled a small wall that separated the garden from the street and scurried after her. He skidded around the side of the house and into a surprisingly large back garden with a long, narrow lawn flanked by flower beds and apple trees. A shed and greenhouse lurked at the back of the garden, in front of a tall fence with a gate on it. Behind the fence was moorland.

"Gerry! Come back!"

The woman was halfway across the lawn but picked the worst possible time to glance over her shoulder. Angus saw the washing line in front of her, but she didn't. Suddenly her legs flew up in the air and she landed with a thud on the grass, literally clotheslined.

Angus jogged over to her. She lay on her back, staring up at the sky, groaning. "You okay, Gerry?"

"No," she croaked. "I've been decapitated."

He stifled a smile, then offered Gerry his hand. After a second, she took it, and he hauled her upright. "Here's me thinking you knew your way around a clothesline, Gerry."

CHAPTER 69

ANGUS huckled Gerry along High Street towards the police Land Rover, where Nadia was waiting. She leaned casually against the vehicle, her arms folded.

"And who's this then?"

"Geraldine MacAuley," he replied. "Aka the Knicker Snatcher."

"Only once have I stolen a pair of knickers," Gerry protested. "And that was because it was dark at the time."

He pulled open the back door of the Land Rover. "Mind your head, Gerry," he said, helping her inside. Nadia slammed the door shut.

"At least a menace is off the mean streets of Silvaig," she said.

"I'd better get her booked in."

"Good, you can give me a lift to the station. My car's parked there."

"Aye, no bother." A sudden jolt shot through him. "Where's Gills?"

Nadia frowned. "Gone. Said something about visiting the bookshop to speak to Lachy about Chichester. Why? What's the matter?"

"Nothing. I just—" He shook his head. "It doesn't matter." He climbed into the Land Rover, that nagging sense of anxiety returning with a vengeance.

"Stinks of wet dog in here," Gerry complained. "Listen, Constable MacNeil. We don't have to take this any further, do we? What if I told you I had some information?"

"What kind of information?"

"Information about the murder."

"Aye?"

"Aye. I saw someone the night that young lassie was done in."

"Really?" He was only half-paying attention because his mobile was ringing in his pocket. He pulled out the device and saw Gregory Stewart's name flash up on the screen. When he'd spoken to the old screenwriter who'd written *The Suffering*, he hadn't expected to hear from him so soon, if at all. Many of the cast and crew who worked with Eleanor on the movie were dead. Of those who were still alive, how valuable would their recollections be after thirty years? He held up a finger to Gerry then lifted the phone to his ear. "Mr Stewart, thanks for getting back to me."

"Got a few names for ya," the old man said.

"That was quick work."

"Yeah, well, gave me an excuse to look up some of my old buddies. We took a stagger down memory lane. You got a pen handy?"

Nadia watched him curiously as he fumbled for his notepad. He balanced it on his knee and fished out a pen. "Go ahead, sir."

"So, the guy who worked in the prop department under that asshole Hawkeye was Charles Gilbert."

Angus scribbled the name in his notebook.

"The rest were all women, apart from the Scottish guy I mentioned in our previous conversation."

Angus gripped the pen a little tighter. "What was his name?"

"My old friend Cody Vaughn, a co-writer on *The Suffering*, got to know him quite well," Stewart continued. Whether he hadn't heard Angus or was ignoring him, he couldn't be sure. "It was the eighties, the era of Charles Manson and satanism and all of that shit. They dabbled in the black arts together. Got up to all sorts of mischief. There was one time when—"

"Mr Stewart," Angus cut in. "What was his name?"

"What? Oh right, my apologies. His name was Neville—Neville Boules."

The hair on his forearms stood on end. "Neville Boules? Are you sure?"

"Of course. Like I say, Cody knew the guy well. He said it was Neville who made the doll for the movie."

He thanked Stewart and cut the call, his mind racing.

"Eh, excuse me!" Gerry piped up from the back seat. "I was about to give you some vital information here. So, I was in Glenruig that night, visiting a friend. I remember because it was Halloween. It was about two, three in the morning, and I was outside having a smoke."

"Gerry!" Angus snapped. "Can you shut up!"

She hunched forward, staring at him with ratlike eyes. "Naw! I'm trying to tell you I saw someone. This guy running past. Proper wrinkly old coffin-dodger."

"Aye, right." He sighed.

"Who's Neville Boules?" Nadia asked.

"He's the guy who made the clay corpse Eleanor used in *The Suffering*." He turned to her, his whole body now tingling. "He ran the bookshop in Glenruig with Lachy."

"That's him!" Gerry yelled from the back seat. "That's the guy I saw."

Both Angus and Nadia swivelled in their seats and stared at the woman. "It must have been a ghost you saw, Gerry, because Neville's dead," Angus said.

She tutted, as if Angus were a complete imbecile. "No, not him. It was the other one I saw. Lachy Campbell."

CHAPTER 70

A fresh wind nipped the tips of Gills's ears as he walked towards the book-shop. His whole body seemed to ache from the hike up Glen Màma, but the pain was concentrated in his thighs and calves. He'd changed out of his walking gear and was now wearing his comfortable cords, trusted old brogues, tweed jacket, and mismatched socks.

The village was now mercifully free of press vehicles. White horses reared and whinnied out in the bay. Black-headed gulls veered above the choppy sea, buffeted by the wind. In the distance, the Cullins thrust upwards like daggers into billowing, soot-grey clouds. Gills, though, was not paying attention to the scenery. His mind was on James Chichester and Dòmhnall MacRuari, two powerful men connected across centuries by strands of genetic code. There was even a physical resemblance between the pair, judging from illustrations of the Druid he'd viewed on Google Images.

Gills wanted to know more about *Na Sgàilean*, Dòmhnall's elite unit of warriors, and hoped Lachy could help him find more source material.

Muriel and Agnes, the Highland cows, glowered at Gills from their field as he walked past. "Has anyone ever told you ladies it's rude to stare?"

The cows continued to glower.

"Clearly not," he said, crossing the road to the bookshop. The bell jangled a flat note as he opened the door and went inside. He walked up to the counter and found Issy the cat curled up asleep next to the heater. Smoke spiralled from a squashed cheroot dout, which lay like a slug in the ashtray on the counter, but there was no sign of the bookseller.

"Lachy, it's me, you old reprobate!" Gills called.

He waited for a beat, then rounded the counter and walked towards the back of the shop. He paused in front of the velvet curtain. Many times he'd speculated what lay behind the claret folds. Now was as good a time as any to find out. Gently, somehow nervous, he prised the drapes aside. "Lachy, you in here, old bean?" he croaked.

When there was no answer, he pulled the curtains farther apart and stepped inside. The room was larger than he'd expected, and stuffed with mouldering cardboard boxes, cleaning equipment, and sagging shelving filled with more books. Gills's shoulders slumped. It was all a bit of an anticlimax. He walked across to a battered old workbench and examined a venerable apothecary cabinet that sat there. At random, he slid open a drawer. It was filled with feathers: crow, buzzard, thrush, starling, and various others he didn't recognise. Shrugging, he closed the drawer and tried another. This one contained scraps of material of different sizes, apparently cut from items of clothing. The next drawer to the right contained an array of buttons, whilst the one above was filled with pins. He never had Lachy down as a haberdasher. "Everyone needs a hobby, I suppose," he muttered, closing the drawer.

On a whim, he decided to take a peek in one more compartment. He clasped the small wooden handle and pulled. The drawer contained locks of fair hair. He let out an involuntary gasp and whipped his hand away, as if burned.

Fingers tingling, he reached into the box and lifted out a length of hair. The strands felt dry, and appeared almost translucent when he held them up to the light. Gills's heart was racing. Why would Lachy keep human hair in a drawer? To make a wig, perhaps? A new business venture—Campbell's Haberdasher and Perruquier?

Aye, must be something like that, Gills thought, returning the lock of hair to the drawer and slamming it shut. Only then did he notice the contraption that sat next to the apothecary cabinet. It looked like an old safe, but was, he realized, a kiln for firing clay.

Hinges squealed like a rabbit caught in a snare as he opened the kiln door. The interior was dirty and blackened through use, but empty. He backed away, and his eyes fell on a grimy tin bucket under the workbench. It contained scraps of dried clay. His knees cracked as he bent to examine the contents of the bucket. He raked through the coarse shards, digging with his fingers like a dog searching for a buried bone. A few inches down, entombed amongst the dusty fragments, was a small clay head. The skull had cracked, but its eyes stared up at Gills, two dark voids that set his heart racing. He wiggled the head free from the powdery debris. Underneath he saw what looked like a torso, arms, and legs. He placed the head down on the floor and scraped down further. His numb fingers became coated in dust as he hauled out more severed limbs, partial heads, and dislocated bodies. The bucket, he now understood, contained aborted clay corpses, like tiny macabre foetuses.

He stopped digging and sat back on his haunches. His heart thumped against his rib cage. Sweat prickled the nape of his neck. He pressed the pads of his hands to his temples. Suddenly little details that seemed insignificant at the time leapt to mind. Like when he'd heard Lachy chatting to someone in this room. He'd presumed the bookseller was talking to himself, but now . . .

And then there was the way he never spoke about Neville in the past tense, despite his partner having been dead for over a year.

Gills hauled himself upright, muscles fired by adrenaline. Lachy knew all about Chichester and the Druid. He'd compiled the laird's family tree. Had his all-consuming grief at losing Nev led him to make a Faustian bargain with the entity that lived inside Chichester? Gills recalled how broken Lachy had been after Nev's death. The colour had faded from Lachy until he'd looked like a sepia-tinged photograph. The Druid preyed on the vulnerable, those crippled by loss, despair, envy, and greed. How lonely must Lachlan have been to allow this to happen?

Gills flicked his tongue across his dry lips. "Christ, Lachy! What have you done?"

Suddenly he caught a whiff of cheroot smoke. Slowly, he turned around.

Lachy stood less than a meter away, an ancient-looking hammer held at his side. He stared at Gills with dilated pupils, the nicotine yellow orbs infused with a strange light.

Gills stepped back until he came up against the workbench. He fumbled behind him for a weapon. His fingers closed around the handle of a chisel. Lachy's face was expressionless as he raised the hammer and stalked forward. Gills was so terrified, he was hardly aware of swinging the chisel. He watched the silver blade sweep in a tight arc towards Lachy's ear.

Too tight, as it turned out.

The chisel whistled a millimetre past the bookseller's nose. His momentum sent him sprawling towards Lachy, who shoved him back up against the workbench. Gills barely had time to raise his hands before the dirty hammer came down. He was aware of a dull thud, then pain exploded across his skull. Bright lights danced across his vision. Something warm slithered down his face.

Then he slumped to the floor.

Gills woke with a thumping headache, ten times worse than a Hogmanay hangover. The floor where he lay seemed to rise and fall. Bile swilled in his stomach. He coughed, rolled over onto his side, and vomited. Only after his guts had stopped wrenching and his eyes had stopped watering was he able to assess his situation. He was trussed up, legs bound with thick rope, hands tied behind his back. Just as Angus had described in his vision. He whimpered. Dried blood was plastered to the side of his face.

With difficulty, he rolled into a sitting position, and the reason he had thought the floor was moving became apparent. He was on the deck of Lachy's boat, *Lenore*. Christ! He'd been so stupid. Angus had warned him to stay away from boats and the sea. How could he forget that Lachy had a vessel?

Gills's head hurt so much, he'd forgotten to be scared. But now he remembered. Fear turned his limbs to icy mush. He could see Lachy's thin form at the helm, but the bookseller kept pulsing in and out of focus. Gills tried to speak, but the words tumbled out in a nonsensical jumble. Concussion, he guessed. Maybe a cracked skull. The least of his worries.

He thought of Angus, and the tears he'd held back began to flow. He'd failed the boy. And now he was going to perish. He laid his head back against the gunwale and felt the spray on his face. He thought of the peaty taste of whisky and the smell of Caitlin's hair. He thought of raucous pub sessions with Uisdean and hours on the sidelines watching Angus play shinty. He closed his eyes and smelt the musty scent of his favourite books. He felt Bran and Sceolan lick his hands, and even remembered Jock, a scruffy terrier he'd had as a child, dead now half a century.

So many memories. Most of them good. Some bad. Some worse. Sad to think they would all soon be erased. Boozy field trips with his friends from the historical society. Scoring the winning goal for Glasgow University to win the Littlejohn Vase. Walking the Incan trail to Machu Picchu with his old girlfriend, Sonja. Hours spent in the library poring over velum and brittle manuscripts. All of that would blow away like dust.

He thought of that first glimpse of Caitlin in the Park Bar and was struck by the bitter irony of everything that had transpired. He'd fallen for a woman who was in love with his best friend. Yet it was him who had been more of a father figure to her son. He'd loved Angus and accepted what Uisdean could not—that the boy was a seer. He had forced him to *see*, only for Angus to presage Gills's own death—at the hands of Lachy, of all people.

The chug of the boat's motor suddenly died. He opened his eyes and saw Lachy stagger towards him.

"You don't have to do this," Gills tried to say, but the words came out disjointed.

Lachy grabbed him by the lapels and hauled him to his feet, his face still expressionless. Those faraway eyes reminded Gills of Uisdean in the care home, as if Lachy were here but not here. There would be no reasoning with him, no appealing to his better nature, because this was not Lachy. This was not the man who sat smoking cheroots with Issy the cat in his lap, or holding forth on the dire state of Scottish football. Gills was a threat—a cricket chirping. And he had to be silenced.

Gills, though, refused to go quietly. He bucked and flailed as Lachy hauled him towards the side of the boat, but the hands gripping him were too strong. He lashed out and caught Lachy with a firm headbutt. Blood burst from the old man's nose, but he didn't even flinch.

"Wake up, Lach!" Gills roared. "Nev wouldn't want this!"

The appeal did not register. Lachy's eyes were completely blank. Blood streamed over his lips and down his chin. He made no effort to wipe it away. He lifted Gills from the deck and levered him over the gunwale. There he snagged, half in, half out of the boat. Lachy's face was inches from his. He seemed to look straight through Gills, his pupils like piercing black arrowheads. Blood from his burst nose dripped onto Gills's cheek. Out of the side of his eye, Gills could see the cold, impersonal waves. The white-tipped crests reached for him on the swell, as if trying to grab him. Flecks of briny spray splashed across his face, like froth from a salivating dog. Lachy worked his hands under his legs and heaved. Gravity did the rest. Gills's body flipped and he dropped like a sack of coal.

He landed headfirst and the cold drove all thoughts from his mind. He thrashed and tugged like a salmon on a hook, but the rope did not budge. He kept his mouth closed as he sank, but soon his lungs were burning from lack of oxygen. Above him, slivers of light penetrated the murk. Lachy's blurry shadow watched his descent into darkness. Gills jerked and kicked, but his strength was waning. The light grew dimmer, the thread that held him to life thinner.

He pictured Caitlin walking barefoot on the shore, sandals dangling by her side, the accidental brush of her hand against his. The warmth of her touch. Would he see her again soon?

In his death throes, Gills clung to the promise of Tír na nÓg, the Celtic otherworld of joy and beauty. He wanted to believe that death was a continuum, the passing from one realm into the next. But then Uisdean was in his head, hammering him with nihilism, and a terrifying doubt seeped into Gills's mind.

He clamped his lips shut to stop the water entering. Now was not the time for doubt, but he couldn't help it. Death was the great unknowable.

There was a roaring in his head. He opened his mouth and expelled the last dregs of oxygen from his lungs. Salt water flooded into him. He watched air bubbles shoot towards the surface—his soul escaping his body.

We are but vessels, he thought. *Without a soul, we sink.*

CHAPTER 71

FIELDS flew past outside the window. Sheep gnawed at fodder left out by the farmers, and smoke rose from the chimneys of drab crofts.

Angus gritted his teeth. He shouldn't have let Gills out of his sight, but he'd been distracted by Gerry and the leopard-print top. How could he have been so stupid?

"Calm down, Angus," Nadia said. "We don't know this Lachy guy has anything to do with the murders."

He said nothing, but in his heart he knew. Lachy had a boat—*Lenore*. When Nev was alive, he'd regularly see them sailing across Glenruig bay, heading for Skye, or round the coast to Eilean Shona. In his vision, he'd seen Gills plummet headfirst into the sea. He'd been thrown from a boat. But he could tell Nadia none of this.

"Lachy knew Chichester from compiling his family tree," he said instead. "Nev died last year, and he's not been the same since. If Chichester is the leader of some death cult who preys on the vulnerable—as you yourself suggested, Nadia—then Lachy is a perfect candidate. And he's linked to the clay corpse through Nev. They were partners—both business and romantic—for years. Seems logical they would have shared a passion for black magic. Christ! Now that I think about it, the bookshop has a whole section dedicated to the occult." He shot Nadia a quick glance. "And Gerry saw him, Nadia. She's a lying wee toerag, but I think she was telling the truth this time."

He squeezed his toe down on the accelerator again, powering along the lochside. The sea swelled up in his peripheral vision, the waves taunting him. *Too late, you're going to be too late!*

"When you put it like that . . ." Nadia said. "I'll try Gills's mobile again—"

Angus stamped his foot on the brake and the Land Rover skidded to a halt in front of the Glenruig Inn. He was out and running before the engine stopped, ignoring the startled walkers sitting outside the pub drinking afternoon pints in the cold. He saw Lachy's boathouse, the back doors leading to the sea ajar. A little distance away was a small jetty, used by yacht owners who moored their vessels in the bay. Tied to the jetty was a steel-grey Zodiac inflatable with an outboard motor. He leapt down a steep embankment onto the shore and pelted towards the jetty. The structure swayed under his feet as he ran down its length towards the Zodiac. He crouched and tugged at the mooring rope, precious seconds draining away as he unwound the coarse braiding from the cleat. At last, the rope was free and he was able to jump on board. The motor was an old-looking Yamaha. He grabbed the starter cord and pulled. The old Yamaha emitted a puff of black smoke and growled into life. He slammed the engine into gear, and glanced up to see Nadia sprinting down the jetty. The inflatable was already a couple of feet from the floating berth. Her legs buckled under her as she landed with a thud in the bow. She winced and pulled herself into a sitting position. "Graceful as always." She glared at him. "You could have waited."

"No time," he muttered, his words drowned out by the roar of the engine. He swung the vessel out into the bay. The bow lifted off the surface as the inflatable loped like a grey wolf across the waves. Nadia gripped the grab rope and ducked down to avoid the gouts of spray spitting over the bow.

He stared out to sea and tried to choke down the despair that was threatening to engulf him.

Don't give up. He would never give up on you.

He gritted his teeth and arced the inflatable to starboard, setting a new course towards a small cluster of islands that lay off the southern tip of Sleat. A breath of diesel fumes whispered to him on the breeze. The inflatable pounded around the lee of the first small island, disturbing a couple of fat grey seals lounging on the rock. They took fright and hefted their bulk into the sea.

Another island loomed out of the waves: veined weather-beaten rock studded with barnacles, like the face of an old woman. The engine snarled as he banked around the rock, sending a slash of salt water into the teeth of the island. His eyes scanned westward—nothing that way but a thick shape-shifting bank of clouds.

Suddenly he heard Nadia yell. "There he is!"

He wrenched the inflatable in the direction of her outstretched finger, and spotted the *Lenore*. The clinker sat broadside to the swell less than two hundred yards away, her red hull glistening like blood. There was movement on deck: two figures locked together. He recognised Gills's unruly mop of hair. He was being forced over the side of the boat, like a wrestler thrown from a ring.

Then he was falling. Angus watched in horror as Gills's body dropped head over heels into the sea, exactly as he had seen in his vision. The waves swallowed the splash. And his friend was gone.

He slammed his fist down on the engine. "No!" he cried. "No!"

Angus curled his free hand into a fist as the inflatable bounded across the waves towards the *Lenore*. Lachlan Campbell stood stock-still as the gap between them narrowed. How long since Gills had gone overboard? How long could he survive in the freezing sea?

The inflatable flew across the waves, howling, as if it, too, sensed the kill. Forty yards. Thirty, twenty. Still the old man did not move. Lachy's face was covered in blood. Gills had gone down fighting.

Angus swung the inflatable parallel with the *Lenore* and slammed the engine into neutral.

He took one look at Lachy, then threw himself into the sea. The cold hit him like a punch, but he absorbed the blow and kicked hard, propelling himself downwards. Salt stung his eyes as he stared into the murk. Down he went. Deeper. Colder. His hands looked spectral as he frantically pulled, as if trying to prise apart the darkness. A scream was trapped like an air bubble in his chest. Each stroke, each thrust of his legs, gnawed away at the frayed thread of hope. His lungs started to burn. Soon he would have to return to the surface for air. But if he did so, that was it. The thread would snap. And Gills would die.

If he isn't dead already.

That cynical voice, which sounded like his father's, sucked the fight out of him. He could feel hope seep away along with his strength. But just when all seemed lost, he saw something shimmer in the darkness. White hair, the ghost of a face. He kicked once more, his limbs fired with renewed vigour. Down he swept, his hands reaching, grasping, flailing. His fingers clamped around a bicep and pulled Gills towards him. The old man's body was limp, his eyes closed as if he'd decided to take a midafternoon nap.

He snaked a hand under Gills's oxters and launched himself upwards. His legs shot back and forth like pistons, his one free arm clawing the water. By now his lungs were ablaze, and the effort of hauling the inert weight only increased the strain. Above, a dim light permeated the surface, but it still looked a long way off. A shrill ringing began in his head as his brain became starved of oxygen.

From somewhere, he heard the words of his swimming coach, Mr. Latimer. *When fatigued, rely on technique. And for God's sake, Angus, kick!*

He closed his eyes and focused every muscle and sinew on his form. And he did exactly what Mr. Latimer had told him. He kicked. Kicked with everything he had. Kicked until there was nothing left.

The ringing increased to a high-pitched scream, but then he felt the water pressure slacken. He opened his eyes and the light was almost dazzling. With one final thrust of his legs he broke through the surface. Choking, gasping, he sucked in a huge lungful of frigid air. Still panting for breath, his arms and legs screaming from the effort, he paddled to the inflatable. Nadia appeared above him, her face a terrified mask.

"Oh God! Oh God!" she muttered, reaching for Gills and heaving him aboard. Angus clenched the grab rope and hauled himself into the Zodiac.

Gills's face was pale blue, mouth slack. Nadia rolled him onto his back and began chest compressions, counting out each push with a jagged hiss. When she reached thirty, she stopped, pinched Gills's nose, and breathed into his mouth. Angus watched his friend's chest rise, then deflate like a popped balloon. Tears welled in Angus's eyes as Nadia resumed the compressions. And suddenly he was back on the beach that warm summer's day, pumping on the chest of Ethan Boyce. The boy's bones had felt so fragile, Angus feared they might break.

He shook his head to clear the memory, and saw Nadia once more lean forward and blow into Gills's mouth. She resumed pounding at his chest, even though they both knew it was now hopeless. "Come on, you daft old bastard," Angus groaned. "Just breathe!"

No response, not even a flicker. He slumped down onto the deck. Tears blurred his vision. "Come on, *a'bhalach*," he whimpered. "Just breathe. Please, just breathe."

He heard a choking sound and Gills's body seemed to twitch. Angus scrambled onto his knees, hardly daring to believe what he'd seen. The old man's chest then convulsed and a gush of salty water erupted from his lips.

Nadia grabbed Gills by the shoulders and levered him onto his side so he wouldn't choke on his own vomit. He spluttered and coughed, his whole body trembling as he evacuated what seemed like half the Atlantic from his lungs.

When he'd finished retching, Angus helped him into a sitting position. He locked eyes with Nadia. "Thank you," he croaked, struggling to get those simple words out. She gave him a faint smile.

Angus pulled Gills into an embrace.

"I saw my soul leave my body," the old man whispered.

Angus squeezed his bony shoulder. "It must have returned."

They broke apart and he watched as Gills's tremulous smile froze on his face, his eyes snagged on something over Angus's shoulder.

Slowly, he twisted around and saw Lachlan Campbell standing on the deck of the *Lenore*. His face was slack and emotionless, eyes like those of a dead fish. He raised a shaking gnarled hand. In it, he held a bright red flare gun. The barrel was pointed straight at Gills.

"Put the gun down, Lachy! It's over."

The old man's arm tensed. His finger tightened on the trigger, but then he swung the flare gun towards his own face. His lips parted wide and he shoved the barrel into his mouth.

Gills threw out a hand. "No!"

Angus heard a pop, like a firework going off. The bookseller was lifted clean off his feet. His face was infused with a sulphurous orange glow. Then his head exploded.

CHAPTER 72

AS Angus drove the Land Rover into the courtyard of Dunbirlinn, he had the eerie sense of events coming full circle, spinning around like the arms of the symbol Faye had drawn in her sketchpads.

The walls of the castle towered above him as he stepped from the Land Rover. High above the battlements, the MacRuari flag whipped and cracked in the wind, as if the wolf depicted on the crest were alive.

For a second he stood staring up at the ancient stonework. The castle was in darkness, save a dim light shining from the arched window of the topmost tower. Angus recalled the room with its beautiful and terrifying apocalyptic fresco.

He set off towards the great oak doors, shoved them open with his shoulder, and stepped inside. The smell of dampness and rot leached from the walls, along with a faint feral stink that reminded him of a fox's den he'd once stumbled upon in the hills above the cottage.

"Mrs MacCrimmon!" he yelled. "Mrs MacCrimmon!"

The housekeeper had made a habit of appearing unannounced, but now, when he would have welcomed the sight of her sullen, wrinkly old face, she was nowhere to be seen. Instead the only eyes watching him were those of Dòmhnall MacRuari from the portrait hung on the wall.

Angus walked to the foot of the grand staircase, guarded by the suits of armour with their long Lochaber axes. The red carpet under his feet felt soft and sticky as he climbed the stairs. Shadows pooled in corners and crevices. Somewhere he heard scurrying and scratching. Suddenly a dark shape swooped down from the rafters and flashed inches over his head. He threw out an arm, almost tripping and plummeting down the stairs. The black entity came to rest on the bronze bust of a consumptive-looking gentleman.

A crow. The bird cocked its head to the side and gave Angus the same penetrative stare.

He heard Gills's voice in his head. *They say the crow presages death, old bean. Hardly an auspicious omen. Perhaps you should turn back?*

He shook away the thought and again started to climb. The crow fluttered like a black flame, gliding ahead as if leading the way. Angus, though, knew where he was going—the room at the top of the tower. His pulse quickened, feet slapping on the floorboards as he hurried past Faye's room, along narrow corridors, and through shadowy annexes.

At last, he reached the foot of the spiral staircase he and Stout had climbed when interviewing Chichester. Again, the sense of coming full circle was palpable. The crow perched on a sconce, let out one last caw, then flew straight at the wall and vanished.

"What the f—" he exclaimed, then realized that rather than disappearing into thin air, the bird had flown out of an arrow loop.

He placed a foot on the bottom step of the spiral staircase. He had no idea what awaited him at the top. Had all his life been narrowing to this moment, as Gills had suggested? Perhaps not, but he was certain of something—Chichester was no mere mortal. Cancer of the type he had did not miraculously go into remission. Whatever was inside the laird, it had come from that otherworld, a realm of the supernatural, of things once known but now lost. *Dà-shealladh* was a product of that same world and it was part of him, woven into his very being, like the subtle pattern on a length of Harris Tweed. Dòmhnall MacRuari had straddled the liminal space between these worlds, and so did he.

His breathing shallow, Angus began to climb. The staircase was illuminated by dim shafts of moonlight from the arrow slits. His fingertips traced the scabrous stonework, footsteps echoing around the space. He ascended, his heart rate increasing with each laboured step. He thought of Faye, climbing these stairs so she could lie on her back and stare at the fresco. Had she pictured herself amongst the carnage? One of the damned plunging into the lake of fire, or a tortured soul being devoured by some beast? Or was she the figure above it all, gazing down with wise eyes, knowing that this, too, would pass—that green shoots would sprout from the blood-soaked soil? His legs felt clumsy and wooden as he reached the top landing. The door to the room at the top of the tower was open a couple of inches and a shaft of light fell across the floor. His fingers trembled as he pushed the door wide and stepped inside. Hundreds of candles stood on every surface, dancing and swaying in the wind from the open window, below which Chichester was sprawled.

Above Angus's head, the fresco seemed alive in the candlelight, the warring creatures massacring each other. The boy at the centre of the chaos continued to sit against the tree trunk. The pages of his red book seemed to turn as he read on, oblivious.

He dragged his eyes away from the scene of destruction and back to the laird. Chichester wore a charcoal suit that hung off his bones. His hands were covered in blood, ragged strips of skin hanging from his knuckles. He'd pummelled the stone floor so hard, the white bone underneath was visible. His lips were drawn back over yellowing teeth, and his hair, once a thick wolf's pelt, was now thin and straggly, clumps of it lying on the flagstones at his feet. Angus took a step towards him and saw something silver glint from his arms—the Fairy Horn of the MacRuaris. Chichester cradled the artifact like a child with a favourite toy.

"James Glas," he breathed.

The laird slowly turned his head and looked up at him with bloodshot eyes. Angus almost took a step back. Chichester's face was thin and leathery, like Lindow Man, a twisted bog body.

"Angus Dubh," he rasped. Even from a few feet away, he smelt Chichester's rancid breath. It was the spoiled-meat stench of the morgue.

A wave of pity swept through him, cloaking, but not erasing, the disgust. The laird grunted as he pushed himself up, then slumped back against the wall. He seemed to have lost half his body weight. Angus thought of the cricket after the horsehair worm had bored its way out. There was nothing left of Chichester but a dried-up husk.

Again, Chichester tried to haul himself up. This time he managed, although the effort had him wheezing. He stood, swaying in front of the open window, a bag of bones in a three-thousand-pound suit. Angus inched towards him and held out a hand. "Come away from the window, James."

Chichester looked down at the horn held in his bloody hands and frowned, as if surprised to see it there.

"James, what's happened to you?"

The laird's hollow cheeks and sunken eyes gave Angus the impression he was talking to a corpse.

"Like the prophecy said, my line will wither and die. If only I'd accepted that, all those years ago, then all this might have been avoided."

The corpse laughed, a throaty death rattle. "We're hardwired for survival. When whittled down to our core, we'll do anything—promise anything—to live, Angus Dubh. I thought I could cheat death."

"Something happened to you in that cave where your ancestors perished, didn't it?"

"I wanted to tell you, Angus. I really did. But I couldn't. It wouldn't allow me."

"Then tell me now."

Chichester traced his gory fingers over the fairy horn. "Its roots were already inside me, planted deep in my genetic code. Like my ancestor Dòmhnall MacRuari, all I did was allow it to flourish. I let this corrupt thing grow inside me."

Chichester raised his head and glared at Angus with bulging bloodshot eyes. "I saw it in you, too. The old knowledge is seeded in your DNA. But it's a different strain to mine. You're not alone, Angus. Christianity declared war on the old ways, then our dissociation from nature diluted the lore of our ancestors even more." His talon-like hand curled into a fist. "It's still there, though. Lying dormant inside us."

Angus inched towards the laird. "Is that what you told Betty Duncan?" His lip curled. "Is that what you told Joe Carver? Jonathan Boyce? Lachy Campbell?"

"You don't understand, Angus. I had no choice. The old gods demand payment in blood."

Questions swirled around Angus's head, like the bats in the woods outside the Old Manse. Here, standing in front of him, was someone who could answer them.

A grotesque smile appeared at the corner of Chichester's rotten mouth.

"I sensed their vulnerability, like a wolf picking off the weakest in the herd." He threw out his arms. "You want a rational explanation? That I fed them a potion? Or injected them with serum? Or made them drink my blood like some hokey Dracula?" He pointed a shaking finger at him. "It doesn't work like that, Angus Dubh! The irony is, your ancestors two thousand years ago would understand. But you don't."

"Then explain," he pleaded.

"Pluck the right string, and you can make people do anything. The artist wanted to express through a brushstroke a truer reality. The carer accepted her son's birth defect was caused by man's corruption of the earth. Her sacrifice was an act of purification. Mr. Carver tasted in fine malts the profound connection he'd always craved, that same alchemy that turns water and barley into something so complex, it embodies the very land itself. He gave himself to the sea in the end—returned his body to its origins so that he might be reborn."

"What about his wife?" Angus growled. "Was Barbara *reborn*? Was Lewis? Was little Ethan?"

"Yes," Chichester answered simply. "We all are." He spun a bloody finger in the air. "It's always spinning."

"And Lachlan Campbell? Which of his strings did you pluck?"

"The power to peer beyond death, to reach into that otherworld and speak to his lost love. People never truly die, Angus, but the thread that connects us to them has become frayed. They exist, just outside our grasp, floating on an umbilical cord of silk."

"Did your pawns know what they were doing? Did you?"

Chichester's whole frame began to shake. Angus fancied he could hear his bones rattling.

"Yes," he sobbed. "But it's a whisper on the wind, Angus, a dream you can't wake from. This black dread hangs at the edge of your consciousness. You try to convince yourself it's not real . . . but part of you knows it is, has known all along." Tears leaked from Chichester's eyes like melting wax. "And you know, too, that you had a choice. That you let it take root."

Angus writhed in the currents of emotion swirling inside him. Pity, remorse, rage, anguish. Part of him wanted to rip Chichester apart, but another, stronger, voice told him this bag of bones in front of him had suffered enough.

"This thing growing inside you," he said. "I want to speak to it. I want to speak to *an Draoidh*."

Chichester looked up and met his stare. "Unfortunately, as you can see, he's left me, ripped out root and branch."

He again spun his finger in the air. "He has a new host. And he will grow, and the cycle will begin again until the scales fall from our eyes."

Angus took another step towards the laird. "Who is the new host? Tell me!"

Chichester inched back until his calves came up against the window ledge.

Angus heard the crack in his voice. "Who killed my mother?" He reached out a hand towards Chichester. "Please, I'm begging you. . . ."

"That I don't know. Believe me, if I could ease your suffering I would, Angus Dubh."

The laird looked down at the hunting horn. "This instrument has not sounded a note in centuries." He traced his shaking bloody fingertips over the swirling patterns carved around the horn. "I wonder, if I blew it now . . ." He raised the horn to his lips.

"No! Don't! Tell me! Who is its new host?"

Chichester closed his eyes and sucked in a grating breath. Then he toppled backwards out of the window. Angus threw himself forward and made a grab for the falling man. His fingers clutched only cold air. He hauled himself up and peered over the window ledge. A dark shape plummeted towards the rocks below. But before impact, a dolorous sound arose, an unearthly note that echoed around the cliffs and ramparts.

Like a dying wail. Like a summons to war.

CHAPTER 73

ANGUS stood in the mortuary anteroom, trying to ignore the whiff of form-aldehyde and bodily decay. James Chichester's would be the third autopsy he'd endured recently. Three—the sacred number of the ancient Celts, the ever-spinning cycle of life, death, and rebirth. In a place like this, it was not so hard to believe human bodies were mere hosts, garments to be worn then shed.

Beside him, Nadia zipped up her white disposable gown. "You ready?"

"Aye," he croaked, then followed her through the double doors into the cutting room. Nadia halted abruptly and Angus almost walked into her. He glanced up and hissed a Gaelic curse. There were two gurneys in the room. One of the corpses was covered in a white sheet. Dr. Kelly and her assistant were bent over the other gurney, upon which lay the headless corpse of Lachy Campbell. Angus felt his gorge rise. Ragged strips of flesh and gristle hung from the old man's neck, the skin charred around the wound margins. Lachy had been transformed into *Coluinn gun Cheann*, the headless bòcan of Gaelic folklore.

Angus stepped forward beside Nadia. A faint sulphurous stench of gunpowder seemed to hang in the air above Lachy's corpse.

Nadia gave him a quick glance and screwed up her nose. "Does the otherworld that Gills talked about smell like that?" Nadia asked.

"I think they all do—Hell, Jahannam, Hades."

"At least Chris Kelbie won't be remembered as a killer," Nadia murmured.

Orla nodded to her assistant, who scampered to the foot of the gurney and pulled a white sheet over Lachy's gruesome corpse.

"That one was straightforward," the pathologist said. "Cause of death was about as obvious as they come. This one, however . . ."

She beckoned Angus and Nadia over to the other gurney. Although it was cold in the room, Angus's hands were clammy. The sound of his own shallow breathing reverberated inside his head as the assistant removed the sheet that covered James Chichester's body.

Angus felt the air leave his lungs. Lying on the slab was a twisted, broken body, barely recognisable as a human being. The corpse's mouth hung open in a silent scream, the blackened eyes wide in terror, as if staring into the dark maw of the otherworld. He thought of the bag of bones in the three-thousand-pound suit he'd spoken to in the tower at Dunbirlinn. Chichester had been a husk of a man, but this was altogether different. Rather than someone who died a mere thirty-six hours ago, he could have been looking at a corpse that had been decaying for months.

"My God!" Nadia gasped. "He looks like Lindow Man. Is it even James Chichester?"

"It's Chichester all right," Orla said. "We ran the DNA to be sure. It's also a paternal match to Faye."

"What happened to him?" Nadia asked.

Orla sounded unusually hesitant. "The fall shattered almost every bone in his body, but James Chichester would appear to have been dead long before he jumped out of that window."

For a long second, no one spoke. "Believe me, Orla, he was still alive," Angus said. "I was there."

"Then this can't be James Chichester," Orla declared. "I've already completed an internal examination. This body is riddled with cancer. The disease had spread to all major organs, literally to his marrow. The flesh is . . . corrupted, as if blood hadn't profused the tissue for a long time. When we die, the decomposition clock begins, bacteria begin to break the body down. The rate of decay is affected by a number of different factors, such as temperature, body position, or whether the cadaver is in or outdoors. Sure, in some circumstances decomposition can occur rapidly, but not this rapidly." She shook her head. "I mean, just look at the skin discoloration and putrefaction. You mentioned Lindow Man just now, Nadia, and bog bodies are a good analogy. If I performed an autopsy on this body without knowing any of the circumstances, I'd say he's been dead for years but preserved in some acidic oxygen-depleted environment.

"Whoever's been living in Dunbirlinn, whoever brought the wolves back to the Highlands . . . it wasn't James Chichester."

A fine drizzle fell from drab clouds, veiling the town of Silvaig in a damp miasma. Nadia had barely spoken since they left the morgue, and it wasn't until they were seated at a booth in the Jac-O-bite that she looked him in the eye.

"Maybe Chichester was part of some secret trial of a new cancer drug?" she said, wrapping her hands around her coffee cup. "Although Eleanor told us he refused to see any doctors and, as far as I know, the search teams at the castle haven't found any medication."

Angus gave a small shrug. "Who knows?"

Nadia glared at him. "You do, I think."

He reached for his own coffee and took a sip, stalling. "Why do you say that?"

"Copper's intuition. Angus, I've always thought you were keeping something back from me, even when we were cadets at Tulliallan. You'd give me that same blank stare that you're giving me now, and I'd have no idea what was behind it."

"I was just trying to be dark and mysterious."

She turned from him and stared out the window. "Don't do that, Angus," she said.

"What?"

"That Scottish male thing of trying to make everything into a joke."

"Chichester was raving mad at the end, Nadia. Nothing he said made sense." He pictured the laird cradling the Fairy Horn of the MacRuaris and the abject despair in his eyes.

"And Lachy, what made him raving mad?"

"Grief after Nev died," Angus said. "I think he believed if he made the ultimate offering to the old gods, they would let him speak to Nev in the afterlife."

"But was he coerced by Chichester? And if so, why would Chichester make Lachy sacrifice his own wife and daughter?"

Because Chichester never comprehended the depths of *An Droaidh's* devotion to the old gods, he thought. Before he leapt from the tower, Chichester had told him he'd believed he could cheat death. If Chichester had known the payoff for his own life was the death of his wife and daughter, would he have made that Faustian bargain? Angus wondered.

When whittled down to our core, we'll do anything—promise anything—to live, Angus Dubh. . . .

"Perhaps Gills and I were wrong, Nadia. Perhaps Chichester had nothing to do with any of this. Like the newspapers are saying, he was driven mad by grief and took his own life."

Nadia nodded, but her eyes were fixed on the middle distance. ""Don't grieve,"" she said after a long pause. "'Anything you lose comes round in another form.'" She tore her gaze away from the window and gave him a faint, self-conscious smile.

"Rumi?"

"Aye."

Angus waited for her to elaborate, but Nadia again appeared lost in her own thoughts. "Perhaps Kelbie was right," she said at last. "Perhaps everything is reborn."

He reached across the table and placed his hand on top of hers. "Someone once told me that in our appetite to label the universe and everything in it, we've sacrificed a deeper, innate knowledge."

"Gills?" she said.

"No. Chichester."

She emitted a grim chuckle. "I want to ask you something."

"What?"

"If I ask it, will you tell me the truth?"

"You'd know, even if I didn't, Nadia."

"It was her horse, wasn't it?"

He winced. "Aye."

She held his gaze for a long second, then reached for her bag and jacket. "I have to go back to Glasgow." She stood, shrugged on her coat, then leaned across the table and kissed him lightly on the cheek. "Take care of yourself, Angus Dubh."

CHAPTER 74

ANGUS stood in front of his mother's headstone, hands thrust deep into the pockets of his long black coat. Wind scoured the graveyard like icy fingernails. A storm had hit last night, lashing the west coast with a fury the old folk in the village said they'd never seen. The sea had surged, flooding low-lying houses. Roofs had been blown off barns, trees uprooted, and boats tossed onto the beach like kindling. Branches had been snapped off the ancient yew that towered over his mother's grave, but the tree stood firm. Stoic. Enduring.

Tears nipped at the corners of his eyes. He placed a hand on the cold granite headstone. "One day I'll find who took you from us," he whispered. "I promise."

Behind him, Gills gave a polite cough. Angus turned and in the distance spotted the hearses wending their way from Dunbirlinn towards the graveyard. "It's time," Gills said.

Calum MacCrimmon's fingers moved with deliberate precision across the chanter, every note of the melancholy pibroch true. No mean feat, considering how cold it was at the graveside. Most of the mourners were wrapped up in thick black coats and gloves. The piper was the only person dressed in full Highland regalia—kilt, plaid, long hair sporran, spats, and Ghillie brogues. On his head he wore a black Glengarry bonnet with a silver cap badge that held in place a pheasant feather.

Angus glanced around the small group. Gills gently tapped out the notes of the piper's tune, as if on an invisible chanter. The staff from Dunbirlinn were gathered. Mrs. MacCrimmon stood off to one side, holding Bessie's reins. Somehow, Angus thought, Mrs. MacCrimmon knew the truth about the horse. The white mare's head was bowed, fogged breath and a mournful whinny escaping from its mouth. The old housekeeper's face was set like stone as her son at last brought the pibroch to an end and tucked the bagpipes under his arm.

A balding Church of Scotland minister gave the sermon, a rushed, impersonal affair, as if he were keen to finish and get back home to the warmth. Out of the corner of his eye, Angus spotted Ewan Hunter slip into the cemetery. The ghillie wore a suit that was a little on the tight side, but he was freshly shaven, his hair was cut, and he was sober. Ewan met his eyes and gave a slight nod.

The minister muttered some more cursory words and intoned a prayer before the three caskets were lowered into the ground. He then invited Ashleigh to step forward and play. His wife settled herself on a stool beside the clarsach. Her fingers had healed after she'd cut them in a fall whilst out hill running. Her hair fell in rivulets over her shoulder, brighter than any display of autumnal leaves. The mourners could not take their eyes off her. Even the minister appeared transfixed. He flashed her an encouraging smile. She lifted her hands and began to play.

The music soared around the graveyard, plaintive and haunting. Each note seemed to hang in the air, laden with emotion. Angus glanced up. Coming from the vicinity of the clootie tree, he saw thin tendrils of tenebrous smoke twist into the sky. The shadow drifted on the wind towards the graveyard. He smelt a faint acrid scent. The pagans were returning Chris Kelbie to nature.

He watched the smoke tear apart on the wind, then returned his attention to Ash. She swayed slightly, lost in the music, a little half-smile on her lips. For a long minute after she stopped playing, nobody spoke. At last, the minister stepped to the graveside, then invited the mourners forward. They filed past and dropped handfuls of soil into the graves, the sound like fingernails scratching at the wooden lids of the coffins.

Snow started to fall, soft flecks that danced in the air.

Angus walked over to Ewan and shook his hand. "Good to see you, *a'bhalach*."

Ewan stared at Faye's grave, fighting back tears. "I wanted to say goodbye to her."

"It's tough, but you'll be glad you came."

Ewan looked down at his polished shoes, nodding. "I wanted to say goodbye to you, too, Gus. I've enlisted in the army."

Angus hid his surprise well. "Good for you. When do you leave?"

"Next week. The training centre's in Catterick."

"Nervous?"

Ewan gave a half-laugh. "Absolutely bricking it."

He gave the lad's shoulder a brief squeeze. "You'll run rings around them. Fresh start, right?"

"Aye, fresh start." The ghillie turned and joined the rest of the mourners dribbling out of the graveyard.

Angus walked over to Ash and helped her pack away her clarsach. "That was beautiful," he said. "It was kind of you to do that."

She zipped up her clarsach case and slung it over her shoulder. "Listen, I'm going to give the wake a miss."

"Oh? Okay. Is . . . everything all right?'

"Aye, I'm fine. Just don't fancy it." She rose on her tiptoes and brushed her lips against his. "I'll see you later."

She turned and walked away, hair billowing in the wind like the tail of a comet.

He smiled faintly, then turned and walked over to Gills at the graveside. He produced Chichester's hip flask from his inside pocket, unscrewed the lid, and poured what was left in it over Chichester's casket. Out of the corner of his eye, he saw Gills wince.

The hip flask did not self-replenish, as at times he'd speculated. When it was empty, he threw it on top of the coffin.

Angus turned and wound his way through the graveyard. Police ticker still flapped from the MacRuari mausoleum. Crows muttered in the yew tree. Behind him, he heard a *thwack*, followed by a wet sucking noise as the grave-diggers got to work shovelling the mounds of damp soil over the coffins.

Ethan Boyce's headstone stood near the outer wall of the kirkyard, some fifty yards from his mother's. He crouched and placed his hand on top of the gravestone. He caught the scent of a familiar sweet perfume on the breeze. "Goodbye, Faye," he said.

"Be seeing ya, Constable MacNeil," came the reply, but when he glanced over his shoulder, there was no one there.

He returned his gaze to Ethan's gravestone.

"Sleep tight, wee man," he whispered.

CHAPTER 75

WITHOUT the reporters around, Glenruig had returned to something approaching sleepy normality. Rutted verges and discarded coffee cups indicated the passing of the press pack, like the aftermath of a rock concert. Only the police tape across the door of Campbell & Boules bookshop hinted that all was not quite as it should be.

The mourners from Chichesters' funeral were drifting towards the Glenruig Inn. Gills and Angus joined the black procession, but they had yet to enter the pub when Angus felt something reverberate in his pocket. He pulled out his mobile phone, which he'd placed on vibrate mode for the service, and saw Ashleigh's name flash up on the screen. Her voice, when he answered, sounded fraught.

"Angus, are you at the wake?"

"Just heading in."

"Look, I've had some terrible news. The *Silver Darling*, the ship Grant Abbot was on, went down last night in the storm. All crew lost."

Ash skidded the Clio to a halt outside Nualla and Grant's house at Ardnish. Nualla's VW Beetle was still parked in the drive, but the front door hung wide open.

"Christ, that's not a good sign," Ash muttered. She yanked up the Clio's handbrake and sprang from the car. Angus levered himself out and followed her into the house. Ash had stopped in the hallway, and he almost ran into the back of her. "Ash! What the—"

Looking around, he saw the house was in disarray. A sideboard in the hall had been ransacked, the drawers yanked out and upended. Crockery lay smashed on the floor, next to framed photographs of Rosie. One had been taken at Rosie's christening and showed Nualla and Grant standing by the baptismal font with the baby, flanked by the godparents—him looking awkward in a kilt, and Ash grinning widely, although the smile never reached her eyes.

"Nualla!" Ash yelled, darting from room to room. "Nualla! Are you in here!"

Angus picked his way over broken objects into the living room. Grant's vinyl collection, of which he was so proud, was strewn across the carpet. A new-looking iPad sat on the coffee table, next to a sofa that looked as if it had been attacked with a knife, the lining slashed.

Ash appeared at the door to the living room, breathless. "She's not here. And neither is Rosie. Christ, Angus, what's happened? Do you think it was burglars?"

"Maybe, but they must have been looking for something specific. If not, why leave the iPad, or the TV?"

They returned to the hallway and Angus took out his phone, intending to call it in. "Damn, no reception," he muttered.

"Her car's still here. And so's Rosie's pram," Ash pointed out. "Oh God, Angus! I've a bad feeling about this."

They clattered out of the house, jogged down the driveway, and crossed the road. Some fish farm workers were on the cages feeding the salmon. Angus waved frantically to get their attention, but the cages were out on the loch, a hundred yards away. He cupped his hands around his mouth and shouted. "Have you seen a woman and child pass?"

The two men squinted at him and appeared to shrug.

"Angus, they're too far away," Ash hissed.

"Are you looking for Nualla?"

They both spun around, startled by the voice. Another fish farm worker had emerged from a small hut, a copy of the *West Highland Mail* under his arm.

"Aye, have you seen her?" Ash asked.

"Not five minutes ago," the man said, stroking his bushy beard. He pointed a thick dirty finger. "She was heading that way along the shore with the child—"

Ash was running before he even finished the sentence.

"Thanks," Angus said, then turned and ran after his wife. His mind spun back to another beach a fortnight ago, to the dark mound lying on the sand that he'd hoped was a dead seal.

Not again, please not again.

This beach was not the soft sand at Smirisary where Faye had lain. The polished shoes he'd worn for the funeral crunched over dried seaweed, shingle, and drifts of flotsam and jetsam that had been coughed up on the shore by the storm. Ash was some fifty yards ahead and extending the distance, her arms and legs pumping in perfect harmony. She'd changed out of her funeral clothes and wore leggings, a hoodie, and Nike trainers. There was no way he could keep up with her. Soon she rounded a rocky outcrop and disappeared from sight. A minute later he reached the cliffs and scrambled around their edges, spray from the waves wetting the legs of his dress trousers. Beyond the cliffs was a small cove, where Ash stood, staring at something on the shingle. He leapt down from a rock and jogged over to her. "What is—?"

The question died on his lips. Lying on a small patch of sand was a pile of clothes. Faint ghostly footsteps led from the clothes a short couple of meters to the sea.

Ash grabbed his sleeve. "Oh God! Where's the baby!"

Angus involuntarily raised his hands to his head. His fingers tugged at his hair. Five minutes, the fish farm worker had said. That was all. Without another thought, he kicked off his shoes and threw his suit jacket to the ground. Ash might be the better runner, but he was the stronger swimmer. He sprinted towards the sea, thrusting his knees up to his waist as he ran through the shallows. He knew the water was freezing, but he didn't care.

Only when he dived into the waves did the cold hit him, a stinging blow as if he'd been slapped. He gasped, broke the surface, and kicked hard out into the sea. His arms lashed the surface as he swam. Waves danced all around him, making it difficult to get his bearings. He paused, treading water, then dived down. His eyes stung, but he kept them open. Even then the visibility was poor, the sea murky from silt and debris churned up by the storm. He could only see a few feet in front of his face. Lungs burning, he resurfaced, sucked in another lungful of air, and dived again.

This time he swam down farther, until he felt the thick strands of kelp that grew from the seabed like an underwater forest. And there, in between the writhing stipes and blades, he thought he saw Nualla's face, her eyes wide open and staring. He kicked towards her and reached out a hand. Suddenly the kelp seemed to billow inwards. He saw a flash of silver, like the glint of a seal's tail, and when he looked again, the face—if it had ever been there—was gone.

He floated there for a second, suspended in the depths, his head frantically darting around. Eventually he could stay underwater no longer. He let out a frustrated howl and kicked for the surface.

His arms felt like sodden logs as he swam towards the shore. His feet eventually touched the stony bottom and he lurched from the sea, panting, his clothes plastered to his body.

Ash stood on the shore, her face twisted in horror and pain. "Where are they?" she yelled. "Did you see them?"

He put his hands on his thighs and doubled over. "I couldn't find them," he gasped. "I'm sorry . . . couldn't find them."

Ash sank to her knees. "No," she whimpered. "Not Nualla. Not the baby . . . not wee Rosie." Angus knelt on the shingle, facing his wife. Her skin was as white as the snow on the mountains surrounding the loch. The colour had even drained from her lips. Her eyes shone with tears and disbelief at what had happened.

He leaned forward and pressed his forehead against hers. "I'm sorry, *a ghràidh.* They're gone. The water's too cold for anyone to survive this long."

Ash's shoulders started to shake. "No, Angus. They can't be gone." She sprang to her feet and rushed towards the water. "No!" she wailed, wading into the sea. "No!" The scream ripped from her lungs, a feral shriek that sounded more animal than human.

Angus leapt up and splashed after her. She was waist-deep when he grabbed hold of her.

"Ash, stop!" he roared. "There's nothing you can do!"

"Get the fuck off me!" She lashed out at him, but he caught her wrists and pulled her towards him.

"Stop," he pleaded. "Ash, they're gone." His wife stopped thrashing and crumpled against his chest, body heaving as she cried.

He held her tight as the waves crashed around them. Even as his legs went numb from the cold, he did not move. Over Ash's shoulder, out in the slate-grey waters of the sea loch, he saw a dark shape bob to the surface. For a heart-stopping second he thought it was Nualla, and that somehow she had survived. But then he realized it was only a seal. The creature stared at him with sad brown eyes. As he held the seal's baleful gaze, he was struck by the strange sensation that she shared their sorrow. Her look was one of utter desolation.

As suddenly as she had appeared, the seal vanished, swallowed by the uncaring waves.

Gently, he prised Ash off his chest and held her upright as they stumbled towards shore. Over the sound of the waves crashing on the shingle he heard a keening sound. At first he thought it was a seabird—an oystercatcher or herring gull.

"Wait! Do you hear that?" he asked.

Ash knitted her brow and stared up at him, her face smeared with tears and grains of sand. "What?"

The cry came again, this time a kind of mewling that sounded like no bird he knew.

Ash's fingers clutched at his arm. The sound seemed to be coming from behind a curtain of rock that thrust down from the hillside onto the beach. "Angus, that's a child!" she gasped.

She released her grip on his arm and lurched up the shingle, her feet slipping as if she were walking on ice. Angus staggered after her as fast as his numb legs would allow. He was vaguely aware the mewling had stopped. Could it have been a bird after all? Or the wind whistling around the hillside? He heard his father's voice in his head. *It's the hope that kills ye, son.* Flecks of salty phlegm flew from his lips. "No, Dad," he hissed. "It's the hope that keeps you alive."

He gritted his teeth and ran, arms pistoning back and forth. His legs felt like the wooden limbs of a puppet. He saw Ash disappear behind a claw of rock, and scrambled after her. He rounded the crag and the wind suddenly died.

Ash was crouched on the sand a couple of meters away. He took in their surroundings at a glance: a small sheltered hollow carved between the rocks and overhung with wizened trees, a halo of charcoal-coloured sky above.

His gaze flitted back to Ash, who was gently lifting something from the sand. She turned to him, a small body cradled in her arms. Tears streamed down his wife's cheeks. For a brief second he thought the worst, that the child was dead. But then Ash gave him a tremulous smile.

"Is she okay?" he gasped.

Ash drifted over to him, her teeth chattering, the baby cradled in her arms. Little Rosie smiled up at him with her rosebud mouth. Slithers of light seemed to shimmer in the baby's light brown eyes.

Angus placed his arm around his wife's shoulders, steering her back towards the shore and a life he somehow knew had changed irrevocably. Out at sea, he spotted the seal again. She gazed at him with wide melancholic eyes, then flipped, her sleek body shimmering in the cold light for an instant, before she disappeared beneath the waves.

EPILOGUE

GILLS stood in the vast gloomy hallway of Dunbirlinn and stared at the portrait of Dòmhnall MacRuari. It was the first time he'd seen the painting—the first time he'd been in the castle itself, for that matter. *An Droaidh* glared down at him with pitless eyes. His gaze felt more real, more disturbing than portraiture had any right to. He'd seen that same abyssal stare in Lachlan Campbell's eyes. Had Jonathan Boyce, the poor bugger who'd been made to stare into those gaping hollows and paint them, been driven mad? he wondered. Or had this originally been a self-portrait? Had Dòmhnall stared into his own soul and painted its abyss?

Gills turned his back on the painting. He could not look at it any longer. "Hello!" he called. "Is anybody here?"

The only reply was the echo of his voice. Perhaps his trepidation was the psychological aftereffect of almost drowning? Being so close to death, he'd realized how fragile human life was, and how feeble the body was against the immensity of the sea.

He stood for a long minute, unsure what to do next. His visit was ostensibly to inventory the contents of Dunbirlinn library for Silvaig University. Chichester had been a collector of rare manuscripts, and it was Richard Blackwell, the rector, who had suggested Gills make an initial assessment of the collection. Gills had jumped at the chance, not only because of the potential discoveries, but also because he would lay his hands on the books Lachlan Campbell had sold to Chichester. When he'd left the Old Manse, he'd been like a child on Christmas morning. Now, though, a cloying sense of dread had replaced the thrill he'd felt on the journey to Dunbirlinn. It had begun the second he'd driven through the gatehouse with its iron-toothed portcullis and glanced up at the tower from which Chichester had plummeted to his death. A mere fortnight ago, a family had swept through these halls, their minds on the minutiae of life. Now they were all dead. He couldn't shake the irrational feeling that the castle was somehow to blame.

Gills had made up his mind to return to his car, when he sensed movement out of the corner of his eye. He spun around and saw a silver-haired wraithlike woman standing at the foot of the staircase. A wolf-headed broach glinted from the lapel of her tweed jacket.

"Gilleasbuig," the old woman said.

"Mrs MacCrimmon . . ." he croaked. "You startled me. I'm here to—"

"I know why you're here," the housekeeper said, cutting him off. She strode past him, head held high, back ramrod straight, the posture of a woman half her age. "Come," she barked.

Gills followed her farther into the castle, eyes darting around, senses heightened. They walked through an arched doorway and into a lofty banquet hall filled with weapons and military memorabilia. "I hope you don't mind me intruding," Gills said.

The old woman cast him a cool glance. "This way," she said, leading them past a display of taxidermied wild animals.

Scores of lifeless glass eyes observed their passing. Gills gestured to a prowling stuffed wolf. "They've not found them yet. The laird's wolves, I mean."

Mrs MacCrimmon did not dignify the comment with a response. She led them from the banquet hall and into a draughty corridor illuminated by shafts of light from a trio of arched windows. She stopped in front of an oak door blackened with age, and turned to face Gills. "You're a renowned folklorist, Dr. MacMurdo. You know the legend."

"Which?"

"That wolves are shape-shifters." She gave him a thin smile. "Perhaps they're something else now."

The smile faded.

"Or perhaps I can't take any more killing on top of all the killing that's been done. Those wolves are the last of the laird, all that remains of his line."

"Err, quite so," Gills replied, unnerved by the old woman's glare. "Anyhow, what will you do now, without the laird to serve?"

Her lip curled. "I was never serving the laird. I was serving this castle, and its history."

She flung open the door and stood aside to let Gills pass. "You'll find everything you need in there."

Gills edged past her into the library, his natural curiosity overcoming the palpable apprehension he'd felt ever since driving into Dunbirlinn. He took in the opulent leather furniture, the vibrant Persian rugs, the gleaming walnut bookshelves, and felt the bitter stirrings of library envy. He let his satchel fall to the floor before perambulating the room, his fingertips brushing the spines of the books. Each had a subtly different texture: some were smooth and worn, others brittle and cracked; some were spongy to the touch, whilst others were rough as a burlap. He spotted first editions by the Scottish Makars William Dunbar and Robert Henryson, sitting alongside works by Blake, Chaucer, and Milton. The books were neatly grouped by subject—science, fiction, art, philosophy, anthropology, history—and indexed alphabetically. As well as being erudite, Chichester had clearly possessed a systematic mind bordering on the compulsive.

Gills was suddenly overwhelmed by the enormity of the task ahead. Dunbirlinn had always been in private ownership, so no one really knew the extent of the library. One thing was certain—cataloguing all the books here would take him years, time he would rather not spend in Dunbirlinn. Despite the initial thrill of seeing the library, that sense of unease was reasserting itself with every step he took. Behind the musty scent of books, he smelt a faint rotten odour, as if the walls of the castle were decaying.

He paused in front of the impressive Scottish history section and felt the warm comfort of familiarity. Many of the same books graced his own shelves, but his were dog-eared copies, the poor relation to these rarefied editions. His eyes scanned the titles, searching for anything on the MacRuaris that Chichester might have bought from Lachy. However, after half an hour of intense browsing, he had drawn a blank.

He stepped back from the shelves, his brogues sinking into a thick rug. Despite the cushioning, the floorboards creaked beneath his feet. He glanced down and saw that the rug was slightly out of position, a slither of pale tan mahogany visible against the deep reddish-brown wood that was exposed to light. Clearly, someone had moved the rug recently, without returning it to its original position. A little odd, Gills thought, when everything else in the library was shipshape. He rocked on the balls of his feet, his movement answered by another creak. A loose floorboard. Hardly surprising—the castle was eight hundred years old, after all.

He moved away from the history section, but as he examined the rest of the collection, his eyes kept returning to the rug. It was large, perhaps ten feet wide by twenty long. If only to satisfy his curiosity, he walked back across the room and crouched beside the rug. He gripped the fringe tassels and began to roll the rug up. A ghostly rectangle of lighter coloured wood emerged. He glanced over his shoulder, wondering how he could explain should Mrs. MacCrimmon return. *Best be quick*, he thought, returning to his task.

He had only furled about a quarter of the rug when the unmistakable frame of a trapdoor was revealed. Gills's heart thumped in his chest. Grunting with the effort, he rolled the carpet away from the trapdoor, then sat back on his haunches. Sweat prickled his hairline, and his throat felt parched. The trapdoor appeared barely wide enough for a man to fit through, but this was no new addition. The iron ring handle attached to the wood looked ancient.

A voice in his head told him to leave it, that he would find nothing good down there—only more water, his feeble body plummeting further, deeper, down into the darkness. But what then, was life, if not the search for knowledge in the face of darkness? What was the point of any of it without knowledge?

Gills's hand shook as he took hold of the ring and pulled. The door yawned open.

Alas, there was no water, but rather a set of stone steps disappearing down into the pitch blackness. He wrinkled his nose at the fetid odour rising from the space. Even as his brain told him not to, he found himself shuffling towards the dark pit. He took out his mobile and placed one foot on the top step. Then he started to descend, with only the light from his phone to guide him. He placed a hand on the wall for balance. The stone felt cold and moist, alive. Darkness closed in around him, the beam from the phone barely penetrating the gloom. He glanced back up at the wan rectangle of light and imagined the trapdoor slamming shut, imprisoning him in this dank otherworld.

Fighting a gnawing panic in his chest, Gills shuffled down the stairs. At the bottom, an alcove cut into the wall held an old storm lamp. A flint kerosene lighter sat next to the lamp. It looked as if it should be in a museum, but when Gills thumbed the notched wheel, a steady flame spat from the lighter. He placed his phone down, then touched the flame to the lamp's wick and heard a faint sigh as the oil ignited. He lifted the lamp, turned, and held it aloft, illuminating the room with a sulphurous orange glow.

Gills let out an involuntary gasp. If the library above was a place of order and structure, this was a place of chaos and madness. An upturned chair lay in the centre of the room, surrounded by books with their pages ripped out and torn to shreds. What looked like claw marks crisscrossed the low stone ceiling, instantly bringing to mind the adulterous wife Dòmhnall MacRuari was said to have imprisoned in the castle.

Gills fancied he could hear scratching as he crept farther into the room, his pulse throbbing. Brittle manuscript pages crunched like bone under his feet. He swept the lamp downwards and saw that many of the pages were heavily annotated, illegible sentences scrawled in the margins and words underlined. He lifted a book at random. It appeared to be a grimoire on the invocation of demons, but only a few pages remained intact. He dropped the book to the floor and spun in a tight circle, the lamplight spilling onto the walls. What he saw there sent a shudder through his body. A large symbol had been carved onto the wall in manic slashes, the cuts so deep that the shape stood out in sharp relief. Knife hilts and snapped blades littered the flagstone floor, testament to the unbridled force needed to create the image.

Gills stood, transfixed by the writhing energy of what he knew was a triskelion, the ancient emblem of life, death, and rebirth. A symbol of the old gods, he'd seen it before, carved into a standing stone in a three-thousand-year-old megalithic tomb in Ireland. He'd seen the symbol two decades ago, as well, when he'd gone to the school to collect Angus after Caitlin's murder. He pictured Angus in the classroom, a crayon gripped tight, his hand moving in a circular motion. He'd crouched by the boy and placed a hand on his shoulder. Angus had not even reacted. Instead he had continued scribbling with his crayon, eyes fixed on the page, immersed in the triple spiral he had been drawing. It was the same emblem gouged in the wall of this dank chamber. The triskelion.

Gills held the lamp closer and flinched, his face contorting in horror. A set of eyes seemed to emerge from the centre of the symbol, the pupils bored deep in the rock. It was surely an optical illusion, but his hand holding the lamp trembled. The flame cast an eerie glow on the carving, transforming the hacks and slashes into a scarred, leering demonic face with knotted brow and sunken cheeks. Gills was frozen to the spot, more terrified now than he had been on the boat with Lachy, more terrified than he had been when he was sinking to his death.

He stepped backwards, almost tripping over the upturned chair. The lamplight fell on another old manuscript, but unlike the others, this one looked to be intact. Its cover was the rust red of dried blood and plain, but for the embossed image of a hybrid creature—part wolf, part griffin, part snake—devouring a human being.

"It can't be. . . ." Gills breathed, falling to his knees. The codex was fitted with bronze corners, and a metal clasp attached to the fore edge looped over a peg on the lower cover. The peg appeared to be made of bone.

Gills placed the lamp on the floor and traced a hand over the book. The cracked leather felt warm, as if blood pulsed just below the surface. Gills ran a tongue over his dry lips. Ever since he was a young scholar at Glasgow University he'd heard his professors make reference to a lost book that had once been owned by the Lords of the Isles. Known as the *Leabhar Ruadh nan Fhithich*—the *Red Book of the Ravens*—it was purportedly penned by the first druids, before the holy caste had decreed that their mysterious teachings should be taught orally and never be written down.

Gills's fingers fumbled with the metal clasp. He was shaking almost uncontrollably now, whether through fear, excitement, or a combination of both, he couldn't be sure. The *Leabhar Ruadh* was real! Within his grasp was a book that could answer the questions he and Angus had agonized over for years.

The clasp suddenly flicked open, displaying a frontispiece of a mighty bull, an important animal in druidic sacrificial rituals. The pages themselves were a creamy calfskin vellum that felt alive, as if reacting to his touch. As he turned to the first page, Gills had the strange sensation that the book was reading him, rather than the other way round. He could feel a terrible energy, as if the book were siphoning his darkest thoughts through his fingertips. He tried to yank his hand away, but it seemed stuck fast. When he looked down, he saw the page was blank but for a sentence in some archaic form of Gaelic. He didn't comprehend the words, but they wrangled inside his head and forced themselves from his lips. Only when spoken aloud did the words make sense. Whether warning, prophecy, or instruction, Gills did not know. But as he trembled in the lamplight, the old man knew one thing for certain. Fate had brought him to this dark chamber. Fate had brought Angus to him.

And their work was only just beginning.

ACKNOWLEDGEMENTS

THE idea for *The Unforgiven Dead* came to me in spring 2016, but in many ways this book has been lying dormant inside since childhood. I grew up in the West Highland town of Fort William, nestled at the foot of Ben Nevis, the UK's highest mountain and also home—legend has it—to an ancient goddess known as the Cailleach. This is an area steeped in myth and legend: where glaistigs haunt lonely waterfalls, where selkies emerge from deep lochs to shed their seal skins and dance as humans under the moonlight, and where the host of the Unforgiven Dead, sinners too evil even for Hell, shoots across the night sky, searching for souls to devour.

Growing up, I encountered this otherworld only faintly, in stories told by older folk and in the books of Highland fairy tales my parents owned. I soon left for university in Glasgow, where I studied Scottish literature and history: the literature, a varied menu of Sir Walter Scott, Irvine Welsh, Robert Louis Stevenson, and James Kelman; the history encompassing everything from Bannockburn and the Highland Clearances, to the Picts and the formation of Alba. Academia appealed to me, so having completed my degree, I stayed on at university to take an MPhil in early medieval Celtic studies, where I delved deeper into the history, beliefs, and mythology of the Celts. I mention this merely to illustrate the cultural well I drew upon whilst writing this novel. History has always fascinated me, but a love of Scottish literature led me away from academia and into journalism and, ultimately, fiction writing.

Fast-forward fifteen years, and I had moved to Northern Ireland with my family and was working as a newspaper subeditor. On a trip home to visit my parents, I rediscovered those Highland folktales from my childhood, ones barely touched upon in my studies, sitting on the same shelves. As I read about shape-shifters, giants, and seers, I was struck—angered, even—that so many of these tales only survived thanks to a handful of Victorian folklorists who had recorded them. I felt a keen sense of loss: no doubt, what remains is but a fraction of what there once was. Just as Christianity had swept away the old gods, three hundred years of the British government's attempts to tame the "wild Highlands" had decimated Gaelic language and culture. By dusk that evening, my goal was clear: to write a Highlands-set crime novel that leveraged the area's rich canon of folklore and myth as part of a grounded supernatural detective story unlike anything in the genre.

By the time I had the manuscript ready to submit to agents and publishers, almost two years had passed. During this period I must thank a number of people who read early drafts, including Donnie "Barcelona Ceilidh King" Nicholson; my mother, Kathleen Ross; and author and mentor at the Irish Writing Centre, Louise Phillips, who provided feedback on the first few chapters.

My big break came in late 2018 when my manuscript came across the desk of Inkshares CEO and publisher Adam Gomolin. I will be forever grateful to Adam for taking a punt on this raw and untested author. Without him, *The Unforgiven Dead* would be a pale imitation of what it has become. He has worked tirelessly on this project during a tumultuous period for the publishing industry as it wrestles with the challenges of the global pandemic. Adam's confidence in me as a writer, his positivity, and his unstinting dedication over three years and eight—yes, eight!—drafts have been invaluable. The owl of Minerva flies only at the fall of dusk, indeed, my friend. . . .

The team at Inkshares—and the wider Inkshares community—have all been incredibly supportive. Thanks to my copy editor, Kaitlin Severini; the eagle-eyed Avalon Radys; and fellow Inkshares authors Chris Huang and Noah Broyles for their notes and kind words.

Thanks also to Adam McNamara for pointers on how cops actually talk (like regular people, funnily enough).

Many thanks to the freakishly talented Tim Barber at Dissect Design for his incredible work on the book cover.

Special thanks to Sorcha Groundsell for her insightful feedback on the manuscript and her help with Gaelic spellings and pronunciations. Any mistakes are entirely my own.

I would also like to thank the characters of *The Unforgiven Dead* who have come to life in ways I never expected during the writing process. Angus Dubh for letting me share his pain; Gilleasbuig MacMurdo for his wit, wisdom, and free hand with the drams; Ashleigh MacNeil for her strength and compassion; and Ewan Hunter for baring his tortured soul. We'll be seeing these guys again soon.

The publication of *The Unforgiven Dead* marks the culmination of a thirteen-year writing journey that began in my early thirties. Beside me every step of the way has been my wife, Roz. When I've been on the verge of quitting, her support and belief has pulled me back from the brink. Without her, I could not have done any of this.

GRAND PATRONS

A. B. Rae
Jonathan Oates
Sandra Bruce

INKSHARES

INKSHARES is a community, publisher, and producer for debut writers. Our books are selected not just by a group of editors, but also by readers worldwide. Our aim is to find and develop the most captivating and intelligent new voices in fiction. We have no genre—our genre is debut.

Previously unknown Inkshares authors have received starred reviews in every trade publication. They have been featured in every major review, including on the front page of the *New York Times*. Their books are on the front tables of booksellers worldwide, topping bestseller lists. They have been translated in major markets by the world's biggest publishers. And they are being adapted at the biggest studios and networks.

Interested in making your own story a reality? Visit Inkshares.com to start your own project, connect with other writers, and find other great books.